THORNS AND FANGS

Thorns and Fangs

Book 1

Gillian St. Kevern

Dedication

To my mother, sister, grandmother and stepfather who don't understand why I write what I write but who have always encouraged me to write.

Acknowledgements

I relied heavily on the support of my friends to write *Thorns and Fangs*. Zenia kept me going through the first draft, while Faith assured me I had a story worth editing. Julia and Kamilah gave me invaluable second opinions during the rewrite, and Tali Spencer and Samantha Lamb generously shared with me their professional expertise. Zoe, Sara, Meg, Bree, Achim and Sera's enthusiasm to read the finished story kept me going. Raevyn and the team at NineStar Press gave *Thorns and Fangs* a home. To all of you, thank you. This is a lifelong dream, and your help made it possible.

Chapter One

I will never be the same again.

The premonition was a cold whisper against the back of Nate's neck. It spread like frost, cool tendrils sliding down his shoulders to take root in his spine. Hard to shake off, even harder to ignore.

Nothing will ever be the same.

"So your regular doesn't show. It's not the end of the world, Aki." Nate turned, but no one stood next to him. The mixologist polished glasses at the far end of the bar, and the couple nearest Nate were only interested in each other. He was alone.

Or as alone as possible in the most popular club in New Camden.

The house DJ had turned up the lights and music to fill the gap left by the live band, and the dance floor was packed. Nate only had to stretch out his arm to touch someone. Strobe lights caught the lingering dry ice from the stage show, and the teasing play of light on the insubstantial mist gave the dancers a hint of its incorporeal mystery. Nate loved that, loved the thrill as he stepped onto the floor, as if the dancers might vanish before he reached them. The warmth of the bodies brushing against him always gave him a rush of triumph.

Tonight, with the premonition clammy on his skin, it looked more like smoke. Nate glanced over the bar. The red emergency box resembled an ordinary fire alarm. It was only when you noticed that the contents included a string of garlic, a flask and a sharpened wooden stake that the words registered—In Case of Vampires, Break Glass.

Vampires. I've been here six months and haven't even seen a single bat! Nate snorted, turning back to the dance floor. New Camden might be home to the biggest population of supernaturals in the world, but none of them were getting in without strict adherence to Century's dress code. The club's security system was better than some banks, thanks to its unique nature (and New Camden's unique risks), but management believed "better safe than scandal" and for very good reason. The club existed only through a very careful balancing act. It had the respectability afforded by success, just risqué enough to titillate its clients without alarming them. Security was a selling point, from the uniformed bouncers, prominently positioned at the front of the house, to the plainclothes security guards who mingled with the guests, and the alarm built into Nate's wristband that connected directly to Department Seven, the branch of law enforcement that dealt directly with supernatural threats.

"Dracula himself couldn't get in here without a spot check." Except for the occasional newspaper headline about an empty tomb or werewolf attack, New Camden was just another big city. And the sooner Nate kicked this weird feeling of danger and remembered that, the better.

"Did I hear 'pick up for table three'?" Aki leaned against the bar beside Nate. "You're never going to make your repayments slacking off like that. Look at me. A round of seven cocktails, and that's only the start."

Nate looked over his fellow host's head to table three. A cluster of girls in evening dresses. A hen do, or maybe college girls on a rite of passage. "Sucks to be me. You with a table full of girls, and me with only one client to my score."

Aki was instantly suspicious. "It's not even been a half hour."

"Forty minutes." Nate smirked. "Blow job, bonus, and I got time left over."

"No way." Aki snatched Nate's wrist. "Show me your band."

Nate grinned, letting Aki see the wristband. The thin strip of plastic hadn't left his skin since he'd started working at Century. Where Aki's displayed a thin green line down the middle, indicating that he was available, Nate's was a dull black, invisible in the dark. Until the internal timer finished its slow countdown, Nate was a free agent.

"Un-fucking-believable." Aki dropped Nate's hand. "I don't know how you do it."

Nate stretched, enjoying the tug of his tight clothing against his body. "I'm just that good."

"Just that desperate." Aki shook his head. "I have got to teach you standards."

"There's nothing wrong with my choice of clients."

Aki raised a perfectly trimmed eyebrow. "Would I have done the guy?"

Nate bit his lip. He'd seen the man at the bar, toying with his glass as he watched two of the other hosts grind against each other on the floor. His blond hair was so thin it gave the unfortunate suggestion of baldness, and he was short enough anyone could see it. The older hosts definitely had. They made a point of avoiding eye contact.

Nate had ducked his head as he approached the guy. He couldn't hide his height, but he'd emphasized the country drawl he usually downplayed. His youth did the rest. Presented with a challenge within his abilities, the man eagerly proved himself. He'd gone for a blow job in a partially lit corner of the club, fucking Nate's mouth with overcompensatory fervor.

Method and means left much to be desired, but Nate got a kick out of being on display. Secure in himself, he'd played up to the guy, getting him off with charitable ease. In return, Nate got a bonus and hadn't needed all his allotted cooldown time to freshen up. He considered his remaining twenty minutes of freedom worth it. But Aki?

"Only if it was the end of your shift," Nate admitted. "And it was a slow night."

Aki drummed his fingers against the bar. "How did I know? From now on, only hot guys count to the tally."

"So no drink orders?"

Aki gave Nate a sour look as the mixologist slid a tray of drinks across the bar to Aki. All he was going to get from his table was drink orders. "Fine. Reset from now," he said, struggling to lift the tray. "And no poaching. I saw you looking at the girls."

"They're looking at me." Nate placed a hand beneath the heavy tray to steady it. "What are you going to get out of them besides make-up tips? Customer satisfaction above personal kicks."

"Don't quote training at me. I've been here an entire month longer than you." Tray firmly in hand, Aki started toward his table.

Nate grinned at his back. Bickering with Aki was one of the perks of the job. Only a couple of months younger than Nate, Aki used his status as a New Camden native to win arguments. He lived up to the fast-talking, irreverent stereotype of the city, hands and mouth constantly in motion—when he wasn't looking at his phone.

He was also extremely easy to wind up. Nate settled back against the bar, feeling the most like himself since he heard the whisper. *Leave it to Aki*. And he still had fifteen minutes of freedom.

The chill went through him before the voice spoke. Nate stood before a force implacably deep, so powerful it would change his entire world. As he struggled to understand the warning—the voice. Rich, warm, and inviting, it spoke straight to Nate's core, stirring instincts Nate didn't recognize as his own. He stared at the speaker, all poise forgotten.

The man smiled. Like Nate, he was dark haired and athletic. His slate-gray shirt and dark jacket clung to his trim form with the intimacy of expensive tailoring, and he stood with a confidence that made Nate, tall and broad shouldered, feel shorter. Somewhere in his late twenties, he looked from Nate's metallic studded T-shirt to his face. The smile deepened into amusement. "Don't tell me you've never had a man buy you a drink before."

Nate looked down to the two glasses on the bar beside him. A lime wedge and a generous splash of mint leaves marked it as his preferred on-the-job drink. "A mojito?" He deliberately leaned against the bar.

Nate realized his mistake at once. Hosts didn't accept anything they hadn't seen made. Century commissioned safety wards from the best magic-users in the city, but they were designed to combat hungry werewolves or starved vampires, not mundane threats like drugging.

How can I refuse the drink now? Nate looked up to find the man's smoky eyes locked on his. *Date rape drugs? This man doesn't need to resort to anything beyond that smile.* "Either you just read my mind or you've been watching me."

His companion was as impressed as Nate should have expected. Not at all. "Watching you," he said, white teeth suddenly bared as his lips drew back. "Or rather" —he sauntered closer— "watching *this*."

Nate tensed a moment too late. The man's hand was cool despite the thin fabric of Nate's T-shirt, a confident pressure as he followed the curve of Nate's back to grip his ass beneath his tight jeans and squeeze roughly.

Smile sharp at Nate's discomfit, the man retrieved his own drink from the bar. "Finish your drink and join me upstairs." His voice held the expectation of obedience. "All of it. I don't want to taste your previous client." Before Nate could react, he turned and strode toward the stairs.

"Easily avoided." Nate raised the glass to his lips. He hadn't just brushed his teeth; he'd changed his T-shirt, too. "Go fuck yourself." If the guy thought the steep price of drinks included other compensation, he would be very disappointed.

People didn't come to Century for a quick fuck. They came for an experience. A few years of legalization was not enough to remove the stigma of prostitution, but Century took the stigma out for a few classy cocktails, a change of wardrobe, and sent it home at the end of the night with a decent bill.

The result? A club that attracted attention—even in the city infamous for the largest population of supernatural creatures in the world. Its hosts were as much a part of the club's successful branding as its location—a beautifully refurbished theater in the downtown area—or the music, the envy of many a festival planner. The air of exclusivity created by the steep entry fee extended to the hosts. They were attractive, came with a high price tag, and had full powers of veto. The man's assumption of Nate's compliance was an instant no.

And yet...

Now that the shock passed, Nate saw the possibilities. Century attracted those experimenting with something new. Nate was used to gently guiding. Someone so confident they rejected the niceties entirely? Not only rare, but promising.

Promising enough to overlook the guy's attitude?

The central staircase was crowded with spectators watching the stage. The man parted them without effort. He didn't gesture. He simply moved with his destination so firmly in mind that everyone else compromised.

Fuck. Confidence like that is as dangerous as it is hot. A sharp clink of ice drew Nate's attention to the fact that his glass was already half empty.

Half empty? When had that happened?

Nate's mouth twisted. Even aware of the man's effect, he was not immune.

Nate threw back the last of the drink and shouldered through the milling crowd. *This place is packed. God, how closely had he been watching to see my earlier client?* The thought excited. Nate took the staircase—a beautifully restored relic of the building's theater past—two ornate steps at a time.

The man waited at the entrance to one of the theater boxes, which were extremely hard to secure without a sizable deposit or the right connections. *This man doesn't just know what he wants,* Nate realized. *He gets it.*

And at that moment, he wanted Nate.

"You took your time."

"It's my time to take." Nate deliberately slowed his pace. "I'm not on the clock right now."

The man's eyes darted from Nate's face to his wrist. Even his apology intrigued, delivered sincerely but with no lessening of his self-assurance. "I'm sorry, Nathan. If I'd realized, I'd have waited."

And he knows my name? Nate should have been annoyed, not charmed. "I hope you'll make it up to me."

The wicked smile that met his words put an end to any internal confusion. "I certainly intend to." The man stepped aside, and Nate squeezed past him into the box.

Century's boxes were a nod to the building's past, but their furnishings were set firmly in the present. A queen bed occupied most of the box, the pulsating light from the dance floor reflecting dully on the slick black synthetic sheets. Nate squeezed past the bed to the railing at the very edge of the booth. Two sleek armchairs waited, but Nate opted to rest against the rail.

He watched his client shrug carelessly out of his jacket. The shadow of the partition between the boxes obscured the man's face. The lights caught his eyes and gave them an almost inhuman gleam.

The premonition came back to Nate in one heartbeat. So strong, it was hard to believe he'd forgotten it in the shock of their meeting. Nate rubbed his palms on his jeans, unsure what to do with himself.

His companion seated himself in one of the armchairs. As he moved, he brushed the tablet left on the low coffee table between the chairs. The device flickered on automatically, revealing Nate's club profile.

Nate seized on the distraction gratefully. "That explains how you knew my name—but not my drink of choice."

The man smirked, slipping a sleek wallet from his pocket. He withdrew a card, motioning for Nate to hold out his wrist. "Like I said, I've had my eye on you."

"On specific parts of me." The green light on Nate's wristband flashed on, only to immediately turn red as the man swiped his card over the embedded sensor within the band. His fingers firmly closed around Nate's wrist, holding it in place as he entered his selection, the pressure making what should have been a routine transaction dangerous.

Nate tried not to think about having that firm pressure applied to other parts of him. As his client's details flickered over the feed, he forced himself to speak. "Emeric Hunter. That's an unusual name."

"Call me Hunter." The man kept a firm hold on Nate's wrist even as he finished with the band, forcing Nate to lean in to enter his confirmation code. Nate's face was now a mere hand's width from

Hunter's chest, and the subtle scent of the aftershave the man wore enhanced his vaguely autumnal scent.

Nate was halfway through his confirmation code before what he'd agreed to hit him. Three hours at the highest rate Nate could sign off on without a manager's approval and the performance bonus? "You don't have to. I didn't lose that much time."

Hunter tapped in the final acceptance but did not relinquish Nate's hand. Instead, he leaned leisurely against the cushioned back of the armchair, drawing Nate toward him. Nate reached for the back of the chair to keep his balance. *Toying with me.* Nate felt his heartbeat quicken. *Everything he does is deliberate.*

"You'll be earning that. When I said I'd make it up to you, I wasn't thinking of the money."

My kind of client. Nate bit down the words, but he was sure Hunter had noticed the effect his proximity had on Nate's breathing. Case in point, Nate hummed as Hunter slid his free hand over the metallic studs embedded in his T-shirt.

"Tell me, Nathan. You're in your early twenties?"

Nate arched into the touch. The studs felt hard against his skin. "Just turned twenty-two, actually."

"Remind me how tall you are?" Cool fingers brushed bare skin as Hunter found the edge of the T-shirt.

The chill of his touch was a surprise. "Six foot one." Nate liked it, the contrast between Hunter and his own hot skin leaving pleasant tingles in the wake of Hunter's touch. "Uh. Century's not that big on specifics. I can be whatever you want me to be."

Hunter laughed, a low chuckle. *Damn, but his voice is hot.*

"That's a bold claim, especially given how broad those shoulders of yours are." He finally released Nate's wrist. "Take off your shirt. I want to see you."

For the first time since meeting Hunter, the advantage was Nate's. He did not intend to waste it. The live band had returned to the stage with a light show that punctuated their performance. Stepping back into the reflected glow, Nate took a moment to get into the beat of the song. He swayed, letting his hand travel over the metal studs just as Hunter had done earlier, before teasing the edge of his shirt up. "I'm shorter on my knees."

Hunter's expression was hard to discern in the shadows, but Nate caught the distinct impression of amusement. "You really are eager to please. Lose the shoes, too."

Nate had paused as Hunter spoke, lulled by his words, but with a spike of annoyance, he pulled the shirt over his head. *Eager?* "I take pride in my work." He kicked off his sneaker so roughly it took his sock with it, tugging the remaining shoe free with bare toes.

Hunter laughed as he stood. He crossed the distance between them with an unhurried stride. "Now, Nathan." He ran his hands along Nate's shoulders in a show of tactile appreciation of the form before him. "For what I have in mind, that enthusiasm of yours is perfect. Stand straight, feet together."

Nate obeyed unthinkingly. Hunter took a step back, stance almost that of a critic appraising an art piece. Nate should have been flattered, but as Hunter's gaze skimmed over the six-pack he took such pride in and came to rest somewhere near his shoulder, Nate had a realization. "You've got something specific in mind."

Surprise glittered in Hunter's eyes momentarily, but the hand he laid on Nate's shoulder changed the mood from "caught red-handed" to "co-conspirators" with ease. "I have plans. I want to make sure they go perfectly."

As if anything this man does could be less than perfect. Nate caught himself before he leaned into Hunter. Appearing needy in front of this client was out. "Special occasion?"

"Yes, actually." Hunter dropped the hand on Nate's shoulder to the small of his back. Nate glanced down to watch him lace the fingers of his free hand through Nate's own. *Does he want to fuck me or dance with me?*

Fortunately, Hunter answered that question with his mouth on Nate's neck. He was sleek and practiced, every bit as cool as his fingers. Nate couldn't hold back a gasp as he felt the scrape of teeth against his skin.

"That's right, Nathan. I want to hear what I do to you." Hunter lowered his head to follow the line of Nate's neck muscle. The light brush of cool lips was quickly followed by his tongue as he moved to suck Nate's collarbone.

Nate moaned. He clutched at Hunter's shirt with the hand not tangled in the man's. *Enthusiastic, not needy!* "You're way too good at this." The man had barely touched him, and Nate was hard enough to regret choosing tight jeans. "How special an occasion?"

Hunter chuckled. His breath teased skin still wet from his mouth. "My brother. It's his anniversary in a week." He squeezed Nate's nipple before bending his mouth back to its work.

He wants me for someone else? It stung. Nate tightened his hold on Hunter's shirt, keeping the man's attention on his chest as he willed the disappointment from his face. "A birthday present?"

"Close enough." Hunter released Nate's hand. As he stood, he ran his fingers down Nate's side before firmly pushing him backward.

Nate was confused until his legs encountered the edge of the bed. He sat, reaching for Hunter's waist.

The man shook his head. "Business before pleasure. I want to be sure you have what I'm looking for."

Nate rolled onto his stomach on the bed so Hunter had an unobstructed view of the tight contour of his backside, framed to perfection by the skintight jeans. The silky sheets delicately brushed his sensitized chest, and the pressure of the bed against his arousal added extra breathiness to his reply. "Most brothers would be satisfied with a voucher. Shopping around like this—" Nate paused, looking back over his shoulder, to make sure Hunter's eyes were on him as he slowly, deliberately ran his hands over his ass. "Makes me wonder who the party's really for?"

"Naked. Now." That rough note in Hunter's voice had not been there earlier.

Hearing Hunter's interest only peaked Nate's own. Not until his jeans and briefs had joined his T-shirt and shoes across the booth, did Nate realize he'd lost a prime teasing opportunity. Arranging himself on his knees, he looked back to gauge the reaction of his client.

"Well?"

"Your confidence in yourself is not misplaced. You're a fine piece of work, Nathan." Hunter's fingers lingered over Nate's tight cleft, sending shivers down Nate's spine even as his cheeks glowed at the compliment. Hunter pressed his hard length against Nate's rear. "I'm going to enjoy you." Then, suddenly, his touch moved away, and something hit the sheets near Nate's hand. "Prepare yourself."

Nate stretched out his hand and encountered Century's in-house lube. "Shouldn't the birthday boy enjoy the present first?" He leaned on one elbow so that he could watch Hunter as he squeezed a generous amount of the slick into his palm.

Hunter snorted, not taking the bait. "As I said, it's got to be perfect. Come on, Nathan. Show me you know how to work that fine ass of yours." His hand rested on his trouser front, lightly stroking the erection beneath.

Nate moaned. In other circumstances, he would spin out the preparation, put on a show for his audience, but Hunter's voice spoke straight to his straining cock. He pressed in two slick fingers to coat his entrance, adding a third almost immediately. Ignoring the protest of his tight ring of muscle, Nate pushed himself back onto his fingers. "God, Hunter. I'm tight, so tight—" He grunted, scissoring his fingers to stretch himself wider. "You're gonna feel so good in me."

"Like that. Just like that." That plastic rustle had to be a condom. Hunter was also preparing himself.

Was he even going to last long enough for Hunter to take his ass? Nate gritted his teeth, continuing to work himself open. His fingers hit that sweet spot inside of him, and Nate cried out, clutching the sheets with his free hand. "Ah— I'm ready! Ready." Breathlessly, he spread his legs wider, bracing himself against the bed. "Hunter, please..."

He felt the bed dip as Hunter joined him, but rather than the rough coupling Nate craved, Hunter gathered him gently against a hard, cool chest. “We’re not short of time.” Hunter caressed Nate’s chest with a lightness that did nothing to alleviate the need throbbing through Nate. “You don’t have to hurry on my part.”

“I want— I mean, I like it rough.” Nate tried to remember his training through the heady haze of need—customer satisfaction—but he could feel the length of Hunter’s cock against his back. “You won’t hurt me. It’s— I need. Want you now.” He rocked against Hunter, trying to elicit an answering reaction.

Hunter took Nate’s hips in his hands, squeezing them in warning. “Tell me what you want.” If Nate had not been so focused on his own need, he might have wondered at his odd tone. “Only what you want.”

He expects me to talk at a moment like this? Nate’s hips jerked helplessly. “You. In me. God— You’re gonna feel so good. Stretching me, forcing me to take all of you—” He rocked back again, and this time was rewarded with an answering surge. “I like it like that. Like it rough.” Was that imagination or had he made the older man catch his breath? “I want the burn as you use me.” A pleading note entered his voice as he gripped the sheets to stop himself from reaching for his leaking cock. “I want to feel you tomorrow, remember how it felt to do this.”

There was an almost animalistic snarl from his companion. Before Nate knew it had happened, he found himself on his back on the bed, Hunter’s lithe, athletic form inches above his own, straddling his waist and pinning his wrists to the bed.

"Do you mean that? It's not simply the job?"

It took Nate a moment to catch his meaning. "God, no." He tried vainly to thrust up against Hunter. "I'd want you to fuck me regardless."

Nate was proud of his strength, of the muscles he'd developed lugging hay bales and crates and honed in Century's employee gymnasium, but he couldn't move Hunter an inch. That realization gave him pause, even through the throbbing, consuming lust, and he looked up to catch Hunter's gaze.

"You're not the birthday present," Hunter said, perfectly still above Nate, his erect cock resting against Nate's. "You're going to be the party favor. There will be three of us, we'll enjoy you together."

The whimper that escaped Nate was pure need. *Being on display, used while others watched?* He hadn't even known this was something he wanted, but man, did he want it. "God, yeah—"

"Mostly we'll be using that tight hole of yours. I need to know you'll enjoy it."

Knowing it was fruitless did not stop Nate from trying to thrust up against Hunter again. "Let me show you. Fuck me, fuck me good. I can take it—"

Hunter let go of Nate's wrists. "Hold onto the headboard," he ordered crisply, kneeling between Nate's eagerly parted legs. He gripped Nate's hips firmly. The older man's cock was proudly erect inside the condom, and Nate watched through lidded eyes as Hunter positioned himself, cock teasing Nate's entrance. "Don't let go until you've come."

It was not comfortable, but Nate reached behind him. "I'm ready.

C'mon, Hunter. Fill me—" With a grunt, Hunter pushed in, every inch as hard and unrelenting as Nate hoped. He moaned, and his fingers clamped down on the headboard.

Hunter gave him a moment to adjust before thrusting shallowly. "Like that?"

Nate answered by using the leverage granted by the headboard to impale himself further onto Hunter's cock. It stretched him to his limit, but the burn was worth the gasp it elicited from his companion. "Yeah. Just like that."

"You are a piece of work." Gripping Nate's hips, Hunter went to work with vigor. He set a steady rhythm, slamming Nate back against the mattress with every thrust. Nate locked his legs around Hunter's hips, willing himself wider, wanting more of the older man. The burn was fading fast as Hunter found his prostate with unerring accuracy. Nate's untouched cock bounced against his stomach with each deep thrust, precome dribbling across his clenching muscles. "You're really getting off on this aren't you?"

"Thought...that was the point..." He wasn't going to last long at all, not like this. Nate moaned again. Normally the burn worked to slow him down, help him last, but each of Hunter's rough thrusts pushed him ever closer to that rush of pleasure. Sensation engulfed him. Blood pulsed in his fingers where they clamped on to the headboard, pulsed in his neglected erection, pulsed through his entire body in time to Hunter's rhythm. He didn't know whether to tell Hunter to slow down or beg him to take him faster. His hips jerked erratically, seemingly of their own accord. "Fuck, you feel so good! I want you deeper."

"That's the way." Hunter paused. Nate groaned as he felt the man pull out. He looked up to catch the man's smoky gaze, Hunter's eyes deliberately traveling from Nate's flushed face and straining body, to his cock, head shiny with need. All it would take was one touch where he needed it most.

"God—"

"Look at me."

If Nate had thought the man was sexy earlier, that was nothing to him now. Hunter's gray silk shirt hung open in disarray, and his erection, pressed against Nate's thigh, provided evidence of his passion. As Nate licked his lips, the man smirked. He swung Nate's legs over his shoulders, and Nate lifted himself, eager to assist.

Rather than give him what he wanted, Hunter rocked his erection between Nate's legs, teasing his hole with the head of his cock. "You like being claimed. I'm getting off on your reactions almost as much as I am taking your tight hole."

Oh, fuck. "Don't tease me! I need—" What did he need? "Your cock in me, I need you to fill me."

And Hunter did. He slammed into Nate with enough force to raise Nate off the mattress with each thrust, balls slapping against Nate's bare skin. Nate felt himself slipping ever closer to the edge with every movement Hunter made. "You— You're so—"

His climax hit suddenly, white spots dancing in his vision as his body arched taut and tingled. Heat splattered his chest as he shot. He heard Hunter exclaim, but transported by the intensity of his finish, Nate could not make out the words.

He came back to himself moments later. Hunter thrust shallowly against him. No words now. Nate reached for the man's hips, heard him gasp at the touch, the steady rhythm of his movements becoming erratic.

Feeling his own power, Nate let his fingers caress Hunter's ass. At Hunter's next inward thrust, Nate clenched tightly around him. Hunter moaned, as raw as Nate could have hoped. He plunged forward again and again until he leaned his cool forehead against Nate's chest, spent.

They remained that way for several long moments, harsh breathing seemingly as loud as the music of the distant band. And then Hunter laughed, a low chuckle as he pulled out. Nate barely had time to regret his absence before he was tugged up to rest against Hunter's chest. His client's smirk glittered in the intermittent light from the floorshow as his fingers encountered the come coating Nate's stomach.

"You'll do."

Nate felt a warm rush of pride at those words, even as he shivered at Hunter's cold touch and the cooling fluid. "Told you I could take it."

"You certainly did." Hunter brushed Nate's sweat slick hair from his temple before casually leaning in to take his lips. The kiss was entirely unexpected, and Nate responded to the meeting of their lips breathlessly. "And with business concluded," Hunter said, cool breath teasing Nate's neck as his mouth traveled lower. "Pleasure."

Chapter Two

"We boring you, Nate?"

Nate started. Days later, the glow had yet to fade. Hunter had left him exhausted, satiated, and with a bad habit of zoning out of conversations in favor of reliving their night together. "You, boring?" Nate reached hastily for his cocktail. "That's like asking the guy who cleans the crocodile's teeth if he sleeps on the job."

Beatrice considered him from across the booth. She preferred uncomfortable to pretty, wearing her dark-brown hair in a severe bob and choosing clunky frames over contacts. "Clearly I need to sharpen my teeth."

"You're always so mean, Bea. Nate might be coming down with something." Everything about Mandy was generous, from her ample curves to her golden blonde hair. She even frowned as she pressed a hand to Nate's forehead. "I don't think you have a fever."

Beatrice leaned back against the wall that divided their booth from the one next to it. Just like the boxes, the ground floor booths recalled the club's prestigious history. The wood used to make the tables and dividing walls had been salvaged from the renovation work and polished until they shone even in the club's discreet lighting, and the cushioning of the seats would not have looked out of place in the original theater. The complete contrast to the stark lines of the bar and dance floor shouldn't have worked, but it did. "Any excuse."

Mandy snatched her hand back. "I was worried!"

"No need. I'm fine, promise." Nate patted Mandy's arm and was rewarded with a grateful smile. "So, Bea. They solved the vermin problem in your building?"

Beatrice shook her head. "Not exactly. Six-B said that if the landlord didn't do something about the rats, they would, right? Well, the rats are gone, but there's a lingering smell of sulfur in the lobby, and seven-B swears they heard demonic barking. We think six-B summoned a demon-dog. Only problem now? The night watchman's missing, presumed eaten."

"How can you joke about that?" Mandy shuddered. "That's horrible!"

"Sorry." Bea's expression was catlike as she raised her regular gin and tonic. "I forgot I had to take your delicate country sensibilities into account."

"That poor man! Just doing his job..." Mandy's eyes were suspiciously bright. "You'd never find a demon dog in Happy Valley!"

Was she about to cry? Nate stretched a hand toward her.

"You're not the only small-towner at the table." Bea's sharp glance stopped Nate's movement. "Well, Nate? What does your hometown keep in its closet?"

She didn't know. Nate forced himself to relax, taking a sip of his drink. "Every town has a ghost story or two."

"But they're only stories." Mandy's vehemence was surprising. "Unlike New Camden..."

"The DJ set is going to finish soon. If we want to dance—" Nate's wristband vibrated with a summons. *The manager's office?* Nate patted Mandy's shoulder as he stood. "*Timing*. The boss calls. I'll find you two on the dance floor—if I survive."

Has my distraction been reported? Nate took the backstage stairs two at a time. He had to get Hunter out of his head. As the man's deadline approached, Nate had replayed the night over in his head until it took on the unreal quality of a dream.

The strange feeling of foreboding returned to trouble Nate intermittently. *Just imagination.* Nate took a moment to compose himself before raising his hand to knock on the office door. *It's not real. It can't be real.*

He was the ordinary one after all.

"Do I get points for turning myself in— Hunter!"

The man had been in Nate's head so much that seeing him on the sleek leather sofa of Denise's office was jarring. He looked up from the paperwork on his lap. "Nathan. You didn't forget then." His voice was just as rich as Nate remembered.

Nathan was aware that his smile was too wide to be cool. He brought it back under control with difficulty. "You left it late. Another night, and I'd have written you off as a no-show."

Hunter's smile showed he knew how empty the threat was. "I had intended to return before. As I was just telling Denise, you made an impression." He held out the papers for Nate's manager to take.

Nate glowed, Hunter's absence instantly forgiven. Clearly, he'd been sick. Or was Hunter always this pale? Nate had an intimate knowledge of the man's body in the dark, but this was the first time he'd seen him in the light.

"Sit down, Nathan." Denise waved him toward the sofa's contingent of matching armchairs clustered around the coffee table at the center of the office. She stood beside her desk, which broke up the circle at one end, glancing through the papers with a frown.

Nate took advantage of her distraction to covertly study his client. Hunter more than lived up to his promise. The stark lines and strong colors of the navy peacoat he wore contrasted interestingly with the long, dark hair that fell carelessly over his forehead. His mouth was fascinatingly voluptuous, and it took Denise clearing her throat to call Nate's attention away from it.

"We don't usually allow house calls."

Nate sat up straighter. Denise's word was final. She was in her midforties, with immaculate auburn hair set in a 1930s-style wave. She wore a pastel green skirt-suit over a white V-neck blouse, accentuating a bosom that made the world a better place just by existing.

"I take it Mr. Hunter already mentioned his proposal?"

"He brought it up in passing." Was that the sticking point? Denise had been Century's most popular *domme* until she found her life partner amongst the clientele and retired. The owners had fought hard to retain her as manager and not once regretted it. Denise knew everything about the job. Her controlling tendencies enabled her to keep a volatile cast of hosts and hostesses on a tight leash but made her a stickler for procedure. "I might be indentured, but I can promise you client satisfaction isn't going to be an issue here."

"Indentured?" Hunter asked.

Oh, fuck. "Industry slang. It's nothing."

Denise eyed Nate sternly. "Our employees represent a sizable investment to the club. Nathan's wristband, for example, is synched to his vital signs and can only be removed with specialized equipment."

Hunter's eyes flickered to the wristband with new appreciation. "That sounds costly."

Denise's smile was thin. "It is. To ensure against employees leaving us prematurely, we offer a lump sum payment against their future earnings. Until they've paid it off, newer employees are limited in what assignments they can accept."

Nate scowled. *Why not say I still have learner plates?* "Experience is not going to be a problem. Hunter knows I perform."

"Indeed, I do." *Was Hunter amused? This just got better and better.* "I can say with certainty that Nathan is absolutely right for what I have in mind."

Had he heard right? Nate stared at Hunter openmouthed.

"It's Nathan's safety that is at issue here."

Sent rocketing to cloud nine, then cruelly tugged back to earth? This conversation was giving Nate the worst kind of whiplash. "Denise—"

Denise shook her head. She was inflexible where issues of employee risk were at stake. "Mr. Hunter has indicated some extreme preferences." She turned back to Hunter. "There's no possibility of allowing a senior staff member to accompany Nathan? Our discretion—"

"Impossible." Hunter's tone was unequivocal. "I mentioned special considerations. My brother is shy. An uninvolved spectator would be out of the question."

Nate had managed to forget the brother. "You're going to a lot of trouble for him."

Hunter shot him a sideways smile. Nate forgave him for having a brother. "He's had a rough year. He needs to remember how to enjoy himself."

"Commendable thought," Denise said, "but our policy is nonnegotiable."

"The statement of intent is intended to cover any contingency rather than insist on it." Hunter leaned toward Denise slightly. "I want the evening to unfold as naturally as possible. For that, Nathan's cooperation is essential. He will not be asked to attempt anything he's uncomfortable with."

Just what is in those papers? Nate held out his hand.

A distracted Denise gave him the document. "It's one thing to make that promise, another to ensure it. The heat of the moment—"

Eager to discover what he might regret doing in the heat of the moment, Nate flipped through the pages. It wasn't the usual Century contract. The bulk of it was taken from the club's legal pages, but it was printed on proper legal letterhead with various amendments. Nate skimmed over the privacy clause, raised an eyebrow at the fee (*Aki will flip!*), but it was the terms of service that made him pause.

Employee agrees to perform or participate in sexual activities, up to and including anal penetration, blood play, bondage, multipartnering, oral gratification...

"Hell, yeah!" Nate realized belatedly that he'd spoken out loud. "I mean—"

Denise's gaze was sympathetic but firm. "It's Nathan's eagerness that means we must refuse. It is entirely too likely that he will push himself too far."

"A possibility that I am anxious to avoid." Hunter stood, drawing Denise's attention to the paper he still held. "But one that I've accounted for. Our medical coverage—"

Denise shook her head. "Entirely out of the question."

That was it. Nate couldn't protest without painting himself as too eager. Not that it made any difference: Denise had spoken.

But Hunter wasn't giving up. "It would mean a lot," he said with a simplicity that made Nate and Denise look at him in surprise. "To have you *say yes*." He held Denise's eye with a directness that seemed somehow scandalous.

"Yes, well." A rosy blush appeared in the cheeks of the woman who'd seen it all. "I suppose, the circumstances... Providing Nathan agrees."

"Of course," Hunter agreed, smile smooth as freshly churned butter. He looked to Nate with every expectation of agreement.

Denise never compromises. Not on safety. Nate frowned. *What if the weird feeling wasn't my imagination?*

"Nathan? Tell me you're not having second thoughts." Something that reassured implicitly layered Hunter's enquiry.

Nate found himself smiling instantly. "No second thoughts here. Where do I sign?"

* ~ * ~ *

If Nate had struggled to concentrate before, that was nothing to the difficulty he had now, knowing he would be meeting Hunter in a matter of hours for round two.

"White?" He held the T-shirt to his chest, metallic lettering glinting in the wardrobe's artificial light. "I wore white last night. I don't want him to think I'm boring. But he always wears dark colors." Nate held up a red T-shirt with stark black block print. "Maybe he doesn't do bright?"

"No one cares what you wear." Aki didn't look up from his phone. His outfit for the night was draped over one shoulder. "You're going to be naked within ten minutes of getting there anyway."

Nate looked back to the racks of clothing set out in the wardrobe. Century's targeted branding extended to the clothes its employees wore. The racks contained a mix of the latest styles, designer labels, and the one of a kind indie creations that Aki preferred. Nate had never had trouble finding something.

Until now. "Those ten minutes are crucial."

"White's great. Go with that."

Nate nodded. "Red it is." He slid the shirt off its hanger.

Aki slipped his phone into his pocket with a glare. "Why even ask me to help?" He pushed the curtain of the dressing room aside roughly. "I don't know why I put up with you."

Nate followed Aki into the cubicle. "Because no one else will go running with you." That discovery still amazed him. Aki loved to exaggerate, waving his hands as he talked. Nate had him pegged as an actor. When Aki revealed he worked at Century to fund a degree in sports therapy, Nate had thought he was joking.

"Like I want to run with a turtle. You get slower every damn time." Aki needed a moment to navigate the long sleeves and buckles of his chosen top, but conversation resumed the moment his head was free. "Today. What were you doing, running backward?"

Aki took running seriously. When he ran, it subsumed his habitual fidgeting. Aki's slight form moved with a focus that amazed anyone who'd talked to him for more than five minutes.

Nate plodded along behind him, typically managing only two or three circuits of the park compared to Aki's ten, but the running track wound its way through parkland so densely planted, it felt like forest. Nate loved the earthy smell rising up from the leaves that lined the path as much as feeling the sun and wind on his skin. He'd never be good at running, not like Aki was, but he'd take the park over the sterile atmosphere of Century's gym any day. "I stopped to see what the blossom was. Didn't know you got spicewood this far north."

"Unbelievable." Aki peeled his jeans off. "Still, I will take your bizarre fascination with plants over listening to you stress about tonight."

Nate stepped out of his jeans. The worn denim was comfortably loose, but not up to club standards. "Who says I'm stressed?"

Aki's silence was so loud Nate reached over and roughly ruffled his hair.

"Maybe I'm a little nervous—"

"You're shitting yourself."

"—about doing a good job for a client I want to impress—"

Aki dug his elbow into Nate's stomach. "A client you're

completely and embarrassingly infatuated with."

"Am not." Nate let go of his T-shirt to grab at Aki. His friend was faster, but Nate's longer arms gave him the advantage, and Aki was trapped against Nate's chest in no time. "Am I?"

Aki's reply was muffled as he struggled to free himself from Nate's pin. "Maybe you'll get lucky and Mr. Tall, Dark, and Improbably Perfect has a thing for huge losers, but I doubt it." He escaped, shooting Nate a dark look as he finger combed his mussed hair out of his face. "After all, you said there was someone else?"

"Yeah." Nate pulled his shirt on. "There is." He hadn't told Aki that he was a present for Hunter's brother.

"Maybe that's a good thing." Aki grimaced. His tone was apologetic as he worked his belt through his pant loops. "You're more nervous about this than you were your first night."

Nate tried to shrug. "I've had this weird feeling ever since I met the guy. Like— I don't know. Something big was about to happen."

"Listen to yourself. It'd be funny if it wasn't so tragic. You're crushing on a guy hopelessly out of your league here."

Aki's certainty made Nate feel lighter. He folded his discarded jeans neatly, placing them over the back of the dressing room chair. "You're right. I should just enjoy tonight. Orgy with at least one hot guy. Could be worse."

"Four people isn't an orgy. It's group sex."

"Whatever. You're totally jealous."

Nate deserved the T-shirt Aki threw at him. "I don't care what it is just so long as you stop going on about it!"

Nate smirked as he picked Aki's shirt off his head. "No

promises." He shook it out before folding it, tucking the sleeves in, and smoothing the shirt down. He looked up to find Aki watching him. "What?"

Aki shook his head. "You can take the boy out of the country, but you can't take the country—"

"So Ma raised me properly." Nate stepped into his fresh jeans. "You should take notes. Not everyone enjoys tripping over your possessions."

"How hard is it to watch where you walk?"

Luckily, the noise of the sound crew testing levels on the stage above reminded them there was no time to waste. Otherwise, they might have had a real argument.

* ~ * ~ *

Denise had refused Hunter's offer of a private car, choosing to put Nate into a taxi herself. "You don't need to leave for another hour."

"I'm just marking time here. I want this over with." Nate pulled the seat belt closed.

"Nervous? You can cancel." Denise rested her arm on the taxi door. "Due to the unusual circumstances of Mr. Hunter's request, I won't mark it down as a no-show."

Denise is second-guessing this, too? Nate bit his lip. "Yeah, I'm nervous, but only because it's a first. I want to do this."

"The taxi will be back to pick you up at six, unless you call for an earlier pickup. Got your phone?"

Nate held up his mobile. "Charged, and the number's already in it. I'll be fine, Mom."

Denise sighed. "I will be very glad to have you back. Akihiro is already complaining about covering your regulars."

Nate smirked. "Beatrice. He'll learn to love her."

"Mm." Denise believed that as much as Nate did. "Be careful tonight, Nathan." She shut the car door.

The taxi came to a discreet stop at the corner of a long residential street in the hills overlooking New Camden. Nate let it pull away before walking down the wide pavement. The houses he passed were varied colonial-era wooden houses, modern creations of steel and glass, and the occasional art deco extravagance. All were immaculately maintained.

Do these people mow their lawns or iron them? Nate couldn't spot so much as a stray leaf.

He wiped his palms on his jeans as he reached 21 Rueful Crescent. The gate stood ajar before a built-in garage, skillfully engineered to look like a seamless addition to the Victorian townhouse resting above it. Nate climbed tiled steps to the front door, so crisply white that Nate fought the urge to wipe his hands again. *Paint doesn't stay that fresh in New Camden without a lot of attention.*

That attention was evident in the lavender bushes, cut into stark squares and placed in uniform terracotta pots that lined the stairs. The paned glass windows glittered in the fading afternoon sun. Nate shifted his overnight bag to his other shoulder and rang the doorbell.

The chimes were startlingly loud within. Nate snatched his hand back. *At least no one can miss that I'm here.*

But as the last peal faded, Nate was still on the doorstep. The evening air was chill on his bare arms. Nate glanced back to the street, conscious of how out of place he looked. *Maybe there's a back door?*

The house extended almost the full length of the property, but Nate spotted a thin cast-iron gate in the niche between it and the fence separating it from the house next door. He squeezed through it sideways to find a shady path, its broad stones almost entirely covered by thick moss.

He was rewarded at the end of the path by the delicious smell of damp earth and ozone. Nate breathed in the rampant garden. No one had trimmed these plants into shape. Ivy almost entirely consumed a small garden shed, and the knee-high grass of the lawn ran riot, liberally peppered with dandelion and clover. The lemon tree's branches were heavy with fruit, and briars swarmed the dividing wall.

I shouldn't be here. The neglected backyard contrasted so completely with the front that it was clear no one was meant to see it. Even so, Nate lingered. There was something human in the tangled growth, and Nate knelt with interest beside the herb boxes, the only part of the garden that had been cared for.

Someone here cooks. Nate frowned at the basil—*Outdoors? In this climate?*—but nodded at the parsley, rosemary, and chives. *Ma would approve.* About to stand, he paused. No surprise to see sage and fennel among kitchen herbs, but putting deadly nightshade so close to the edibles?

Nate stepped over for a closer look. “Mugwort.” He held the leaf of the less familiar plant between his fingers. “Yarrow?”

It looked less like someone was a keen chef, and more like there was a witch in residence.

“Can I help you?”

An elderly man stood in the back door. Instead of a witch’s broom, his thin fingers held a spatula.

Nate wanted to laugh at the apron that hung innocuously over his crisp suit. *What was I thinking?* “Sorry.” Nate stood, brushing his hands on his jeans. “I tried the front, but no one answered.”

The man’s gray hair was smoothed back with gel, and the pristine folds of the suit beneath the apron indicated that this was the careful hand that maintained the house so perfectly. His eyebrows, however, ran rampant above sharp, hazel eyes, giving him the suggestion of an owl. “Are we expecting you?”

Fuck. Where did you even start? “Yes. At least, Hunter is. He, uh. Hired me—”

“Ah.” The bushy eyebrows relaxed. “You would be Nathan.”

“Just Nate is fine.”

“I’m Godfrey. I wasn’t expecting you for another half hour. If you’d like to come in, I’ll show you to your room.” The man led Nate into a hall that gleamed with polished wood. “You find me in the midst of dinner preparations. On that note, Master Emeric neglected to inform me of your dietary preferences?”

Nate was guiltily conscious of the Red Bull and energy bar in his bag. “I eat anything.”

Godfrey stepped into the kitchen. Nate had a brief impression of gleaming steel surfaces and steaming pots before the butler emerged. He'd removed the apron and led Nate down the hall without preamble. "That certainly makes things easy."

The scent of wood polish in the hall mingled with something older. It reminded Nate of raking dead leaves in autumn, musty but not unpleasant. He lingered in the hall, trying to identify it. "You don't have to go to any trouble."

"It's no trouble, I assure you." Godfrey led the way up an exquisitely carved staircase with a speed at odds with his age. "With the night ahead of you, you'll need a good dinner."

Nate caught his foot against a stair. Hunter had informed his extremely proper butler that he'd hired a prostitute?

"I've placed you in the Green Room." Godfrey didn't miss a beat. "It's a touch removed from the rest of the house, but you'll have privacy." He stopped before a door on the third floor. "I trust this suits?"

The cool green of the pinstriped wallpaper and the crisp white of the bed linen and ceiling were a welcome break from the dim hallways. Nate set his overnight bag down on the bed. "It's great."

"The Green Room offers a fine view of New Camden." Godfrey drew back the curtains to display the nightscape. "You'll find the bathroom through that door. If you need anything—"

"No way. Is that a bell pull?" Nate caught himself. "I didn't think they had those outside of books."

Godfrey smiled with urbane amusement. "This house is something of a fossil."

"It must take you a lot of work."

"Us old relics have to stand together." Godfrey patted the wall. "I must attend to dinner. Don't hesitate to ring if you require anything."

Nate nodded. "Thanks." He was sure they both knew he had no intention of using the bell pull.

* ~ * ~ *

Lights were coming on in the city below. Nate shivered in the breeze. The evening had turned from cool to cold, but he hesitated to close the window. It took the faint conversational murmur drifting up from the street for Nate to realize why.

This house is too quiet. It shifted and moved, the same way the farmhouse did—the way all old houses did—but the wooden murmurs only highlighted the lack of other noises. Human noises. *Are Godfrey and I the only people in this place?*

Nate pulled the gray hoodie from his bag, tugging it on over his head. The chill reminded him of the basil in the garden, and he settled on the bed, phone in hand.

[How's the pruning going?]

His brother's reply was prompt. *[Slower without you.]* This time of the night, Ethan would have just gotten home, waiting as Ma put the final touches on dinner.

Nate snorted as he typed his response. *[With the bank paid off, you can afford help, you know. Rube'd do it.]*

[No.]

Nate laughed. That was so like Ethan. *[Rube's a good guy.]*

[Doesn't know plants.]

[According to you, no one knows plants.] Nate rolled onto his stomach, settling the pillow beneath him to better text. *[What if there's an early bloom?]*

* ~ * ~ *

A bell sounded sonorously downstairs. *Dinner?* Reluctantly, Nate relinquished his phone.

He met Godfrey on the stairs.

"Excellent. I was just coming to collect you." The butler guided Nate down the dark hall toward a thick door, the murmur of conversation just audible behind it. "As this is your first time, I'll run over the house rules. No real names, no identifying details, and no discussing the night's business." Before Nate could even blink, the man bowed him into the dining room.

Electricity lit the chandelier, and the people seated at the dining table wore modern clothing, but in every other respect, Nate felt as though he'd stepped into a historical photo. The room was grand, the oak table able to accommodate far more than the four seats placed around it. Nate took the unclaimed seat at the foot of the table with unease. *Where's Hunter?*

His fellow diners only increased Nate's confusion. He sat opposite an attractive woman of mature years, wearing a chic black dress with a startling cashmere scarf tossed around her shoulders. The woman to her left was equally striking, but in a thoroughly different way. Her vibrant copper hair was coiled in a tight bun, and she studied Nate from behind a severe fringe and thick-rimmed glasses. However, her lipstick choice was as bright as her hair, and the lace choker at her neck undercut the formal lines of her pantsuit.

Then there was the young man on Nate's right. He wore a casual gray cardigan over a faded paisley shirt, an oversized woolen scarf looped around his neck.

Nate looked, trying not to be obvious about it. *The brother?*

"You're new." He returned Nate's stare with undisguised interest. "Are you going to be a regular, or is this in honor of the occasion?" There was a mocking tilt to the last words.

The woman at the head of the table set down her wineglass. "You know the rules. No business."

The man blinked at the reprimand, and it was a moment before he smiled. "Old habits are hard to break. It's been a while since we've had fresh blood." He seemed unwilling to leave the subject entirely, eyes sliding to settle on Nate's wristband.

"Are you from New Camden?"

Nate turned toward the copper-haired woman gratefully. This question he could answer. "Moved here six months ago. I'm still settling in."

She laughed. "It's that much of a challenge?"

Conversation proceeded smoothly. The clatter of cutlery heralded Godfrey's return, pushing an old-fashioned trolley. He set a plate before Nate, whisking off the silver lid to reveal a meal that would not have looked out of place in a five-star restaurant. Crisp oven-roasted vegetables were paired with generous slices of poached chicken, steamed asparagus, and a buttery sauce on the side.

Nate breathed it in happily. *Is this really for me?*

Nate's dinner companions did not share his enthusiasm. They

murmured their polite thanks as the butler placed their meals before them, but shared glances as soon as he left.

"Asparagus again." The younger woman shrugged. "Godfrey does it impeccably, but even so."

"You're lucky." The hipster poked his plate. "I got brussels sprouts."

Nate took a closer look at the meals. They were all different. The brunette had an oven-baked salmon fillet with roast vegetables, while the redhead had lamb chops on a bed of pumpkin and roast yam with the asparagus on the side. The guy had slices of roast chicken, replete with mashed potatoes and thick gravy, clearly more welcome than the brussels sprouts.

"If you want to swap ..."

The brunette shook her head. "Dinner is specified in our contracts. Now, as I was saying, you must visit the theater—"

* ~ * ~ *

"So bad they're ironically great." The hipster leaned back against his chair. He and Nate had discovered a common interest in music, although not the same type of music.

"I still wouldn't pay cash to see them play." Nate shifted back to allow Godfrey to set a tray in front of him. Coffee, complete with sugar bowl, and tiny jug of cream. "Sure, The Unholy Noise hasn't aged well, but you're going to see a legend, not the boy band of the moment—"

Godfrey cleared his throat. "I hate to interrupt such a lively conversation, but it is time."

I'm the only one getting coffee? Nate watched as his companions stood. The ladies followed Godfrey out of the room together.

The man smirked at Nate's confusion. "Still beats selling burgers," he said, unwinding his long scarf as he followed the others. For a brief moment, two red marks were revealed, standing out starkly against the man's pale neck. Then the door shut behind them.

Nate stared at his coffee. The twin marks had looked just like—

Bite marks.

The rattle of Godfrey's trolley recalled Nate's attention to his coffee. He gulped down the lukewarm liquid. "Sorry, I got distracted."

"There's no rush." Godfrey didn't chat as he cleared the table, for which Nate was grateful. Once the idea had taken root, it was difficult to dispel.

It's not possible—is it? A lot was odd about the night's transaction. *Or am I jumping to conclusions?*

Only one way to be sure. Nate finished the coffee and stood. "I'm going to go back to my room to freshen up."

Godfrey nodded. "Do you remember the way?"

"I'll find it."

Nate took a deep breath and opened the bathroom door.

He was met by the same pinstriped green wallpaper as the bedroom, and an ornate antique bathtub that stood on wrought iron claws. Modern comforts were provided in thick, fluffy towels that hung from the railing beside the sink and the showerhead over the tub. It had its own toilet and medicine cabinet. The only thing it lacked was the mirror.

Nate let out a slow breath, trying to think past the cold chill that had settled in his chest. *Vampires.*

He was in a house of vampires.

Chapter Three

Dinner was over.

A black car waited outside the house. Nate watched from the window as the three dinner guests filed into it. *Dinner guests or dinner?* It was so obvious in retrospect. The only thing the guests had in common were that all three of them covered their necks. Nate swallowed. *Does that mean three vampires?*

The man was last. He lingered a moment, looping the scarf around his neck as he stared up at the house. Godfrey bowed from the steps, and the car pulled into the street.

The surrounding houses didn't so much as twitch a curtain. And why should they? *Vampires, in a nice neighborhood like this?* Nate rested his hand against the wooden window frame. *How can I ask for help? No one will believe me.*

He bit his lip and then regretted it. The last thing he wanted to think about right now was teeth!

They didn't kill the dinner guests. Nate took a deep breath and left the window. *I'm a professional. I can handle this.*

They'd covered this in training. Any irregularity in a job meant you got out of there as fast as possible. It would be easy. Tell Godfrey he wasn't feeling well and call the taxi.

It's true, too. Since making his discovery, a cold weight had settled in Nate's stomach. *I'm never going to get hard wondering if I'm gonna be eaten.* And weren't vampires technically dead? *Okay, that's beyond gross.* Why make excuses? He could just slip out the backdoor.

So why didn't he?

Nate flinched at the knock. He took a deep breath, forcing himself to relax as he opened the door. "Listen, Godfrey, I– Hunter!"

The sheer physical presence of the man went through Nate like an electric shock.

Hunter smiled, eyes sweeping over Nate. "Nathan. I'm glad you could make it."

Nate stood taller. "You don't get an invitation like this every night." *What am I saying?*

"Indeed." Evidently happy with what he saw, Hunter placed cool fingers on Nate's cheek. The memory of having those cool fingers stroke him to completion came back to Nate with an immediacy that made his blood rush. He didn't protest as Hunter dropped his hand to take Nate by the wrist. "Now that we have our present, the party can really start."

Hunter's teeth were bone-white but not sharp, and the preemptory tug of his hand as he led Nate into the hall thrilled. Getting hard while thinking about fangs was not the problem he'd envisaged. "Party favor," Nate reminded him. "Presents are only for the birthday boy."

Hunter laughed. "I knew I'd made the right choice. Now" –he slowed his pace as they reached the stairs– "I told you I had something specific in mind, but I didn't tell you how specific." He outlined his intentions.

Hunter's voice painting an erotic picture in the dark was the hottest thing Nate had ever heard. "You can talk specifics to me anytime." *Do I get off on danger? What is wrong with me?*

"Up for the challenge? Good." Hunter halted before a door on the second floor. A thin crack of light stole out from under it. "My family is a little off-putting," he said as he relinquished Nate's hand. "They can come across as a little weird sometimes, but they'll not harm you."

That sounds like vampires all right. Nate willed himself firm. He had to tell Hunter that he knew. "Hunter—"

"Be yourself and follow my lead." Hunter opened the door and stepped into the lit room.

Fuck. What do I do now?

The stairs were right there. A smart person would just keep walking. All Nate had to do was move.

And yet...

'I'm glad you could make it.'

Glad. And Nate was wearing the dull gray hoodie that was only in his bag because he'd forgotten to take it out.

Goddamnit! If six months of hooking hadn't made him immune to this, nothing would!

Nate stepped through the door. *At least, as ways to die go, I could do worse than a vampire orgy.*

The room was too luxurious to be anything but the master bedroom. Nate got a general impression of the same antique wooden furniture that characterized the rest of the house, but his immediate attention was on the two men Hunter approached.

Nate had seen men like the first man before. They hung in museums, in clunky gilt frames with ornate frills entirely at odds with the brutality contained within. This man could stand on a pile of his enemies' bones as naturally as he now rested against the Victorian mantelpiece, and the bones would have suited him better. His black suit did not tame his powerful physique. His features were sharp in the way of a finely honed blade, refined over centuries into something cool and immovable. He took in Nate without even the pretense of surprise.

The second left a lot to be desired. He wore the same black suit as his companions but lacked their confidence. Instead, its snug contours emphasized his sallow skin, vague brown hair, and overly delicate features. Even his eyes were an indecisive blue-gray color. They flicked over Nate rapidly, halted as they reached the wristband. The only interesting thing about him was his mouth, too wide for his thin face, which registered his abrupt discomfiture. "Hunter. You didn't." Obviously, the brother.

Hunter shot Nate an amused smile. He'd anticipated this. "Bed."

The king bed occupied the opposite end of the room. Nate tugged off his shoes and hoodie before he sat on the immaculately smooth duvet.

Hunter sauntered over to the other men. "Now, Ben. Nathan's a friend of mine who has very kindly agreed to join us tonight."

Ben raised his gaze to look at Nate across the room. His mouth twisted. "Agreed?"

The museum piece laid a hand on his shoulder. "You know your brother better than that. Emeric puts a surprising amount of care into his mad schemes." He nodded to Hunter. "Continue."

Hunter did. "You've had a hard first year," he told Ben. His tone was intimate, and Nate had to strain to hear. "None of us will argue that." He placed his hand on Ben's other shoulder. "Why make it harder by torturing yourself with thoughts of what you cannot have? Enjoy what you can."

A guilty pink tinged Ben's cheeks at the touch.

Seeing Hunter's effect on someone else made Nate uncomfortably aware of how readily he'd caved to that same touch. *Guy's infatuated. No wonder he doesn't like me.*

"This is not my idea of enjoyment." Ben's reply was stiff.

"Emeric's not wrong," the older man said. "Better you master all weapons available to you than allow them to master you."

That startled Ben into a second glance.

Now I'm a threat? Nate lounged insolently. He was comfortable with his sexuality, but he'd never wielded it like a whip before. He liked the feeling, looking over Ben's slim form before catching his eyes in calculated challenge.

Ben chewed his lip, but his eyes were deliberate. "I don't want—"

"To hurt him? You won't." Hunter leaned in. Nate very nearly missed his next words. "What you were, you will be."

You will be what? That doesn't make any sense.

The elder vampire spoke, cutting through Nate's thoughts. "The choice is entirely yours, Bennet."

You say that, but... Nate would have bet his entire exorbitant fee for the evening that the final choice was this man's alone.

Ben's reply was measured. "If this means no more of Hunter's presents..."

Hunter laughed. The reflected glow of his smile was visible in Ben's cheeks. "Watch closely. You don't want to miss this."

We're on. Nate scooted back on the bed as Hunter approached.

Hunter settled Nate's hand on his waist as he straddled the younger man. "Keen to get the party started?"

"Someone has to." Hunter's sheer confidence was a welcome antidote to the unexpectedly formal atmosphere of the room. Nate's libido was back in full force. "Why not us?"

The first touch of Hunter's mouth and Nate forgot they were putting on a show. He moaned as Hunter lavished the erogenous zone of his neck with expert ease. *Knows my neck better than I do. Does being a vampire give you a sixth sense for this?*

He looped his arms around Hunter, breathed him in deep. With the scent of his cologne came the memory of lying tangled amongst Century's black sheets, but as Nate rubbed against Hunter, he noticed something else.

The amorphous soil-like smell of leaves in autumn he'd smelled in the corridor. Nate hissed as Hunter ran cold fingers up the inside of his T-shirt. *Do vampires have a smell?* The newspaper articles and vampire novels never mentioned that.

Hunter pushed Nate back against the bedspread. "Mind if I unwrap your present?"

Ben snorted. "Please yourself." He hadn't moved from his place at the other end of the room. Beside him, the older man—*Sire? Vamp-daddy?*—unhurriedly loosened his tie.

Hunter tugged at Nate's T-shirt. Belatedly, Nate remembered he was getting naked and raised his arms to let Hunter strip him. The brief flight of the red cloth to the ground was a flash of brightness in the dark room, drawing the attention of their watchers like a red flag to a bull. *Or was that blood to a vampire?* Nate, usually more confident without clothes, suddenly felt naked.

Hunter ran a fingernail down Nate's chest with distinct satisfaction. "I chose very well."

Think too much and I'll never do this. Nate cupped Hunter's well-defined ass and pressed him against his denim-covered erection. "I was feeling underdressed before. Now?"

Hunter ground against Nate with a smile that should have been illegal. "Do you want company?"

"Mm." Nate joined Hunter in a lazy rhythm. "I want you to take your shirt off. Slowly."

Off-script, but the glint in Hunter's eyes as he ran his hands over his shirt to the buttons at his neck said he approved. "Like this?"

"Just like that."

Still riding Nate's hips in a decadent rhythm, Hunter divested himself of shirt and tie with artistic flair. *Guy can work a room.* He had Nate's professional approval. But the other two?

Hunter's family had followed his lead, discarding their jackets. Ben had removed his necktie, but it hadn't done much for the overheated flush of his cheeks or the obvious bulge in his pants.

Lost cause. Handed his wet dream on a platter, and the guy didn't do a thing about it? Nate couldn't help his thrill of victory. He gripped Hunter's hips tightly, and Hunter rewarded Nate by grinding his erection against him. Men like Hunter were not interested in lost causes. *His loss, my gain.*

But Nate could never resist a lost cause.

"View's better over here." His statement was no less of a challenge for the breathy tone in which it was delivered.

Ben glanced at Nate, weighing his expression for a moment. His thin mouth pressed into a decided line as he stalked over to the bed.

Hunter greeted Ben with a kiss that left Nate in no doubt that vampire brothers did not equate to actual siblings. Intense, but too unpracticed for real intimacy. Hunter pulled away before Ben was ready, leaving the younger vampire wanting and willing to be guided onto Nate's hips.

Nate raised himself into a sitting position, hands on Ben's waist, as Hunter pressed firmly against Ben's back from behind. "Told you it was better than watching."

Ben's eyes flickered shut behind long lashes as Hunter's mouth dropped to explore his neck. He was too caught up in Hunter to notice Nate had pulled his shirt free and started to unbutton it.

That changed the second Nate's fingers skimmed his bare skin.

Ben gasped. He surged forward, eyes bright and surprised. Nate was just as startled. *Too much?* The hard length pressing against Nate's stomach said otherwise. Nate placed an experimental hand on Ben's stomach.

Ben bit his lip. Nate could feel the shift of his muscles as he fought to keep himself still, but he couldn't repress his shiver as Nate brought a second hand to caress his smooth skin.

Fuck me. Nate let his fingers skim slow, soothing circles, watching Ben's overly delicate lashes flicker shut. *Guy's a dam waiting to break.* Ben moaned soundlessly as Nate worked his way up, long fingers tangling in the bed sheets as he fought for control of himself. *God, just think of what he could do with that control!*

Nate shifted. Ben's reactions went straight to his cock, trapped within suddenly too-tight jeans. It demanded attention, but Nate couldn't take his hands off Ben. Just the slightest contact elicited response, pure sensual need warring with iron self-control.

Hunter's low chuckle came as a surprise. Nate had entirely forgotten the older vampire until the bed shifted as he moved, slipping Ben's shirt free of his unresisting shoulders. "If you like his fingers, think how good his body will feel against yours." He paused to press a kiss to Ben's shoulder. "Or his hot mouth—"

"Hunter." The reprimand was fierce, but Ben's distraction couldn't prevent his body hungrily reacting to Nate's fingers. He raised himself up to press his body into Nate's touch like a cat demanding attention.

And we're barely getting started! When he lets go...

It was all Nate could do to stop himself from jerking his hips up at the thought. So maybe he could get into sharing Hunter. Ben wasn't built, but the sheer determination required to hold back the sensual need that vibrated from every part of his body gave his slight form an attractive power entirely its own.

"On your knees." Hunter slapped Ben's rear playfully. "I want Nathan's pants off."

Just in time. Nate had felt Ben's reaction to the slap. If his pants had been tight before, now they were a prison.

He levered himself up as Ben inclined forward. Face to face with the bare skin he'd been exploring, Nate couldn't resist. He pressed his mouth to Ben's navel, laved the cool skin with his tongue. Ben's moan was breathless. Nate bent his mouth to see what other sounds he could draw from the man. Only six months of practice at this allowed his fingers to undo his fly themselves. Ben's subtle reactions were so interesting that Nate's attention was entirely focused on every hard-fought admission of need.

Hunter divested Nate of both jeans and boxer briefs smoothly. "Very nice." Hunter's approval was so pointed that Ben shifted to look down at Nate's cock, hard and glistening. "You're next, Ben. Nathan, undo him."

Ben was still as Nate positioned his hands at Ben's waist. "You mind?"

Ben's gaze was unreadable. "Do it."

Carefully, Nate eased Ben out of his crisply laundered trousers, and Hunter immediately whisked them off. Ben lost his balance, falling back onto his ass on the bed.

Nate snickered.

He regretted it immediately. Ben glared, making no move to restore proximity.

Oops? "No harm done." Nate rolled onto his stomach so that he could position himself between Ben's legs. Hunter had left Ben's tight briefs intact, and Nate pressed a teasingly chaste kiss to the bulge trapped beneath the cotton. "Let me make it up to you."

Ben buried his hand in Nate's hair. "God," he said as Nate tongued his erection through the fabric. "Your mouth—"

Nate smirked, hooking his fingers beneath the elastic band of the briefs. “I know. Both a blessing and a curse.”

Ben’s fingers tightened in warning. “You’re more attractive when you’re not talking.”

Hunter’s chuckle behind them was accompanied by the rustle of clothing. “Play nicely now.”

“I always play nice.” The reminder that Hunter’s gaze was on them made Nate ever more eager for what was to come. He caught Ben’s eyes as he continued to stroke him. “Can I taste you?”

Ben’s fingers clenched in Nate’s hair. The answer was evident in every line of his body, but he still took a moment to gather his reply. “Yes.”

First time someone’s gone down on him? Can’t be. Nate carefully drew the briefs aside. Ben might be hesitant, but his cock sprang up to meet Nate without hesitation, tip wet with precome. “Not bad.” He ran his thumb up the dorsal vein. Long rather than thick, Ben would feel so good inside him. He lightly flicked his tongue over Ben’s head and then took the tip into his mouth.

Ben’s gasp was roughly cut off.

Nate glanced up to see Ben had placed his other hand across his mouth. His blue-gray eyes betrayed the need he didn’t want to voice. *Definitely more attractive like this,* Nate decided. *Time to show him just what this mouth can do.*

Engrossed in his task, the lube-slicked finger that caressed his rear surprised Nate. Hunter planted a cool kiss on the small of Nate’s back and pressed that same slick finger inside, working his entrance with slow care.

Nate hummed his approval around Ben's cock. His words weren't intelligible, but his want was understood. Hunter added a second finger, then a third, finger-fucking him with elaborate attention.

Now we have a party. While Hunter worked him open, Nate concentrated on taking Ben's length inside his mouth, alternating between licking and sucking. The pace was too slow for his taste, but knowing what Hunter intended, he appreciated the man's care.

Ben's slow ministrations had an added effect Nate liked even more. His obvious verbal pleasure woke something in Ben. No longer trying to stifle his enjoyment, he dropped his hand to the base of Nate's skull, urging his mouth forward as his hips moved in shallow thrusts.

So responsive. Nate eased off Ben's cock to swipe his tongue over Ben's balls, eliciting another gasp. *He really needs this…* The thought of giving him what he so obviously desired should not have been as hot as it was, but Nate gloried in his power. He ran his tongue gently back up the underside of Ben's penis, finding Ben's gasp of need as much of a turn-on as Hunter's expert fingers, and the knowledge that they were on display. Senior vampire had not commented, but Nate felt the cold weight of his gaze on his bare skin.

And then Hunter found that spot inside Nate that made it impossible to think. "You like that, don't you, Nathan?" Hunter worked more moans from Nate, voice conveying distinct satisfaction. "You'd like it even better with something else inside you." Hunter sounded oddly coy. Was it the atmosphere of the house or the silent presence of the third vampire?

Nate pulled his mouth off Ben as Hunter withdrew his fingers. “Yes, please.” Now Nate was doing it! *This is going to be the politest fuck of my life.*

If he survived it.

“You should have the honors, Ben. It’s your anniversary.”

Ben’s eyes traveled down Nate’s body and up to Hunter. “Nathan,” he said, trying to pretend his cheeks weren’t a deep shade of red. “Do you—”

“Yes.”

Hunter laughed. “Nathan knows what he wants.” He tossed the tube in his hand to Nate. “You’re in good hands.”

“Literally.” Nate spread the lube over Ben’s cock by pumping him. He had to admire their handiwork. Ben’s cock was slick and jumped at his touch. Caressing Ben’s sac, Nate was surprised when Ben’s hand closed over his own.

“Thought you wanted me inside you.” He managed an authoritative note despite his breathlessness.

Nate grinned. He trapped Ben’s wrists beneath his hands, spreading them wide. “Want me to stop?” He exulted in the way Ben’s body squirmed underneath his.

“Not what I meant.”

Ben’s impatience was flattering, but the quiet reserve he retained while naked, aroused, and trapped beneath another man really intrigued. Nate released Ben’s hands to kiss his mouth. “This what you had in mind?” He pressed Ben’s cock to his entrance, pushing down before Ben could reply.

Hunter had done an expert job of preparing him. Nate took Ben’s length in one slick move. *God, it's like he's meant to be inside me.* He took a moment just to savor the feeling of being filled.

"You!" Ben's hips jerked up. "You feel so—" He placed first one hand, then the other on Nate's body, experimenting before he allowed himself to feel.

Slowly, Nate began to move. "You have no idea how hot you look right now." It was the truth. What Ben lacked in Hunter's sophisticated charm, he made up for in a distinctly different way. He looked good flushed with passion and straining for more of Nate, but it was what he still held back, contained within his half-lidded glance and the fingers tightly locked around Nate, that really got Nate. "How good you feel inside me." At his next downward thrust, he tightened around Ben.

Ben's entire body jolted with need. "That—"

"See, Ben?" Ben's eyes flew open as Hunter leaned in. The older vampire smiled, cupping Ben's chin before kissing him. "I knew you'd like your present."

Nate eased off Ben entirely. He had been right about the view being better up close. The pallor of the two vampires emphasized the evidence of their arousal. Ben's wispy hair had spilled over his face, but Nate resisted the urge to pull it back. *My turn soon.* He watched Ben run shy hands over Hunter's body, ignoring the urgent throbbing of his cock. He had to pace himself. Pace Ben.

Not that Ben was thinking of pacing. "Maybe it's not your worst idea," he said, stroking down Hunter's well-defined stomach toward his cock. "But I could use some more convincing—"

Hunter drew Ben's hand back. He made up for the man's

disappointment with a rough kiss. “I have something particular in mind.” He crouched back to command Ben’s gaze, trapping one hard nipple with his thumb. “Do you trust me?”

“Absolutely.”

Nate winced. Too immediate. *Has he forgotten he’s got an audience?*

Hunter was pleased, leaning in for a more leisurely exploration of Ben’s mouth. “Then trust you’ll like this.”

Nate was very relieved when Hunter pulled back. The other two might have forgotten, but Nate was aware of the silent presence of Vampire Sr. He didn’t dare glance to see what the man thought of the slip. Instead, Nate wasted no time slicking Ben again.

This time Ben helped guide Nate onto his erect cock. “How’s that?”

Nate waited until he had Ben inside him. “You feel great.”

Ben tried to thrust up, but Nate held his hips tightly. “Wait.” He shifted carefully so that he lay on top of Ben, his own erection trapped between their bodies.

“For?”

The dip of the mattress answered Ben’s question. Nate felt Hunter’s weight press against his back, the light pressure of his breath on Nate’s neck. “If only you could see what I do.” Hunter extended his hand to stroke Ben’s cheek. “You do wanton extremely well.” As Ben squirmed against Nate, Hunter squeezed more lube into his hand. Nate felt a cool touch at his entrance. “Ready for me, Nate?”

Nate eased off Ben so that only the younger vampire’s tip rested inside him. "So ready."

Hunter kept a tight hold on Nate's hips as he pressed inside. Even liberally coated with lube, his cock wasn't an easy fit. Nate caught his breath as he was stretched.

"Hunter, you're hurting him!"

"It's cool." Nate sought and found a hold in the bedspread. "Keep it slow. I got this." *I can do this. I can totally do it.*

Hunter continued to work his way inside. The pressure was uncomfortable, but the feeling of being that full was something else. "I'm going to start to move. Nate?"

"Try me."

Hunter set a challenging rhythm, his hands firm on Nate's hips as he thrust up. At the down stroke, Nate was plunged onto Ben. The two cocks constantly shifting within him stretched him wider and wider.

"Fuck—"

Hunter eased off Nate. Both the vampire's cocks bounced against his ass as they were freed. Nate could feel their excitement, their eagerness for him as they strained against him, and he wanted more, even as his breath caught up with his wildly racing heart.

Hunter spread his hands with lube, cupped his hands around both erections. He probably intended to give Nate time to recover. The sight of Ben, biting his lip as he watched Hunter stroke his cock, Hunter's gray eyes watching both of them as he licked those indecent lips.

"I'm ready."

Knowing he'd done it once, it was easier to relax as Hunter joined

Ben inside him. Nate gripped his thighs, spreading himself further and succeeding in taking more of Hunter's erection.

"That's it." Hunter continued to work his way in with short thrusts. "Doesn't he feel good, Ben?"

Ben moaned.

Nate opened his eyes to see Ben's flushed face, wispy hair stuck to his forehead. His blue-gray eyes locked on Nate, shining with need. Unbelievably hot, and Nate craned his neck to watch Hunter move behind him.

Hunter smirked at him, but there was color in his cheeks and a definite lusty note to his voice. "Nice and slow. We got you."

Nate gasped agreement. As his body relaxed, the sensation of having his ass penetrated by two men began to feel less raw, more right. "Oh god. Fuck. You feel incredible, I can't tell you— Oh fuck. More!"

Hunter obliged and set a mean pace. Ben rocked up against Nate as much as he was able, while Nate braced his hands against the mattress. The sensation inside him was building, growing with every movement.

Finally, Hunter paused, drawing out to lube himself again. Nate gasped for breath, appreciating the brief respite, even as he missed the feeling of being filled. Ben, not privy to Hunter's repositioning, made a needy sound of protest. "Hunter—"

Hunter's rough hands gripped Nate's hips tightly, legs nudging Nate's even further apart. "Now." In one stroke, he plunged fully into Nate.

White light exploded behind Nate's eyes as he cried out. They'd pressed against his stimulated prostate at exactly the right angle, resulting in a wave of pleasure so intense his entire body shook. Nate gloried in it and the feeling of being completely full. Hunter stayed still.

Nate, unable to move, urged him on. “More. I need...more. Fuck me, fuck me just like that.”

But Hunter remained unmoving.

Nate gasped as the pleasant burn faded to simply burn. “I need it, need more.”

Hunter pressed closely against Nate’s back as he reached down, linking his fingers through Ben’s. “Didn’t I tell you to trust me?”

There was no question of the trust in Ben’s expression. Wonder and something more intimate were written across his face. “This is why...?” He squeezed Hunter’s hand.

Nate was glad that he couldn’t see Hunter’s face. If his expression mirrored Ben’s, Nate did not want to know about it. *This is way too personal.*

The vampires began to move in perfect unison. They didn’t need words, establishing a see-saw rhythm. Nate grunted as the slow build began to move through him once more. His body had adjusted to accommodate the two cocks, and the feelings of fullness and pleasure were even more intense. But even as he felt totally filled, Ben and Hunter thrusting into him in turn, he felt weird.

Empty.

Ben let out a keening sound, arching desperately up. Hunter slowed as Ben ground frantically, lukewarm seed spilling deep within Nate. The younger vampire threw an arm over Nate’s shoulder, burying his face in Nate's chest as he came with a muffled sob. Nate looped his arm around him in response, gently ruffling Ben's hair. *Just how embarrassed is he gonna be when he realizes who he's clinging to?* Still, the contact felt good.

If momentary.

Hunter's hand slid between their bodies, Nate's cock twitching at the slightest touch of his fingers. "Want me to do something about this?"

Nate groaned as Hunter pumped him once and then stopped. "You said 'play nice.'"

"I didn't say that applied to me. Get on your knees. I want to come in you."

Ben scooted back without prompting as Nate positioned himself. He didn't have time to wonder if Ben was watching. Hunter lined himself up then drove in. Nate could easily take Hunter's girth, but the punishing pace Hunter set and the change of position created plenty of friction. The treatment was rough, but Nate reveled in being able to take it and give back. Hunter grunted in approval as Nate found purchase enough on the mattress to move back to meet Hunter's thrusts, drive him deeper.

"Forgot...how good you were at this."

It should have been all the praise needed, but Nate gasped, relentlessly grinding back against Hunter. He didn't want to think, he wanted to *feel.*

A strong hand supporting his shoulder allowed Nate the purchase he wanted to meet Hunter's thrusts. Startled, Nate looked up.

He'd completely forgotten the presence of the oldest vampire. His hard cock protruded from his neat suit trousers and pressed into Nate's cheek, the tip dribbling precome. Clearly, he'd liked what he'd seen. His other hand gripped Nate's hair, leaving no doubt what he intended.

And I thought Ben was cold. Nate licked his lips as the man positioned himself carefully, cupping the base of Nate's skull with care at odds with his silence. Nate parted his mouth obediently. The older vampire pushed inside, stopping just at the point where Nate had to work to accommodate him. He waited until Nate had relaxed his throat, thrusting once experimentally before deciding that Nate was ready.

"Hunter."

Hunter had stopped when the man joined them, but at that order, he began to move again. Each stroke drove Nate forward onto the older vampire's cock, shallowly at first, but quickly escalating to deep thrusts as their urgency increased. No question of thinking now. It was all Nate could do to keep up with Hunter's rhythm, the cock working farther into his mouth with each breath, and his own aching need. All it took was Hunter's hand, gently grasping his erection. Nate jerked into his touch, crying out as he came with such intensity that for several long moments he was aware of nothing but his climax.

When Nate came back to himself, Hunter was pulling out of him, come dribbling down Nate's crack. He barely had time to process the sensation before the fingers in his hair reminded him that he was in the middle of something. The elder vampire's cock sought readmission at his lips. Dazed and satiated, Nate let himself be mouth-fucked.

There was the murmur of conversation behind him. Nate focused on taking the older vampire's erect length as far as he could. His nose brushed the fabric of the trousers, and he caught the mingled scent of fabric softener and cologne, along with that same earthy smell that Hunter and Ben shared. Nate breathed in the scent, rather than listen to the postcoital cuddling behind him. *I'm never going to smell fresh soil without remembering this...*

The tightening of fingers in Nate's hair was all the warning he got. The man came, staying in Nate's mouth until he'd exhausted the last of his seed. Nate laved him with his tongue before the man pulled out, mindful of the crisply laundered suit.

In reward, the man patted Nate's head briefly. "Hunter did not choose badly."

Uh.

Thanks?

The older vampire did not join the other two. He made himself comfortable on the side of the bed, and they came to him. Ben curled up catlike in the space beside him and laid his head on one leg with a nearly imperceptible sigh. Hunter knelt between his legs to tuck him back into his trousers. The man rested his hand on Hunter's head. Only then did Hunter lean back against the man's legs. The older vampire's suit still had the iron-crisp lines intact, a detail that struck Nate as strangely hilarious.

Nate realized they never touched Count Vampula without seeking permission first. They always sought the slight incline of his head before reaching for his hand, or waited to be touched instead. Nate enjoyed some power play as much as the next guy, but this...

Either they're into some extreme BDSM play or vampires are fucked up. Nate was strongly inclined toward the latter.

Chapter Four

Deep in the house, a clock chimed twelve.

The senior vampire laid his hands on Hunter and Ben's heads briefly. "Delightful as this was, I have matters to attend to."

Hunter stretched, flaunting his lean, athletic body without even trying. "Give me half an hour, and I'll join you. I'm up to date on the New York files, and de Silver brought the Conrad case with him."

Ben sat up. "Those are my projects."

Hunter glanced down with a curving smile. "Not tonight."

Vampire Sr. nodded. "You have been so long devoted to your tasks that you have allowed yourself very little leisure. Tonight, at least, is yours."

Ben collected himself as he stood. "I'm grateful." He made it sound as though he accepted a difficult request, but Nate, granted an unobstructed view of his back, thought there was less tension in his form.

Since they convened for family time and forgot Nate, he had ample time to observe the vampires in their natural habitat. *I'm like some kind of investigative reporter. Literally going undercover.* He'd taken full advantage of the luxurious duvet, careful to wipe himself off before slipping beneath it, but its warmth didn't counter the strange chill that had settled over him.

The hell is wrong with me? Before Nate could answer his question, Hunter's eyes alighted on him.

"Going to take your present with you, Ben?"

He meant it as a joke, but Ben, startled, locked eyes with Nate. His uncertainty was so obvious that Nate made the decision for him, coming to stand beside him.

Ben took his presence with quiet gravity. "If there's nothing else, we'll go." He bowed briefly before leading the way into the dark hallway, not fast enough to escape Hunter's laugh.

Nate stuck close to Ben in the dark. Sympathy had replaced antipathy. He could leave in the morning, but Ben was trapped in the dead house with his unachievable crush.

Or was Nate just grateful to be out from under Hunter's knowing gaze?

They didn't talk in the hall. They padded over floorboards that were cold on Nate's bare feet. Occasionally their skin brushed, adding a thrill to the journey. It felt more like they were awkward schoolboys stealing away illicitly than grown men who'd just fucked.

If I don't stop documenting every surreal aspect of this evening, I'm gonna be here forever. Not on Nate's to-do list.

"Here." Ben opened the door, pausing to turn on the light, and Nate stepped past him into the bedroom.

This was the most comfortable room Nate had seen in the house yet. Bookcases, holding a sound system, DVDs, and models, in addition to books, took up most of the room. The walls had posters for movies that had come out that century. A phone charged on the desk. Of more immediate interest was the bed. While the grandiose wooden frame had obviously come with the house, the duvet was thick and fluffy, warm instead of decorative.

"We have many spare rooms. I can ask Godfrey—" Ben halted to watch Nate climb beneath the generous duvet.

"Sorry," Nate said without apology. "It's cold."

Comprehension flickered over Ben's face. "Right. I forgot." His arms had settled across his chest.

Is that why the house is so cold? Vampires don't feel it? Nate patted the bed. "Keep me company?"

Ben took the invitation cautiously. Nate waited until he'd settled beneath the duvet to loop an arm around his shoulders. Unexpectedly, Ben rested his head on Nate's side. "You're very warm."

Nate smirked at the reminder of Ben's enthusiastic reaction to his body heat. He was happy to be different things for different clients, but "convenient source of body heat" was new. "You're nothing like I imagined a vampire."

The only hint of Ben's alarm was the alert flicker of his eyes. "You knew? I thought—"

"Worked it out at dinner." Nate squeezed Ben's shoulder. "Hunter wanted it to be as normal as possible."

Ben's mouth twisted. "Normal?"

Had using Hunter's name been a mistake? Nate shrugged. "Comparatively speaking."

Ben didn't buy it. He sat up, forcing Nate to shift to meet his gaze. "Vampires aren't comparatively normal."

"Okay, fine. You're weird as fuck…but you're a good fuck.

Happy?"

Ben's expression remained fixed, but his mouth twitched. Was he going to laugh? Cry? Frown at Nate as though he had just been presented with a puzzle he was determined to solve? "I'm not sure that even qualifies."

Ben's tone was emotionless, but his cheeks were pink. Inside he was a real person. For the first time since Hunter's betrayal, Nate didn't feel quite so alone.

"It qualifies. Trust me." He replaced his hand, shaken off as Ben sat up. "Your first time with a group?" Ben hesitated. "It's cool. Even with the mountain of nondisclosures I signed, I still wouldn't tell."

For a second, Nate thought the nondisclosures offended Ben more than the question, but he gave a short, barked laugh. "First time, period. I did the drunken making out at parties a few times but never had a serious boyfriend."

"You're shitting me. Never?" Nate was really glad he'd gone for the cuddling. A first-timer needed aftercare. That was a basic. "Is that why you held back?"

Ben tensed again. It was so subtle that if their earlier activities hadn't tuned Nate to his reactions, he'd have missed it. "I didn't realize it was noticeable."

"Noticeable to me." Nate let his fingers stray over Ben's shoulder, skin as smooth beneath his fingers as the sheets they sat on. Just like before in the master bedroom, he felt the minute vibrations of Ben's attraction to his touch held in check by his reserve. "But then, I really like a guy with control."

"Do you?" Ben's smirk was skeptical. He'd summed up Nate's

intentions and was unimpressed.

"Yeah." Lazily, Nate let his fingers skirt across the small of Ben's back, making his angular shoulder blades twitch at the unexpected touch. "I like the challenge of it." He pressed his mouth to Ben's shoulder, letting his tongue aggressively caress Ben's skin. "I like pushing that control to its limit," he said, keeping his mouth close so that his breath stroked the sensitized skin with every word. "Seeing how far we can go before need overcomes restraint."

Through his fingertips, idly stroking the bumps of Ben's spine, Nate felt him shiver, but his voice was completely cool. "With you, I can't imagine that's very long."

"Is that a challenge?" Nate planted a farewell kiss on Ben's shoulder before moving up to his neck. "'Cause I, for one, am up for it." The thought of it had his cock stirring, and Nate sucked greedily at Ben's collarbone. "I want," he said, pausing to work his way up to Ben's jaw, "to push that control of yours all the way. Watch as you lose yourself in the rush."

Ben's eyes had fallen shut as Nate worked his neck, but they flew open in shock when Nate took his mouth. They'd kissed, but only in passing. Ben's lips parted as soon as he felt Nate's tongue, and though Nate explored Ben's mouth first, Ben wasted no time catching up.

Must have been a hell of a good drunken make out! Nate hummed in approval as he felt Ben's fingers fasten on his shoulder, drawing their bodies close. Ben didn't kiss, he demanded. Nate took the hint, pressing Ben back against the mattress, feeling Ben's arousal stirring against his stomach.

Ben didn't break the kiss, but he grunted, a sharp, impatient little sound that was entirely at odds with his collected self. *Guy's got no idea how hot he is when he lets go—lucky for me.* Nate's erection was rapidly becoming harder, fueled by Ben's proximity. *I want to last long enough to test his control; I got to shift—*

The instant that Nate tried to move, however, Ben's fingers tangled in his hair, pulling him back to Ben's mouth with an urgency that was irresistible. *Like I even want to resist this. Fuck.* Ben sucked at Nate's tongue as if he intended to keep it, and Nate rocked against him. Ben's mouth was cool but not unpleasantly cold. The contrast in temperature to the heat Nate felt and Ben's slick tongue gave another layer of stimulation to the kiss. *Like the bite of chilled lube before body heat kicks in.* Nate moaned as Ben darted his tongue over Nate's lips. *How do I feel to him? If my touch is hot, my mouth must be searing.*

Ben's fingers dug into Nate's shoulders, and then suddenly there was the cold bedroom air between them, Ben holding Nate at arm's length. "For someone who intends to test my control," he said, again master of himself and the situation, "you seem to be very close to losing control of yours." He deliberately arched up, his erection brushing Nate's.

Fuck! The contact was enough that Nate thrust into it needily, but Ben held himself unmoving. *Guy must have nerves of steel to not react to that. I can feel how hard he is!* "That mean you accept my challenge?"

"Challenge is too big a word. With your obvious enjoyment, it's easy to see you won't last long." Ben's eyebrow raise was pure come-on.

"That's where you're wrong." Ben had the same uncanny strength his brother did. Nate couldn't move out of his hold, but he could rock his hips, thrust his hard cock against Ben's in a rhythm that was slower than either of them wanted. "I don't hold back what I feel. Doesn't mean I can't hold on. You, on the other hand, are fighting yourself." Just as Ben adjusted to the tempo Nate had set, he paused. They both felt Ben's hips shift, seeking the contact his body wanted. "That's a losing battle right there."

Ben paused, assessing this new threat. "You're a jerk."

"Want me to keep going?" Nate stayed as still as Ben had. He was achingly aware of every slight movement of the body beneath his and of his own need, growing stronger with every moment. He had even more respect for Ben's control. "Tell me to move."

"Nate—" What was that expression? Ben stared up at him. Want gave way to regret, and then the walls that Nate had fought so hard to bring down were back up. Ben let go of Nate and sat up. "I can't."

"You've got nothing to be shy about." Nate settled on his side. "Trust me." Even now, Ben had an aura of self-command that prevented his nervousness from being a mood-killer. "In fact, I think you'd enjoy telling me what to do."

Surprise flickered in Ben's eyes, followed by a guilty flash of red across his cheeks. He got his composure under control quickly, however, smoothing his mouth into a determined line and meeting Nate's leer sternly. "Not possible."

"Why not?" Nate made sure his tone was curious rather than demanding. Stopping just as things were getting good was frustrating, but the evening wasn't about his satisfaction. Ben had the self-assurance of a goddamn master, but Nate couldn't forget he was new to this. "Too soon? Or not your kink?"

There went Ben's composure. Still, it was interesting to note that even pink with embarrassment, naked, and half-hard, he could answer as clearly as if he were making polite dinner conversation. Taking it slow had definite compensations. "I like...the idea. But we can't. Because I'm a vampire."

"You guys have rules in place?" Nate would not put it past Vamp-daddy to have a strict "no power games without me" policy in place. He was the type.

"No, it's...compulsion. If I told you to do something, I wouldn't be telling you to do it. I would be compelling you to do it."

Nate raised an eyebrow. "You know I want to fuck you, right?" He wasn't hiding his erection.

Again, Ben stared at him, mouth slightly open. It was a moment before he collected himself, frowning at Nate but not taking his eyes off him. "Vampires survive through blood magic. Our bodies convert the blood we consume into the power we need to survive. We're constantly emitting it at a low level."

"We covered this in training, I'm pretty sure. Or maybe I saw this on *Buffy*."

Ben's mouth twitched briefly. "It's more like *Star Wars*, actually. Not the Force, the Jedi mind trick. Or it would be if it wasn't for my sire's power."

He's a geek? Geekpire? Nate suddenly realized that Ben had paused to allow him to react. "Yeah, I'm gonna need an explanation."

Ben resettled himself as he thought. "Basically, the older the vampire, the more he's consumed to sustain himself, the more powerful he is."

Ben's posture suggested this would take a while. Customer satisfaction, Nate reminded himself. "That's every vampire movie ever."

"Don't get me started on vampire movies." Ben settled his shoulders resolutely. "But you get the idea. Saltaire's only turned three of us in his lifetime—"

"No way." Nate sat up. "Mr. Personality is Saltaire? As in the fucking millionaire, Saltaire?"

"It'd be wise to be respectful!" Ben nudged Nate with a bony knee. "You're only here because of his generosity."

Knowing that his hunch about the senior vampire being the key to the evening was right did not make Nate feel any better. "Fuck me. Saltaire." Every other week there was a paragraph in the paper detailing how he'd spent an exorbitant amount of money on a painting, donated to a hospital, or shunned a journalist. He was famous for his love of solitude, appreciation of the finer things in life, and refusal to pose for photos. All New Camdenites knew him by name, but no one had ever seen his picture. Now Nate knew why. "No wonder I had to sign the Mt. Everest of nondisclosures."

Ben prodded him a second time. "Pay attention."

"I'm listening." As Nate sat up, the same sadness he'd seen earlier flashed across Ben's face.

"Saltaire's old," he said stiffly. "And he has shared his power with only a few. Hunter and I have a greater share of power than most vampires our age."

"You're telling me I screwed vampire royalty?"

The sadness was gone, replaced by that indefinable expression. Ben took a moment before he replied. "Most vampires have to concentrate to compel someone to do what they want. Hunter and I, we just have to speak, and the words function as a spell."

"A spell?" For the first time since leaving the master bedroom, Nate felt something of the room's chill on his skin.

Ben shifted back, drawing the sheet around him. "Any living thing with blood in it is susceptible to blood magic. When I told you to 'pay attention' before—"

Nate could feel his blood thumping in his chest with sudden awareness of danger. "You *compelled* me?"

"Not intentionally." Ben's fingers dug tightly in the bed sheets. "It's easy—too easy—to forget, especially in conversation like this. Please, be—" He cut himself short.

Believe me. Nate's mouth twisted. Ben hadn't finished his sentence, but Nate was inclined to obey. *Or is this my genuine reaction? Everything the guy does says how much he hates this!* Ben didn't look at Nate, but the tenseness of his body said how much he feared Nate's reaction.

As he should! Yeah, Nate enjoyed being told what to do, but it was still his choice!

Or was it? Nate was uneasily aware of how he'd reacted to Hunter's proprietary attitude. *Finish your drink and join me upstairs.* He swallowed. "If Hunter told me to do something—"

"You'd do it," Ben said simply. "I'm sorry, Nathan."

"It's Nate." Grimly, he thought back. Hunter was not as careful with his words as Ben. There had been other orders: *Take off your shirt. Stand straight. Touch yourself—*

All of those I'd have done anyway! Does it matter? It mattered. Running his hands over his arms in a futile effort to ward off the chill, Nate discovered it mattered a lot. *Tell me you're not having second thoughts! Is that why the premonition?*

"I'll call someone to collect you." Ben slid off the bed to fetch the phone on the desk. "Or maybe you'd prefer to do it yourself? I can go—"

"No!" Nate's voice sounded far too loud to his own ears. "No. I'd...rather not be alone." Not with Hunter and Saltaire around. Ben, at least, was sympathetic. Nate patted the bed. "I know none of this was your idea."

Ben stayed where he was. "I compelled you, Nate. I could do it again."

"But not on purpose." Was that why Nate did not resent Ben's command the same way Hunter's upset him? "And nothing I wouldn't have done anyway."

"But you can't be sure of that."

Nate paused. Sitting up had felt like his natural reaction. When Hunter had given him the drink on the other hand...? *That wasn't my choice.* But at the time, it had felt so natural Nate hadn't even questioned it. His shoulders sagged. "I can't." The admission was so terrifying his mind struggled to take in all the implications. *If I can't be sure of that, what else can't I be sure of?* Nate's chest constricted with alarm. *He wanted me for his brother...* Had Hunter's determination to give his brother a good time extended as far as making sure Nate would want to follow Ben?

Ben's smile was flat. "That uncertainty. It changes everything. Tomorrow you'll be wondering if you chose to stay or if this is my influence... If anything you felt tonight was real."

That coffin has sailed. But it was the bite in Ben's voice, alarmingly real, that troubled Nate. "Is that what happened to you? Vampires...they're not immune to this, right? Or...is that how you became a vampire?"

Ben stared at him. Braced for loathing, Nate's sympathy seemed to have caught him off guard. "No. Saltaire turned me to save my life."

"But?"

It was fascinating. Ben's mouth, pressing flat before twisting unhappily, said as much about his feeling as his words. "Created from his blood, I can't help but be influenced by him. He's aware of this. Keeps a careful distance to allow me as much autonomy as possible. I should be grateful." Ben shook his head. "All I can think is that this isn't real freedom."

"Jesus." Basic training had given Nate no idea of how fucked-up vampires were. Being eaten looked like a favor in comparison. "I'm—"

"That is what you risk if you stay." Ben looked directly at Nate. "Do you see now why you should leave?"

Nate stared back. How had he ever imagined that Ben was a poor echo of his brother? He didn't have Hunter's smooth confidence. He didn't need it. The finality in the set of his mouth was enough. Nate slowly got to his feet. Ben was right. He'd earned his fee. There was no reason to stay and every reason to leave.

Ben did not try to stop him. His mouth twisted as he turned aside, arms folded across his chest. Steeling himself against the desertion he'd encouraged?

Nate bit his tongue. *If I go now—* It'd be proof to Ben that he could not hope for more than solitude. *He'll be alone. No—worse than alone.*

But what choice do I have?

It was then Nate realized he had a choice.

If I was compelled, I wouldn't feel this conflicted. If I was compelled —Nate looked from the door to Ben's back, still turned firmly toward him— *I'd already be out of here.* Scarcely daring to breathe, Nate set his hand on Ben's arm. *Where the fuck are my self-preservation instincts?* He felt a chill down his spine that had nothing to do with the cool skin beneath his fingers. *Am I afraid of him, or for him?* The walls Ben erected as defense might as easily become a prison.

As before, there was an instant reaction to Nate's touch. Ben's fingers dug into his skin in an effort to hold himself unmoving. "You don't know—"

"What I'm doing?" Nate let his hand skim over Ben's shoulders. "This is kind of my area of expertise, remember?" He let his hands work soothing circles, keeping the pressure light.

Ben's fingers landed on Nate's so hesitantly that if it wasn't for their cold he might have missed them. "You're not afraid?"

"Not of you." Nate turned Ben around to face him, brushing Ben's wispy hair off his forehead. Somehow, the gesture felt more intimate than their previous contact had been. Ben's gray-blue eyes met his solemnly, waiting. "You won't make me do anything I don't want to do." No wonder Hunter had wanted to test Nate's eagerness. Looking for someone who matched Ben's needs, so that even if his brother slipped— "That's what Hunter meant when he spoke to you at the start of the night. Why he brought me here. To show you that you don't have to be afraid."

Ben blinked. "Did he tell you that?"

Nate shook his head. "I'm right though, aren't I?" He took hold of Ben's hand, giving him a tug toward the bed.

This time he took the hint, sitting on the edge of the bed but careful not to brush against Nate. "You really want to talk about this?"

Nate squeezed his hand and then let go. "Yeah. I want to understand what happened tonight. I think hearing your side will help." Will help Ben. Nate had always prioritized the emotional over the logical, to the frustration of many of his teachers, family, and friends. *Is Aki right? Is this my need to be needed getting me in trouble?* Nate pulled the duvet around him, doing his best to look encouraging. If his instinct was right, Ben needed an ear more than anything. "So?"

Ben shifted to sit cross-legged, as sedately as if they were having a business meeting. "There's a saying amongst vampires. 'What you were, you will be.'"

A naked business meeting. In bed. Nate's mouth twitched, but Ben continued without any waver in his composure.

"The living change, grow. The dead...don't. Hunter wanted to show me that I might not have the experience, but I still have the desire...and I can satisfy that without hurting anyone."

It was a neat explanation, but something about it still seemed lacking. "Sure that's all? Seemed like Hunter went through a lot of effort for tonight."

Again, Nate saw the slightest tensing in Ben's shoulders. "You care a lot about Hunter. That's why you came tonight."

"I came because Hunter's hand was on my cock."

Ben choked. "Not what I meant!"

How does someone live in New Camden and remain this inexperienced? "Hunter's a client. A seriously hot client with an excellent credit rating, but still a client. I'm not here to get my kicks. That honor's all yours."

Ben's mouth twisted as if he'd tasted something unpleasant. "My anniversary."

"Could be worse. My last birthday my cake got lost in the mail, and I had to work."

"A vampire's anniversary remembers his death."

Nate froze. "Jesus. I'm sorry—"

"It's all right. You obviously don't know about the night world." Ben's smile was at odds with his words. "It's nice, actually. The reminder there's a world out there that doesn't end at dawn."

I knew it! He needs this as much as the physical contact. Nate sat up, mirroring Ben's upright posture. "Being a vampire's pretty heavy, huh?"

Ben's thin mouth turned up at the ends. "You have an amazing gift for understatement."

"One of my many talents." Nate bit his lip. "Look, I hope this doesn't come off wrong, but you got nothing to worry about where Hunter and I are concerned. He went through the effort of getting to know me only so I'd be relaxed tonight."

Ben went very still. "I'm that obvious."

"So's he." Nate met Ben's startled glance with a smirk. "I don't want to spoil the present, but he went to a lot of effort. Trust me on that."

Ben turned away quickly. "It's not. You can't—" He stopped, his shoulders radiating tension.

"Hey." Nate settled his hand on Ben's shoulder. "I'm a pretty good listener. Try me."

Minutes passed. The only sound was the shifting of the house. Then Ben sighed, a soft sound, almost hidden by the wooden creaks. "Nondisclosures?"

"Discretion's part of the job." Nate kept his tone mild. "So. How long have you had a thing for Hunter?"

"Years now." Ben's laugh was short. "He was my first crush. My only crush."

Now Ben's lack of experience made perfect sense. What gangly high school student or college kid could compare to that level of sultry self-importance? "He wasn't interested? Because of the vampire thing?"

Ben nodded. "That and I was just a kid. My father was Hunter's housekeeper. We lived here. Hunter traveled a lot, but when he was home...he just had this aura of excitement and danger."

"He's not short of charisma."

Nate felt Ben's muscles relax beneath his hand. "I suppose not.

Anyway, Hunter was kind. Told me I reminded him of the family he'd lost, hoped I'd consider him a brother. If he'd been cruel, I'd have got over it, but kindness—" He shook his head. "I must sound pretty pathetic."

"Don't let it stop you. Hunter's something else."

Ben turned back to look at Nate. His angular shoulder nudged Nate's arm. "Is that your professional opinion?"

Nate grinned. "Yeah, actually. And it's my professional opinion that Hunter's noticed that you're not a kid anymore. He's into you."

Ben bit his lip. After a moment, he shook his head. "Impossible."

"Tonight—"

"Hunter died without ever having fallen in love. He's not capable of it. Not in the sense that I want. He cares about me as much as he can care about anyone—or wants me to think that, which is basically the same thing."

"It's something." Nate patted the other man's arm. "More than some relationships I've seen."

"It gets worse. Because Hunter was turned by Saltaire too, there's overlap between us. So far it's latent, but if we did what we did tonight without a proxy" —Ben looked down— "the attraction between us, it would be—"

"Compulsion?" Nate frowned. "You just don't get a break."

"It's not so bad. I was never very social, so solitude isn't anything new." Ben picked at the sheet. "I occupy myself with our projects, mostly."

Overworks himself? Nate remembered Vampire Senior's comments at the start of the evening. "Is that your family's solution to the problem?"

Ben shook his head. "Saltaire prefers to avoid humans altogether. When he can't, he speaks as little as possible."

"I wondered about that." Usually Nate's most authoritative clients were among the more vocal, enjoying the sound of their own instructions. "And Hunter?"

Ben's mouth pressed together tightly. "Hunter cares only that his partners are willing. As long as they're satisfied, he forgives himself the occasional slip."

But Ben does not? "That explains so much."

Ben went still. "Explains what?"

Nate patted Ben's arm. "There were a few things that happened at the club that didn't make sense. Now it does—"

"If he made you do this—" Ben's quiet manner had not prepared Nate for his anger. He moved fast, halfway to the door before Nate had slipped off the bed. "He's going to regret ever being turned—"

Nate wasn't sure if pulling rugs out from under client's feet was covered by Hunter's long legal disclaimer, but he was willing to risk it. Ben stumbled forward but didn't fall, and Nate got to his feet, braced for Ben's anger. "It's not like that!"

Ben spun around to face Nate. "If he compelled you, there wouldn't be a choice. No matter what you think or feel—"

"Hunter said things weirdly. Like finding out if I liked bottoming." Nate let his fingers rest lightly on Ben's shoulder. "Set things up to see how I'd react. Most clients wouldn't waste their time. They'd ask. Hunter...I think he didn't want to lead me."

Ben was silent. His anger had appeared suddenly, but it wasn't so readily abated. “You’re sure?”

Nate leaned in to kiss Ben’s forehead. “You ask me to do that?” He brushed Ben’s hair out of his eyes.

“No.”

Nate rested his forearm on the door above Ben’s head, close enough that Ben could feel his body heat, but not his skin. The room was cold, but Nate bet the chill only made him seem warmer in comparison. “You forget.” He let his hand trace the contours of Ben’s chest down to his stomach. Ben arched into Nate’s touch, confirming his guess. “That vampire thing aside, you and your brother are sexy as fuck.”

Ben leaned back against the door. “I know the expression, but I wasn’t aware that ‘as fuck’ could be used as an actual term of measurement.”

“Watch and learn.” Nate let his hand drift lower.

Ben caught it before it could dip between his legs. “You don’t have to do this.”

“What if I want to do this?”

“I—” Ben frowned at him. “What is this?”

“An opportunity. You’ve been holding yourself back from contact with people, afraid of compelling them.” Ben was still, his eyes fixed on Nate’s face. *Listening*. Nate wanted to lean in and kiss that serious mouth, but it had to be Ben who moved first. “What we did with Hunter… You didn’t tell me what to do.”

Ben snorted, folding his arms over his chest. “You really want to test me?”

Ben’s move. Nate swallowed, taking his eyes off the rise and fall of Ben's chest, and looking at his face. "Hey. Sex with me was not terrible, right?"

Despite Ben's posture, his mouth was lopsided, as if he fought a smile as well as the inclination of his body to lean into Nate. "It was not."

Nate's pulse quickened. "So why not? You got nothing to do tonight but me."

"I'm not sleeping with someone whose seduction technique amounts to 'why not?'"

Nate laughed. "I'm not trying to win your heart. Why overcomplicate it? The longer we're together, the more I see of you. And to be crude?" Nate stepped back so he could deliberately run his eyes over Ben's lithe form.

Nowhere near as developed as Hunter, but in the older vampire's absence, Nate could see he'd been unfair. There was appeal in Ben's leanness. Was the reserve Nate had classed as inexperience something else? Ben met his brazen gaze without budging, and Nate had to grin in appreciation.

"I like what I'm seeing."

"I gathered." There was pink in Ben's cheeks, but his manner was deliberately cool. His eyes did not drop below Nate's shoulders. He'd noticed Nate's erection and was even more aware of his own.

Nate made his smirk a challenge. "That worried about giving me an order that I can't refuse? I've got on the job certification in bondage, and I think I remember enough of scouts to tie knots. Want me to gag you?"

He got the reaction he was hoping for, Ben's fingers cruelly tangled in his hair. "Pass. Somehow I can't see you as a very good boy scout."

Do all vampires have that predatory air, or am I just lucky? "Yeah? Let me show you how I do my best."

Challenge accepted, they fought with mouth, tongue, and teeth, trying to force the other to give way with rough kisses. Nate had the first victory. Ben gasped as Nate caught and sucked Ben's tongue, giving it the same treatment the other vampire's cock had received. Ben retaliated by taking the battle to Nate's sensitive neck.

"Fuck—" It was confirmed. Vampires came with an internal radar tuned to all Nate's weak points. Pulling Ben close, Nate didn't care that he was losing their battle. Ben worked his neck mercilessly. Occasionally Nate felt something sharp skim his skin. Ben didn't employ his fangs, but the knowledge that he could gave an undercurrent of danger.

When something firm pressed into Nate's stomach, he had to glance down to see who the erection belonged to. He slipped his hand down to caress both hard cocks in turn. "Like that?"

Ben rocked up in time with Nate's deliberate strokes. "Didn't think I'd enjoy someone jerking me off. But you—"

"I'm just that good."

Ben's lips caught Nate's earlobe. He felt teeth. *Fuck.* The involuntary jerk he gave at the touch was only too obvious given how tightly their cocks pressed against each other.

Ben's low chuckle confirmed that Nate was in trouble. "You'll do."

In pure self-defense, Nate thumbed the tip of Ben's penis,

playing with the sensitive ridge, and it was Ben's turn to buck at the touch. Nate glanced around the room. "Lube?"

Ben leaned across Nate to pull open a bedside drawer. "It's lucky you're hot," —he tossed Nate the thin tube— "because your technique is terrible."

Nate gave Ben cause to reconsider his technique, running a deliberate finger down the length of Ben's frenulum before twisting the cap off the lube. "You admit I'm hot."

"If you think I'm going to feed your ego, I" —Ben arched back as Nate caressed his sac with slick fingers— "I'm not falling for that."

"No? Then I'll settle for hearing you say my name when you come." Nate wrapped his hand around Ben's base, pumping him once over his entire length. Now that they were lubed, he wrapped his hands around Ben's ass. Their cocks lined up, and began to thrust against him.

Ben learned fast, slipping his arms around Nate to add to the friction. "You...you're far too confident—"

There was exhilaration in the simplicity. Or maybe the simplicity was the appeal. Nate gloried in the physicality of it. Ben was shorter, but he didn't hesitate to push back. The more forcefully Nate caressed him, the more urgently Ben responded.

Ben gasped in Nate's mouth. "Nate—"

"Just like that." Nate kissed him hard, trapping Ben's lip with his teeth and working at it with his tongue. He felt Ben's moan vibrate through his entire body. *What will he sound like, coming with my hand on his cock?* Nate's hand reached between them.

"Wait!"

Too fast? Nate drew back. *Was that compulsion? I'd have stopped anyway.* Nate pushed the thought aside. For this to work, he had to trust Ben. "You all right?"

Ben drew a steadying breath. He lifted his eyes directly to Nate's. "I want," he stopped abruptly. Nate watched Ben's tongue travel across his lips. "Before. I was inside you. I want to try that."

Nate squeezed Ben reassuringly. "You're sure?"

Ben's jaw set as he nodded. He'd clearly already made up his mind. "I want to know what it feels like," he said. "You can show me."

Nate let go of Ben's hips, giving him a gentle nudge toward the bed as he retrieved the lube. "Yeah. I can."

Usually guys wanted to get off in Nate. When they didn't, they were usually those with more extreme tastes, who wanted a harder fuck than they felt they could ask their partner for, getting off on the humiliation so much as anything else, or the rare virgin, using the club's make-believe to counter their hesitation.

Ben was a different prospect entirely, so different that Nate didn't begrudge him the interruption. He was quiet as Nate greased his fingers, but didn't hesitate to move when Nate drew him close. They lay side by side on the bed as Nate worked him open. Inexperienced but not vulnerable, it was impossible to treat Ben with anything but respect. "Tell me if you want to stop."

"What part of that sounded anything like stop?"

Nate leaned in to suck at Ben's lip. "Impatient, aren't you?"

The thick curtains blocked sound as well as light, but an incongruent note slipped through. They both paused as the siren wailed closer.

"Hate sirens. Always make me think something bad's going to happen," Nate said once it had passed.

"If you're hearing one, something did."

"Not the point." Nate flicked Ben's shoulder. They still made him think of Pa, even after so much time.

Ben shifted against him, hard length nudging Nate's own erection. "Leave me waiting and something bad will happen to you."

His face showed determination as he positioned himself according to Nate's directions. "I'm ready."

"It's sex, not an exam." Nate settled a hand loosely on Ben's hip, giving him a reassuring pat. Ben was above him, legs on either side of Nate's waist, and Nate used his other hand to line his penis up with Ben's hole.

Ben glanced down at him. "You're very gentle suddenly."

Ben should get an award – seriously, about to be taken for the first time and still wondering if he's being patronized? Nate thrust up so that his cock slid over Ben's entrance, so he could feel Nate's need between his legs. "I like it rough and fast. Doesn't mean I can't behave when I want." He continued to rock, drawing a soft moan from Ben. "You...you're worth doing right."

It was criminal. Nate was sure Ben had no idea how hot he looked, need warring with trepidation as he took hold of Nate's cock. He lowered himself without any more hesitation.

Ben was inherently private, but lack of experience with intimacy meant he had no guards against this. Nate gripped the sheets hard, holding himself back from thrusting up. He watched the play of emotion on Ben's face, the wonder as stretched muscles gave way to the sensation of another's warmth. His focus was inward and personal, intent on his own pleasure.

Nate felt every inch of his control tested. Ben was tight around him, muscles clenching and relaxing as he experimented with being filled, and Nate heard himself moan before he was aware the sound had left his mouth.

Ben glanced down through soft lashes and tightened again. The realization that he could draw such a response out of Nate gave him new confidence. Locking his gaze on Nate's, Ben licked his lips deliberately and began to move.

"Fuck," Nate groaned. Despite his good intentions, his hips jerked up. Ben adapted to meet Nate's urgent thrusts, taking more of Nate inside him with every upward motion. He was perfectly in control, setting the pace just a little bit slower than Nate needed. *Does Ben get off on that the same way I do?* Stringing out his partner until reserve gave way to bare passion.

Nate bit his lip, using the sting of pain to keep his head clear of lust.

"Like that?" There was challenge in Ben's tone. His pace had quickened erratically, and Nate reached up to take firm hold of Ben's thighs.

"Didn't peg you for a tease—"

Ben gasped suddenly, a shock going through his body. His hands clutched at Nate's chest as he sank forward. Nate's momentary alarm that he'd hurt him gave way to understanding as he took in Ben's glassy look and the rough sound as his hips moved back against Nate's cock. The change in angle had found Ben's sweet spot. Holding

Ben tightly in place, Nate thrust up against him and drew another unbelievable moan from the man.

"H-hell. *More—*"

That was the end of self-control for either of them. Nate urgently rolled his hips against Ben, who responded in kind. He used his body with abandon, plunging down on Nate's cock with no thought but the pleasure building within him. The intensity of his cries only spurred Nate into taking him harder. Ben's body arched shamelessly, his mouth falling open in breathless abandon. He moved as one with Nate but still remained distant, lost in his own pleasure. Nate ached to claim him.

Ben's eyes flickered open in shock as Nate grabbed his hand.

"Touch yourself," Nate said, too close for gentleness. He pulled Ben's hand to his cock, wrapping their fingers around it and pumping it roughly. "I want to see you come."

For a brief second, he thought Ben might resist, but his hips jerked, cock jumping in Nate's fingers. The next moment, Ben's seed coated Nate's stomach and hand as Ben sobbed his name. Ben's climax felt incredible around Nate, and he cried out, hips rising off the bed entirely as he slammed into Ben.

They lay locked together for the longest time, each unwilling to break the spell and come down. Even their breathing seemed synchronized. Moving felt wrong, so Nate offered Ben a kiss of apology before grabbing a towel from the en suite.

The brief separation allowed the thrill of reunion. Nate took pride in the fact that Ben needed no invitation to join him beneath the covers. As he settled on Nate's chest, Nate took the chance to stroke his fingers through Ben's long fringe, hair improbably thin and fine. "That— You are something else."

Ben allowed Nate to settle him on top of himself, burying his face against Nate's neck. "I didn't know it could be like that."

Not much of an achievement, given it was his first time, but Nate basked in it all the same. "You are going to make some lucky bastard deliriously happy someday." His fingers stilled in Ben's hair, the comfortable stirrings of satisfaction and exhaustion creeping up on him. Nate let his eyes drift shut. "Think I'm jealous."

Nate felt Ben's cool lips brush his temple. "Forget tonight." The words were so gentle Nate might have thought he'd imagined them. "Forget me."

Nate slept.

Chapter Five

Good sex was sex you felt the next day.

Nate felt it. He hauled himself out of bed and down the long corridor of the employee dorm, feeling the burn in his tired muscles. The floor-length mirrors of Century's sleek futuristic shower only displayed a paltry smattering of bruises. Nate explored them all. *Six months. I should be over the souvenir stage.* He snorted, turning away from the mirror.

There was nothing better than the combination of latent endorphins, aching muscles, and that moment when the hot water first hit... Nate stayed still, letting the water pound his skin remorselessly. The room was empty, meaning he had the luxury of taking as long as he wanted.

Something lingered.

Something the water could not wash away.

Nate ran fingers through his hair. *Amazing sex and an equally amazing paycheck.* No reason he shouldn't be happy. Right?

A distant whine intruded into his thoughts. Nate reached for the soap. *New Camden's got too many damn sirens.*

* ~ * ~ *

No one was in the break room, either. Nate buffed the apple he'd chosen for breakfast on his T-shirt, drumming his fingers on the small kitchen counter as he waited for the coffee to brew. The break room was never empty.

The buzz of voices in the hall was a relief. Aki flung open the door, leading a general surge toward the coffee machine. “Coffee? Nate, you’re a lifesaver.”

Nate stepped back. *The entire night staff?* He’d wanted company. This was pushing it. “Where were you?”

“Denise called a staff meeting. Tried to wake you, but you were out like a rock.” Aki looked up from his mug, expression sour. “If rocks drooled. Good night?”

“Great night.” Unprecedented opportunity to brag, but all Nate wanted was to bury himself in the everyday. “There wasn’t a meeting on the schedule.”

“Guy got murdered last night. Graphically. He was in the business.” Aki shrugged. “We had the whole no chances, anything weird tell security, don’t sign your soul over to any demonic entities spiel. Like basic training, only without the education videos.”

“Ugh.”

“Come to think of it, the guy had black hair and hazel eyes like you. You’d better be careful in case this killer has a type.”

He’s got to be joking. Right? Nate turned the apple over in his hand. “There’s been other deaths?”

“Not yet. But it looked like a ritual that was interrupted. Chances are good he’s only the first.”

Nate shivered. “How can you be so flippant about it this early in the morning?”

"Morning? It's past two." Aki shook his head. "And before you say anything, don't. No one cares how great your night was."

"I wasn't going to—"

"How can you even bring it up in the circumstances? I think that's totally inappropriate."

Nate wasn't going to win this.

[Late frost. Worried about new growth. New Camden?]

Had news of the murder made it as far as Little River? Nate leaned back on his bunk with his phone. The last time he'd sent Ethan a message, he'd been in the greatest danger of his life and had no idea.

[Cold but fine. Slept in so I got no idea about a frost.] Nate hesitated over the send button. How did you tell your brother you'd had once in a lifetime sex with a vampire family? At least Ethan wasn't likely to flip out. Ma on the other hand... *[Last night's house call? Only a goddamn vampire! Nothing happened, but in retrospect, kind of freaked out.]*

Sent. Nate bit his lip. He was still digesting the night. Without Hunter's presence and the eroticism of the situation acting on his impulses, he reviewed the night with decidedly mixed feelings.

It seemed like ages before Ethan's response flashed across his screen. *[Spider ferns need light. But be careful. Don't leave it by the window overnight.]*

Seriously? Nate wanted to pitch his phone against the wall. There was not flipping out and then there was this. *[You care more about that stupid plant.]*

His wristband vibrated. Wanted in the lobby? Something about last night...

The message scrolled away before Nate had caught all of it. He dropped his phone into his pocket and stood. *Just as well.* Last thing he needed was to fight with his brother.

Stepping into the club, Nate had to admit it wasn't Ethan's fault he didn't understand. Even with the lights on and the cleanup crew working on the floor, Century was a universe away from the sleepy country town Ethan inhabited. Add in the nature of last night's call, and in a day or two, Nate himself would have trouble believing it.

"Nathan."

"Just Nate is fine." Nate felt relieved—then immediately foolish. *It's daylight. Was I really expecting Hunter?* He came to a halt before the waiting man. "What about 'what happens at dinner stays at dinner'?"

The man smiled. He'd swapped out his cardigan for a more businesslike black blazer, but the shirt beneath it was thrift-shop paisley with a high collar. "House rules don't apply to business. I'm Peter de Silver. I take care of Hunter's finances."

Nate shook his hand and tried not to think about what the collar concealed. "Anything wrong?"

"That's my line." Peter raised an eyebrow at him. "I understand you left without being paid this morning."

"Fuck me. I did, too."

Peter held out a credit card that Nate recognized. "I take it you're not dissatisfied with the transaction then?" He held Nate's hand as he swiped the card and entered in the details, just like a proposal in a period drama.

The perfect surreal note to end an entirely surreal encounter. "No. No, not at all. I barely remember getting into the taxi." Nate okayed the details.

"Hunter anticipated as much." Peter hit the final confirmation button.

There. Contract fulfilled, job over. Things could go back to normal. *And not a moment too soon.* "So—"

"My card." Peter held out a crisp rectangle. "Just in case."

Nate paused. It was only the quizzical look in Peter's eyes that made him realize how silly the hesitation was. *I get cautious now? When it's all over?* "Sure." About to slide the card into his pocket, he paused. "ARX? The insurance company?" *What did vampires need insurance for? They're vampires!*

Peter's smile was faintly self-congratulatory, and Nate hoped his thoughts weren't visible on his face. "It keeps us busy. New Camden, especially. We offer complete coverage against supernatural threats, so you can imagine how in demand we are."

ARX reduces the supernatural threat by giving it a steady job? "I can see Hunter in a suit. Other than that—"

Peter smirked. "Hunter's a field agent. Investigates claims and, where possible, eradicates the cause. We're the only insurance company to include extermination among our services. Really gives us a competitive edge."

Something of the chill of the townhouse came back to Nate suddenly. He shivered. "I can see that."

"You should consider us." Peter brushed something off his sleeve and pulled his blazer straight. “I imagine that your…business has risks.”

Nate’s smile was flat. “Century’s got us covered. Insurance contract tailor-made to account for every on-the-job contingency with a solid firm, and they pay part of our premiums.”

“That’s too bad.” Peter shrugged, looking away from Nate’s faded denim jeans. “Our rates are really quite reasonable.”

A dig at my clothes? Really? “I’ll keep that in mind.” Nate tucked the card into his pocket. *How does he know I didn’t buy these preworn in a thrift shop?* “So—”

“I’ve passed this place a million times.” Peter glanced around the club. “Have to say, it’s not what I expected.”

Nate walked him to the door. “You have to see it at night. Totally different atmosphere. And the music’s unironically great.”

Peter laughed. “Maybe I will.” His smile was self-deprecating. Club too mainstream? Or did its iconic status give him a smug hipster kick? “Business allowing. Nights tend to be our busy time.”

“Ours too.” Nate watched Peter slide into a waiting car.

It pulled away from the pavement immediately, swallowed by the usual peak hour rush. Nate lingered on the steps, surrounding himself with the chatter of passing pedestrians, the day cleaning crew saying their good-byes behind him, and the burst of music from a passing car. It was a new night. No vampires. Time to kick that lingering feeling of unease for good.

Nate should have known better. Century offered many things but normality was not on the night's menu. Even in New Camden's unique melting pot of culture clash, progressive attitudes, and paranormal diversity, murder stood out.

"Graveyard killing? It's a cult. That simple." Aki gave his opinion with the authority of a New Camden native.

Beatrice disagreed. "Male prostitute. Cults are traditional."

"Maybe he was an ex-member? Or a newbie who didn't pass initiation?"

"More likely. Getting out of a cult is like getting out of a gym membership—"

Nate had never realized just how confining the table booths were. "Can we change the subject?"

"Please!" Mandy looked pale. "I'm not going to sleep tonight. Mom called twice today. She's convinced I'll be sacrificed to some eldritch horror."

Nate patted her hand. "Mine, too. I told my brother I was fine, but no. She has to check."

"You two delicate blossoms can relax. New Camden's finest are on the job." Beatrice leaned in, her oversized plastic bangles clattering against the table. "Don't all look at once, but the guy over there? Talking to the barman?"

Aki craned his neck to see. "Brown hair, bomber jacket?"

"I said 'don't all look.'" Beatrice waited for everyone's attention. "I told you about six-B summoning a demon dog? He's the officer who took my testimony."

"No way." Mandy looked again. "He's one of them? He looks...normal."

"Don't count on it." Nate had a bad feeling. The sirens had warned of something happening.

"Makes sense they'd investigate the clubs," Beatrice continued. "Don't make it obvious you're checking him out. They say werewolves can hear across a crowded room—"

The man turned. Nate looked away immediately, but took with him the impression of a hard, considering gaze and eyes curiously light in the dim club. The hair on the back of Nate's neck stood up. He was relieved as one of the security team ushered the man toward the back stairs. *I have no problem believing he's not entirely human.*

"He's not a werewolf," Aki said immediately. "Not enough facial hair."

"Maybe he shaves." Nate toyed with the glass in front of him.

"I didn't say he *was* a werewolf," Beatrice said. "But he's definitely *something*."

"I wish they wouldn't let people like that in here." Mandy shivered as she picked up her cocktail.

Aki put down his drink. "He's doing his job. Protecting us."

"It's like my father always says, 'if it's not human, it's not right.'"

"Does your father also—"

Nate put his hand on Aki's shoulder. "You never told us what happened to the demon dog, Bea."

Beatrice met his eyes. For a moment, Nate thought she was going to call him on his overly obvious subject change. Instead she leaned back against the wall of the booth. "It's what happened to six-B. Three a.m., Thursday, the fire alarm goes off. Smoke and sulfur everywhere, but no fire. Fire department broke down the door to six-B. They found a pentagram, a half-eaten sack of dog biscuits...and that's it. The occupants? Gone."

Nate whistled. "Botched banishment ritual?"

"Looks like it. Landlord's had the cleaners in, but the rotten egg smell got into the internal AC. It stinks like anything, but it hasn't stopped him leasing six-B."

Mandy blanched. "Someone actually wants to live there?"

"Central location, close to the metro, decent rent." Beatrice shrugged. "New guy is old, keeps pigeons, and smells like bird shit. I think he's trying to drown out the sulfur with guano."

"I am never visiting you after dark again!"

Beatrice's smile was pointed. "I'd take demon dogs over walking under that bridge of yours any night."

"Don't remind me!" Mandy grimaced. "I'm dreading going home tonight."

Nate's wristband vibrated. "Just as I was starting to think I'd lucked out, and Denise had forgotten me." He put his hand on Mandy's shoulder as he squeezed past her. "You take the subway home, right? Want company? I'm on a half-shift, I can see you home."

Mandy looked pathetically grateful. "Thanks, Nate. I'd— That means a lot."

* ~ * ~ *

"Against all expectations, I survived—" Nate came to an abrupt halt in the doorway.

Slouched on Denise's sofa was the man Beatrice had recognized. The synthetic office light and familiar surroundings did not diminish his presence. Nate was uneasily aware that the man's sharp gaze was on him.

"Nathan." Denise was brisk. "Gunn is here from the police."

"Officer Gunn, Department Seven." The man's grin showed an unnecessary amount of teeth. "I have some questions about last night."

Nate sat. "Last night?"

"You can tell him anything." Professionalism alone couldn't account for Denise's abrupt tone. Nate glanced up, surprised to see that her ample lips were pressed together thinly. "The nondisclosure agreement you signed was invalidated when Mr. Hunter failed to apprise us of the nature of those using your services."

They already knew.

"You're not surprised." Gunn's tone was conversational. "When exactly did you work it out?"

"At the house." Nate glanced at the man sideways. He felt oppressed by the man's gaze, reluctant to look directly at him. "But it didn't change anything. I'm fine."

"We can't say the same for Michael Brook." Gunn placed a snapshot on the low coffee table. "Seen him before?"

Nate studied the photos. A man about his age raised a beer in a toast to the photographer. He had a bad case of red-eye, a vacant grin and wore a Canucks shirt. "Not that I know of. Maybe in the dark at the club..." He glanced at Denise, hoping she had some idea of what was going on.

“As far as we know, Brook had no connections to Century.”

“Then why ask me?”

“You were observed leaving twenty-one Rueful Crescent by taxi at five fifty-eight this morning.” Gunn’s hair was scruffy, and there was visible stubble on his chin, but he rattled off the facts with certainty. “Taxi company stated that you arrived there five thirty-four p.m. the previous day. You spent over twelve hours in the company of Saltaire’s colony. I want to know what happened in that time.”

Nate stared at him. “Colony?”

“Plural for a group of bats.” Gunn leaned back against the sofa, one arm draped casually over the back. “Bats, vampires...”

“That’s the stupidest thing I’ve heard all day. You get a murder of crows, but a colony of vamp—” Nate’s brain caught up to his mouth belatedly. He swallowed, placed his hands on his knees. “I’m not saying anyone got murdered last night.”

“I am.” Gunn allowed his words to grow big enough to fill the room before he continued. “You’ve seen the newspapers. I’ll spare you the gory details, but we know Brook didn’t meet a natural end. Your hosts are connected to the case.”

Nate’s mouth felt heavy. “Connected? How?”

“You arrived at the house alone. Were you the only guest?”

“There were four others. Two women, Hunter’s accountant. The butler. You didn’t answer my question.”

“And influence your account?” Gunn grinned. “I’m looking forward to this. First time I’ve heard of anyone spending a night with a vampire and insisting nothing happened.” He stretched out, resting his heavy boots on the coffee table.

The movement rattled the papers on the table. Nate recognized Hunter's request form. "That—"

"I've told Officer Gunn everything." Denise crossed her arms. "Mr. Hunter's use of mind control on both of us, the fact that he was alone with you for three hours in the club. You don't owe him any protection, Nathan."

"I thought Century's privacy clause extends to nonhumans."

"Not when the nonhuman doesn't disclose their status or abuses their power. Those rules are in place to ensure your safety—not so that I send you off like a lamb to slaughter!"

"Hunter plays by the rules—but only so far as it's convenient to him." Gunn spoke with a confidence that drew Nate's attention. He indicated the request form with his foot. "Interesting reading. How was the blood play?"

"Nonexistent," Nate retorted. "They'd already dined."

Gunn removed his shoes from the table, sitting up. "None of them fed?"

"I told you. Nothing happened. Nothing vampiric." Admitting that still felt wrong, but Denise and Gunn were absolutely still, waiting on his words. "The idea was to give...the brother...as normal an experience as possible. That meant pretending they were human."

"Show me your neck." Gunn was alarming at the other side of the coffee table. At Nate's back, he was even worse.

Nate tugged his T-shirt down. "No unexplained marks. I checked when I showered."

"That doesn't make sense." Nate was grateful for the hand Denise set on his arm. "Why would Mr. Hunter visit Nathan twice before abducting him, if not—"

"He didn't abduct me," Nate protested.

Gunn abruptly turned his back on the two of them. "Compulsion. If he was preparing a witness, he wouldn't need to drink—"

"That is the opposite of what he wanted!" Nate clenched his fists. "Hunter came to Century because he was looking for someone Ben's age. Someone with features Ben found attractive, who he could relax with and forget being a vampire. Someone who didn't need to be compelled to do things."

Gunn looked sharply over his shoulder. "Hunter tell you that?"

Nate held his gaze. "No. But I know it's true."

The empty feeling he'd not been able to shake resolved itself suddenly. Hunter's odd manner, Ben's unrequited attraction to the man—Hunter had chosen Nate because of their superficial resemblance. That clarity brought another fact into sharp relief.

"Oh god. Brook—"

"Exactly." Gunn hooked his hands through the belt of his beaten up jeans and looked down at Nate. "Hunter shopped around before he fixed on you. Brook worked in a bar that catered specifically to vampires. They were observed together roughly two weeks ago. Brook was reported to be distracted and moody ever since."

Nate could feel Denise's gaze. "I was distracted because the man is a fucking sex god," he said, lifting his eyes to hers. "And he'd promised me a foursome."

The manager sighed. "He wouldn't have needed to coerce Nathan. Or any of the staff. In the short time he was here, Mr. Hunter left an impression."

Knew it! Aki was totally jealous.

"That doesn't eliminate compulsion. Saltaire's colony knows how to be discreet." Gunn sat back down, leaning across the coffee table to watch Nate closely. "Still. An account of the night from someone free of the effects of a vampire's bite should be something."

"You here for my information or your kicks?"

"Your dinner companions left at ten. We already know about their regular arrangement with Saltaire. What happened next?"

"I watched them leave from the third floor. Hunter came to take me downstairs— I really have to do this?"

"It would help Officer Gunn a lot." Denise listened as intently as the officer. She leaned on her immaculate desk. "It was then you provided your services as laid out in the contract?"

Nate was grateful for the out. "And then I provided my services. That's really it. I went back to Ben's room with him—"

"Who else was in the room?"

"Hunter, Ben." Nate stopped himself from saying 'the Vamp-daddy.' "An older man that Ben told me later was Saltaire."

"Didn't smile, imperialistic mannerisms, made the room heavier just by existing in it?"

Nate blinked at Gunn. "You know your vampires."

"It's my job. What time did you leave the group?"

Like I had the chance to look at the clock! "I don't— Wait. A clock struck midnight. Saltaire said he had business, and Hunter volunteered to help. It was Ben's anniversary, so they gave him the night off."

Denise seated herself on the arm of Nate's chair. "Ben's the brother?"

"Vampire brother." *Of all the things to get defensive about!* Nate took a deep breath. "Anyway, I went back to Ben's room. We talked for a bit before...getting back to business."

"How long were you together?" Gunn questioned with extreme viciousness.

"A couple of hours? I don't remember."

"A gap in your memory could be proof of—"

"They didn't mind-work me! You want the blow-by-blow, fine." Nate met Gunn's challenge. "We started out with some basic aftercare. I asked about the vampire thing. Ben was surprised I knew. I made some comment about Hunter, ticked him off. We argued until I told him we could be making more productive use of our time." Nate shrugged. "You want the R-rated version, Denise will have to charge you."

"Spare me." Gunn's mouth was an unimpressed line. "You were together all night?"

"Well, yeah. I mean, I fell asleep. I don't remember seeing him when the taxi arrived, but I barely remember the taxi."

"Nathan is not a morning person," Denise agreed. "He slept through our last fire drill and today's meeting."

Gunn ignored this evidence against vampiric intervention. "You've got no idea when you fell asleep?"

"I wasn't exactly checking my watch." *Did a vampire piss in this guy's cereal? What the hell is his problem?* "Could have been an hour. Could have been two or three. The sirens didn't help any."

"Sirens?"

"Killed the mood." Nate shrugged. "I've never liked the sound of them."

He wasn't sure he was even heard.

"Only one call-out near Rueful Crescent last night." Gunn frowned. Turned inward, the man's attention was less alarming. Nate was startled to realize the man was only in his late twenties. Before he could study Gunn further, the man's head whipped up, fixing Nate with his tawny glare. "Bennet was with you when you heard the sirens? Did he leave your sight during the three hours you were alone?"

"No. The other two, sure. Ben's the only one I was with the entire time."

Gunn stood so suddenly he almost upended the table. He contained himself with effort, shoulders as tightly clenched as his fists. "Your information has been valuable," he said through gritted teeth. "If you think of anything else that might be relevant, you can reach me at this number."

Nate tucked the card into his pocket as Gunn swept the papers on the table into the pocket of his bomber jacket. "That's it?"

"We need a formal statement; we'll be in touch." By the time he reached the door, Gunn had recovered himself. "Some friendly advice. Don't accept any more requests from Hunter. There's no such thing as a tame vampire." He slammed the door behind him.

"Friendly?" Nate shook his head. "The hell—"

The arms around his shoulder shocked him into silence. "I am so sorry, Nathan. If I'd had any idea—"

Oh man. It is just not my day. Nate awkwardly patted the arm of the scariest woman he knew. "Honestly, I'm fine."

"If anything had happened to you, I would never have forgiven myself." Denise squeezed him tightly then waved him back toward his seat. "Now, your report."

"Report?"

"Standard procedure in the event of an irregular call." Denise sat behind her desk. "Unlike Officer Gunn, I will be requiring the R-rated version."

~~*

Nate was now in trouble twice over. First, for not calling the instant he realized his clients' nature and again for not following Century's protection rules. "Seriously, Denise. They're dead. What STD is going to survive vampires?"

"You're going to Nisha now," Denise ordered. "She is giving you every test she has, and you're not working the floor until they're all back."

"But Denise—"

"I'll make room for you in laundry. Go, or I'll march you to medical myself."

The in-house doctor was unsympathetic as she stuck Nate with needles. "Rules are rules. And really, if you dislike injections so much, you shouldn't hook up with vampires. What are needles compared to fangs?"

"I didn't know they were vampires when I signed on." Nate held his hand over his newest puncture wound as directed. "How long am

I stuck in laundry?"

"A week to ten days. Enjoy it. It'll be your first time off since you started here."

"This isn't time off. This is torture." Nate tugged his shirt back on over his head. "Can I go already?"

* ~ * ~ *

At least Beatrice and Mandy were normal. Walking from the subway station, Nate threw himself into their usual pattern of conversation with gusto. He was disappointed when Beatrice came to a halt in front of an apartment building.

"This is my stop."

The stark industrialist design of the 1970s style apartment building was undercut by the creative additions of neighboring street artists. Nate tried but couldn't make out even a faint scent of sulfur. "Want us to see you to your door?"

"Please. I'm a native." Beatrice plunged through the automatic door without hesitation.

"Bea always carries mace, a crucifix, and salt. Chances are, she'd wind up protecting us," Mandy said. She twisted the edge of her bright pink cardigan between her fingers.

Still freaked out about the demon dog? Nate patted her arm as they turned back down the path. "Knowing Bea, I think you're right."

They left the busy and well-lit main road for a seedy side street beneath a traffic bridge that plunged the footpath below into complete darkness. Nate was relieved to emerge to discover a tidy brick apartment with functioning lighting on the other side.

"I hate that bridge." Mandy dug in her handbag for the key. "Thank you, Nate. I must seem pretty silly, but—"

"Don't apologize," Nate patted her on the shoulder. "You should complain about the lack of light. That bridge is a crime scene waiting to happen."

Mandy found her key. "Do you want to come in for a coffee?" She paused before the door.

'If it's not human, it's not right.'

Nate shook his head but couldn't shake the memory of her words. "It's late. You get off to bed, Mandy."

The hell is wrong with me? Nate climbed between the cold sheets of his bed in Century's employee dorms, thoroughly annoyed. *The one thing all day that goes my way and I turn it down?* Mandy was pretty, pliable, and genuinely into him. Maybe they didn't agree on everything, but who did? A week ago, he would not have hesitated.

At least this day's over.

"That was fast. Hit it and quit it?"

"Sorry, Aki. If I'd realized you were sleeping, I'd have made more noise."

"The foursome's not enough, you have to wake me up to relive your out-of-hours exploits, too. It's official then, you guys are dating? Or are you doing the benefits thing?"

Nate's life. "I didn't stay, Aki."

"Obviously. But you fucked her, right?"

Nate didn't reply.

The bed frame creaked as Aki levered himself to the edge of his bunk to look down at Nate, despite the lack of light. “You didn’t?”

“We didn’t.”

“Did she not—”

“Coffee. Think she wanted to, but I don’t know.” Nate shrugged, even knowing Aki couldn’t see him. “Didn’t feel it.”

“What’s wrong with you lately? You and Mandy have been doing the sickening small town sweethearts thing for months now. Beatrice agrees with me; it’s revolting.”

“Beatrice hates anything that doesn’t come in a cocktail glass or with a designer label.”

“Not the point. I thought you liked Mandy.” Aki paused. “Tell me it’s not the house party guy.”

Nate blanched. “Hunter? No.”

“Good. Because I’m not tall enough to shake sense into you.”

Nate snorted. “You’re not tall enough to shake sense into a Chihuahua.” He adjusted his pillow so he could rest his head on top of it but still cradle one arm around it. “I’m over Hunter. Saw him with someone else. I don’t have a chance.”

“Sucks, man.” Aki’s fake sympathy was improving. “But you shouldn’t take it out on Mandy.”

“You just said we were sickening.”

“Completely nauseating. But don’t let that prevent you from being all domestic and gross.” The bunk shook slightly, Aki settling onto his back.

“Sacrifice appreciated. But it’s not that.” Nate toyed with the edge of the duvet. “I’m up for having fun, but I don’t think I could date anyone I couldn't take home to meet the folks."

"You are so provincial, it hurts."

"That's common sense! Everything going to plan, you want your date to become family."

Aki's laugh was hollow. "Family. I told mine I was gay, Dad was all 'Door's over there.' We're not even friends on Facebook."

Nate sat up. He'd noticed Aki never mentioned family but put it down to Aki's habitual irreverent attitude. *What else have I missed?* "Sorry, Aki. I didn't know."

"I try not to dwell." The bunk creaked again. "Is that why you only date girls?"

So much for sleep. "We're getting weirdly personal tonight. But if I met the right guy, sure. Ma's religious, but she's..." Nate bit his lip. "Flexible."

"Mandy's got perfect daughter-in-law written all over her. No mother in the world would disapprove."

"Something she said tonight made me think." Nate settled back against the wall. "Maybe we're not as similar as I thought."

"Tonight?"

"It bothered you too, what she said about supernaturals."

"That." Aki shifted. "Yeah. I guess it struck close to home. It's not like anyone chooses to become a werewolf, or a vampire—"

"Some people choose."

"But you don't know that until you get to know them, right? That kind of prejudice is... Well, it's complete and utter bullshit, that's what it is."

"Aki—"

"But then we're all jaded in New Camden. Unlike you pure country folk who think *lemures* are nothing more than a group of cuddly, long-tailed monkeys."

"We did *lemures* in training. Roman ghosts, right? Didn't get buried and mad about it?"

"Malignant spirits. You won't see one wearing a toga." Nate wasn't surprised to feel the bed frame rattle, his friend dragging himself to the edge of the bunk again. "You paid attention to training?"

"It's pretty interesting. The history of it and how New Camden ended up with a mix of monsters because of all the different cultures living here. Like the vampire who stalked a guy here from the Amazon and then settled in Founder's park? The parasol—"

"*Patasola.*"

"Patasola." There was something Nate couldn't place in Aki's tone, and he hurried on. "When you get down to it, they were human once. Until something went wrong."

"There's 'wrong' and then there's 'dead and lusting for human flesh.' And not in the way that gets us paid."

"Very wrong. But it's like you said before, you got to get to know a guy."

Nate was surprised when Aki's hand brushed his shoulder. "I don't know how you can go from every country stereotype to this in the same conversation, but it's cool. Sorry if I gave you a hard time today."

Nate snorted, patting Aki's hand. "Maybe you should try to let go of your anticountry prejudice. You're seriously close-minded."

"I'll come down there and kick you. Don't think I won't." Aki gripped Nate's shoulder tightly and then let go.

Nate listened to Aki resettle himself, feeling that maybe he'd accomplished something after all. "What's stopping me kicking back?"

"I'm banking on that old-fashioned country courtesy."

"Bad news, Aki." The wooden slats that held Aki's mattress were loose enough that Nate could push them up easily.

"Jerk! Shattering illusions without warning! What's next? Gonna tell me it's not actually quieter out there?"

"Clearly you've never tried to sleep through the dawn chorus. Or been hauled out of bed because the cattle got out overnight and you have to stop them from eating the lawn."

"At least our garbage trucks take mess, they don't leave it."

A week ago, Nate would have left it there. Now...

He bit his lip. "Anyone says there's nothing odd in the country, they're full of shit."

"I thought that was cows?"

Despite himself, Nate smiled. "No. Everywhere you go, you got people that aren't like everyone else."

Now he had Aki's attention. There was no movement at all from the top bunk. "What do you mean?"

"Ethan's different."

"Your brother?"

"My brother."

"What, he's got...second sight or something?"

"We don't actually talk about it. It's just there." Nate hesitated.

"I've never tried to explain it. But it's part of him. Like the color of his eyes, or the music he likes."

He tensed at Aki's sudden shift, but it was only so that Aki could lean down and stab Nate with his finger. "Is that why I've never met him? I thought you said he was an antisocial weirdo."

"He is." Nate swatted Aki's hand away. "He drove me all the way here and left the second my suitcase was on the pavement. He didn't even stay long enough to eat. Said the place felt wrong."

"'Cause he stands out?" Aki sounded sympathetic.

"'Cause he's an obsessive compulsive weirdo who is allergic to fun, people, and leaving the goddamn farm."

"You sound so close."

Nate snorted. "I got a text this afternoon. Told him I'd spent the night with a house of vampires, and his response? He reminded me to take care of the stupid spider fern! It's like—"

"Vampires." Aki's voice was hot and angry.

Nate remembered belatedly Denise's injunction of silence.

Chapter Six

If there's one place in New Camden guaranteed vampire-free... Nate pulled on his thick workman's gloves and surveyed the community garden with satisfaction. *Score one for normality.*

There was no greater challenge to the surrounding monochrome buildings than this riot of life. The aluminum fence exploded with color, the rusting metal decorated with a lively conversation between rival street artists.

Within its bounds, the garden made a strong argument of its own. The rich brown of the topsoil contrasted favorably with the lighter, grittier dirt that was the base of New Camden. The entire spectrum of greens was represented, from the new leaves on apple trees, so fresh they might have sprouted that morning, to the stalwart, unvarying green of the lavender, the dark, mossy sheen of the ivy that clung to the shady side of the equipment shed and the mottled yellow-green of the decomposing vines on the compost heap. The smattering of blossoms was a footnote to the steady succession of spring flowers that had come and gone already. Then there were the volunteers themselves.

"Just in time, Nathan." Mrs. Ikeda greeted him from the picnic table where she presided over the old lady collective, busy scrubbing dirt from newly harvested potatoes. "There's the potato bed to do."

Nate glanced away from Mrs. Enver's blinding headscarf to the vegetable patch. It was a mess of vines and trampled dirt, the women having made sure that not a single potato escaped harvest. "You like to keep me busy."

"Since you missed the fun of the harvesting, it's only fair we save you something." Ms. Heller smirked. She was a short-haired septuagenarian whose arch manner projected "retired school teacher" so strongly Nate forgot she was an ex-policewoman.

"You don't mind?" Mrs. Ikeda paused as though she'd only now realized how much work clearing the patch was.

Nate grinned. "Leave it to me."

No one had taken Nate's preferred shovel from the communal shed. He swung it lightly from hand to hand as he headed for the vegetable beds. *Finally. Things are looking up.*

It had taken effort to haul himself out of bed before Aki, but avoiding the dreaded v-word was worth it. He'd even managed to fill his flask from the break room coffee pot without anyone dredging up the latest developments in the Cult Killing. In this case, ignorance wasn't just bliss; it was sanity.

Best of all, the strange feeling of inadequacy that had haunted him ever since the premonition was finally gone, replaced by the blue sky, the midmorning sun, and the breeze lazily stirring the leaves of the willow. Nate breathed it in with relish. *Dracula never gardened—*

"No such thing as your common garden-variety psychopath," Ms. Heller resumed. "But I agree with the papers. There will be more victims."

Nate froze.

Mrs. Ikeda leaned in. “Disappearances have been up lately. The radio—”

“I tell my son he’s mad not to set a curfew for his girls. A city like this...”

“But the victim was male—”

“The victim could bleed. That’s the sum of it.” The other women deferred to Ms. Heller’s certainty. “A necromancer doesn’t care for male, female, human, animal. They’re only interested in power.”

“Necromancer? The papers—”

“A cult means a group. They meet indoors where they can’t be observed. No, this man was killed *in situ* and that means—”

Nate hurried past them to the potato bed.

Hopefully anyone noticing his haste would put it down to enthusiasm. Weren’t the other volunteers always saying that if there was one person who could be counted on for the hardest jobs, it was him? Nate applied himself to raking with energy, but it was too late.

Something of the coldness of New Camden had crept in with the gossip. The soil, so full of promise earlier, now held the distinct aroma of wet leaves and the memory of the townhouse. Nate paused to work a rock loose from the garden. It wasn’t Hunter his thoughts returned to, but—

Something rustled in the undergrowth behind him. Nate swung round.

Brown eyes blinked at him impassively from behind thick-rimmed spectacles.

Nate bit his lip not to swear. “Kenji. You got to warn a guy before you do that.”

The child considered Nate thoughtfully. He wore his grandmother's windbreaker. It covered all of him except for the tip of his very muddy sneakers. He held something carefully in his clasped hands. "Grasshoppers are insects because they have six legs."

"Stands to reason. Shouldn't you be at school?"

"Holidays. Guess what I caught."

Nate changed position so that he could talk to Kenji as he dug. "Is it an insect?"

"Correct."

"Grasshopper?"

"Yes," Kenji said unwillingly. "But it only has five legs."

The resulting discussion on the vagrancies of the insect kingdom lasted until Mrs. Ikeda spotted Kenji crawling through the compost in pursuit of a beetle. He was dragged home for a bath, the old lady collective dissolving in Mrs. Ikeda's wake. Possibly, they'd wanted to leave earlier but hesitated to make the first move. Nate didn't blame them. The demure Mrs. Ikeda held such firm sway over the community garden that even Father Baumann, priest of the church the land belonged to, deferred to her. *And who could blame us? Ikeda could put the fear into a necromancer, no sweat.*

Finally, it was just Nate. He peeled off his gloves as he surveyed the vegetable patch, now neatly raked and composted, ready for the planting of the sweet corn. *Still think we've left it late...*

A voice cleared behind his shoulder. "Another garden, another meeting."

Just as well he'd already put the shovel away. "Jesus— Godfrey?"

He coughed. "Right the second time." He was prim, although it was hard to tell whether he disapproved of Nate's casual heresy or was simply doing his job. He wore a generous coat over his suit, and he had a canteen slung over his shoulder, but he radiated "butler" nonetheless. "I trust I did not disturb you?"

"No, I...no." Nate gestured vaguely toward the vegetable bed. "I was just about to leave."

"Then I arrived at just the right time." The man's smile was polite. "I mentioned the sad state of our garden to Father Baumann as I was stocking up on holy water, and he thought I might be interested in meeting one of his volunteers, a very keen gardener who might have time for some part time work."

That explained why a vampire's butler was hanging out at a church—if not why he needed holy water.

Godfrey's words caught up to Nate. He looked up from the canteen in shock. "You want to hire me?"

"If it does not conflict with your...existing obligations." The butler smiled genially. "I imagine that your days are mostly free?"

Nate bit his lip. "My manager would have to sign off before I could accept." *No way Denise is going to agree to this.* The thought made Nate feel better. "I think I'm booked."

"A pity." Godfrey radiated exactly the right amount of disappointment without being pressing. "Still, if anything changes, you'll let me know?"

Nate snorted. "Sure." *And when hell freezes over, I'll get in touch.*

* ~ * ~ *

"You're not seriously thinking about it, are you?"

Nate started guiltily away from the spider fern. "What? No!"

Aki considered him from behind his textbook. He preferred to read on his back on the top bunk, legs against the wall and his head upside down over the side of the bed. He claimed it helped him remember. "Do I need to go over why vampires are a bad idea?"

They were talking again. Supposedly, this was an improvement.

"This has nothing to do with Hunter, all right?" Nate misted the fern one last time before turning to the rest of his collection of houseplants. "I've never had a patch of garden entirely my own. The farm is Ethan's. I mean, it's left to both of us, but it's his, no question. And the community garden's great, but you want to plant anything, you have to get approval at the quarterly meetings, and they always have those when we're working." Aki's expression was, if anything, even more skeptical. "Honest."

"I can't tell if you're trying to convince yourself, or you're actually this weird." Aki shook his head.

"Says the guy who grew up in weirdness central. Seriously, you're from New Camden."

"Making me all the more qualified to know a freak when I see one. And I see a freak now, fussing with his weirdo plants."

Nate spritzed him with the mister. "Everyone's got a hobby. You like running."

Aki tried to deflect him with his textbook. "Fuck off! This is a library book." He sat up. "You realize you were really lucky to walk away from that job, right?"

Nate leaned against the wall. "Yeah. I know." The spider fern's tendrils extended over the side of its pot, and Nate gently guided the new growth toward the light offered by the window. “Trust me. I have no desire to go back there.”

“Then what is it?”

Nate bit his lip. “You ever get a feeling like—”

Aki’s phone alarm blared. “No rest for the wicked.” He let his textbook slide from his hand. “Why’d you have to get relegated? It’s always so boring without you.”

Nate rolled his eyes, returning the mister to the desk that neither of them used. “At least you’re on the floor.”

“Not my fault you apparently forget all your training the moment a vampire bats his eyes at you.” Aki paused in the doorway. “You forgot one.”

“What?”

Aki nodded to the line of plants on the windowsill. “You didn’t water the last one.”

Nate looked from the plant back to Aki. “You’re kidding. The *cactus*?”

They were still arguing when they reached the dressing room.

“It rains in the desert!”

“Sporadically! Anyway, he’s fine for at least another week— What now?”

“Plants don’t have gender!” Aki paused. “Please tell me you haven’t named them.”

“Not formally—”

Aki shook his head. “I don’t want to know.” He shut the dressing room door on Nate.

Not worth it. Nate made his way down the hall to the cleaning closet. All the good of the garden was rapidly being undone. As he pulled the nondescript coveralls over his T-shirt, he tried to remember the smell of the soil and feel of the sun, but the stringent smell of disinfectant was too strong.

Nate hated cleaning.

He hated how boring it was. How the basic hourly for cleaning was only a fraction of what he could make on the floor. He hated how on cleaning, no one even saw him. The black coveralls could have been an invisibility spell. He had to skirt the cart around club-goers carrying on conversations and more intimate transactions as though he wasn't even there.

Most of all, Nate hated the fact that everyone else was having more fun than him.

Tables were fine. Wipe down the surfaces, sweep beneath, and he could exchange opinions on the game playing on the kitchen radio with the bar staff when he dropped off the dishes.

The booths were another story—crumpled sheets, used condoms, the lingering smell of sex. Nate tried to concentrate on cleaning, but his mind insisted on recreating the time he'd spent in one of those same booths with Hunter. Some of the best sex he'd ever had.

And yet...

Nate shook himself firmly. *I am too young to be this jaded.* Seriously, who was he— Aki? *Should've taken Mandy up on the coffee. I've been single too long.*

The laundry room was uncomfortably humid, but thanks to Ma's training, Nate had his share of the night's load pressed and back on the wardrobe racks in record time. He glanced at the clock. It was still early enough that there would be a good crowd above. *Too bad Aki chose tonight to be a pain.* His passion for running translated well to the dance floor, and the two of them had met some of their best clients that way.

What am I thinking? I don't need Aki to have a good time. Nate came to a decision. So what if he wasn't working? He had a free ticket to the best party in town, and for once, he could enjoy it on his terms.

A drink and a set on the dance floor later, Nate leaned back against the bar. Endorphins and alcohol mingled in his system in the best possible way. It was early enough that there were plenty of energetic partners on the floor and late enough that inhibitions were thoroughly lowered. *This is the best idea I've had in days...*

So why can't I make myself believe it? Nate replaced his glass on the bar. Time he faced the facts. The problem wasn't Denise. It wasn't Aki. It wasn't even vampires.

The problem is me.

The chill was just as surprising the second time, like someone placed an icy hand on his shoulder. Nate took a deep breath, squaring his shoulders before he turned. *Last person I want to see right now is Hunter.*

Ben's blue-gray eyes were a shock. He stood at the edge of the dance floor. His eyes widened as Nate looked up, but his surprise was momentary. As Nate watched, Ben subtly adjusted his posture.

Shoulders back, hands tucked in the pocket of his jacket, he could have been a club regular.

With a smirk, Nate sauntered across the floor to join him. He kept his eyes on Ben, noting with amusement the brief flicker of his tongue across his lips. *Out of his element, but like hell is he gonna admit that.* Nate slowed his pace. He could match Ben's control any night.

"No one takes getting caught staring gracefully," he said. "But I got to admit, that's the closest attempt I've seen."

Ben raised an eyebrow. "You're that sure I was staring."

"Gonna tell me you're here to dance?" Nate let his gaze fall deliberately to Ben's clothing. The casual T-shirt and jacket combination looked better on him than the stiff suit from the anniversary party but still overdressed for the dance floor. "I might call your bluff. And then where would you be?"

Ben's mouth twitched. "Presumably on the dance floor."

The mental image was immediate. Ben's cool skin would contrast with the heat of the surrounding dancers, making every brush of their bodies in the pulsing light an electric shock. Unable to resist, Nate let his fingers rest on Ben's arm, feeling the familiar thrill of contact. "Fun as that would be" –Nate tugged at Ben's jacket sleeve– "you'll suffocate in this. Far too hot."

Ben blinked. Something indefinable flickered in his eyes, and his mouth twisted.

Fuck. Vampires don't do temperatures! Nate squeezed his arm in apology. "Sorry," he said as he withdrew his hand. "Wasn't thinking. So, if you're not here to dance, why are you here?" *Like I don't know.* Nate had no desire to see Hunter, but given the way the two vampires felt about each other, he knew he couldn't be far away. *Better accept it. Only pleasure I'm getting tonight is vicarious.*

In any other circumstance, that would be a fate worse than death. Knowing how deeply Ben felt his isolation from the world? *You'd have to be a complete asshole to resent the guy getting a taste of happiness.* The memory of Ben's expression as he looked up at Hunter returned to Nate, and with it, the same tug at his insides. *I want someone to look at me like that—but Ben needs it.* If Nate had facilitated the two vampires getting together? *Job well done.* He scanned the club for Hunter.

"I'm not—" Ben hesitated. "Looking for company."

Nate snorted. Anyone else, that level of straitlaced unease would be irritating. Ben made it endearing. "I know. This isn't exactly your scene." And then as Ben blinked, expression growing fixed, Nate frowned. "You're here alone?"

Ben's fingers tightened on Nate's arm. "You're making a lot of assumptions," he said, "for people who've just met."

Nate shrugged. "You forget. We had one hell of an introduction."

Ben didn't share Nate's smile. "You remember?"

"Of course. I meet a lot of people on this job, but a client like you stands out, Ben."

How had Nate imagined Ben soft? His grip hurt. "I told you to forget."

"You can't tell someone to for—" Nate swallowed. His throat felt uncomfortably tight. "You compelled me?"

"We need to talk." Ben kept his grip on Nate's arm tight as he glanced around the club. “Somewhere private.”

He compelled me. After everything they’d talked about, everything they’d done together? Nate pulled his arm back but couldn’t shake Ben’s hold. “You think I want to talk to someone who mind-wiped me?”

“Nate.” Ben looked at him with a directness that Nate was completely unprepared for. “You could be in a lot of danger.” He marched straight up to the nearest table booths, bringing Nate with him. “You’re finished with this table,” he said to the bemusement of the host and the guests he was entertaining. “Go.”

The host stood clumsily, the girls with him putting down their glasses. As they squeezed past Nate to join the crowd on the dance floor, Ben let go of Nate’s arm. Nate slid into the booth without protest. Seeing Ben’s power exercised so casually gave him chills in a way that nothing at the townhouse had. His legs shook, and Nate was grateful for the solidity of the table. “You seriously just controlled them.”

“Keep your voice down.” Ben took the other side of the booth, leaning across the table. His tone was soft, and Nate looked up at him in surprise. “Don’t call attention to yourself. You never know who is watching.”

“Yeah. Don’t want anyone to look over here and see you mind-working me again.”

“It was absolutely necessary.” Ben sat back, stiffly. “Please, Nate. A man is dead. Another is missing. I don’t want you to be the third.”

“You don’t mean—” Nate’s breath stuck in his throat. “Brook.” Suddenly Gunn’s insinuations seemed very real.

"They found his body on my father's grave." Ben looked down. His voice was brisk and controlled. "Someone is sending us a message."

"Who?"

Ben shook his head. "We don't know. Yet."

"You must have some idea." Nate caught himself belatedly as Ben winced. "Relax. No one's gonna hear us over the music."

"Our enemies have heightened hearing." Ben caught Nate's eye and held it with a serious stare. "Saltaire isn't popular in the night world."

"I wonder why."

"I told you he was old and powerful," Ben said firmly. "That's only half of it. He was a soldier in life. He's made himself a war in death, too, against anything that preys on humans. He has countless enemies."

"No way." Things were starting to make sense. "The insurance company is really a front for his war on vampires?"

"You know about ARX?" Ben's fingers dug into Nate's arm. "What else are you hiding?"

"Let go! Jesus– I only know about ARX because Hunter's accountant told me about it."

"Peter? He was here?"

"Yeah. Stopped by yesterday to give me my fee– Are you all right?"

Ben had let go of Nate's arm. He slumped back against the wall of the booth. "I'm too late. I'm sorry, Nate. I hoped to keep you out of this."

"That's why you wiped my memory? To protect me?"

Ben nodded. "You're of no use to our enemies if you don't remember our ways. Coming here tonight was a risk, but after the news— I had to check that you were safe. I didn't anticipate this."

Nate snorted. "Hate to disappoint you," he said, reaching for one of the abandoned cocktail glasses. "But I'm fine." He was not going to let Ben see how rattled he was.

"Yes," Ben said. "You are."

Nate glanced up from the drink.

Ben watched him closely. "I'm aware that you must feel that you have no reason to trust me right now—"

"You think?"

"—but it's very important that you tell me how you resisted my command, Nate. You don't know the danger you're in."

"Alone in a dark corner with a vampire and you want to talk about danger—" Nate paused as Ben's meaning registered. "You're right. I remember everything."

"You see why this is so important." Ben's voice was quiet, but Nate heard every low, insistent word clearly, even over the pounding of his heart. "The house is warded against magical intrusion. If you were enchanted, you could not have entered, and there was—" Ben looked down, but was not fast enough to conceal the pink spreading across his cheeks. "No way you could have concealed a crucifix on your person."

Nate eyed him with a feeling of disbelief. *Death and enchantment, he's all business, but thinking about a guy naked rattles him?* Despite it all, Ben had not faked his uncertainty in the bedroom. *Does that mean the rest of it was meant?*

"Please, Nate. If I'm going to protect you, I need to know." Ben placed his hand on Nate's arm. "What are you?"

Nate shook him off. "Don't even start."

"Nate. I'm serious."

"So am I." Nate glared at him, gripping the stem of the cocktail glass hard enough it hurt. "I'm normal. One hundred percent regular human here."

Ben frowned, settling his hands in front of him. "That can't be possible."

"Maybe you're just not a very good vampire. You think of that?" Nate took a sip and grimaced at the saccharine taste of the drink. *Figures. I need something strong, and instead I get a fucking Shirley Temple.*

"I'm not joking! It's your safety at stake here." Ben took a deep breath. By the time he'd let it out again, he'd assumed control over himself. "Maybe asking you to confide in me was too much, but I really do want to know you're safe. If nothing else, please promise that you'll keep what happened at the house to yourself."

So you and Hunter can play mind games with someone else? The retort stuck in Nate's throat. Ben's eyes fixed on his, and his fingers were wrapped tightly together. Nate bit his lip.

"You mentioned a nondisclosure agreement. Please tell me you haven't told anyone about the party—"

"Nate!" Aki parked himself at the end of the table. "I was waiting for you to come off shift! You could've told me—" He paused to take in Ben's presence, sizing up the expensive cut of the jacket and Ben's pale skin. “Don’t tell me you found another vampire.”

“*Ix-nay on the ampire-vay,*” Nate hissed, but it was too late.

Ben’s anger lacked Aki’s dramatics, but was somehow more impressive. He drew himself up, walking away without a word.

It took Aki a long moment to recover. “What was that? You didn’t actually—”

Nate rested his hand on Aki’s shoulder as he levered himself out of the booth and after Ben. “Don’t.”

Nate caught up to Ben halfway down the next block. “Ben! Let me explain.”

Ben kept up his rapid pace. “How about explaining how your extreme lack of self-preservation has not prevented you from making it this far in life?”

“Hey! If either of us has the right to be angry here, it’s me! You didn’t give me time to break the nondisclosures before you tried to erase my memories! Not that the agreements were valid.” Nate had to jog to keep up with Ben. “Hunter broke those by not being honest about what I was signing on for. Gunn said—”

Ben stopped so suddenly that Nate came dangerously close to slamming into his back. “Gunn? You talked to him?”

“Yeah.” Nate glanced around, conscious that their conversation was gathering curious looks from other nighttime pedestrians. “Dropped by the club last night,” he said, lowering his voice. “Had some questions for me.”

“Did he?” Ben crossed his arms.

"I did you a favor. It's only due to my good memory that Gunn hasn't called you in for an interview."

"Not in public," Ben said, the firmness with which he took Nate's arm not allowing any disagreement. "Come on."

They walked three blocks in angry silence, ignoring the buzzing of Nate's wristband. Finally, they reached a thin, barely lit path squeezed between two tenement blocks. Nate toyed with a strand of the ivy that engulfed one wall, while Ben perched on the other, directly below a flickering streetlight. He listened silently as Nate outlined his interview with Gunn, his arms crossed.

"I'm not a fan of Gunn or his methods. But he is right about Brook's death. We're looking into it, of course." Ben's mouth twisted. "Brook wasn't exactly discreet about seeing Hunter. Every customer at that bar must have heard about it. Even more reason for you to be careful."

He's serious about protecting me? Nate bit his lip. Ben had tried to make him forget even before he'd learned about Brook. "I'm more likely to be careful if I remember I need to be careful."

Ben raised an eyebrow. "And yet here you are, alone in an alleyway with a vampire. Is that careful?"

Nate had picked his T-shirt with the crowded dance floor in mind, not the cool evening air. He ran his hands over his bare arms, trying to ward off the chill of Ben's words. "The vampire's you. There's a difference."

"No difference." Ben's answer was immediate. "Vampires bring death. It might not be intentional, but it's a fact all the same."

"Funny. Gunn said the same thing." Nate hesitated. "Seemed like the guy's got a serious grudge against you."

"Merely doing his job." Ben shrugged out of his jacket. "My feelings for Hunter give me a motive in Brook's death, coupled with the location of the body. It makes sense that he would fix on me. Here."

Nate looked down at the garment. *Am I missing something?*

"It's cold." Ben held the jacket out awkwardly, looking like he didn't know what to do with it or himself. "Take it."

Oh no. He's not getting away with this that easily. Nate crossed his arms. "You telling me to take it—or compelling me?"

Hurt flashed through Ben's eyes. "It's not something we can turn off or on," he said stiffly. "It's the wording. Talking to you is so natural...I forget." He hesitated, still holding the jacket out.

Nate didn't move. "You didn't forget back at the house. This is your second failed attempt."

Ben's mouth twisted. "You're more upset about my failed attempt to control you than you are about Hunter's successful use of compulsion. If you needed any proof vampires were dangerous, you've got it there!"

"Hunter can go fuck a cactus for all I care. You did that knowing full well what it's like to be controlled." Nate crossed his arms over his chest. "I'm not upset. I'm fucking furious."

"I did only what I thought necessary." Ben fingers tightened in the jacket. "You don't understand what's at stake."

"You and your brother's ability to prey on people might be compromised. Yeah, big loss there."

Ben stared at him. He tugged his jacket back on, movements

sharp and annoyed. “I don’t care what you think of us, but don’t underestimate the danger you’re in. Two men are dead, Nate.”

“Two?” Nate’s anger could not keep him from feeling the sudden chill in the air. “I thought you said one was missing...”

“These cases only end one way.” Ben pulled his jacket straight, once again the master of himself. “You don’t want to hear it from me, maybe you should listen to your friend.” He looked back down the path, toward the main road. “He’s looking for you.”

Nate’s wristband continued to buzz. “Following the GPS. He’ll be here soon.”

“Not soon enough. You don’t need GPS, Nate. You need something that’ll offer real protection.”

“Good idea.” Nate hooked his hands in the back of his jeans. He wasn’t going to let Ben see him shiver. “Next time I see Gunn, I’ll ask him what he recommends.”

“Whatever Gunn’s motives are for taking this case, your welfare is not among them.” Ben pulled his jacket more tightly around himself. “Be careful, Nate. I can’t emphasize that enough.”

“Nate?” Aki’s thin voice was just audible at the entry to the alley.

“Over here!” Nate glanced toward the call. “What is your deal with him, anyway?” he asked, turning back to Ben. “I’m sick of—”

He was alone in the alley.

“Nate! Would it have killed you to let me know you weren’t getting murdered?” Aki collided with him at speed.

Nate thumped him on the back. “I’m fine.”

“Against every law of god and man! Seriously, what is the first rule of horror movies? Don’t go anywhere alone!” Aki relaxed his death grip slightly. “Where’s the vampire?”

“Ben.” Nate steered Aki back toward the mouth of the alley. “You just missed him.”

Aki’s relief was palpable. “You shouldn’t scare me like this, you big lump. What if something had happened?”

“It didn’t.”

Despite himself, the night must have got to Nate. Aki glanced at him sideways. “Did you want it to?”

“What?”

“You ran out of the club very quickly. You a fang-chaser, Nate? I won’t judge.”

“No. And also, no.” Nate waved his arms in emphasis. “The guy tried to mind control me!”

“Tried?”

Nate came to a complete halt, fingers grasping at empty air. He still had no idea how he’d resisted Ben’s command, but not Hunter’s. “Clearly he’s not a very good vampire.”

“A good vampire’s an oxymoron! Seriously, no such thing, Nate!”

“Whatever.” Nate wrapped his arms around himself. “Let’s get back inside. It’s cold out here.”

Still upset about the argument, it took Nate a few minutes of walking to realize that Aki was silent. With a sigh, Nate reached out a hand to Aki’s shoulder. “I’m fine. Honestly.”

Aki glanced up in surprise at the touch. He managed a faint smile. “I wasn’t kidding about you scaring me earlier.”

Nate shrugged, letting his arm rest around Aki’s shoulders. He was startled to realize just how far his friend had come alone in the night to look for him. "So maybe running out of the club after a vampire wasn't the smartest thing I've ever done."

"Why'd you do it at all? I mean—the sex was that good?"

Nate bit his lip. It was hard to explain exactly what had prompted his pursuit. "I guess I was annoyed," he said at last. "I mean, we talked about some important shit. I thought— Well, I guess I thought wrong. I wanted to know why."

"A vampire doesn't need a why. That's the entire point of vampires."

"Ben's different. Or I thought he was." And that stung.

Aki elbowed Nate. "Hey. It's like I always say. They're either—"

Nate snorted. "Straight, taken, or an undead hell-creature bent on devouring your soul."

Aki thumped him on the shoulder as they reached Century. "Cheer up. Not like you have a soul worth devouring."

Nate squeezed Aki's arm. "Thanks, Aki."

~~*

The joke wasn't as funny the next morning. In fact, the sight of the newspaper in Aki's hands made Nate feel positively ill.

"Told you it was a serial killer." Aki shook out the paper as he turned to read the further developments on page three. "At least this one looks nothing like you."

Nate blanched. "He might not be dead."

The look Aki sent him was pitying. "He's dead. Has to be." He looked back at the paper. "No signs of forced entry, and the apartment was neat and everything. The first victim finished his shift at the bar and left everything all neat and tidy, too."

"That's a pretty weak connection—"

"There's more. Brook was found on the grave of an ARX employee who was murdered a year ago. This guy, Peter, worked for ARX, too." Aki shook his head. "Kind of ironic, considering they sell insurance— Where are you going?"

Nate couldn't afford Starbucks with his hours cut, but it was worth it to be away from Aki—and from the front-page picture. Peter looked just as Nate had seen him last, smiling knowingly as he looked over his shoulder at the camera, hands tangled in the ever-present scarf.

He wouldn't be coming by the club now. The concert he'd bought tickets to, none of that—

"Vampires are bad news. Looks like the message is finally getting through." Gunn pulled out the free chair at Nate's table and sat.

Too late to take my Frappuccino and run? "If you're here to deliver another friendly warning, you're too late." Nate sat up. "Ben beat you to it."

"That so?" Gunn grinned at him offensively. "At what time did Saltaire's servant deliver his warning?"

"Is this official police business?" Nate glanced around. Gunn wore the same battered jacket and jeans of their previous meeting and was overdue for a shave. He could not have been any further from the crisp recruits of the news reports, but Nate was sure they stood out. "Can you do this in Starbucks?"

"It's just a question. Won't hold up in court." Gunn flicked a color copy of Peter's photo across the table at Nate. "I dropped by for your opinion of de Silver's disappearing act. Didn't expect Bennet's visit, but it makes sense. He needs a new donor."

Nate held the photo out for Gunn to take back. "For your information, Ben came by to warn me."

"Of what?" Gunn didn't take the photo.

Nate paused. He put the photo down. "He didn't say exactly. Just that someone was missing. Now I know who."

Gunn was silent. Nate was acutely aware of the interest in his sharp hazel eyes, hinting at a mind at odds with the officer's slovenly appearance.

"I'm not lying."

Gunn's smirk was ironic. Nate immediately felt foolish. *How many times had the man heard that?*

"Strangely enough, I believe you. Or would if I didn't know better than to trust anyone." Gunn leaned back in his chair, eyes on Nate. "I don't know what role Bennet plays in all this, but he's in deep. And he's unusually interested in you."

Nate tried to shrug off his discomfort. "Being concerned is hardly a crime."

"Vampires, Lesson Two. They don't change, Nate. In life, Bennet Hawick was a self-interested little sycophant, and in death, he's continued that trend. No friends, no hobbies, only leaves the mansion on ARX business. And you're telling me that he breaks the habit of a lifetime to be nice to a stranger?"

Nate casually picked up his drink. "What can I say? I give great head."

For the first time, Nate thought he saw a crack in the officer's façade as Gunn tried to work out if he was serious. "Brook bought the weapon that killed him," he said flatly. "Carried it with him to the cemetery as punctually as if he had an appointment. You know what that means?"

"Suicide?"

"Brook's wounds weren't self-inflicted. Compulsion."

Made to show up to his own murder? Nate pushed his drink aside. "That's sick." And hastily, "But nothing to do with Ben! He wasn't there."

Gunn draped an arm over the back of his chair. "You feel a need to protect him. Why? Good sex isn't worth dying for."

"This isn't misplaced loyalty." Nate glared. "And no one compelled me to say that."

"Not from lack of trying. That is" —Gunn grinned again— "going from the very interesting account Mr. Fujino gave me of your evening."

Goddamnit, Aki. "He exaggerates."

Gunn smirked at his obvious discomfort. "Does he? Mr. Fujino seemed to think it was only his civic duty."

Civic duty my ass. "You want to talk about people acting out of character? Start there." But that thought led to others. "Peter worked for Saltaire. If they wanted him gone, they had tons of opportunities at the house."

"You're thinking in terms of human reasoning. That's your first mistake." Gunn kicked his boots up on the table. "Whether the undead act civilized like Saltaire's brood or are as basic as a newly turned revenant, they're all instinct. Whatever you want to call 'em—

natural or unnatural, animal or monster—they're only in this world at the cost of other lives. When the moment of survival comes, they always go for the one thing that'll keep 'em alive longer. No exceptions."

People were definitely staring at them. Nate swallowed. "You said they were colonies."

"Shut up. I'm enriching your vocabulary."

Nate could take being intimidated. But laughed at? "What's your problem with vampires? You get compelled?"

A muscle tightened in his neck, but Gunn suppressed it and smiled. "Swing and a miss. I got a better question for you, Nate. What didn't Ben tell you last night?"

Nate resisted the urge to pick up his cup. Gunn didn't need to know how nervous he was. "I hope you don't expect me to answer that."

"De Silver wasn't any ordinary accountant. Saltaire oversaw his education personally, and Hunter was training him for a field position. If Bennet hadn't died when he did, it's likely de Silver would have become part of the family."

"You're implying that Ben resented him?"

"I'm implying that whoever's behind Brook and de Silver's deaths knows their vampires. De Silver's exact position wasn't widely known, and believe it or not, Hunter's generally discreet." Gunn's chair scraped the ground as he stood. "Here's hoping our mystery gift-giver doesn't know why Hunter hired you." Gunn nodded farewell with a grin that showed an alarming amount of teeth. "You're not the sort of present one can return."

Nate's anger warred with his shock and alarm for a few seconds. He stood, almost colliding with a startled woman in his attempt to catch up to the officer. "Hey! I—"

Gunn was not on the footpath. No sign of him on the road. Nate looked up and down the street, but it was pointless. The officer was simply gone.

Chapter Seven

The cold night air burned Nate's throat. It had an aftertaste of smoke, a scummy stickiness like that of the fire escape rail he rested on. The vibrations of the DJ set he'd come outside to avoid rattled the rusty stairs. The reinforced emergency door shut out the club's sound, if not the street's. Somewhere in the dark, a woman laughed, and a man murmured in response, low and attentive.

Nate's lip curled. *I cannot win.* Gunn's insinuations lingered, and he'd argued with Aki. Seriously argued, leading to Nate spending his break on the hated fire escape, ignoring his phone.

The shrill wail of a siren filled the night. Nate's fingers clenched around the rail. *Just perfect.* The sound got straight under his skin. They'd been going all day. Every police car in the city must have driven through downtown at least twice.

To think I would ever miss hearing the frogs at night. Christ. I must be seriously homesick. Nate would choose the endlessly repeated marshy bellows traveling across the smooth slope of the field all the way up to the porch where he sat with Ethan over the mosquito-whine of the sirens a million times. He looked up, but instead of stars scattered like seeds across the sky, Nate saw only the bland expanse of light pollution. The absence caught in his chest. *Bus depot's only one subway stop away. There's always seats going out of the city. I could be home in a matter of hours.*

Nate smirked, imagining Ma's surprise at seeing him, even as he toyed with the edge of the wristband. He wasn't leaving. He knew that. The farm—

It all came back to the farm.

Nate straightened. Aki wouldn't stay mad at him forever. If Gunn paid him another friendly visit, Nate would refer him to Denise for daytime rates. And the vampire clan—

"Can bite me."

Not the best choice of words, but Nate didn't care. He was through with Hunter, and Ben—

He wasn't going to see Ben again.

Brakes screeched, followed immediately by a blaring horn. Nate glanced toward the street. He saw a car lurch forward, engine revving in annoyance at the sudden start and stop. And in the gap left by its absence, he saw a familiar figure walk calmly into the night crowd.

Nate was down the fire escape and on the street in seconds. "Ben!" He lost precious seconds waiting for a break in the traffic. By the time Nate reached the opposite footpath, there was no sign of the vampire's diminutive form. Nate jogged down the street in the direction he'd taken, scanning the crowd for Ben's wispy hair. *Goddamnit, where is he?*

"Watch it. Jerk!'"

Nate doubled back to duck down a side street toward the angry voice. He had a hunch.

He was right. Nate dodged the angry man getting to his feet and wove through the bystanders who'd stopped to gawk.

"Young people these days. No manners..."

"See his face? No expression, nothing!"

An older woman shuddered, turning to her male companion confidingly. "If you ask me, drugs—"

Nate barely avoided a second collision. He put on an extra burst of speed to catch up to Ben at the next corner. "Ben! The hell are you doing?"

Ben continued his unhurried pace.

"I'm serious here. Did you even see the car?" Nate caught his arm.

Ben turned. His eyes slid over Nate without recognition. He didn't expend any energy, stretching out his arm as an afterthought, but the casual shove felt like a punch.

The sting of the concrete as Nate collided with the pavement had the harsh shock of reality. Nate anchored himself in the throbbing of his grazed palm. The night felt as unreal as a nightmare, but the pain made it real. Which meant that the danger—

"Ben!"

Nate limped after him.

"I thought it was zombies who did the whole brain-dead thing. Vampires are supposed to be smart."

Ben reacted to Nate's commentary the same way he'd reacted to the last set of traffic lights, the righteously angry driver, and the jeering pedestrian—not at all. It made Nate sick. The farther they walked, the more deserted the streets became.

"Your point about vampires being creepy fucks is well and truly made. Seriously, snap out of this!" Nate didn't expect it to work, but he was getting desperate. Ben acted as if—

"That's it, isn't it? Someone's controlling you."

Just like Brook. Knowing what had happened only made it worse. *This was everything Ben was afraid of—and he'd been unable to prevent it.* "Chances of you staying put while I grab some holy water?"

Ben kept walking. His steady pace led them directly toward Old Town, where the evenly distributed and well laid out streets of broader downtown reluctantly conceded to the winding stone roads of the original city.

Not that there'd be a church open this time of night. Nate started to jog as Ben reached a bridge. He couldn't risk losing the vampire to the next dark turn.

Wait. Where there was a bridge, there was usually water—

If this doesn't work, we're screwed. Nate didn't let himself think about it. Tackling a vampire off a bridge was bad enough without making it worse with anticipation. He ran, colliding full on with Ben.

The chill of the water was as much of a shock as the impact of the fall. Nate's shoulder collided with the rock of the riverbed, and he let go of Ben. Air forced its way out of his mouth and water rushed in to replace it. He choked and struggled to find "up," so disorientated, it took the sound of his own spluttering breath for Nate to know he'd reached the surface. The sodden coveralls dragged him down as Nate staggered to his feet. He glanced up—

—and felt a fear colder than the river.

Ben stood on the bank. The streetlight illuminated clearly the feral light of inhuman eyes, the sharp edges of his fangs visible as he bared his teeth.

This is it. The instinct Gunn had warned him about, the change the premonition had foretold. It was inevitable. So inevitable, Nate could not even make himself move.

Ben shook himself with obvious effort. “Nate.” His voice was tight and angry, but it was his. “What was that?”

“Oh thank god. You’re *you*.”

~~*

“Blood magic, worked expertly,” Ben said from his position on the bank. The street lamp flickered behind him. His waterlogged clothing clung to his form, giving him the stark outline of a silhouette in a noir film. “A necromancer with a strong claim on me.”

Nate rolled his eyes as he wrung more of the river water out of the sleeves of his work coveralls. *This is the thanks I get?* “You’re welcome.” Having got as much water out as possible, Nate worked his arms back inside the sleeves. It was even colder out of the river.

“Welcome?”

Nate couldn’t see Ben’s face to know if he was serious. “I saved your life.”

Ben turned to look at Nate. After a moment, he spoke. “You did.”

Unbe-fucking-lievable. Nate shrugged the clinging uniform fabric over his shoulders and jerked the zipper up. “Going to tell me it doesn’t count ’cause you’re a vampire?”

“No, actually. I hadn’t realized. After the way we parted, I didn’t think you’d want to see me again. Let alone help me.” Ben sounded puzzled.

Nate forced his hands to uncurl from around the zipper. Adrenaline pounded in his veins, spoiling for a fight, but Ben wasn't his enemy. "I've thought about last night. Brook being murdered on your father's grave, the guy you snack on being abducted, Gunn's immediate assumption you're involved with this– Maybe you had reasons for doing what you did." As Ben's shoulders relaxed, Nate hastily added, "Not saying they're good reasons–"

"No," Ben agreed. "That would be expecting entirely too much." After a moment's pause, he held out his coat. "Not that this will do much for you right now," he said. "But at least it'll keep the wind off." He proffered it awkwardly, like a kid picking up his prom date.

Afraid of rejection? He's really not how I imagined vampires. Nate draped the coat over his shoulders. While the damp coat was hardly warm, the weight was somehow comforting. "Thanks. With all the unnatural hazards in this city, I would hate to catch my death of cold."

Ben's mouth twitched. "The necromancer will be looking for me. So if you want to give hypothermia the chance to set in, you should stick close."

"If you think I'm leaving you here–" Nate paused. "You're not going to try to convince me to leave?"

"If an unplanned river dive isn't going to shake your martyr-complex, I don't know what I can do." Ben shrugged. "Besides, there's no guarantee you'll make it home safely. At least if you're close, I can fool myself into thinking that you're safe. Come on. A moving target is harder to locate magically."

* ~ * ~ *

"It's as dead as you are." Nate looked from his blank phone to Ben, who had deemed their current position beneath a traffic overpass safe enough to take stock of their situation. "Yours?"

"A lost cause." Ben returned the phone to his pocket. "Not that it matters. My family has other ways of finding each other."

"Chances of them finding us some place warm and out of the wind?" *What I wouldn't give to be under the showers at Century now...*

Ben shook his head. "It'll be harder for the necromancer to control me a second time, but not impossible. I'm a threat to anyone around me."

Big shock there. Nate's mouth twisted, and he wrapped his arms more tightly around his body. Ben had opposed Nate's use of the SOS button on his wristband for the exact same reason. A little thing like Nate retaining feeling in his limbs wasn't going to sway him. "We can't spend the entire night dodging people."

"We don't have to. We've got places throughout the city set up for situations exactly like this." Ben started walking. "The nearest one's about five minutes away. I can create a protective circle to keep us safe."

Safe is good. All the horror stories they'd been fed during basic training were coming back to Nate with a vengeance. Every noise made him jump.

Ben, on the other hand, was alert but not panicked, knowing instinctively which noises he could ignore and which deserved a glance. He led the way through dimly lit side streets that followed the overpass until they reached a section beneath the bridge that was loosely fenced off.

"You're sure about this?" It was just a wire fence on three sides, with a Dumpster resting against the concrete pillar that supported the road, but the scene made Nate's skin crawl.

"It's spelled to keep people away." The thick padlock on the door fell open as soon as Ben touched it. "Once I invite you in, you won't feel the repul— Stay back!"

"Ben!"

A shaggy form loomed up out of the shadow of the Dumpster. It had thick, matted gray fur and growled as it leapt at Ben.

"Look—"

Ben was moving even before Nate finished his warning. He turned sideways, avoiding the creature's leap so neatly the move looked synchronized. He caught the thing by its scruff, forcing its head up.

For the first time, Nate recognized it. "It's a man!"

"Was a man." Ben tightened his grip on the man's neck viciously. "Now it's less than an animal."

The man snarled, baring unnaturally sharp teeth. They were too big for his mouth, and his eyes were devoid of anything but pain. He clawed at Ben, trying to shift his body free of the disabling hold.

"Stay where you are," Ben continued. "Revenants are hunger in a human shell. They don't care what they kill, only that they kill."

Nate couldn't take his eyes off the struggling man. He'd seen hungry before, but not like this. The man was a collection of skin drawn tightly over angular bone, layers of clothing loose around him.

His hair was matted, thick as fur. "That's a—"

"Vampire at its most basic." Ben's voice was thick. As the man dug his fingers into Ben's arm, he hissed a warning, displaying fangs as cruel as his victim's. The man lunged clumsily at him, and with a grunt, Ben flung out his arm, sending the man hurtling into the concrete pillar. He was there before the man slid all the way to the ground, sending him back into the wall with a sick crack.

Nate had seen a video once, of orcas playing with a seal before they killed it. It was like that, the man left in a limp puddle, a dark stain on the wall behind.

He picked up that guy like he was nothing! And just—oh god. "You killed him!"

"He's been dead for days now." Ben lifted the lid of the Dumpster. "Since before Brook." He lifted the Dumpster lid, rummaging hastily through the contents. A bundle of sticks fell to the ground, the pungent smell of decay overcoming the burnt rubber and petrol smell of the road. "Compromised," Ben said, flinging a bunch of herbs after them. "And the necromancer knows we're here."

"He struggled. He didn't want to die..."

Ben paused. His expression softened, and he shut the Dumpster. "That's not life, Nate. He had no thought, no will beyond his creator's."

Nate let out a shaky breath, allowing Ben to pull him back onto the street. "You're saying the necromancer deliberately killed someone—"

"To make himself a servant?" Ben frowned. "He's not the only fatality. We've been investigating disappearances from homeless shelters throughout the city for about a week now. I think we found the cause." He led Nate through a series of sharp turns, navigating the streets with certainty.

At least one of us is calm. Nate swallowed. He couldn't get the man's face out of his mind.

"The necromancer knows I'm getting tired," Ben said conversationally. "He'll try to control me again. As soon as we find somewhere with space, I'll show you how to draw a protective circle."

"Me?" That jarred Nate out of his frozen state. "I can't do magic!"

"You can do this. You have to." They hit a main road. Ben looked up and down before turning onto it. "Any circle I draw is compromised by the necromancer's hold on me. Without a token, I've got no resistance beyond my will."

"A token?"

"Those twigs might not have looked like much, but they were mountain ash, imported from Romania," Ben said. "They're prized for their ability to ward off ill will. We can't stop, Nate."

Nate held his ground. "I think I know something that can help."

How had Nate missed the creepiness of Mason's Park? Granted, he was there in the dead of night, accompanied by a vampire who *technically* hadn't killed a man and pursued by the necromancer who had.

It's better if I don't think about it.

"This is it?" Ben looked up at the tree in front of them.

The dark obscured most details, but the bulk of the oak spoke for itself. It towered above them, outlined in black against the lights of the surrounding city. Resting in the hollow between two great branches was the reason they were there. A small bush, bobbing lightly in the night breeze.

"It's called a flying rowan." Nate placed his hand against the oak's trunk. *If this is just an old wives tale, we're screwed.* "Supposedly it—"

"Guards against witchcraft and is especially potent against dark magic." Ben turned his cool gaze on Nate. "There a witch in your family?" His eyes caught the moonlight in a way that wasn't entirely natural.

Nate swallowed. He remembered Ben's mouth, distorted by its extra teeth. "My brother's really into plants. This can help?"

"It might save our lives." Ben held out a hand. "There's a Ziploc bag in the pockets of the jacket. How'd you even find this?"

"Aki and I run here every other day." Nate pulled the bag out of the jacket. "Candles, salt, matches— This exorcism on the go?"

"In our business, it pays to be prepared." Ben tucked the bag under his arm, balancing candle, matchbox, and match with the ease of practice.

"Insurance? Or vampirism?"

Ben looked at him. "First, build the circle. Counterclockwise, around the tree." He passed the lit candle and salt to Nate.

Following Ben's directions, Nate spread the salt in a continuous circle. "Dabbling in witchcraft... Ma would have a fit if she could see me."

"She'd rather you were pursued by revenants?" Ben's voice came from above.

Startled, Nate craned his neck to look. Ben was perched on one of the thick branches on either side of the rowan. He pulled a small knife that glittered in the dim light out of the bag. Watching him cut twigs from the rowan with brisk, businesslike movements reminded Nate of Ethan pruning. "My brother knows. I mean, I told him about the vampire stuff, not...what we talked about."

"And?"

"He reminded me not to leave the spider fern by the window overnight."

A cluster of rowan twigs fell to the ground near Nate. As he picked them up, something fell down his neck. Nate put a hand up to discover a bunch of tightly curled white blossom.

"You weren't kidding about your brother liking plants." There was a moment's silence, followed by a thud from the other side of the tree. Nate tucked the blossom into his pocket and made his way around the trunk to see Ben dusting the dirt off his knees from his landing.

"You okay?"

"Vampire," Ben said shortly. "Give me those twigs."

Hypothermia no longer seemed a distant threat, but rather than burn the twigs as Nate hoped, Ben poked them into the ground at intervals along the circle. "Their inherent power augments the circle, and this placement draws the oak into the circle, too. Nothing's getting into this circle uninvited."

Like hell I'm inviting anything like that man inside. "What about these?" Nate still had a handful of twigs left.

"Keep them." Ben was silent as he stood, reaching immediately for the oak's trunk. "If the necromancer succeeds in taking me over again, they'll be your only defense."

Nate stared at him. "Are you okay? 'Vampire' is not an answer."

"Worry about yourself." Ben leaned against the tree. He should have been shivering, but he was as indifferent to the wind as he was Nate's concern. He had one hand on the oak, the other pressed to his neck. His already pale skin had lost all its color, and his eyes were glassy. "The necromancer will be here soon. When that happens—" He jumped as Nate laid a hand on his arm.

Ben's skin had been cool in the mansion, but not clammy like this. Nate tucked the twigs into his pocket, raising the candle to see better. "Fighting his control now?" Ben hesitated, and Nate squeezed his shoulder in warning. "Lying's not gonna protect me either."

Ben's smile was rueful. "I deserve that. Yes." He paused to swallow. "It grows more concentrated the closer he gets."

His movement drew Nate's attention to a splash of darkness on his neck. "What's that?" Nate tipped Ben's chin up to display two open cuts, a mirror image of the marks he'd seen on Peter's neck. "Fuck."

"A mirror wound," Ben said quickly. "It doesn't hurt." His shiver as Nate's fingers brushed his skin said otherwise.

"This is how the necromancer controlled you?"

"A vampire has no defense against blood magic, not when it's—"

"Blood you've drunk." *That's why Peter was taken!* "Shit."

Ben looked down. "I'm really sorry Hunter dragged you into this."

"Sorry you can't mind control me? Give it a rest, for fuck's sake."

Ben's gaze jerked back to Nate. "I wanted to protect you. Not control you!"

"That's not your choice to make!"

Ben glared. "My entire existence puts everyone around me at risk! The only way I can live with that knowledge is by limiting the danger I pose—"

"I'm worried about my carbon footprint, too, but you don't see me mind-wiping people." Nate shrugged, forcing himself calm. "Far as I'm concerned, a sane vampire with his heart in the right place is worth the risk."

"That's what makes us more dangerous." Ben was angry, but his eyes were no longer clouded. "At least revenants are feared. You saw me kill a man tonight, and instead of doing the smart thing and running, you want to help. That's the true curse of the vampire right there."

"Watch who you call a curse." Nate squeezed Ben's hand. Still cool, but the skin had lost its awful clamminess. "Feeling better?" He tipped the excess wax from the candle and used it to fix it against the oak's roots.

"Actually, yes."

Don't sound so surprised, geez. "You need to let go more." With both hands free, he pulled Ben into a loose hug. "You can't fight the necromancer if you're fighting yourself, too."

"I've heard that before." But Ben sighed, and Nate felt his weight against him. "Your safety rests on my ability to keep control. Don't push that, Nate."

"I don't need to be protected from you." Just like it had the night of the anniversary party, Nate felt the tension start to ease from the tightly wound body he held. "I don't know vampires, but I know people. Holding yourself in constant check is killing you."

"I have to." Ben's reply was muffled, somewhere in the vicinity of Nate's neck. "Saltaire—"

"You're not Saltaire." *Thank god.* Nate only just suppressed his shiver. *World only needs one of those.* "What works for him isn't gonna work for anyone with a functioning heart." Ben's expression of wonder as he'd finally allowed himself to feel came back to Nate in one painfully sharp heartbeat. "You can't lose that."

"You're advocating for Hunter's approach, indulging every whim so that they're all equally unimportant?"

"It's not one or the other—"

Ben shook his head. "It won't work, Nate. You could never be a casual encounter for me."

Nate felt as if he'd been plunged back into the river. Emotion swirled through him in a dizzying rush, and it was difficult to breathe. *He doesn't mean it like that.*

Ben was the sort of person to whom casual hookups would never appeal. That was all it was. He didn't mean anything else.

Even if the thought of that anything else made Nate's heart race. *Is that the reason nothing seems right anymore?*

"Ben. I mean. You—"

Ben pulled away from Nate abruptly. He looked beyond Nate, into the dark. "They're coming."

Nate took a deep breath. He could do this, show Ben he didn't need protection.

Cool fingers gripped tightly around his hand. "You're safe," Ben said. "Don't let them make you think otherwise."

So much for impressing the guy. But Nate couldn't mind Ben's touch when the pressure of his fingers provided a certainty Nate lacked.

There was a steady rustle, feet on grass. It grew louder, heading directly toward them. Nate looked in the direction Ben turned, trusting the vampire's senses. For a long moment, there was nothing, not even the sound of the breeze whispering through the trees.

Nothing? Nate breathed out. *Shows what can happen when you let imagination run away with you.* He shifted, glancing to the side as he tried to shake off the oppressive night air.

Moonlight reflected in eyes as wild as a stray dog.

"Shit—"

Nate collided with the oak. His back stung but the pain didn't register, his attention taken by the figures.

There were three of them, a bearded man and two women with knotted hair and clawlike nails. Their ragged clothing was torn and bloodstained, and their movements were strangely jerky, as if the impulse to move came from outside and not their own movements. They made no sound at all, but they spread out as one to circle the tree.

Their mouths were too hungry, always working. They bared their teeth, licked their lips, and snarled, always creeping closer. The nearest woman smiled, but the invitation of her lips became immediately undone by the sharp edges of the teeth she revealed.

"Stay against the oak," Ben said. "Remember they can't cross the circle."

Nate glanced down. The three revenants stood just before the line drawn by the salt. "It's working?"

"Be confident in your work," Ben squeezed Nate's hand again. "It's powered by your belief."

Unbelievably, Nate—the normal one of the family—had done magic. *Who knows what else I can do?*

The woman stayed where she was, but her companions prowled the edge of the circle. They shot dark looks at Ben, hissing as they did. Occasionally, they made short darts toward them but always stopped at the edge of the circle.

"What are they doing?"

"Probing the circle for weak points," Ben said. "Failing that, they're trying to trick you into stepping out of it."

Nate took his eyes off the staring woman to glance at him. "That a fact?"

"You forget." Ben looked at the male revenant with a strange expression. "I've had practice."

No amount of practice is going to stop Ben pitying these things. Nate took a deep breath and tried to imagine them as Ben saw them. Not monsters, but as victims of supernatural attack. His gaze followed the dark stains on the woman's chest to the bloodied patch on the man's back. Days ago, they'd been ordinary people. And now...

If possible, that was even more terrifying.

"How do you do it?" His voice sounded more abrupt than Nate wanted, and he pressed on, hoping that Ben wouldn't notice. "Stay so calm, I mean."

Ben turned a measured gaze on him. "You'll laugh."

"Try me."

"I used to read a lot of comics, loved action movies, TV shows." Ben took a deep breath, leaning against the tree. "Whenever I was in a situation like this, I imagined a voice-over narrating it for the viewer who'd just tuned in. Break down the threat, go over the stakes, round it off with a throwaway line—somehow, it made things more manageable."

"I knew it! You're a closet geek."

"You asked." Ben's shoulders hunched. "Anyway, it's not like I do that now."

"You don't?"

"Used to it."

The thought gave Nate chills. Ben turning into Saltaire or Hunter—or worse, the creatures circling them with predatory interest—gave him chills in a way the revenants did not.

"See what I mean? Focus."

"I got this." The conversation had taken the edge off the circling revenants. They were still there, but a degree removed. "You know, back at the mansion, I felt like I was channeling Attenborough. Undercover, observing the vampires in their natural environment."

Ben looked at him sharply.

"Not saying you're anything like these monsters!" Nate waved a hand toward the revenants and then snatched it back hastily. The three creatures had immediately honed in on him.

"You were right the first time." Ben turned away once more, back toward Nate. "Vampires aren't anything to be happy about." He paused. After a long moment, he added in a much quieter tone, "My friends don't know what happened to me. As far as they know, I just vanished."

"You're serious?" *Ben had cut himself off from any contact?*

"I tell my family I see my friends occasionally, but since they don't know what I am, I can't invite them to the house." Ben's mouth flickered cynically. "With the lengths Hunter went to arranging the party, I hate to think what he'd do if he knew."

"I can picture it now. Vampiric playdates. Truly terrifying."

Ben had positioned himself at the edge of the circle, as far from Nate as he could get. "Don't make me come over there," he warned.

"You're welcome to," Nate said. "I'd like the company." The circle didn't provide a barrier against the constantly shifting leaves or the restless gaze of the revenants, tracking every movement with famished intensity.

Ben bit his lip.

"This shouldn't involve an internal debate." Nate leaned back against the tree.

"You'd really want me near you?" Ben stuck his hands in his pockets, awkwardly attempting diffidence. "You saw what happened earlier."

"Yeah." Nate took a deep breath. "Freaked me out big-time." He wasn't going to forget the man's limp form, lying still as blood pooled around him. Or Ben, walking through the streets with no knowledge in his eyes.

"I can smell your fear. So can they."

Nate winced. There was an answering rumble as the revenants jostled for prime staring position at the edge of the circle. Even without looking at them, he could feel the weight of the revenants pointed interest on his neck. *If I ever manage to sleep again, it'll be a miracle.* "I'm afraid of them. Not you."

"You can't trust me," Ben warned. "The vampire in me is reacting to those creatures. Every instinct I have is telling me to fight."

"You forget. I've seen how well you keep your instincts in check." Nate bit his lip. Was Ben right? By encouraging him to let go, was Nate just making it easier for Ben's hold on his humanity to give way?

"Your generosity of feeling might be an advantage in your work, but it's going to destroy you in the night world." Ben sounded distant. He'd leaned back against the oak to keep a watchful eye on the women. "There's no room for kindness or sympathy tonight."

But being an ass, A-OK. Nate bit his lip. The night weighed down on him, the pressure of the revenants hunger so strong that resistance felt ultimately futile... *Is this what Ben meant?* "What if that kindness is what stops you from being like those monsters?"

"Everyone in this park is dead because of me, Nate. Except you."

Nate blinked. "You do realize how skewed that logic is, right? Because—"

"You're right about one thing. I can't hold back forever. And when that happens—" Ben continued as if he hadn't heard Nate.

Perhaps he hadn't. His gaze was unfocused again, and he rubbed at his neck. Nate hastily scrambled to his feet as Ben took a clumsy step toward the edge of the circle.

"What are you doing?" He grabbed Ben's arm just before the

vampire crossed the barrier. “Wake up!”

Ben reacted with a snarl and preternaturally sharp teeth as Nate jerked him backward.

Fuck! I don’t have a chance! “Snap out of it! They almost got you!” Nate used his weight to pin Ben against the tree.

The revenants’ screeches filled the air. They hissed and bared their sharp nails, surging against the barrier. Nate, his eyes shut, felt their attacks in an awful pressure that squeezed down on him from above. It was hard to think, hard to breathe, paralyzed by overwhelming fear. Ice-cold fingers closed around his wrists. *Don’t think.* Nate knew how strong those deceptively delicate fingers were and that the teeth only inches away from his neck— *Don’t think!*

“That’s twice tonight you’ve saved my life.”

Ben! But Nate couldn’t feel relief just yet. “What is it?” He forced out each word.

“Blood magic, warped by its wielder’s dark desires into something with almost a life of its own.” Ben’s voice was quiet, but his unmistakable calm lifted Nate’s panic. “Necromancy’s hard to resist even with training.”

“Of course it is.”

The sympathetic downward slant of Ben’s sideways glance was welcome but brief. Ben turned away from Nate to scan the park. “No one’s here.” He sounded puzzled.

“What’s wrong?”

Ben looked at Nate blankly.

“Besides the obvious.”

“For the necromancer’s power to negate the oak’s protection, he has to be close. Within this clearing," Ben said. "This doesn't make sense."

"Talk me through it?" Nate squeezed Ben's shoulder. "I am serious about what I said before. I don't want to see you end up like these things. And talking seems to help."

For the first time that night, Ben's mouth quirked up in an honest smile. "Not like I've got anything better to do."

They sat between the oak's roots, backs wedged as far back against the tree as they could get. There was something inherently reassuring about the solidness of the bark. Between that and Ben's cool presence beside him, Nate's heart rate had fallen to something approaching normal.

"Not much to tell. These attacks target us, but we've got very few leads. Whoever this is knows our methods. Someone we've worked with in the past or—"

Nate glanced at Ben. "Someone in ARX?"

Ben frowned. "Peter's role in the domestic arrangements was known only to a few."

Nate raised an eyebrow. "I worked it out at dinner."

"Brook." Ben's frown increased. "I didn't know Hunter was planning anything, so for them to... Anyone we associate with is at risk, the risk increasing in proportion to the importance of the relationship. Saltaire distances himself from human contact. Hunter negates the risk by—" Ben paused.

Nate could infer the rest of the sentence by the color in Ben's cheeks. "Associating with a wide amount of people, none of whom mean anything?"

Ben glanced at him worriedly. "It's just how Hunter is. For someone to realize Brook was different, they must know Hunter really well. They didn't know why Hunter spent time with Brook, clearly, otherwise—" Ben caught himself.

"Otherwise I'd be dead?" Even with the comforting bulk of the oak behind them, the possibility seemed real. *Can't think that.*

"I'm—"

"Apologize again and revenants or no fucking revenants, I'm walking."

"You can't tell me you want to be here," Ben shot back immediately.

"Better this on my terms than safety on someone else's. If I'm in danger, I want to know."

Ben stood. "Still think these are your terms? Let me show you something, Nate." He stood. His voice sounded thick.

"This a practical demonstration?" Nate followed him to his feet.

"If you like." Ben smiled, allowing Nate an even better view of his fangs. "It's animal instinct to fear death. A natural reaction. But humans are fascinated by it." The curve of Ben's lips was accentuated by the starkness of his fangs, their cruel tips. Nate shivered as Ben's cold fingers stroked over his neck. "You can't pull away."

Nate found he couldn't take his eyes off Ben's bared teeth. White as bone, there was something hypnotic about them, and Nate's heart pounded in his chest like six a.m. roadworks. "I don't want to."

The vampire leaned closer, until his breath brushed Nate's lips.

It was all Nate could do not to shiver as Ben wrapped cold arms around him. The coat slipped to the ground as Nate settled his arms around Ben.

And something cold and sharp poked his neck.

Fangs.

"That's your carotid artery." Ben spoke deliberately to ensure he would be heard. "Severed, you'll bleed to death in a minute. I do it, you won't have time to notice." He pressed his fang fully against Nate's skin.

Nate couldn't move.

"You're only alive right now because of my control." Ben ran his tongue deliberately over the newly sensitized skin. "You have no defenses against me ripping out your throat."

Don't react. Nate concentrated on the softness of Ben's touch, not the iron strength that lay beneath. "I have your control." Instinct told him that as long as he believed it, Ben would. *If seeing's believing, doing has to be twice as good.*

Slowly, allowing the vampire to read his intentions, Nate shifted so that he could press their mouths together.

Ben was still except where his fingers gripped Nate's shoulders tightly. The vampire could not immediately refute this argument, and Nate took the time to make his point, exploring each curved fang in turn with his tongue. As Ben's hand relaxed, moving over Nate's shoulder, he felt a surge of triumph. *I'm finally getting through!*

The wind sliced right across Nate's exposed back, and with it, the low growl of the revenants. Nate had forgotten them, and he remembered their presence with a shock of fear.

And then suddenly Ben's teeth were pressed against his neck as Nate felt himself thrown against the oak.

"Don't move!" Distorted by anger and teeth, Ben's voice was almost unrecognizable.

I couldn't even if I wanted to. Nate's head ached from his collision with the oak. *I'm no match for a vampire's strength.* The coldness of the night weighed him down, the speed of his heartbeat only making the unresponsiveness of his body more obvious. *Fuck this! I'm not afraid.*

Very carefully, Ben pulled back so that he was holding Nate at arm's length. His gaze was unreadable, and his arms shook. Was that ravenous growl Ben or the revenants? "Stay here."

"What—"

This time, the meeting with the oak was even more brutal. The pain of impact jolted through Nate's body. Ben dropped him, and Nate fell to his knees, stunned.

"The hell—" Something dark crossed Nate's blurred vision. He looked up to see Ben leave the circle. "Ben!"

The three revenants launched themselves in an instant attack. The man howled as he threw himself at Ben, taking the brunt of Ben's unnatural strength. He was viciously beaten back, and as he fell to his knees, Ben grabbed the hair of one of the circling women, flinging her to the ground. Before she could rise, Ben came down with a kick that resulted in a bone-like crack.

"Jesus Christ." Nate reached blindly for the oak. The revenants fought wildly, without any thought of self-preservation, but Ben's reasoned fighting style was terrifyingly efficient. Leaving the long-haired girl broken, Ben dealt the man another sharp blow, and the second woman charged him from behind.

I have to help! Before Nate had made it onto one knee, the woman's triumphant shriek changed to an anguished wail. Ben used her momentum to overbalance her, catching her in an awful parody of support. Before she could struggle, Ben's teeth were in her throat. The scream ripped out of her and dark liquid splattered the ground between them.

Nate watched it fall. *He tore out her throat with his teeth.* The same teeth Nate could still feel pressed against his neck.

The male revenant charged. The girl followed, dragging her broken limbs. Ben tossed the dead woman aside to meet them.

Nate watched the gradually slowing spasms of the woman. No movie death for her. She simply shuddered and went still, the darkness at her throat continuing to pool around her.

I'm going to be sick.

He could smell it even after he shut his eyes, a metallic tang that settled on the back of his throat, and the damp soil felt clammy beneath his palms. Nate clutched the rough bark of the oak as if it were a lifeline. His fingers closed on something soft and he looked down to see the white blossom of the rowan. He picked up the flower. *God. White flower. White teeth—*

It was a nightmare, only there was no waking up.

The clearing was absolutely still.

Ben held the girl in a lock. He did not try to finish her, and she made no attempt to resist. They stood there, unmoving, while the man made no attempt to attack.

Has Ben done something? Nate swayed unsteadily to his feet. *No. It's the necromancer – he's got Ben!*

Unlike the earlier blank mask, Ben's face was drawn with struggle. Aware and fighting. He could resist the necromancer's commands, but that was all.

Frozen like that, he's a sitting duck. Nate swallowed down fear so tight it hurt his lungs. *What's stopping the others?*

Something was stopping them. The bearded man ran a tongue over his bared fangs but made no move toward Ben's unprotected neck. Whatever invisible force had Ben trapped held the revenants in place, too.

Nate watched the man's arm twitch, straining forward only to be jerked back. As he stared, he caught sight of something that stood out strangely against his faded T-shirt.

A wire? Can't be—but what the hell is that? It was taut, trembling with the effort needed to contain the hungry beast. *Thread?* The line looped around the man's wrists, neck and body. *Almost like...*

With sudden understanding, Nate looked to Ben.

The female revenant was restrained by the same red threads as the man. Ben stood stock-still, trying to resist the tug of the cords that circled his neck. They started where the bite marks were on his neck, but spread out to wrap snakelike around his arms and body. Even as Nate watched, another rusty coil was added to the weight already weighing Ben down.

Red. Is this the blood magic? Nate could feel bile rising in his throat. *More like blood puppet show. The fuck!* His fingers gripped tightly about the flowers. *Think!*

This was just the point in the show where the ending theme would play and the voice-over guy would urge viewers to tune in again next week. Nate's lip curled. *Not helpful.* The revenants were hardly going to hold off eating them while the viewers waited to see whether Ben could fend off the unseen puppeteer—

Puppeteer?

Nate looked again. The strings all stretched in the same direction. Above the clearing, his limp feet at least a meter off the ground, Peter's body dangled like a damp sheet on a laundry line.

What's happened to him? The red lines were attached to Peter's fingers, but their source was his neck. It started with the bite, but didn't end there. The gash split Peter's throat almost entirely open, while the rest of his body continued the same tale of ill-use. *That's an entire CSI episode's worth of material.*

Peter's fingers had been worn so thin that it was hard to tell if they were skin or bone, while the dark outline of the trees were visible through his body. *There's almost nothing left of him!* His arms flung out at either side of him, fingers twitching in sporadic bursts of activity. Nate didn't have to glance back to the frozen struggle taking place to know that each twitch corresponded to an action of the revenants. *They're working the revenants through him.*

Worse were his eyes. The revenants had nothing beyond their hunger. Peter had self-awareness. His gaze fixed on Ben with a focus that made Nate's skin crawl. His mouth, the only part of him besides his fingers that moved, gritted in frustration as his lips drew back. *Dead and unable to die was bad enough, but to watch as you are used?* Nate swallowed.

Ben's shoulders were stiff, his eyes locked on Peter's. The thread pulling at Ben went slack as Ben took a lurching step toward the part of the clearing where Peter hung.

He's stopped fighting! Nate glanced around the circle for Ben's knife. *If I can cut that thread...*

Something glittered in the night air.

Another knife?

Its wielder caught three of the red threads on its surface, using the blade to tease them before selecting one.

Ben gasped as he could move again. "Hunter—"

"A knife of pure silver, anointed by a priest and blessed by a virgin. I *told* you blood magic, didn't I?" Nate hadn't thought he'd ever be glad to see Hunter again. The elder vampire spun the blade lightly on gloved fingers. "I also told you we would hunt together tonight."

"This wasn't my idea." Ben resumed his fighting stance. Released from their restraints, the two revenants met the arrival of the older vampire with snarls and renewed attacks.

It was hopeless. Hunter's assurance gave him grace, even while driving his knife through the heart of the bearded man, or helping Ben crack the neck of the woman. As she died, the apparition of Peter started to fade. His face contorted into a snarl that mirrored the dying vampire before he vanished.

Nate sank to the ground. He had no desire to leave the protective circle, even if his legs hadn't felt like lead. He watched Hunter tuck his coat and scarf into order before glancing at the corpse by his foot.

"I recognize the man from our files. The women?"

"Turned recently." Ben rubbed his neck. "Since Peter disappeared."

Hunter nodded. "I anticipated you'd follow procedure exactly and head for the memorial. So did the necromancer. Coming here was a good thought."

Ben didn't correct Hunter's assumption. He glanced towards Nate, then quickly looked away, wiping blood from his mouth. "Another trap? How many more deaths does he want?"

Hunter glanced up at Ben's abrupt about-face. A curious expression flitted over his face as he noticed Nate. And then he smiled, projecting urbane amusement. "It's safe now. Come and join us."

Halfway across the clearing, Nate realized that although Hunter's tone was reassuring, that last sentence was an order. He came to a self-conscious halt before the vampires, looking to Ben. *Compulsion?*

Hunter looked deliberately at the coat draped over Nate's arm. "I take it you enjoyed your present." He showed his own fangs clearly as he leered.

Knowing that Hunter possessed fangs didn't make seeing them less of a shock. Nate dragged his gaze away, only to find Hunter's eyes on him. *Gauging my reaction?*

"This isn't the time," Ben shot back over his shoulder. His glare encompassed both of them. "Nate's in very real danger!"

"It's cool," Nate assured him. "I'll be in more danger when Denise realizes—" Denise. "Fuck! I walked off my shift. Denise will kill me!"

Ben flinched, but Nate's poor word choice didn't bother Hunter any.

"We shouldn't delay. Denise didn't strike me as patient." Hunter wiped his knife clean with a smile. "Give Ben his coat back."

Nate held the coat out to Ben. "Thanks."

"It has to be like this." Ben held the coat awkwardly. "For your safety."

Nate slipped his hands into the pockets of the coveralls. The awareness that Hunter watched them closely made it hard to speak. "And your safety?"

"I'll take care of that." Nate hadn't heard that note in Hunter's voice before. He glanced back. The blueness of the vampire's eyes weren't as bright in the night, but they were just as fascinating. Nate returned Hunter's smile unthinkingly. "Forget what happened tonight. Forget the anniversary party. Forget everything connected with us."

Chapter Eight

"Don't ever scare us like that again! *Nate—*"

No need to ask if I was missed. Nate let Aki barrel into him. His friend's grip was tight enough it hurt, but Nate didn't protest. Aki was warm, a space heater in human form. Nate probably risked frost burn, but he didn't care. His fingers and toes were numb, and he was shivering so hard it had taken him two attempts to slide his wristband in front of the employee entrance lock.

"You asshole! We were so worried— Someone tell Denise he's back! Geez, Nate!" Aki thumped his fist angrily against Nate's chest. "Answer your goddamn phone!"

Every breath, every surge of rapidly changing emotion was proof of Aki's extreme state of existence. He was alive.

I'm alive. Nate pulled Aki close. "I'm okay." Aki was a lifeline that connected him to everything safe and ordinary. "But man...it was close."

"What happened?"

Nate let go, ruffling Aki's hair. "Tell you after I shower. Dived off a bridge. My body's ice."

* ~ * ~ *

Steam rose immediately from the sleek tiled floor, heat radiating outward. Nate watched it fog the cubicle wall before continuing to undress. He'd turned the shower faucet to high. Nate's hand still tingled from where it had encountered the water, but it didn't reach below the surface. The numbing cold had gone deeper than his limbs. He could still feel the silence of the vampires behind him, cold night made even colder by their watching presence.

There was blood on the coverall trousers, a cut Nate didn't even remember. Peeling off the T-shirt revealed even more scrapes and what would soon become bruises, all numbed by the pervasive chill. Nate smoothed down the clothes automatically, pausing as he felt something hard in the pocket.

The rowan blossoms were definitely worse for their journey. Nate set the twig on the sill above the sink with deliberate care. The white blossoms were crinkly, edges browning where they'd been torn. Although only picked a few hours ago, they were badly wilted. No wonder— Nate's hand had closed reflexively around them the entire walk back from the park.

"Especially potent against dark magic," Nate repeated. *Was that why?*

"Back! I got a change of clothes and towel, just like you said!" Aki flung open the shower room door. "And uh...Denise."

"Denise?" Nate looked around hastily, but Aki held the only towel.

The red-haired manager waved him toward the shower with her usual briskness. "I've seen it all before, Nathan. Get yourself warmed up. Akihiro said something about rivers and a vampire?"

"Multiple vampires." Too worn to protest, Nate leaned against the back of the shower. The water rushed over him, the first burn quickly becoming soothing warmth. Nate felt something of the night lift.

Alive.

"Turn around...there." Denise let out a breath. She still wore her business suit. "You weren't fed from, that's one thing. Gunn stressed we should check."

"You called the police?"

"You weren't in our room, the break room, the roof, or the fire escape." Aki sat himself on the tiled floor. "When security said your wristband indicated you'd left the club, I got scared."

"Given the circumstances, I agreed to alert Department Seven. I was on the phone with Gunn when you returned." Denise glanced down at the clipboard she held. "He's given me a checklist."

"Fantastic." *Who brings a checklist into a shower?*

"Don't sulk. Department Seven wouldn't let you take a shower while they interviewed you."

Nate eyed Aki and Denise from the other side of the clear plastic shower wall. *That's a positive?*

Denise consulted her list. "No bites of unknown origin, nothing resembling a knife wound, or the burn of some unholy seal—"

"What happened to your shoulder?"

"The river dive I mentioned? Completely literal." Nate hesitated, but Denise and Aki already knew about the anniversary party. "So." It still felt wrong. "I'm out on the emergency stairs, and I see Ben. He's walking into oncoming traffic, like he's got no idea. He's gonna hurt someone, probably himself, so I chase him down..." Nate shook his head. Even in the showers he used every day, with his best friend and manager there and the hot pinpricks of the shower drumming on his neck, he still felt that cold shock. "Something was controlling him. I guess I panicked, and, well...the river was there."

Denise folded the clipboard across her chest. "That's twice now Hunter's actions have endangered you. If he thinks he can abuse my staff—"

"It's cool. They're...not coming back." Nate took a deep breath, tried to push past the leaden weight in his chest. "Hunter did the vampire compulsion thing to me. Told me to forget. Ben...didn't stop him."

Aki's head shot up, his expression puzzled.

Before he could speak, Denise cut in. "Shouldn't that have worked?"

"Yeah, it should've." Nate nodded to the tattered white flowers of the rowan, looking even more battered against the industrial design of the tiles. "We sheltered under a rowan in the park. It's effective against dark magic. Guess that includes vampires. I had them in my pocket. I remember...everything." Briefly, he filled them in on the feral vampires, the fight, and the awful specter of Peter strung like laundry over the park.

"Just 'cause they want you to forget them doesn't mean they're not coming back," Aki said slowly. He looked to Denise.

The manager nodded. "Gunn will be made aware of this, as will security. Hunter and his family are not welcome on our premises." Hand already on the door, Denise looked back. "Take care of yourself, Nathan. Your shift's been covered, and Akihiro's volunteered to stay with you tonight if you need anything."

Denise's departure didn't lift the atmosphere any. *Fuck it.* Nate gave dignity the finger and slumped against the base of the shower. The water hit him in individual darts, sting soothed almost immediately by the warmth they left behind.

The wounds from the river were another story. His body had thawed enough to feel again. Tired muscles protested even the slightest movement, and Nate couldn't even make himself care that Aki watched.

"You look bad."

"Thanks, Aki."

"No, I mean it. Worse than after Kyle's birthday party, even."

Nate smiled tiredly. "You're comparing vampires to a fucking hangover?"

"You finished the entire bottle and walked most of the way back to our room before you threw up. Even Tanner was impressed, and nothing impresses him."

Nate shut his eyes. "I saw four people die tonight. Yeah, they were already dead, but—" He wiped his hair off his forehead. "That's a big deal, Aki."

"Welcome to New Camden." Aki paused. Nate didn't need to look at him to know that Aki's restless fingers twisted the hem of his T-shirt and his eyes were fixed on Nate. "When you said Ben didn't stop Hunter from wiping your memory, it almost sounded like you wanted him to. Stop Hunter, I mean. Not wipe your mind—"

Nate let out his breath slowly. "I know what you meant."

Aki's question was palpable. "So—"

"Yeah, I guess I did."

Aki let out a harsh breath. "But you said he was—"

"*Taken.*" Nate's mouth twisted. *And wasn't that the icing on the fucked-up cake?* "I know. Or thought I knew. Didn't realize how bad I had it."

"And I thought Hunter was the dangerous one. Sorry, I-I'm sorry."

Had it just been a week ago that Nate had been desperate for Hunter to acknowledge his existence? Strange how quickly priorities could change. "Not as sorry as I am."

"Maybe it's not as bad as it looks. Erasing your memory could have been a sort of…friendly thing. Like he didn't want you to have nightmares or—"

"Aki. I saved his life twice tonight; he slammed me into an oak." Nate scrubbed his hand across his forehead. "There are no mixed signals there."

The water of the shower was interrupted as Aki wrapped his arms around him. "All that proves is that vampires are beyond stupid," he said, voice muffled against Nate's neck. "Seriously stupid. More so than you."

Nate smiled weakly, thumping a fist gently against Aki's side. "You're just saying that—you *dweeb*. You hopped in here with your clothes on?"

* ~ * ~ *

The roof was a far cry from the beach, or even a pool, but some hard-core escapist had dragged a couple of deck chairs up there and made the best of it. A potted palm placed against one of the air vents added some much-needed credibility to the scene, and the afternoon sun did the rest. The overflowing recycling bin full of glass bottles and a smattering of ashtrays attested to the popularity of the club's roof among its employees in the summer months, but in the early spring, Nate and the palm had it all to themselves.

Leaning back in the more stable of the two deck chairs, Nate gazed up at the sky. The weather was uncharacteristically mild. There was even enough sun that Nate could unzip the fleece he wore. No greater contrast to the night he'd passed...

And I still can't shake the cold. Nate stroked the rough stem of the rowan twig. Aki had mocked him for tucking it into his pocket, but while Nate was not going to win any fashion accolades, he felt better. Who knew? Maybe it did work. Against Aki's dire predictions and Nate's expectations, he'd slept solidly, undisturbed by nightmares or recollections of the night.

Until he woke up.

Nate sighed, fist closing around the twig.

"Stopped by to bring you some protection. Didn't realize you had some of your own."

Given how abruptly Gunn had disappeared after their last conversation, Nate was not totally surprised by his sudden appearance on the roof. "Come to gloat? Yeah, you were right about vampires being bad news. It bites. Can we move on?"

"Aren't you a ray of sunshine?" Gunn helped himself to the other deck chair. "I'll admit, I can be officious at times, but do I really deserve a pun that bad?" He still wore the same pair of jeans, but he'd traded his habitual bomber for a quilted jacket in camouflage colors. He folded his arms behind his head and raised an insolent eyebrow. "Heard you had an interesting night."

Nate narrowed his eyes. "You know what happened last night. That's why you're here."

"Department Seven isn't typical police, but we still have procedure to follow. But you're right. I'm not here to take your statement."

Nate sat up. "Don't tell me this is your idea of a social call."

"Possibly. But then I've always been considered antisocial." Gunn's smile was catlike, cruel. "Thought you might be interested in hearing how Saltaire's colony are dealing with last night."

Nate bit his lip. Denise had ordered him to forget the vampires, but—

"That's what I thought." Gunn's smirk was unapologetic. "So. To business." He swung his feet off the deck chair, sat up to face Nate. "Saltaire's lot claim de Silver's abduction is an attempt by a necromancer—probably employed by a rival colony—to gain control of the newest, and therefore weakest, member of the family."

The little warmth the roof had retained vanished. "Ben."

"Saltaire's pet witch will give him the vampire equivalent of a detox. De Silver's blood can't be used against them again." Gunn shrugged. "I'm willing to bet the same holds true for whatever their unknown enemy was attempting on Hawick's grave. Which means our necromancer will be looking for a new line of attack."

"Really."

"Necromancers use blood magic, worked through sex, blood, and bonds."

"Bondage?" Nate was sure he'd misheard. *Then again, the creepy way Hunter and Ben had both deferred to Saltaire—*

"Bonds. Emotional, familial, unfulfilled. In the parlance of ghost hunters, 'unfinished business.' Not whatever you are thinking of."

Nate tried to look as though he hadn't pictured Ben in leather. "If it's strong enough to tie a person to a place, it's strong enough to work on a vampire?"

"Close enough." Gunn smiled. "I'm sure you see where this is leading."

Nate could feel the inevitability like a cold blade against his neck. "Me. Dead in some dark ritual."

"If you're lucky. Ritual murder and magical energies play havoc with the deceased. You might end up haunting an alley or Dumpster. Worst case scenario, you're a low-level vampire like the four you met last night."

"You're doing a lousy job of making me feel better."

"Feel better? I'm trying to keep you alive." Gunn drew a brown paper bag from the pocket of his jacket. "Take this."

The bag was heavy. Nate opened it to reveal an ornate crucifix. Blackened with age, Nate couldn't tell what metal it was. The cross felt cool in Nate's hand, the chain pooling around with surprising smoothness. "I can't accept this. It's—"

"On loan. I got a dozen of them, all regularly blessed. Take it and use it." Gunn stood. He produced a cigarette from an inside pocket of the jacket, pulling his lighter from his jeans. "I'm serious."

Nate hesitantly lowered the cold chain around his neck. "Don't these things work on belief? I'm not exactly religious."

"But you believe in dying flowers and a twig."

Nate put his hand around the rowan. "That's different."

"My neck's on the line, I'm not gonna split hairs." Gunn caught Nate's eye. "Crucifixes are proven deterrents to vampires."

About to drop the cross inside his shirt, Nate stopped. "We're looking for a necromancer."

Gunn smiled at him. It was his most unpleasant expression yet. "Saltaire's colony's been content with keeping close tabs on you, but now they know their enemy's target and his only remaining line of attack. I don't know how long you're going to be allowed to be a loose end."

Nate's hand closed reflexively around the cross. "You're seriously suggesting—"

"Saltaire's from a time when a man could be executed just for looking at a superior wrong. Killing you wouldn't be a precaution. It would be his duty."

Despite the daylight, Nate shivered. Saltaire's manner during sex had been nothing if not dictatorial. "I'm guessing Saltaire did his duty."

Gunn shrugged. "New tricks, old dog."

"And no kennel club willing to take him."

Gunn showed his teeth in unabashed enjoyment of Nate's annoyance. "Try not to get turned. Putting you down would lower my mood for at least five minutes."

"Yeah, that would really suck for you." Nate hesitated. He wasn't sure he wanted to ask this. "Department Seven. What's that mean exactly?"

"A bit late for you to start to worry, kid. But don't fret about my credentials. Number one requirement for any department member is the ability to hold their own against throwbacks like Saltaire."

Nate couldn't remember seeing any thick chain around Gunn's neck. "What's yours?"

"A life of virtue is its own reward."

"You could just say 'none of your business.'"

"I like my answer better." Gunn exhaled slowly, the tobacco smoke lingering around him. "You don't believe I'm virtuous, Nate? I've got the badge and everything."

Nate dropped the crucifix beneath his shirt. "I could sooner believe that anyone in Saltaire's family gives a shit about my life, except as it potentially makes things inconvenient for them."

"Attaboy."

"You encouraging my continued existence or pissing off Saltaire?"

"I can't do both?" Gunn shrugged. "Saltaire's continued existence is inconvenience enough. The fact he's a vampire pretty much means any effort to investigate him could spark another political incident."

"The Auckland Protocol?" Nate knew the basic gist of the first moratorium on human-vampire relations. "That's just politics—"

"Saltaire's old blood. Can't take a shit without it being of interest to the rest of his kind. Any suggestion of weakness and every vampire in this city will be on him." Gunn tapped his cigarette on the arm of his deckchair. "Like undead sharks after blood."

On him—and the rest of his family? Nate bit his lip. "There's nothing you can do?"

"Auckland Protocol only holds up so long as no humans are killed. We can't pin any of our six victims on vampires yet, but their involvement gives us some leeway to investigate."

Nate's hand stroked the hard crucifix through his fleece. "What is there to investigate?"

"Bluntly? You."

Nate had been afraid of that. "You're not going to get very far investigating me. I've already told you everything I know."

"Exactly," Gunn said. "Now I'm not saying you *should* volunteer to let us use you as bait to draw our perp out into the open. I'm just saying you could *consider* it."

Nate's life. "Right."

"You're in danger either way," the brown-haired officer continued. "In fact, you're in less danger if we're using you as bait since we know exactly when to watch you."

"That is...a point."

Had Gunn's teeth always been that sharp? "You got my number, Nate. Stay in touch."

* ~ * ~ *

"You sure the black doesn't make me look like a wannabe Jet Li?" Aki tapped his foot as he considered his reflection in the mirror.

Nate folded the several T-shirts and pairs of jeans that Aki had discarded prior to his current choice. "No one's gonna mistake you for Jet Li. He's got, what, a full four inches on you?"

"Fuck you. Yeah, cleaning sucks, but you don't have to be a bitch about it!"

Every single time. Nate grinned. He set aside the clothes and draped himself over Aki's shoulder. "Look in the mirror." As Aki watched, Nate let one hand move down, deliberately caressing Aki's body through the silken T-shirt. When he reached the waist of the skintight trousers, Nate let his fingers go beneath. "How's the black look now?"

Aki leaned back against Nate, looping an arm back to pull him closer. "Pretty fucking good." He'd gone commando, humming as Nate teased his cock. "God, Nate. Why couldn't you have been on floor tonight?"

"Way things are going, I'll be lucky Denise clears me at all." Nate continued to stroke his friend. "I got another lecture about 'stranger danger' in addition to Officer Gunn's social call. I'm worried she might relegate me to cleaning until this whole thing's cleared up."

Aki rocked back against Nate. "That could take weeks—months even. Is that where you were after lunch?"

"Nah, I was up on the roof."

"I looked there. You weren't— Fuck, it's gonna be hard doing Brandon without you."

Nate deliberately pumped Aki one last time before he pulled his hand away. "Hard's what we want."

"You know what I mean." Brandon was an artist manager who often flew into New Camden with his acts. He celebrated a successful show with his "regular order," hiring two hosts to put on a show before he fucked them both. "Eddie goes into full diva mode the moment we get going. Like he thinks he can impress Brandon with his vocal range."

"That's not how you get signed."

"Eddie can have his dreams." Aki gave himself a final once-over in the mirror. "Me, I'll settle for Brandon's massive dick."

Nate thumped him on the shoulder. "Don't need to tell you to enjoy yourself."

What is wrong with me? Nate pulled on a new set of coveralls in the small equipment room. He could joke with Aki, fake an interest in the night, but did he actually regret missing out? Brandon's cock definitely more than compensated for any deficits in creativity, but all the same—

The park lingered.

"Fucking vampires."

* ~ * ~ *

Denise showed rare pity and granted Nate's request to be placed somewhere with people. He spent the night on kitchen duty, rinsing seemingly endless trays of glasses and dishes before loading them into the industrial dishwashers, trading insults with the part-time cook, and listening to the college football game over the radio. The work was tedious, but the company helped, and Nate actually felt like he was going to be able to sleep as he climbed into bed in the early hours of the morning.

The rowan twig was definitely on its way out. The blossoms had browned and gone limp, even after spending the night propped up in a glass of water. Nate fingered the blossoms thoughtfully as he set them on the windowsill. *Tossing them doesn't seem respectful.* He would find somewhere to bury them tomorrow.

Sunlight filtered through the summer greenery of the willows, shining like the stained glass of the little Lutheran chapel in the valley. The trickle of the creek that ran through the farm was audible beneath the whisper of leaves in the breeze. Nate smiled up at the canopy, relishing the feeling of the cool grass on his bare feet. It had always been one of his and Ethan's favorite places, and Nate turned at the sound of footsteps, fully expecting to see his brother.

Ben picked his way hesitantly through the grass, in jeans that had to be rolled up and a T-shirt that all but swallowed him. His expression cleared as it settled on Nate. "They said I'd find you out here."

Nate held out his hand.

Ben took it, coming to lean against his side, and they watched the play of the intermittent sunlight on the surface of the water. Nate let his fingers loop through Ben's, content not to question the moment.

The light on the water shone brighter, and suddenly it wasn't light any more but the clean white of bone. Peter lurched out of the creek, his eyes still human behind his skull, as he reached one clawlike hand toward them—

Nate kicked out, jolting himself awake.

"Back—"

He inhaled, taking in the sound of Aki's steady breathing above and the low rumble of the club's internal heating. "Just a dream.

Christ."

He lay back down, feeling for Gunn's cross around his neck. He owed the officer. Having it in his hand, Nate definitely felt better. *I was overdue a nightmare. I mean, fucking hell. All things considered, I'm lucky even to shut my eyes!*

Of all the things for his brain to throw at him. Sure, he was homesick, but Ben being there? "Vampires can't go out in the sun." Everyone knew that.

Nate snorted at the memory of the skeletal figure looming up out of the creek. *Really? There's never more than a few centimeters of water there at the best of times!* Ethan and he had spent many summers vainly trying to dam it up and create a proper swimming hole without success. *But since when do dreams make sense?*

Nate reached under his pillow for his phone before remembering that it had not survived the dive off the bridge. It balanced precariously on the heater grill in a desperate attempt to resuscitate it. Nate pulled the blankets up over his shoulders and settled back down. He'd borrow Aki's phone and message Ethan in the morning.

The dream refused to be shaken off so easily. Once the shock of Peter's skeletal visage faded, the incongruity stood out. Nate hadn't just imagined Ben in jeans and a T-shirt, he'd imagined him in jeans clearly borrowed from his or Ethan's wardrobe, and a T-shirt that Nate had grown out of in high school but never thrown out.

He'd imagined Ben in the sort of detail that made things *real.*

Nate groaned. He rolled over to bury his face in his pillow. *Textbook psychological stuff.* Stripping the vampire of his suit and New Camden sophistication, sticking him in a place familiar to Nate, even dressing him in Nate's own clothes. Obviously Nate's subconscious was attempting to take charge of what had happened to him and sublimate it... *But do I have to make Ben look that good in the process?*

The unguarded expression on Ben's face as he'd taken in the scene beneath the willows, the way the voluminous clothing teased by obscuring the lithe body Nate knew lay beneath, even the curve of his lips as he looked to Nate in greeting... Nate groaned again. *My mind hates me. Only possible explanation.* Seriously, getting hung up on a guy who dismissed him?

Nate reached for his pillow. *That's what hurts the most. Being written off just like that.* He could take the loathing of customers too far gone in self-hate to be able to make love without degradation, or ignore the smirks when people at the park noticed his wristband, but Ben had wedged himself under Nate's skin in a way he couldn't shrug off. *So what if I don't know what I'm doing! Or he could kill me without even breaking a sweat!*

"I saved the guy's life twice!"

There was a snort from above. Nate bit his lip, but Aki's breathing remained even. Good. *Last thing I need is Aki on my case again.* Despite his spirited defense of supernatural rights, Aki vehemently opposed Nate having any further involvement with the vampire family. "Friends do not compel friends. End of." He delivered the verdict with a seriousness that was as impressive as it was worrying. Nate had not known Aki was capable of that much dislike, or that much concern. Nate felt a pang in his chest. Aki had to be seriously scared.

And for good reason. The wild light of the revenant's eyes haunted Nate, even within the familiar confines of the dorm room. *What? Am I trying to give myself nightmares?* Nate shifted, digging his shoulder into the mattress. *Bad enough I'm still thinking about Ben at all.* Hunter's far less threatening and infinitely more casual abuse of his powers had been an instant turnoff. Seeing the brutal truth of Ben's vampire existence should have been the end of it. And yet, Nate's mind continually traveled back to Ben.

What the hell is wrong with me? He's not even that hot! As brutally as Aki would, Nate laid out all Ben's flaws. The weak chin, strangely impressive with the weight of the park behind it. Limpid eyes, either frustratingly blank of any clue to the vampire's intentions or unguarded in a way that made Nate anxious. His too-wide mouth, which—

Nate paused, running a quick mental inventory. Somehow he'd amassed a very complete catalog of Ben's physical characteristics.

"I seriously need to get laid."

Providing nothing else went wrong, he'd be on active duty again in a few nights. *A good fuck—yeah, that'll do it.* Getting hot and dirty with some well-hung guy with broad, beefy shoulders and his own pulse— It would be great. Letting his hand drift beneath his T-shirt, Nate splayed his fingers across his chest.

The fantasy came readily. An older man, authoritative, tanned, with a physique even a straight guy would look twice at. As different from Ben as it got. No nonsense, he had Nate's cock in his hand, stroking him within his pants, even as he ground his own hefty erection against Nate from behind in full view of everyone on the dance floor.

Just like that. The crowd pulsed with the beat of the music, his partner stroking him fast then slow, working him in time to the DJ's beats. Nate imagined swaying back with the music, encountering that hard body with a thrill. Ben would have to be coaxed onto the dance floor. He would be uncomfortable at first, tensing every time someone moved too close, but maybe if Nate found a dark corner—

Nate rolled over, burying his groan in the pillow. "Fuck me."

This was seriously pathetic.

What made it even worse? Any attempt at acting on the connection would end in the vampire family wiping his memory! *No way am I giving the vampires that satisfaction.*

Pleased with his conclusion, Nate settled back to sleep. Couldn't be a splinter in the vampire's collective coffin if you were tired, after all.

He might have been able to make himself believe that in daylight, but at night, with only Aki's steady breathing to distract him, Nate knew there was more to it than that. He'd remembered Ben's rigidity of expression as he'd looked at Peter's tortured shade so often that the memory came instantly. The contrast to the feelings he'd shown Nate as Ben slowly opened up to him was marked. *Serious about protecting me?* The thought lacked the bitter bite of earlier. *"You could never be a casual encounter."*

Words Nate hadn't known he wanted to hear, but hell if he didn't want to hear them again. *Fat chance of that.* As long as Ben considered their association a danger to Nate, he would continue to retreat.

I got lucky with the river and the rowan, but that's it. Revenants? Nate shuddered, hand going automatically to Gunn's cross at his neck. *A crucifix isn't going to impress a vampire. Neither is being the bait in Gunn's trap—even if I could be sure that it's the necromancer he wants to catch.* Nate had to face facts. Ben occupied a world so removed from Nate's that the vampire might just as well have been on another planet, and there was nothing Nate could do about it.

Nothing?

Chapter Nine

Nate leaned his weight against the iron gate. It creaked, but didn't budge. Nate glanced up at the townhouse. The downstairs curtains were firmly shut, while all Nate could see in the second and third floor windows was the empty gray sky of the overcast day. Somehow the reflection made the day feel even colder.

Nate pulled his scarf more tightly around his neck. *I didn't come all this way to give up now!* Shaking off the disapproving shadow of the stiff, Victorian façade, Nate rested his hands on the wrought iron curls. There had to be a catch somewhere, maybe a switch—

Or maybe an intercom unit installed with typical discreetness into the wall itself.

Of course, there's an intercom. Nate shouldered his bag and leaned into it. "Hello? This is Nate. Is Godfrey home?" Nate winced. *What am I, five? Do I want a job or for Godfrey to come out and play?*

"Nathan?" Nothing in Godfrey's polite surprise indicated what he thought of Nate's greeting. "I have to say, I did not expect you to stop by this morning."

"I was wondering if you still wanted help in the garden."

"As a matter of fact, I do. It is good of you to come all this way."

Benign enough, but Nate thought he detected a note of enquiry.

He smiled thinly at the gate. "I'd have called, but my phone fell in a river."

With a mechanical *click*, the gate swung open.

"I'll meet you around back," Godfrey said. "I trust you remember the way."

The butler was as neat as Nate remembered. Even the apron he wore over his suit was crisply ironed and fresh. Despite his advanced years, his pale eyes were alert. Nate was conscious of Godfrey studying him closely. "You'll have to forgive me. I've been rather...preoccupied lately. I can't quite call to mind the details of our arrangement?"

Can't tell how much I remember. Nate shrugged. He set his hands in his jacket pockets to stop himself fidgeting and nodded toward the shed. "Basic maintenance stuff. A few half-days to get the garden in shape, and then a couple of hours every week to keep things ticking over."

Surprise flickered in Godfrey's eyes. "And you're ready to start?"

"Been itching to have a go at those roses. And while ivy looks great, it can do a number on old wood. If I can train it to grow over the terrace instead of your shed..."

"Yes," Godfrey agreed. "I suppose so. Would you like to step into the house while I draw up an agreement?"

Nate shook his head. "If it's all the same, I'd like to get started now." The cross Gunn gave him felt heavy around his neck. Several layers of clothing buried it, but Nate felt sure that the moment he stepped into the house, the butler would know, and that would be the end of this.

"I can't argue with such enthusiasm," Godfrey said. "You'll find everything you need in the shed. I will be back to check on you shortly."

Someone with every intention of taking care of the garden had stocked the shed. Nate leaned in the doorway, weighing the tools. Bought new for the job and used sparingly, if at all. Nate remembered the barn and the rusted collection of tools handed down through generations of farmers. *Am I making a huge mistake?*

Then again, what choice do I have? Nate had to show Ben that he could rely on Nate and plants were the only thing Nate was good at. Besides fucking, which really was not going to help against revenants. *But plants will?* Nate repeated his plan to himself as he pulled on the gloves. Start by proving himself with mundane tasks like the garden and work up from there. Sure, it'd take a while, but once Ben realized Nate was there for the long haul...

The gloves on the door were intended for bigger hands than Godfrey's. They fit snugly when Nate pulled them on, cracked in a way that indicated use. Nate felt better wearing them. Following in someone else's footsteps was a lot easier than striking out entirely on his own. It was true what he'd told Aki, that having a garden of his own appealed. But this garden... Everything depended on this garden.

First, the lawn. The riotous grass would eat the ancient push mower alive. Nate set to work with the long-bladed clippers. The lawn was so thickly tangled that the neighboring grass held up the cuttings, and it wasn't until Nate got out the rake that he could see the progress he'd made.

Godfrey appeared around noon with two neatly cut sandwiches and a cup of tea. “You’ve certainly made progress! I did not expect to see our lawn looking itself again so soon.”

“I’ll have to go over it again with the rake,” Nate said modestly. Once he cut the grass down to size, he’d been able to trim it evenly with the mower. “But a well-maintained lawn makes all the difference.” Part one of the plan had gone even better than Nate had hoped. Removing the ivy and cutting back the roses were more urgent jobs but would make the yard seem bare until the fresh growth came. The neatly mowed lawn instantly repaid attention and would hopefully impress more than just Godfrey. “Do you have a compost bin for the cut grass?”

“The compost was last seen somewhere beneath the ivy that engulfed the shed.”

“That can be my next task.” Nate glanced at the sky as he sat on the terrace steps with his sandwich. “That should take me until midafternoon. Then I’ll head out.”

“So soon?”

Nate ignored Godfrey’s raised eyebrow. *Probably thinks this a ploy to see Hunter.*

“Don’t want to be late to the night job.”

“Very wise.” Godfrey had joined Nate in his break. He sat on a chair set on the back terrace rather than the steps and held his cup of tea with complete poise. “New Camden has never been safe at the best of times, but with the recent unpleasantness...”

Nate felt incredibly clumsy, balancing the delicate china teacup in his thick fingers. “How do you get a job with Saltaire?” he asked.

"I mean...um."

Godfrey looked at him over his teacup but did not question the apparent non sequitur. "ARX is well represented at job fairs and technical conventions. We're currently looking for staff with an aptitude for economics, innovative sciences, or technology."

Nate had barely scraped through remedial math, was only good at the science involved in farming, and his technical knowledge was limited to the use of his smartphone. "I was kind of wondering about the...other side."

"Ah." Godfrey set his teacup down in its saucer. "Recruitment for the domestic side is at management's discretion. Candidates have either years of trustworthy service behind them, a natural talent, or personal circumstances that make them uniquely qualified to take up the task."

"Personal circumstances?"

"Saltaire considers anyone who has survived supernatural attack a good investment." Godfrey smoothed his hand over the apron. "Less risk to others should they succumb on the job. Survivors generally don't have family to endanger by their association."

Ben's father murdered and Ben himself—

"Peter? I mean—" Nate paused. *What do I mean?*

Fortunately, Godfrey was so well trained he filled the gap in conversation fluidly. "Peter first came to our attention as a recently orphaned teenager, the recipient of a Saltaire educational grant. He showed such promise that Master Saltaire personally oversaw his schooling. He entered the company immediately upon graduation and soon took over the management of Master Hunter's affairs. He was the youngest board member we've ever had."

So businesslike. I don't have a chance!

"Were you thinking of joining us as a dinner guest?"

"That'd never work," Nate said. "Ben—"

He realized his mistake too late.

Godfrey didn't express more than mild surprise. "So it is Master Bennet."

"I'm not— I mean, I didn't want—"

"Master Saltaire is still in the city. I can have a quiet word with him and suggest you for dinner. After all, we have an opening."

"No," Nate said with enough vehemence that Godfrey looked vaguely astonished. "I don't want to be helped. This is something I have to do myself."

It sounded ridiculous as soon as he'd said it, yet Godfrey took the statement seriously. "Why is that?"

Nate hesitated. *What's the point? I've already outed myself.* "If I have to be helped, then it doesn't prove anything. I don't want to be made to forget. Even...even if it's safer."

Godfrey smiled benignly and stood. "This has been a most enlightening conversation. You have a lot of work in front of you, Nathan. I won't keep you from it." He nodded to Nate and returned to the house.

Have I ruined everything? Nate set his cup aside, tugging on the gloves. *Nothing I can do but get back to work.* He was committed.

* ~ * ~ *

"Where did you go? I couldn't take notes in psych, I was that worried!"

Any excuse for drama. Nate sprayed the spider fern with the mister and refused to take Aki's bait. "I left a note."

"That told me exactly nothing. I have been texting you all day! Why didn't you reply?"

Nate looked up at that. "My phone's dead, remember?" It rested in plain view of both of them on the built-in heater, as unresponsive as it had been the night before.

It took all Nate's self-control not to laugh at Aki's expression. "Right. I forgot." Aki deliberately plonked himself down on Nate's bunk, leaning against the frame. "Gonna get a new one?"

"Give it a day or two." The spider fern didn't seem to be hurting from its relative neglect. Nate pressed a fingertip into the soil to judge how damp it was. "A guy at my high school dropped his in the can. His mom put it in a bag of rice for a week and that fixed it. Of course, he didn't exactly want it after that."

They both looked at Nate's phone.

"Yeah," Aki said. "I would get a new one. And I am saying this as someone with criminal amounts of student debt, so."

"If it's not working in a couple of days, I'll have to. But man, this is the last thing I need." Nate let go of the fern, looking over to Aki. "Can I borrow yours? Just to send a quick message home. Ma worries if she doesn't hear from me."

"Not until you tell me what you were doing in Old Town this afternoon."

"That's your most pathetic attempt to weasel information out of me yet. I wasn't in Old Town."

Aki scoffed. "So what, you're going to tell me you have an identical twin?"

Nate rolled his eyes. "Yeah, actually. And Ethan was nowhere near Old Town either." Nothing short of the apocalypse would budge his brother from the farm.

"Wait." Aki sat up. "Ethan's your twin?"

"Yeah, he is." Nate suddenly remembered why he had decided not to share that information.

"And you're really...?"

"Identical. Yes."

"Why did you never tell me you had an identical twin brother?"

"The industry we work in?" Nate made a face. "You mention twin and immediately—"

"That is so fucking hot."

Nate winced. *Definitely a mistake.* "No. Whatever you're thinking now, no."

"But—"

When Denise arrived, Aki had given up on Ethan's Facebook details but not photos. "I have been your best friend for months now—"

"What part of 'he doesn't like people' is hard to understand? Seriously, he— Denise!"

The manager rested her hands on her hips. "Although this sounds like a very interesting conversation, it doesn't preclude either of you from attending our debriefing on the new safety measures—especially since they've been introduced with you in mind, Nathan."

Oh god. A staff meeting and it's all my fault? "Sorry, Denise."

"Upstairs, now."

Aki elbowed him as they joined the other staff gathered on Century's dance floor. "Think of it like this. We get what, half an hour of Denise telling us to be careful? Compare that to one of us getting killed. Denise would talk at us for a good two hours."

"Also you'd be dead."

"You want to borrow my phone or not?"

"You're still not getting Ethan's details."

Aki waggled his phone at him. "I find it really sad that you immediately assume I'd have an ulterior motive to wanting to help my friend."

Nate took the phone before Aki could take it back. "Thanks, Aki."

Despite the added security, Century didn't feel different. In fact, it was so relentlessly normal that Nate wondered if the rest of the city was as sick of necromancers as he was. Whether trying to put the recent deaths and mounting disappearances out of their minds or simply making up for wasted time, their clientele kept the cleaning crew so busy it was late before Nate could e-mail Ethan. Wording the message in a way that would inform Ethan but not alarm Ma if she saw it took all of Nate's break. He stuffed the phone into his coverall pocket immediately upon hitting send and pushed the cleaning trolley to the next booth.

Handcuffs, wow. Nate pulled on his gloves to drop the toy into the sterilization bucket. *Seriously, shelling out for Century and that's the best your imagination can do?* As Nate heaved the sheets into the laundry basket, the phone buzzed.

Ethan worried? That'll be a first. Nate pulled out the phone. *If he so much as mentions that damn plant...*

He stared at the message, not comprehending for seconds. *Romeo? Who the fuck is—*

Then it clicked. Nate had used the web app. This reply was meant for Aki.

[Is Nate back?]

It was coincidence. Had to be. They had a lot of mutual friends—none of whom were called Romeo. Nate stayed frozen, trying to remember who he hadn't seen that night that might be legitimately worried about him.

He could only think of one name.

Another message popped up as Nate hesitated.

[It's after dark. If he's not back now, call Gunn.]

[Don't take any chances. He has to be all right.]

Their only club friend that knew Gunn's name was Beatrice, and she'd scolded Nate for his relegation to cleaning at the start of his shift. Gripping the phone so tightly that his hand hurt, he set off through the club.

Aki was taking a tray of glasses to the bar when Nate joined him. "Tell me I'm not in your phone under Juliet."

"OBF," Aki said promptly. "Though if I'd kno—" He paused, the tray sliding out of his grip. "Fuck. Ben didn't—"

Nate caught the tray before any glasses could fall. "He did." He deposited the tray on the bar and turned, wondering how he was going to get the truth out of Aki. "So."

"I knew you'd be furious." Aki's admission was immediate. "But the way he put it— It really seemed like I'd be helping you."

Note to self: do not trust Aki with any secrets. Nate hadn't even tried hard. "Right."

Aki squirmed under Nate's gaze. He couldn't meet Nate's eyes, but he kept glancing back at him, unable to handle not knowing Nate's reaction. *Like being angry at a kicked puppy.* Nate leaned against the bar. "You didn't tell him—"

"That you remembered? No." Aki shook his head. "It was right after you got back from the park. I was on my way to Denise when he caught me. I told him to fuck off, threatened him with the emergency box. He said he'd wait until I'd checked on you, but begged me to hear him out."

Nate had a hard time imagining that. The vampire was controlled to a fault. "Begged?"

"Maybe 'beg' isn't the right word." Aki frowned. "He was weirdly cool about it. Like his tone was detached, but it didn't quite fit what he was saying. Until I told him there was no way I was going to spy on you, and he said it might be all that saved your life."

No way Aki could resist a dramatic line like that. Nate felt the hard knot of his anger start to unwind. "He didn't make you do it, right?"

Aki slowly shook his head. "No. He was really deliberate about not making me. Like, he didn't look at me when he spoke, except accidentally. At the time, I thought he was just trying to hide how upset he—fuck. I didn't say that."

Upset? "Tell me what he said. Exactly."

"Promise you won't go rushing off to find him? That is the last thing we want." Aki glanced up at Nate, fingers clutched at the neck of his mesh shirt. "He said whoever is attacking his family will use anyone close to him as leverage. He doesn't have any living family, so anyone who spends time with him is at risk just by proximity."

The confirmation of what Nate had suspected sent chills down his neck. *He's closed himself off from everyone...but me?*

"Ben wanted to know you were all right without endangering you with his presence," Aki said. "Necromancer's have ways of watching people, so he can't risk anything less obvious."

Less obvious? Nate snorted as he held up the phone. "How long did it take me to rumble you exactly?"

Aki obviously wasn't sure how to take Nate's words. He scrambled to catch the phone as Nate tossed it to him. "You're not angry?"

"I'm angry, all right. Just not at you. It bites, but if it was you in trouble, yeah, I'd probably let Ben talk me into stalking you, too."

"Does that say more about our friendship or your obvious vampire-bias?" Aki's smirk was hopeful, but it faded as the phone buzzed with another message alert. "What should I do?"

"Tell him that I'm fine before he organizes a freaking manhunt. And that if he wants to know how I am, he can get in touch with me himself." Nate thumped Aki on the shoulder. "What's OBF mean, anyway?"

"Depends how sorry for myself I'm feeling," Aki said, already typing out a reply. "But usually it's 'Original Best Friend.'"

Nate raised an eyebrow. "And if you're feeling sorry for

yourself?"

Aki's fingers stilled over the touch screen. "'Only Best Friend.'" He bit his lip.

"You're kidding, right?" Nate looked around the bar. At least half of the crowd knew Aki, and he got some of the best reviews in the club. "You are never short of company."

Aki looked at his feet. "Nate, I'm serious. You— I don't have anyone else like you." He grimaced. "No one else knows about my family."

Nate squeezed Aki's shoulder. "You're the only one who knows about Ethan."

Aki sighed, leaning in to wrap his arms around Nate. "You have got to stop scaring me," he said, voice muffled. "I'm going to get gray hairs, and then I'm going to have to shell out for dye, and it will be all your fault."

Nate laughed, patting Aki's hair. "You look all right from up here."

"Jerk." Aki's boots nudged Nate's shin, but as he heard the rattle of the new tray being set down at the counter next to them, he disengaged himself. "We cool?"

Nate grinned. "Yeah."

* ~ * ~ *

Three champagne flutes on the table, feather duster on the floor, and silk blindfold nestled in the rumpled sheets? Nate smirked as he stripped the bed. *Someone's night is going well.* Cleaning had never gone as well or as quickly.

He caught Aki briefly as he finished his circuit of the club, taking the cart to the storeroom. “No reply?”

“Nothing since. You sure you’re all right?”

“Positive.”

In fact, Nate pushed the cart down the hall feeling better than he had in days. The uncertainty that had plagued him since the park was gone. Sure, he still had an impossible task in front of him and was in all likelihood making a terrible mistake...but he was making the mistake for the right reason. Whatever his intentions, Ben was clearly worried about him.

And he wouldn’t worry if he didn’t care.

* ~ * ~ *

“Ow!” The sudden collision with hard wood was as jarring as it was painful. “Who the fuck put a door there?”

“Nate?” The bunk creaked, and then the light flickered on. Aki blinked down at him. “You— What are you doing awake?”

He was in their shared bedroom? “I think I walked into the door.” Nate rubbed his forehead. He didn’t even remember getting out of bed.

“Oh my god.” Aki dissolved into laughter.

Nate glared. “It’s not funny.” His head throbbed.

“I’m so sorry.” Aki needed a moment to regain his breath. “I locked the door last night.”

“You what?” They both had keys, but they never used them.

“I had a feeling last night that I should lock it. Denise getting on our case again.” Aki shrugged. “I’m always up before you, so I didn’t think— I'm so sorry, Nate. Really sorry. I didn't know you sleepwalked."

"I don't sleepwalk."

"Then what on earth are you doing awake at" —Aki glanced at his phone— "eight a.m.?"

"I—" Nate paused. That was a very good question. "It's too early for this shit. I'm going back to bed." He got back into bed. "If this bruises, you're gonna be in trouble."

Nate's unintentionally early start had one positive consequence. He got to Hunter's townhouse in good time.

"Punctuality is a good habit to cultivate." Godfrey's greeting sounded approving over the tinny intercom. "If you get started, I will join you when I have a moment."

Buoyed by the success of the lawn, Nate decided to attack the overgrown roses, steeling himself for the task as he drew on the rough working gloves. Pruning was necessary, but Nate couldn't help but feel it cruel. Knowing that cutting the plant back with the gardening shears allowed opportunities for new growth failed to reconcile him to the brutal-looking stumps left behind.

"And again, we are in your debt." Godfrey appeared with a tray and a steaming mug of tea. "I could not have made that much progress in an entire day's work."

That revealed more about Godfrey's schedule than his capabilities, but Nate accepted the compliment anyway. "Roses take time, but they repay it," he said, reaching for the mug of tea. "What should I do with the trimmed branches? I don't know New Camden's bonfire laws." He hesitated and then withdrew his hand, mug untouched.

"You'd need a fire permit. More trouble than it's worth." Godfrey shrugged his shoulders readily. "Still, I can easily arrange them to be taken to the dump. Won't you have some tea, Nate?"

Nate shook his head. "I'm on a roll. Think I'll keep going for now."

Godfrey raised an eyebrow. "Do you have anything of protection on you? The crucifix is most common, but given your tendencies toward the natural world, perhaps you've found an alternative?"

Thank everything holy. For a panicked second, Nate thought the aged butler was asking for a condom. "I've got a cross."

"Hold it in your hand. Now reach for the cup of tea again."

Bemused, Nate tucked the gardening gloves under his arm and did as instructed. The cross was warm from being buried under his shirt. It felt comfortable in his hand as he reached for the mug with his other. "This is the strangest grace I've—"

He stopped.

Godfrey watched him closely. "You don't want to take the mug," the butler asked. "Do you?"

Nate shook his head. "I'm sure it's great tea. It just feels wrong."

"I should think so. It contains an extremely unpleasant charm intended to give its recipient nightmares and temporary paralysis."

Nate's hand tightened around the crucifix. "Paralysis?"

"It had to be unpleasant." Godfrey emptied the mug onto the grass. "Any latent magical instinct you possess would only react to a real threat."

"You'd have let me drink *that*?"

The butler coughed. "Better you spend a few days indisposed, than weeks, perhaps months, pursuing a career you are not suited for. Still, your reaction has put my mind at ease." He turned back toward the house. "Come into the kitchen. I've just put the kettle on."

Nate didn't feel confident about the mug of tea set in front of him at the kitchen table. He watched Godfrey don gloves to wash the first cup, following it with a rinse of baking soda and vinegar.

"Traces of evil left to linger over time take on awareness and intent of their own. That particular draught does not pose much danger, but I find that cleaning as you go is a good practice."

First, attempted poisoning. Now, housekeeping tips? "I see."

"Actually, if you do not object, I wonder if I might take you away from the garden for a couple of hours." Godfrey's eyes glinted in the reflected light of the stainless steel counter. "I'm an old man, I don't have the energy I used to. "

Nate was sure he was being played. *But what alternative do I have?* "What's up?"

~~*

Polishing silver was not how Nate had expected to spend his day.

Godfrey showed him how to spread the great dining room table with newspaper before getting to work with a fine cloth and a jar of sharp-smelling polish. "Silver requires regular attention. There are tricks and harsher cleaning agents that will clean it faster, but they damage the patina. As it is the quality of the silver that gives these items their protective value, you understand why that should be avoided."

Spread out before him was a selection of cutlery, teapots, candlesticks, knives like the one Hunter had used in the park, a handful of crucifixes, ankhs, and other pieces of jewelry twisted into shapes that Nate could not identify. "Makes sense."

"Gentle cleaning is key—" Godfrey paused. As Nate leaned forward to take the polish, Gunn's cross slid out of his shirt. The butler reached for it, turning it over in his hand thoughtfully. "Well. How did you come by this cross, Nate?"

"It's on loan." Nate dropped the cross out of sight beneath his shirt.

It was hard to tell what Godfrey was thinking. "Perhaps it was not merely chance that you caught Hunter's eye." He patted Nate on the shoulder and left him to work.

* ~ * ~ *

"Why didn't you just tell him about Gunn?"

In a moment of weakness, Nate had trusted Aki with his plans. Godfrey's apparent endorsement of Nate's choices equally baffled his friend.

"I don't know. I guess it's because if Gunn helped me do this... Well, I wouldn't be proving anything."

"Yeah, like mowing the lawn will really impress a vampire. You know he can't go out in daylight, right? He won't even see it."

"He's a vampire." Nate paused, making a face at the bunk above him. "He's got to have night vision or something."

"I would work on your plan B. Speaking of, I got those library books you wanted."

"Yeah?" Nate sat up.

Aki leaned down from his bunk to pass the books to Nate. "*An Introduction to Accounting, Household Management for Complete Incompetents,* and *So You Want to be a Witch.*"

"Thanks, Aki."

Aki rested his cheek on his arm, looking at Nate sideways. "You're really serious about this."

Nate looked up from the contents of the witchcraft text. "Obviously."

"No, I mean— We've been roommates six months now, right? This is the first time I've seen you pick up a book." Aki studied Nate thoughtfully, still upside down. "You're not just into him, are you?"

Nate closed the book. "No. I'm not." He'd had time to think, time to reconsider, time to doubt. "Part of me thinks I'm crazy, going to all this effort for a guy who I've only just met and—"

"Has tried to erase your memory twice, got you tangled up in some dark magic revenge death thing, and is avoiding all contact with you."

Nate winced. When Aki spelled it out, it sounded even more impossible. "Yeah. That."

"So why? I mean, objectively he does not hurt to look at, and I am assuming the sex is good, but you get enough of that on the job."

"I'm not on the job."

"That makes a difference?"

"I don't know." Nate clutched the book tightly. "This is so far outside my usual field of experience that I have no idea where this is going."

Aki sighed loudly and disappeared from Nate's view. He reappeared a second later, swinging himself lightly over the top bunk. "Fine." He settled himself on the foot of Nate's bed. "Get it over with. Tell me how he makes your heart flutter and you can totally see him meeting your folks. I'll try not to gag."

Meeting your folks? About to protest, Nate hesitated. The dream of Ben by the creek was strangely real. Strangely comforting. "Now that you mention it, I do want to take him home." What did it mean?

"So what is it? His dreamy blue eyes? Aloof personality? Does the vampire thing turn you on?"

Nate ignored Aki. "Objectively speaking, I've seen hotter guys. Fucked most of 'em. Maybe I'm just jaded or something, 'cause I don't even care about that. Ben just—does it for me."

"Personality? You got a hard-on for people who ignore you?"

"Hate it," Nate said instantly. "It's not that. You talked to him. You know how he doesn't let himself feel. When we're together—"

"There's a side of him that only you see?"

Nate nudged Aki with his foot. "What happened to not laughing at me?"

"I said I'd try not to gag. I said nothing about mocking. You continue entirely at your own risk."

"See if I'm ever sympathetic to you again." Nate picked up the book in his lap before setting it back down. "I think," he said slowly, trying to put words to his feelings. "I make it hard for Ben to keep up the vampire thing. And that is good for him. Forces him to be human."

"He's not human."

"No. But he's not a monster either," Nate said. "And I remind him of that. Which is more important than me being safe, or him wanting to fuck me, and that's—"

"Yeah." Aki nodded. "You're totally screwed." He leaned over to pat Nate's shoulder. "Cheer up. It could be a lot worse. You could be hung up on a guy with halitosis and a belly."

That's consolation?

Aki didn't allow Nate time to process his advice. "Plus, the vampire thing? He's not gonna get old and flabby. Assuming you prove yourself, win him over, and don't die horribly, you've got a good fifteen years before the age gap becomes untenable and he dumps you."

Nate stared at his friend. "You've put a scary amount of thought into my love life."

Aki stretched as he climbed off the bunk. "It's like having my own private screening of whatever the latest Twilight movie is. Only with less popcorn."

"So glad you find my problems so entertaining," Nate grumbled as he followed Aki to his feet. "I—"

Something white flickered in their bedroom window. Nate paused, taking a step toward it, but the shape vanished. "Reflection?"

"Nate?"

Nate glanced to Aki, then back to the window. "For a minute, it looked like there was something in the window. A white face."

"Just the lights from the cars outside. Come on. Denise said she wanted to see us before opening."

Nate shrugged and shut the door behind him. His imagination

was getting seriously out of control. Although he'd made a decision not to dwell, what happened in the park still disturbed him. Little wonder he'd see Peter's reflection in the glass.

* ~ * ~ *Chapter Ten

For once, Denise had good news.

"You're putting me back on the floor?"

Denise rested her perfectly manicured hands on her hips. "I hate rewarding reckless stupidity, but Nisha's cleared you."

Nate grinned at her. "Thanks, Denise! You won't regret this."

"I already do." Denise caught Nate's gaze. "Another stunt like that and you're on cleaning permanently."

"Finally," Beatrice greeted him. "Between Aki's hyper tendencies and Mandy's constant peppiness, the cheerfulness was starting to grate."

Nate grinned at her over Mandy's welcoming hug. "Got bad news for you, Bea. After a week on cleaning, I am happy to be back."

"We missed you," Mandy said from Nate's chest. "Not that Aki didn't look after us, of course."

"Of course." Aki looked on with such smug pity that Nate realized he needed to have a quiet word with Mandy before Aki got even more obvious.

Especially with someone as observant as Beatrice around. "Interesting week, Nate?"

"It's been something else. I'm really looking forward to hitting the dance floor tonight."

"Only hitting the dance floor?"

"It's a start."

What a start. As soon as Nate had seen Beatrice and Mandy off, his bracelet blinked red, the feisty managerial assistant that Nate suspected of having dominatrix leanings wanting an hour and a half of him at premium rate. The businessman with the European accent who did something in finance bought him a drink as Nate took his break, voicing his opinion that while Nate's skinny jeans hugged his ass admirably, they would look much better on the floor of one of the upstairs booths.

Tangled in sheets that he might very well have laundered the day before, Nate had to agree. A week without sex had left him eager, responsive to the merest touch, and the businessman had taken full advantage, testing his self-control with a leisurely blow job before fucking him against the edge of the balcony, where anyone on the dance floor might have seen them. Nate lingered on the bed, savoring his physical satiation.

He'd been worried it might be weird. That he might call out Ben's name or not be able to get it up. Luckily, the managerial assistant's generous curves and her floral perfume had made their time together totally different from anything Nate had shared with Ben. Likewise, the businessman was a lot more forceful in bed than Ben, but Nate hadn't been able to resist imagining coming in Ben's mouth. His client hadn't noticed anything unusual in Nate's performance, giving his ass an appreciative squeeze before he left.

But as the rush faded, Nate was aware of a sense of unease. Lying in the tangled sheets, one hand splayed across his stomach, he probed the source of the feeling.

Have I been worried about nothing? Nate bit his lip. *Or is the fact that I can do this a sign I'm not as into Ben as—*

He couldn't finish the thought.

Not being able to perform would have been humiliating, but it would have proved this was no ordinary attraction. Instead, he'd fucked two people and enjoyed it. Nate dug his fingernails into his skin but wasn't able to stop the thought.

Hunter's fault! Before the anniversary party, I never felt empty after—

But it hadn't been Hunter alone at the party. It had been Ben.

Nate let out a sigh, any pleasure from his night's work well and truly gone. The thought of Ben brought with it the same ominous feeling that preceded Nate's first meeting with Hunter, and he shook off the sheets. *Am I going to be haunted by that forever?*

Too late Nate realized that he wasn't alone in the booth. "Ben!"

He stood at the foot of the bed, back to the balcony. The lights of the stage outlined his form but gave no hint to his expression. He held himself totally still.

"Some warning!" Nate struggled to right himself. "How did—"

"I'm not here to enjoy myself."

Nate froze in the process of sitting up. That note in Ben's voice—

"Hunter told me to come. Said I needed to see you for what you were. How readily you let yourself be used." Ben climbed onto the bed.

The mattress dipped. Nate almost lost his precarious balance. He righted himself, only to find Ben practically on top of him. "That's—" It was hard to think past Ben's body as he knelt over him. "I'm not ashamed of what I do—"

Ben's hand on his throat put an end to his sentence. "I smelled you on the woman." His mouth was inches away from Nate's neck. "Saw you with the man." Nate felt every word on his throat. "I wanted to tear you away from him."

Nate believed him absolutely. The hand on his throat was unrelenting, holding him immobile as Ben dropped his mouth to Nate's neck.

He expected the short, sharp sting of teeth. Ben's mouth, fastening hungrily on Nate's skin, was a shock. His tongue rasped roughly along the veins of Nate's throat and dipped into the hollow of Nate's collarbone. As Nate gasped, Ben released his hold on him, tongue continuing its systematic conquest on the other side of Nate's neck.

Was he trying to suck the businessman off Nate's skin? Nate gave up his attempt to sit. He wrapped his arms around Ben, bringing the vampire with him as he sank back against the sheets. "Fuck, Ben. You're so fucking hot like this."

Ben growled. Evidently not what he wanted to hear.

Nate cried out as his skin was caught between unforgiving teeth and held there as Ben's tongue swirled over it. "God. Your mouth—"

He was already hard as he thrust up against Ben, desperate for more. *Is Aki right? Do I get off on vampires?* He was as needy as if he hadn't been touched at all that night.

There was a warning pressure on his hips, and Nate found himself roughly tipped over onto his front. Ben hadn't forgotten his clients even if Nate had. He trapped Nate's body beneath his own, using his weight to stop Nate from angling against the mattress—or even moving at all.

"Fuck—"

Ben twined his fingers through Nate's, the gesture intimate even as it ensured Nate couldn't lever himself out of the position. He licked the back of Nate's neck. "You will feel what I want you to feel—and only what I want you to feel." The tenderness of his mouth on Nate's neck and shoulders was a complete contrast to his strength. Without exerting himself, he had Nate trapped, unable to do anything but whimper as Ben continued his exploration.

"Jesus. Ben, I had no idea you...fuck." He could feel Ben's hard length against his ass, further torture to his already straining body. "Please. Give me more of you—"

Ben did.

Forget his previous clients. By the time Ben decided he was ready, Nate had difficulty remembering his own name. He let out an urgent gasp as Ben's mouth stopped its work, and his weight vanished. "Ben. I want—"

"I know what you want." The protest of a zipper as he tugged it down impatiently had to be one of the sexiest sounds Nate had ever heard. "I'm going to give it to you. On your knees."

Nate looked behind him, but he couldn't make out much more of Ben than his silhouette and the rustling of clothing. He felt exposed, totally at the vampire's mercy—and he loved it. "Condom. Table.

Don't need lube. *Ben—*"

The booth went silent.

A mistake?

Nate shivered as Ben's cold fingers settled to deliberately squeeze his ass cheek.

"You want me to claim you as much as I want to make you mine." There was a note of wonder that was pure Ben, and then the touch was gone.

"Yeah, I..." Nate wished he could see Ben's face. "I want you. Every way you can want a guy, I want you. "

One hand settled on Nate's hip, the other guided Ben's latex-covered erection to his entrance. Just the feel of Ben lining up against him had Nate's cock pulsing with need.

Ben drove into him in one long thrust. He stilled, waiting for Nate to adjust. His long cock felt just as good as Nate knew it would, and Nate rocked back. "Yeah...like that."

Ben refused the invitation to move. Instead, he caught first one, then both of Nate's hands, drawing them behind his back so that Nate balanced precariously on his knees. "I'm not going to use you," he said, a note of warning in his voice. "I'm going to *own* you."

Fuck, yeah. Nate was in the best trouble of his life. "Ben—"

Ben began to move. He left one hand keeping Nate's arms pinned to his back while the other gripped his hip, pulling Nate back to meet his cock, balls slapping against Nate's ass. Every stroke drove Nate closer to the edge, stretching the limits of his endurance and balance. "Oh my fucking god." He was falling and didn't care, heedless of anything except Ben's total command of his body.

"Nate. Nathan. You want— You need me." The vampire's tone was rough, his thrusts increasingly urgent.

Nate struggled through the haze of his need for words. "Y-Yeah, you— I'm gonna come, now, just from you inside me—"

Ben made a low, guttural sound, a growl. Nate felt both his hips gripped as Ben pulled him back onto his length with an intensity that had him seeing stars. He cried out, losing himself as he shot.

He came back to himself, his arms braced against the mattress as Ben slammed urgently into him. The vampire's hips jerked, losing even the erratic semblance of rhythm as he came. "Nate—" With one final moan, he leaned fully against Nate, buried in him to the hilt.

Nate's arms gave way, and he slid onto his stomach, Ben coming along for the ride. "Fuck. That was...incredible." Carefully, he maneuvered so that he could lie face-to-face with Ben on the bed. "You..." Nate brushed Ben's hair out of his face and pressed a kiss to his forehead. "Where have you been hiding that?"

"When I saw you tonight...I just had to." Ben sounded breathless, but his cock was still hard. "Oh, god, Nate, you—"

Nate pulled the vampire more tightly against him. "I got you." He reached between them to stroke Ben. Sliding the condom off, he pumped Ben slowly as he sought the vampire's mouth.

The kiss was as gentle as their earlier lovemaking had been hard and fast. Ben gasped against Nate's mouth, body jerking in helpless need as he came again. Nate cradled the vampire against his chest, and Ben eagerly wrapped his arms around him.

"So...I got the night off Wednesday. You want to hang out? Here, I mean. Obviously, with the necromancer we couldn't go out properly—"

Ben groaned. He turned to bury his face in Nate's neck, hiding although he couldn't be seen. "I came here tonight to end this."

"Getting mixed messages here."

"I'm serious." Ben started to move.

Nate stroked his fingers through Ben's wispy hair before he let go to sit up. The small bedside table held towels in addition to toys and other supplies, and Nate held one out to Ben. "So am I. An attraction like this doesn't happen every day. I want to go for it."

Ben's fingers closed around the towel, but he didn't take it. "It's too dangerous, Nate. Not just because of the necromancer. You saw what happened earlier. The vampire in me— I could have hurt you."

Nate dropped the towel he'd grabbed for himself into his lap and patted Ben's arm. "But you didn't."

"It could have been different—"

"Would Dracula have stopped to put on a condom?"

"I— What?"

Nate rested his hand on Ben's shoulder. "Yeah, you got all territorial and forceful, and maybe you're wondering what the hell you were doing now, but even when you were going all alpha vampire on my ass, you still had control enough to stop and listen."

Ben's fingers moved lightly to Nate's face. "Is that why you weren't afraid of me?"

"I won't lie. When you first showed up, I wasn't entirely sure what your intentions were, but I never thought of running away."

"You should." Ben drew back. "You were afraid in the park. I smelled your fear. The vampire in me reacted—"

"It was the revenants I was afraid of. Not you." Nate used his hand to draw Ben close enough that their foreheads rested together. "I know you don't want to hurt me," he said. "So that's—"

Fluorescent light interrupted the moment. Ben and Nate jerked apart from each other.

Tybalt eyed them sourly. On Nate, the uniform coveralls were forgettable, but paired with Tybalt's beefy arms and close-cut hair, they suggested another sort of uniform entirely. Only the cleaning cart he leaned on differentiated him from security. "Freebies, Nate? You asking for trouble?"

Ben stiffened, going from flustered to authoritarian in seconds. "You will—"

Nate placed his hand over Ben's mouth before he could finish that sentence. "First night back," he said. "Gimme a break."

The man shrugged. "I couldn't care less who you fuck, but if this booth's not clean—"

"One minute. We'll get out of your hair."

"One minute's all you got."

They dressed in silence, Ben pulling on his quiet distance in addition to his clothes. *I can't let him disappear on me again.* Nate fumbled in his haste to pull his jeans on. *Why'd I pick skinny jeans tonight?*

Nate caught Ben's arm as he squeezed past the cleaning cart. "Thanks, T. I owe you a drink."

"What the fuck ever. Get out of here."

Ben was not happy being held, and even less happy that Nate directed him toward Century's back exit. "What are you doing?"

"You shouldn't have come here tonight." Two of the club's security guards leaned against the fire escape. *Shit.* Nate hesitated before guiding Ben across the floor. With any luck, they'd go unnoticed in the throng of people coming and going at the front. "Century's on full alert for anything ampire-vay."

Ben tensed, but luck held, and they made it outside without being stopped. Nate's bare arms drew second glances from the warmly dressed patrons waiting to enter Century, and Nate took the first chance he saw to get them out of view. "Here."

"Most people would actively avoid being followed into a dark alley by a vampire." Ben's tone was hard to read. The streetlight at the alley entrance allowed Nate to see that his mouth was pursed, the rest of his expression giving nothing away.

"I'm not most people."

"You're lucky I'm not most vampires."

"You did a pretty good impression of one just now." Nate's leer was thoroughly unrepentant, even as he ran his hands over his bare arms.

Ben shook his head as he held out his coat. "That is exactly my point. That can't be allowed to happen. We can't happen."

Nate draped the offered coat over his shoulders, enjoying the autumnal scent that clung to the garment. He felt a warmth entirely out of proportion to the coat. *The third time now.* "Why not? I trust you, Ben. And if you'd stop protecting me from what I need to learn, you could trust me, too. I still remember what Hunter tried to make me forget—"

"You can't count on there always being a flying rowan around when you need one." Ben paused, reconsidering Nate. "Is that why you came to the house today? To learn?"

"Godfrey told you?"

Ben's smile was wry. "He didn't need to. It was obvious you'd been there. Your smell was in the hall, the dining room—"

"There are nicer ways to say go shower."

Ben's hand on Nate's chest stopped him. "Vampire senses are heightened. It's not ...unpleasant. Actually, it's the opposite." He stepped forward to breathe Nate in. "You smell raw. Like an animal. Full of lust and life, and I couldn't concentrate on anything. It was like you were physically there." His hand stroked over Nate's chest with definite possessive intent.

Nate owed Godfrey big-time. "You want me physically there?"

Ben snatched his hand back. "That's just the vampire's hunting instinct," he said. "Nothing more."

Nate snorted. "The vampire didn't decide to check up on me at the club."

"You're making a lot out of very little," Ben said stiffly.

"Am I? You could have deputed checking up on me to Godfrey or Hunter. Safer for me, but it would mean admitting you were worried."

"I don't know what's more alarming. Your conclusions, or the fact that you've spent time thinking about this and still missed the obvious conclusion. The danger is too great. You could have died in the park!"

"You've tried to show yourself to me as a monster," Nate said. "But you're forgetting. The dead don't change."

Ben shivered as Nate put his hand on his shoulder but didn't draw away. Just as well. Nate's heart was racing fast enough for both of them.

"You're still human, Ben. With human needs." Nate took courage in Ben's silence. "You cut off contact with your human life. You don't have anyone except for your colony-family. No friends, boyfriends, I have doubts about even acquaintances."

Ben's fingers tightened on Nate's arm. *Hit a nerve?* At least he knew Ben was listening. "If you're implying I'm a friendless loser—"

Nate refused to be drawn. "Maybe your isolation is making you a target. You need people. Tonight proves that, and I want to give you whatever you need. Lover, friend, fuck buddy, I don't care. As long as you're not alone."

Ben's mouth gathered tightly before he spoke. "Is this about my needs—or your need to be needed? You— I saw you tonight." He paused to swallow, tone carefully dispassionate. "You do enjoy" —if the stakes hadn't been so high, watching Ben struggle with words would have been ridiculously endearing— "servicing others."

"I sleep with people for money, which to a big chunk of society makes me a leech. You're a vampire. Maybe we're both bloodsuckers when it comes down to it." Nate let his hand rest on Ben's shoulder. "Yeah, I get off on making people feel good. And for the people at Century, that's all I do. You." He paused as something shifted inside him, a sudden impulse suddenly revealed to be a symptom of something deeper. "I make you feel. That— It doesn't even compare, Ben."

Ben looked at Nate hopelessly. "The danger—"

"I could get mowed down in traffic. Picked up by the wrong client. Get slipped a bad trip in the club. There are a thousand different ways I could go, and if I held back from them all I'd never do anything."

"This necromancer's not an idle statistic, Nate."

"I know. Look." Nate kept his eyes fixed on Ben's. "Pa always said that life was about finding the thing you love and going for it. He refused to give up the farm, even when all the doctors and specialists said it was the only way." Nate swallowed. "He said living without the farm wasn't living. And I'm finally beginning to get what he meant."

"Nate—"

"I haven't known you long. But with you, I think I've found my farm." *Could I do this any worse?* Nate hurried on. "I'll take any amount of revenants if it means being with you. That's how strongly I feel."

Ben's face was blank. He could be holding down anger. He could equally be suppressing laughter. Nate had no way of gauging his mood, except to know that it was only with difficulty and his fingers gripping tightly into Nate's shoulder that Ben didn't show his reaction.

"I think we're good for each other. I've never been interested in learning before— There's only the one thing I'm good at, and it's not exactly the most useful right now." *Fucking the revenants is not exactly on my to-do list.* "But between you and Godfrey...I really think I can do this. And I'm good for you, too." Nate took a deep breath. "In the park. I helped, didn't I?"

Ben licked his lips cautiously. "Provoking the vampire to attack isn't really helping—"

"Before that." All the time that Nate had spent mentally rehearsing this hadn't stopped his mind from going blank. All he could do was press on, watching the surprise in Ben's eyes change to understanding, then a strangely somber distance. "I make it easier for you to express what you feel. More importantly—I push you. Challenge you. With me around, you're in no danger of getting trapped in your ways like Hunter or Saltaire."

"The dead don't change," Ben said. "Nate, please. Listen to me—"

"Dying didn't stop you loving Hunter, did it?" Ben tensed, and Nate pressed on before he could think too closely about his argument. "You care as much—maybe more—than any person I've ever met. Maybe you didn't act on your emotions when you were alive, but you still have them." He let his hands rest on Ben's shoulders, there without being insistent about it. "You don't have to hide them."

Ben's mouth grimaced. "Nate. I can't love you."

"Not because you're a vampire—"

"That's part of it." Ben's confession had the unwillingness of truth. "I became a vampire loving Hunter. That means I will always love him."

Nate's head felt hollow, almost as though he was dizzy. "But he can't—"

"I know. It doesn't make a difference." Ben's slanted smile hurt, as well as the way he shrugged. His fingers were cool on Nate's cheek, and Nate was ashamed to feel heat sting at the corners of his eyes. "Nate. You gave me something I didn't think I could have. For that, I will always be grateful. But you can grow and change—and in time, you will forget."

"Forget." Just the word sounded like defeat. "And what will happen to you then?"

"Nothing. I won't change." Ben stepped into him, and Nate wrapped his arms around him automatically. He felt just right against Nate's body, the perfect height, and Nate realized with a dull ache that this was the last time he would hold him. "It's for the best. You'll find someone who can return your feelings."

Nate blinked, deliberately looking up. They'd covered this at training. Deep breaths, distance. He was in control of his reactions. "I'm not—"

Something moved in the shadows of the surrounding building. At the same moment, Nate became aware of the inexorable chill of the air surrounding them.

Ben felt it at the same instant. The vampire reacted with a speed and strength beyond Nate's ability to resist. Nate was pushed back against the wall, Ben planted in front of him as he readied himself to meet the threat.

The shadowed form dropped from the roof to become Saltaire. The master vampire drew himself up as easily as if it had been a mere step down. "Coupling in an alleyway with a cheap whore, knowing you are being sought by enemies. This is not how I expect the trust I place in you to be repaid, Bennet."

Cheap? The words annoyed, but Nate found himself unable to move.

Ben's fists shook, but he drew himself up to meet his vampiric sire's disapproval. "Sire. Nate risked his life to free me from the necromancer's control. We owe him—"

"Nothing." Saltaire's tone was uncompromising. His eyebrows were thick jagged lines in the dark. They threw shadow across his eyes, making them appear pure black. "No member of my family will be dependent on a human so destitute of choices he prostitutes himself."

Nate tried to speak. The night had become very heavy, and the words died in his throat. The atmosphere around him was choking. Suddenly he understood. The petrifying atmosphere at the townhouse wasn't its age; it was Saltaire.

Ben didn't even flinch. Nate could see his body tense with the effort of not reacting, but his reply was cool. "Hunter would have reached me too late to help. It's only because of Nate that I'm still here."

"A circumstance that does no credit to either of you." The elder vampire didn't need physical height to tower. "Since meeting this man, your attention has been sadly lacking. You've neglected your duties. You've allowed a necromancer to come close to taking control of you. And worse, you've disobeyed my direct orders."

Worse? The last statement stuck incongruously in Nate's brain. *Shouldn't Ben's life be more important?*

"What you say is true," Ben admitted. "But I have taken steps to deal with the situation." Shoulders tensed, he stepped away from Nate. "I've informed Nathan that as of tonight, there will be no further association."

It was hard to say what hurt more, the use of his full name, the formal dismissal, or simply the distance as Ben joined Saltaire in the shadows. Nate was suddenly grateful for the crushing pressure around him.

Though even that was no protection as Saltaire turned his machete-sharp gaze on Nate. "Is that so? Answer me truthfully."

"Yes." The compulsion forced Nate to be honest. His words were naked, his hurt clear. "Ben made his lack of interest obvious."

Saltaire looked sharply at his protégé. "That is only half the task."

"It is enough." Ben didn't turn to look at either of them. "Godfrey is casting runes to locate the necromancer. He might have found something—"

"So far he's found that the necromancer knows exactly how to hide from us and not much else."

Nate tensed. The third voice sounded from the wall right behind him. *Hunter. Now this night really is perfect!*

The vampire flashed his teeth at Nate in a grin before continuing conversationally. "He has a very good idea of how we work. I don't think we'll find him via Godfrey's methods."

"Making it even more imperative that there are no loose ends. Once we force the necromancer into the open, we will have him. But for that to happen..." Saltaire's silence was heavy with meaning.

Nate didn't like the silence at all, but Ben's sharp intake of breath settled it. "I suppose I don't get any choice in this at all?"

Saltaire looked at him as though affronted merely by his interruption, but Hunter answered.

"We can't predict the necromancer's victims should this last link be removed. If Nathan is willing..." He paused to shrug carelessly.

"A trap?"

This was the second time someone had suggested using Nate as bait. *Is it something about me?* “Sure. I don’t give a fuck.”

“You should. It is more than merely your life at stake.” Saltaire’s glare was fierce enough that Nate stepped into the wall at his back.

“Absolutely not,” Ben said immediately. “It’s too much of a risk.”

“I’m inclined to agree,” Saltaire said. “Trusting our safety to one who lives a life ruled by his baser passions...” He shook his head. “We will proceed as decided. Bennet, you will accompany me back to the house. Emeric, as you were the one to start this business, I leave the resolution of it to you.”

Hunter’s hand rested on Nate’s shoulder. “Understood.”

Saltaire nodded in the slightest acknowledgement and then glanced around. Ben straightened immediately, preparing to follow him. In moments, he would be gone.

“Wait!”

Feeling the gaze of all three vampires on him, Nate held out the coat. “You forgot this.”

Ben took it. Nate listened to the vampire pull it on, not trusting himself to look up. “I meant what I said before,” he said. “I am very grateful.”

An hour earlier, they’d tangled intimately with each other, and now Ben was *grateful*. Nate wrapped his arms around himself. “Clear night like this spells a frost. Godfrey needs to cover the basil.”

Ben frowned. “I’ll tell him,” he said, glancing back to Saltaire. “But—”

“We’ve wasted enough time here. We go.” Saltaire made no sound on the concrete of the path. Ben moved as if he were a second, silent shadow. And maybe he was. His movements matched Saltaire's too perfectly to be coincidental.

Compulsion? Nate watched until the last trace of them faded from view. Knowing that Ben didn't leave him of his own volition should have made the blow feel less, not more.

"Service and then some." Hunter's voice was startlingly loud in the dark. "Did I pick too well or not well enough?"

The crucifix Gunn had given him. Nate had been wearing it ever since, and it was now—

"Fuck."

—on the table back in the booth. The businessman was catholic and had objected to it.

Hunter's hand stayed put on Nate's shoulder. He could feel the coldness of the vampire's touch even through the shirt he wore. "It was not my intent to see this go so far." He shrugged, stepping into the streetlamp's light. In sharp contrast to Ben and Saltaire, he flaunted his immunity to the night air, scarf draped loosely around his shoulders and his blazer open. Hunter's eyes, as they turned back to fix on Nate, were clear as ice. "But if it was my mistake, it's my responsibility to fix it."

"By wiping my memory?" Hunter's face was impassive. Nate tried anyway. "That's your answer to everything! It didn't work last time, what makes you think it'll work now?"

"This time you're not in the vicinity of a standing rowan."

Nate's mouth worked soundlessly.

Hunter showed his teeth in quick amusement at Nate's shock. "Godfrey and I worked it out together. He thinks that with proper direction, you might make a decent witch. Provided, of course, our necromancer doesn't kill you first."

"Godfrey said that?"

"Coming to the house was a bold move, but it seems to have won you a supporter."

"For all the good that does me now." Nate caught himself too late. Self-pity never looked good on anyone. He took a deep breath and tried again. "I'm not sorry it happened."

"I hope you remain of that opinion."

Nate glanced up, startled out of his attempt at cool. "You sound like you're not going to wipe my memory."

Hunter bowed to him, a theatrical gesture performed with aplomb. "Saltaire does his best to ensure that we have as much free will as we can, even as his scions. It wouldn't be fair if I didn't do my part and occasionally rebel."

"Scions?" Something in the emphasis he'd laid on the word—

Hunter had stepped back into the shadow. Nate couldn't see his eyes. "Saltaire's reluctance to use his power is great—but the power itself is greater. It was many centuries before I felt myself in his presence, longer still before I understood his choices. Ben is young. He feels his lost freedom keenly. In time those memories will fade, and he will begin to understand."

Definitely a frost in the air. Nate wrapped his arms around himself. "There's really no other way?"

Hunter laughed. "The only way to free oneself from the sire's compulsion is to kill the sire—and Ben owes him too much to want to contemplate Saltaire's second death—or feed until he consumes power equivalent to Saltaire's centuries."

Nate couldn't imagine Ben choosing either of those options. "Being a vampire sucks."

"Possibly just as well." Hunter shrugged. "The power of compulsion is so easily abused that it is only right that attaining it should come at such a high cost."

Says the guy who compelled two people to sign off on his party! Nate frowned at Hunter. "That didn't stop you from using it."

Hunter's shrug was unrepentant. "Ben needed to see that his fear of endangering others did not need to extend to such radical self-deprivation. I think we did quite well on that front." He leered, but Nate wasn't distracted.

"What you say he does," Nate finished slowly. "Is that why—"

"Any relationship where one party does not have the right of choice inevitably sours." Hunter looked up at the night sky. "I am too fond of Ben to want to lose him."

He doesn't—he can't mean that? "Even if it means starving him of the affection he so clearly needs?"

"In a few centuries, he will thank me for this."

Nate felt like the weight of Saltaire's presence pressed down on him again. "If he survives that long."

"Speaking of survival, let's talk about yours."

For the second time in three nights, a vampire held Nate up by his neck.

"Ever since the party" —Hunter casually raised his voice to be heard over the sound of Nate choking— "my brother has been distracted, moody, and secretive. In short, he's been acting more like himself than in the entire year he's been dead."

Nate's lungs burned with trapped air. He struggled to pry Hunter's icy fingers from his throat.

"Your influence seems to be good for him. Which is why I am not going to erase your memory or kill you."

Is this a vampire handshake? Nate shut his eyes. His chest felt like it was going to burst—

"Pay attention. This concerns you after all." With that advice, Hunter let him go.

Nate's hand caught in the ivy, the only thing preventing him from falling. "Was that really necessary?" He rubbed his throat. "A simple 'be careful'—"

"We're dealing with a necromancer," Hunter said. "Reflexes that poor are not going to save you. From now until we apprehend the necromancer, you will not leave Century unless in the company of someone you know. Understood?"

Knowing he was being compelled did not enable Nate to resist at all. "Yes."

"Good. Now, let's get you back inside. You're shivering."

Chapter Eleven

A figure loomed at him suddenly out of the steam.

Nate stepped back. His foot slipped on the wet tiles, and he grabbed the towel rail just before he fell. "Jesus Christ!"

A raucous round of laughter followed his exclamation.

"Jumping at your own reflection, now, Nate?"

"Go easy on the kid. I mean, I see that face coming at me, I'd jump too."

"Thanks, Mike." Nate turned back to the mirror. His reflection had a strangely unreal quality. Him, but not. *This is what I get for only a couple hours of sleep.*

"You've lost weight. And you're pale. Coming down with something?"

"Yeah, Nate's got a serious disease. It's called 'vampires.'"

Nate winced. It had not taken long for their colleagues to connect Denise's increased security measures with Nate's irregular house call. "I'm not—"

"Forget blood suckers. He's got more serious problems." The sheer sadism of Javier's smirk would have looked good on one of the club's doms. On the chef, it gave Nate chills. "Security reported you leaving the club."

"Fuck me." Denise would not take long to match the description of Nate's companion with the information she had on Hunter's family. Nate was as good as dead.

His companions laughed again. "Cheer up, Nate. Least you got a chance of survival with the vamps."

"If I survive long enough for the vampires to take a shot at me." Nate paused, looking back to the other men. "She didn't say anything at closing last night. Maybe she doesn't know?"

Mike shook his head, starting to towel himself off. "There's nothing Denise doesn't know."

"It's psychological," Javier added. "She's letting the pressure build. Mind games, until you crack."

If Aki had made that statement, Nate would have laughed it off, but coming from the older men, it had the ring of truth. "Should I own up?"

"Shave first," Mike said. "You want to look professional when she rips you a new one."

"And hey. You survive, maybe I'll make you something special tonight."

Nate smiled faintly, picking up the razor. "You're a lifesaver, Jay." Confessing that he had no appetite would only bring questions Nate did not want to answer. Bad enough the entire club knew about the vampires. They did not need to know he'd been dumped by them.

* ~ * ~ *

Nate ran fingers through his damp hair. The shave and change of clothes had done wonders. He was recognizably himself. But would that impress Denise? *What am I thinking?* "Nothing impresses Denise."

Nate tossed the towel to his bed. All he could do was project repentant vibes and try not to think about Ben. Even Denise at her worst was better than thinking about Ben.

The crucifix Gunn had lent him was not hanging from the bunk bed where Nate had left it. Nate checked, but it hadn't fallen onto the bed. He knelt to check the floor.

"Weird."

No sign of the crucifix, but there was a broad swath left in the dust beneath the bed. Someone had pulled out Nate's suitcase recently.

"Aki?" What was he looking for, photos of Ethan? Nate yanked the suitcase out so viciously that he had to remind himself that the case was a hand-me-down on its last legs, and he couldn't afford a new one.

His winter coat and long socks were folded neatly, too neatly for Aki to have been anywhere near them. On top of them was a brown paper bag with a logo that Nate didn't recognize.

"Vulcan's Forge?" Nate shook out the bag.

A knife fell into his lap, silver and sleek. A type favored by magic-users, the sharp blade rounded out into a handle, the entire knife made from one piece of metal.

"You don't hide a knife like this under someone's bed for kicks."

Aki wouldn't splurge on a knife. So whose was it?

There was a receipt in the bottom of the bag, carelessly folded. Nate smoothed it out. *How much? The fuck— Who has that much money to spend on a knife? Even a—* Nate looked back at the receipt

—knife of pure silver—

A sick feeling settled in the pit of Nate's stomach. "Please, no."

The payment code on the bottom of the receipt matched the code in Nate's wristband. The only person who could have bought the knife was him. "But I never went anywhere near—" Nate glanced at the address on the bag. "Old Town?"

Why did that— "Shit." Aki had seen Nate in Old Town.

Nate put a hand out to steady himself against the bunk. He felt like invisible strings were tightening around him. Brook had bought the knife that killed him and then walked to the cemetery to be killed—

"No."

There's got to be something! Nate forced himself to think. *I'm not dying like Brook!*

First: get rid of the knife.

Trying to step outside the fire escape was an exercise in futility. Nate strained against an invisible wall until he remembered Hunter's command. *Fuck you, Hunter!* But knowing he couldn't leave the club helped Nate think through the panic. *Could the vampire actually have been useful?*

Nate dropped the knife into the kitchen Dumpster from the roof. *Can't kill me if it can't reach me.* He swiped sweaty hands on his jeans. Not only was the knife outside the club where Nate couldn't get it, but it was unlikely anyone would spot it amongst the rubbish. *Now what?* Training taught them to avoid necromancers. They hadn't covered what to do if one controlled you.

Nate swallowed. *This is way out of my league.*

He needed help.

"Denise?" If there was one thing you could say about mortal peril, it did wonders for perspective. Nate actually wanted to see the manager.

There was no reply to his knock. Nate pushed open the door to find the office empty. Denise's desk was clear except for the landline, a sleek cordless model in the same shade of green as her favorite suit. Nate didn't hesitate.

"Department Seven? I need to talk to Gunn."

"Brook's knife came from Vulcan's Forge, too. You're right. This isn't coincidence."

Gunn's confirmation didn't make Nate feel any better. "Don't sound so happy about my rapidly impending death."

"This is our chance, Nate." He could hear the teeth in Gunn's smile. "Hunt's finally come to us. When the necromancer arrives to find out what is keeping you from your date, he's ours."

Nate flinched as the office door opened. *Just Denise.* "Gunn," he mouthed as she sat on the sofa. Nate returned to the phone call. "How soon can you get here?"

"Relax. Hunter might actually have done you a favor. Rounding up the girls and boys won't take long. We'll be with you in twenty minutes."

Twenty minutes. Nate took a deep breath. "Great."

"Just sit tight. Even your knack for trouble's gonna have a hard time against a vampire's compulsion."

"That's not the consolation you think."

Gunn only laughed at his annoyance. "Don't do anything I would do."

"Don't you mean—"

The dial tone answered that question.

Nate put his thumb over the hang up button and took a deep breath. "Denise, you will not believe—"

There was a glassy quality in her eyes. Something about her posture was off. More like she'd been placed on the sofa than sat there.

"Denise? You're seriously freaking me out here."

She didn't move, her immaculately painted mouth slack and slightly ajar.

"I know club policy on freebies, but there were special circumstances." Nate placed his hand on her shoulder. Her skin felt cold and she slid over sideways. She left a trail as red as her hair on the leather sofa surface.

"Fuck. Denise. You're the manager; you're not supposed to do this!"

911. Nate dialed the number automatically, kneeling beside her. *Ambulance? Police?* "I don't know. She's not reacting, but I don't think she's dead. There's blood— Airway? I'll check."

Nate leaned over.

"Oh my god."

It was as if a dam had been released. A line of red sprang up along Denise's wrist, traveling up the sleeves of her jacket arm in ugly blotches. The fabric wasn't torn, but Denise was coming apart at the seams.

A strand of red stood out among her hair, darker than the rest. Nate hooked his finger around it. He felt a familiar dread as he recognized it, even before he followed its path up and toward the door.

Peter waited in the doorway. He met Nate's eyes without reaction, a faint blue tinge to his mouth. His eyes were purple with shadow, but the haggard edge of the park was gone. He smiled, a slow movement of the mouth that left the lips pressed tightly together and didn't reach his pale eyes. He hooked an index finger as white as weathered bone around the red thread and tugged.

Nate let the phone drop from suddenly unresponsive arms. *This—*

Peter turned and walked out the door.

Nate lurched clumsily after him. The corridor was crowded in preparation for opening, but no one looked twice as Peter walked through their midst.

Nate hurried to keep up. *What is wrong with everyone?* Peter's face had been plastered on the news every night that week! *And he just casually brushed past security like—* Nate swallowed. *Like I'm the only one who can see him.*

Peter waited at the door, rearranging his scarf around his neck. "We're behind schedule."

This is wrong. Nate's thoughts came slowly, as if they belonged to someone else. "I'm not—" Nate stumbled over the words. *Denise—I can't leave her!*

"Supposed to leave? Don't worry." Peter's smile was as mocking as Nate remembered from dinner. "Hunter didn't mean me, obviously."

Sirens sprang up in the distance as they walked down the sidewalk. Nate stuck his hands in the pockets of his jeans, squaring his shoulders against the sound. "Fucking sirens."

Peter glanced at him sideways. "Not a fan?"

"Is anyone?"

"Law of averages. There's got to be someone. But I'm with you." Peter walked quickly. "Bad memories."

Nate frowned. The spring afternoon had taken on a decidedly chill air, but none of the pedestrians in their short-sleeved T-shirts seemed to feel it. The cold had a strangely numbing effect, settling in Nate's limbs and making them heavy and unresponsive. *Just like at the dentist.* Feeling an internal tug, he trudged after Peter, the sirens coming to an abrupt halt behind them.

* ~ * ~ *

The park was obscenely normal. Nate sidestepped one dark-suited man with an espresso, only to collide with a second.

The man shook spilled coffee from his hand with an angry hiss. "Watch your—" He looked straight at Nate and came to a halt. Looking on either side of himself, the man shook his head. "Mad." He picked up his briefcase and jogged after his colleague.

Nate rubbed his shoulder. New Camden had a reputation for rudeness, but that? "I don't care how mad you are, but seriously, a little courtesy?" *The guy looked right through me!*

"What do you expect from someone who buys coffee from a

multinational chain?" Peter waited for Nate on the path. His voice was hoarser than the night of the party, but still his own. "There are three independent coffee shops in walking distance of this park, all with better drinks."

It was hard to reconcile the conversation with Peter's blue lips and bone-like pallor. *Am I imagining this?* The park certainly had the unreality of a dream, Nate's own thoughts as distant as if they were echoes of someone else. "You work for a multinational."

"That's different," Peter said. "ARX didn't go into business for the sake of business. That they're so successful is no fault of their own. We're getting distracted."

Something was off about the situation. Something he was missing. Nate followed Peter off the path and into the forest, trying to identify it. *I had to tell someone something—*

That wasn't it. Why couldn't he think?

The startling crack of a snapping twig drew Nate's attention back to the park. "No!" They'd reached their destination—the oak.

The tree, bare with only the slightest scattering of new leaves, stood as solid and ancient as Nate remembered it. A tattered shred of police tape was caught in its branches. The ground surrounding it was trampled into mud, emergency services, investigators, and sightseers all having left their traces on the dirt. Nothing remained of the vampires—or the rowan.

"You didn't need to do that!" There was a scar where the rowan had been, bark torn away where someone had ripped the roots out. Nate put his hands on the oak's trunk, trying to look up at the damage. "You—" What? There was something connected to Peter, something just out of reach.

"How quickly blame turns to the victim." Peter stood with his hands in his pocket. "Don't you remember the last time we were here, Nathan?"

"Nate." The oak's rough bark was too familiar. Its uneven ridges brought back the uncertainty and peril of the darkness with such force that Nate shivered. "You were—"

"In a place halfway between life and death." Peter looked over to the trees. "I've been here ever since. Can't move forward or back. Not till I've got what is mine."

"Halfway?" Ben might have understood his meaning, but Ben wasn't there. Nate forced down the thought. "Is that why no one saw you in the club?"

"You're only just figuring that out now?" Peter relented. "People believe in absolutes. Good, bad. Black, white. Alive, dead. They close their minds to anything that doesn't fit their blinkered vision of reality. You don't fit, you don't exist. Simple as that. I did my final paper on it. Argued that theologians' embittered defense of life after death, the medical community's efforts to prolong earthly life, even proponents of euthanasia's attempts to cross that line are all expressions of the same thing—a need to force the world to comply with humanity's perception of it. I got an A-minus, but it should have been an A." Peter shrugged. "I take it as a positive. Genius is never recognized in its lifetime."

Nate licked his lips. The more Peter said, the less Nate understood. His tongue was starting to feel fuzzy again, not his own. "What are you talking about?"

"Case in point." Peter's mocking smile stretched skin so thin it took on an eerie translucence in the fading afternoon. "What do you remember, Nathan—sorry—Nate?"

"I remember the revenants." As Nate wrapped his arms around himself, he caught a putrid, sickly smell, not fully disguised by the carpet of damp leaves beneath his feet. *Is that—*

"Is that all?"

Nate shook his head. "Ben was there. Obviously. And you." He stopped.

"Don't say anything." Peter seemed surprised by his own vehemence. His laugh wasn't entirely convincing. "I think pity is the worst, don't you? 'What do you expect, when he lost his parents so young?' Passing responsibility, that's all it is."

"There's nothing wrong with wanting to help someone. When Pa died—" It was a struggle to complete his thought.

Peter's glance was knowing. "Sympathetic neighbors? Offering to help, but relieved when you said no, glad that your tragedy didn't intrude into their cozy reality?"

"Some people genuinely want to help!"

"People like you?" Peter joined Nate beside the oak. "No one could deny the purity of your motives. After all, Ben's lack of interest was crystal clear."

Nate winced. "No crime in looking out for someone."

"No crime," Peter said thoughtfully. "But maybe it should be."

"It's not hurting anyone is it? If you can make someone happy—"

"How real is happiness that relies on someone else, anyway? That's distraction. It doesn't make people change, try harder, grow bigger. It makes them complacent." Peter's fingers tightened on the oak bark. "Fuck that. I passed my driving test. I got a card from his trustees." Peter's laugh was angry. "Won't step up and be a father figure to their best friend's son, but they can sign a card. Yeah. Thanks a lot. I'm really grateful."

Grateful–

Nate's breath caught in his chest. Being handed that like a consolation prize hurt, the pain momentarily breaking through his confusion. "I don't want to be protected."

"Written off?" Peter's glance was bitter. "Do you know how many people say I only got my job because of my parents' death? The scholarship, Saltaire's interest– I'm not even allowed to be my own person!"

The newspapers had been full of clichés. "Model employee," "tragically orphaned," and "legacy." "That fucking bites."

"I don't want pity. I want the credit I'm due. The freedom to not be anyone's victim." Peter stood. "Now do you understand?"

The memory surfaced suddenly. Bone-like teeth bared in a vicious snarl. Nate hesitated.

"I don't want your pity, Nate," Peter repeated. "But I do need your help." He held out his hand. "I think it's time to end the cycle. Once and for all." His eyes had the calm of certainty. "Give me your hand."

Nate held out his hand, his mind still wrestling with Peter's words. "If you're not the victim–" What wasn't he getting? His reactions were just that little bit too slow.

"Neither are you." Peter drew a box cutter from his pocket. It was the kind sold in the Little River General Store, on the same shelf as the fishing tackles and gardening twine, and Nate relaxed. *No necromancer would shop at Little River.* "You choose to help me. Don't you? Say yes." He drew the knife across Nate's palm.

The cut was shallow. Nate looked down at his palm, surprised to find that it stung. "What was that for?"

Peter grabbed Nate's hand before he could pull it back. "You want to help," he said, pressing his hand down over the wound. "Say *yes.*"

A thin red line escaped their hands to travel down Nate's wrist. He watched it with a sense of inevitability. Its ticklish crawl slowed, but didn't stop when it reached the hollow of his elbow, curling up his bicep and disappearing under his T-shirt sleeve. "That—" He could feel a string pulled taut inside him, yanking the word from him. "Yes."

Peter's grin was the white-cold he'd glimpsed in the window. "Formalities over, the fun can begin."

Nate felt the ties before he glanced down. Tightly looped around his wrists and fingers were the same blood red strings that had suspended Peter in the park, controlled Ben, and tangled Denise. His skin felt numb everywhere they touched, cold as Peter's fingers as he used the blade edge to slice through the fabric of Nate's T-shirt and push it back.

"Fun?" Was that his voice? It sounded so distant. *What is wrong with me?* His thoughts moved as slowly as his body, the coldness penetrating even his mind.

"A bleeding heart like you will get something out of this." Peter worked briskly, scoring a line across Nate's bare flesh. "If the satisfaction of helping me reclaim what is mine doesn't do it for you, seeing what Ben feels for you should do the job."

Nate felt his chest squeeze tight in a way that had nothing to do with the blood magic bonds. "Ben doesn't—" He gasped as the sting of the cut suddenly registered.

"Felt that?" Peter frowned. "My bad." He tucked the cutter under one arm to smear Nate's blood in a line across his chest. The warmth of the liquid soon faded, leaving only a cold pressure that seemed to go through him entirely. "Spent so long working with animated corpses, I forgot. This is the first real conversation I've had in a week."

The coldness settled in his lungs and throat. *Like the river*. Nate pushed back the rush of fear. *I'm not drowning—*

"If you can call this conversation." Hand still bloody from his work, Peter gathered a handful of the crimson threads. He closed his fist around them and, in one sudden movement, tugged them hard.

Everything went black.

* ~ * ~ *

Something crept down his forehead.

Nate flinched back instinctively but found himself restrained. The shock startled him awake, straining against the bonds that kept him locked in place.

What the hell?

Just seconds ago, it had been late afternoon, rain clouds gathering in the distance. Now it was night, rain slowed to a steady, depressing trickle. Nate's wet hair was slicked against his skull and his throat hurt when he swallowed. It took effort to move his tongue over his lips, but the rainwater brought some relief. The steady stream down the oak's trunk provided a countereffect to his panic. Another drip ran down Nate's chest, stinging as it passed over the open wound. Nate followed its passage down to his stomach.

I hurt everywhere.

The moonlight didn't penetrate the shadows, but Nate didn't need to see the myriad of thin lines binding him to know they were there. He felt them press into him as he took a shaky breath.

He hurt...but he wasn't shivering. *I should be. It's been, what. Hours?* His T-shirt was long gone, but his jeans were damp even where they rested against the rough tree bark at his back. *Soaked through. So why—Peter. He's controlling me—no. He's controlling my body.*

And if Nate could figure out that much, he could figure out an escape.

Flexing his fingers took effort. Nate had to fight against the strings that cut into his skin as he moved. He gritted his teeth. *SOS button on the wristband—*

There was an answering vibration on one string and then footsteps. Peter had returned.

"I was just thinking an attention whore like yourself—like that?—would want to be aware for this." Light reflected off the rain-slick ground, and then a flashlight came into view. Peter held it in one hand, an umbrella in the other. "I had to go halfway across town to get a second knife. The price one pays for perfectionism."

At least this time, you paid the bill. Knowing he'd put the man out of pocket was small revenge, but Nate relished it anyway. Peter shone the flashlight directly at Nate. Without Peter's rigid control, he would have winced.

"And now the weather. I'm going to have to start over." Peter's umbrella dipped wildly as he pulled up his sleeves. "Still, it's like I always say—when life gives you lemons, murder a hooker."

Now he thinks he's Jack the Ripper? Spare me. Nate's arm stretched out of its own volition. As he tried to decipher the lack of pain, Peter pressed the umbrella into his hand.

"At least you don't disappoint." Peter paused to set the flashlight down. When he stood, he held a bright silver knife in his hand. "I couldn't have chosen better myself. I waited an entire year for that uptight ass to show a flicker of interest in anything beyond his infatuation—an entire year! And only when I decided to make my own opportunity, you show up. I worked it out. It's your complete lack of self-preservation. Someone as married to his responsibilities as Ben can't ignore the obvious danger you pose to yourself. And that could not be any better for my purposes."

The sharp sting of the knife was easier to take than the stinging within. *How many times do we have to rehash this? Yeah, it was dumb, but I really wanted—*

Peter retraced the previous pattern. By now, the flexing of invisible cords was a familiar sensation—or almost. *Something feels different—*

"And your blood, too." Peter licked his fingertip clean. "There's something to be said for having a big heart after all. I was worried there wouldn't be enough of you left when Ben gets here for him to appreciate this."

Not the problem you think it is. But would Ben's indifference be enough protection? Nate shivered so violently the umbrella shook.

"Steady." Peter's command was muffled. A sudden burst of light revealed a shiny monogram—a book of matches. Peter juggled the lit match and the candle he'd drawn from the long pockets of his coat. "Of all nights to rain, it would be tonight."

Nate's hand obeyed, but the shivering remained. Nate resisted the urge to wrap his free arm around himself for warmth. *Does this mean his control is slipping?* Scarcely daring to think about what he did, Nate moved his free hand to rest over his wristband, seemingly supporting the hand holding the umbrella. As Peter dropped the spent match and began a sonorous chant, candle in one hand and knife in the other, Nate hit the emergency button.

Peter was occupied burning a folded piece of white paper. Herbs as thick as overly perfumed potpourri mixed discordantly with the smell of human hair, and Nate gagged on the smoke.

This time, Peter noticed Nate's movement. He didn't pause the chant, but once the paper was entirely burnt, he let his free hand rest on Nate's shoulder, eliciting a shiver that Nate couldn't suppress.

"Odd."

Nate felt the internal stirrings of the strings and held out his hand unbidden. *Don't look at it!* Rather than risk glancing at the wristband, he willed himself to concentrate on every action Peter made.

In a strangely intimate gesture, Peter cradled Nate's wrist, raising both their hands over the flame. Cuts that Nate didn't remember crisscrossed his palm. Peter pressed the knife against a new patch of skin, repeating the gesture on his own palm. Most of his scars were scabbed over or in the process of healing. There was only one new one, and Peter added a second before pressing his palm to Nate's.

Unapproved blood play. Denise is going to be furious—

Blood ran down their wrists, and with a sodden hiss, the candle went out.

The strings pulled tight. *No question of moving now.* He was pushed back against the oak. Peter took the umbrella, sheltering Nate's chest as he began to trace a new pattern.

Nate tried to follow Peter's touch but couldn't. His body felt distant, like it didn't belong to him. Even his thoughts seemed to float somewhere outside his head, the sound of the raindrops hitting Peter's umbrella more real than Nate's own breathing.

The insistent tugging of the strings, that was very real. They continuously shifted, calling Nate's fractured attention to them.

Why?

Nate found the thin lines led his thoughts beneath the soil. Something waited there. *Somethings.* The putrid smell made sudden horrifying sense. *Revenants!* Nate jerked away, but it was hopeless. His body wouldn't move.

Neither did the revenants.

Trapped? No—hidden. Now that he was looking for them, Nate could see the red cords that looped the clearing, laid out in a clear circle. *A trap. That's what this is—a trap for Ben.*

With that realization came an even more chilling one.

I'm the bait.

One red line hung slackly, not moving in response to Peter's chanting. *Sex, blood, and bonds.* Nate remembered Gunn's words. *Unfinished business.*

The thread seemed impossibly delicate as Nate held it. Like it might break at any moment, but it held firm at the tentative tug Nate gave it.

Do I?

The thread was so absurdly thin. Nate turned it over in his hands. He would lose it in the dark, or it would snap—

Nate glanced back.

He was looking at himself. His body was slumped against the tree, held in place by the red lines of Peter's magic. The image was so jarring that Nate immediately looked down.

He could see the damp leaves through his shoes, the dark bulk of the surrounding bushes through his arm. *This isn't supposed to happen!* Nate's hand locked around the string. *I don't even know what this is, but it is definitely not meant to happen!*

The string was solid. With it clenched tightly in his fist, Nate discovered he could hold the panic at bay. *Nothing else that has happened tonight makes any sense. Why should this be any different?* Steeling himself, he looked back.

Seeing his own body from the outside was strange, even expecting it. Propped up against the oak by the lines he looked puppetlike. Nate shuddered. *Denise—*

Before he could fully process what he saw, Peter stood, the

umbrella blocking Nate's body from sight.

Very carefully, holding a breath he hadn't drawn, Nate pulled at the thread he held. He felt the tug as it reached his body, a phantom pain around his heart. *That's real, at least. Or am I the phantom?* He'd ask Gunn later. *The thread's other end—*

Nate's fingers closed around the thread he held. *It's only unfinished on my end. Ben—*

Ben had made his feelings clear. *But the thread—*

He couldn't tell what was on the other end of it, only that it was there.

If it's Ben, then it's my fault this thread is there. Nate gathered his thoughts together slowly. Gunn had said sex, blood and bonds. Not sex, blood and necromancers. *My fault if he gets hurt.*

Keeping a firm hold on the thread, Nate let the string guide him away from the park.

~~*

So, that's not tacky at all.

Nate stood in front of the iron gate to Hunter's townhouse, looking up. The Victorian frame outlined in bright lights would have been the envy of any Vegas billboard. Hell, Century could have taken some tips from them. The old house positively glowed.

Lucky vampires are loaded. The electric bill alone...!

But was it lights? Looking closer at the gate, Nate saw that the candlelike glow formed patterns. Curious, he stretched out a hand, hoping to feel heat. Instead, he encountered resistance.

What the hell—now things decide to get solid?

The string had led Nate through the city without any regard for traffic, buildings, or even people. Nate had pressed through all three as easily as a ghost, trying desperately not to think about what that implied. He hadn't let himself get scared. But now, suddenly, Nate was afraid.

I want to be back in myself! His body might not move, but the numbness kept the rising panic away. Nate's fingers tightened reflexively around the cord in one hand, and immediately he felt ashamed.

Numb won't help Ben. Nate forced himself to remember Ben's cool gray eyes, his determined mouth. He borrowed the vampire's self-control, using it to school his panic. He'd come so far. He wouldn't turn back now.

Keeping the thread grasped firmly in one hand, Nate stepped into the gate. As he pushed, he felt an invisible barrier give.

The lights behind him went out instantly.

Did I do that? The thread led up to the glowing front door, and Nate followed it, pushing back the feeling of dread. *They must have anticipated an attack.* Nate swallowed. *What if they think it's me?*

The memory of the waiting revenants decided for him. Nate didn't allow himself time to balk at the closed door. He shut his eyes and pressed into it.

It felt like the time Pa's city friend had taken them fishing in his boat. Nate's hat had blown into the water, and he'd fallen in trying to retrieve it. His waterlogged clothing had pulled him down, and Nate had needed Ethan and Pa's help to haul himself back into the boat. This time, Nate was alone.

Should I have gone round the back? Nate stopped the thought before it could become a full-on doubt and concentrated on the thread he held. It seemed to shift on its own accord now. Ben was close—

Nate pitched forward into darkness. For a moment, he thought he was lost, and then an alarmed murmur reassured him. The lights had gone out.

I don't need lights to find Ben. He could have located him even without the thread. Nate stepped through the nearest door. This time, there was no resistance.

A fire still burned in the fireplace, its untroubled flicker catching the thick shine of the embroidery on the elaborately upholstered sofas and armchairs. An actual wood fire. *Totally wasted on vampires.* Unthinkingly, Nate stretched out a hand to it. For a moment, he was warm. Then the flames whipped out of existence, leaving a smoky trail in the air and drawing a startled exclamation from the room's occupants.

"The fire, too?" Ben's voice had the firmness of someone who was not being honest with himself. "Could be a sign of a manifestation—"

"I know what it's a sign of." Hunter's confidence didn't sound misplaced. "You're staying put."

A second light illuminated the room. Nate watched as Hunter bent the match to a candleholder set ready on an end table. He had to swallow back an odd feeling as he watched Hunter's hand settle on Ben's shoulder.

"This circle is here to keep you safe, and that is exactly what I intend to see it do."

Safe—that's the important thing. That he's safe.

The circle was drawn in salt and chalk, bordered with candles that Hunter relit, one by one. Their reflected light glittered in the long blade that Hunter's hand rested on, dark peacoat taking on a military aspect in the room. The candle glow also illuminated the armchair in which Ben sat, a revolver on his lap. The table beside him held extra bullets in addition to salt and a box of matches, and Nate felt something in him ease. Ben looked better, not as thin as when Nate had seen him last. Someone had convinced him to feed, and maybe that meant—

Nate took a deep breath. *Maybe Ben doesn't need my help.* He let go of the thread.

Instantly, a harsh pressure pushed down on him. Nate gasped. It felt like the weight in the air before a storm, only a thousand times stronger and more personal.

There was the scrape of a chair against floorboards, then a wooden clatter. Nate looked up to see the bullets from the upended table scatter across the floor. Behind the table, Ben's gaze was fixed on Nate.

"No. Not him."

Hunter grabbed his arm before he could move, but Ben seemed physically stunned, as though he'd been hit. "Tricks. You're not leaving this circle."

They can see me. Nate hadn't even realized how afraid he was that they might not until he felt the relief, and then he almost choked on it. "Ben." His voice sounded faint, even to himself, and Nate forced himself to struggle past the crushing pressure. "Ben, you have to listen. No tricks, this is really important—"

"Nate." Ben's eyes had traveled from Nate's face to his chest and seemed stuck there. "What happened to you?"

"Within the circle," Hunter repeated. "No matter what."

"Hunter's right," Nate said. "It's a trap. At the park. He's waiting for you." The memory of the waiting revenants, buried with their hate and hunger came back to Nate with a rush. "Underground. He's buried them there. Dirt's already disturbed, no one would ever know. I felt five of them. There might be more. He thinks he's fucking Hannibal Lector or something—"

The door swung open, sending a ripple through the room that nearly knocked Nate off his feet. An old storm lantern was raised, revealing Godfrey, his usual dark suit blending seamlessly with the shadows. "The wards are down. Grounds and house—" He came to an abrupt halt as his gaze fell on Nate. "*My*—"

"Nate's brought us a message." Hunter's tone was casual, but his mouth was tight. His hand dug into Ben's arm in a way that must have hurt, but the younger vampire didn't protest. Maybe he didn't feel it? All three of them were motionless. "Please, Nate. Continue."

"Mason's Park. Where the oak tree is. He destroyed the rowan, but that's where he'll be."

"Where who is?" Ben's voice held determination.

Is this a mistake?

"Tell me, Nate. Who is it? Describe him if you don't know his name—"

"It's someone Nate knows," Hunter said slowly. "Someone we all know. His knowledge of Godfrey's wards, our habits—"

Nate nodded. "Peter," he rasped.

Ben's mouth moved, but he made no sound. For the second time that night, he stared as though Nate had just stabbed him.

Instead, there was movement from the darkest corner of the room. Saltaire might have been present the entire time, but Nate had no idea he was there until he stepped out of the shadows, infinitely more threatening than anything that waited at the park. His thick coat was open over a white shirt, a heavy curved blade better suited to a corsair than a vampire at his waist. "De Silver is our necromancer? He's hidden it well."

"I did not anticipate this," Hunter admitted.

"I had some doubts," Godfrey said mildly. "If you remember, we spoke about this a year ago." He looked with special significance at Saltaire.

What is he not saying? A year ago—

A year ago, Ben was a new vampire and his father was dead.

"I put them down to an old man's fancy. After all, he has been with us since he was in school." Godfrey's fingers played over the garishly ornate cross he wore at his neck. "Has he sent you here to state his terms?"

"I found the way myself," Nate said. "I don't know what he wants, but it's not good for Ben. Something about what is owed him—"

Sharp, searing pain flashed across his senses with an immediacy that jarred him back to his body at once. Nate cried out, but the sound was trapped in his throat. He fell to his knees, one hand scrabbling for support in the damp soil. His other hand clutched at his throat. Liquid dribbled between his fingers and splashed to the ground in thick, dark blobs.

Peter's fingers were tight in Nate's hair, the sharp knife now stained with use in his free hand. "Thought I wouldn't notice you using my powers? Fatal mistake. I don't need you alive to use you."

He kicked Nate onto his side, then again in his ribs, nudging him with his foot. Nate could offer no resistance, gasping for breath as he lay on his back. He couldn't breathe, the liquid pooling in his throat—

"It was going to be great. Making Ben watch as you slowly bled out, cursing him with your final breath. Exhibitionist like yourself, you'd have enjoyed it too—but no, you had to rush things."

There was a savage snapping of wood, and Nate shut his eyes, trying desperately to stay calm and will air into his lungs.

"Fine, then. Let's do it your way. Ben isn't rushing here to save you. He's rushing here to turn you. I'm making doubly sure that's not happening."

The rough sound of metal on wood was instantly familiar. Nate opened his eyes incredulously. *I know Pa said that whittling relaxed him, and there is no one in this park who needs to settle down more than Peter, but right now?*

Peter pressed his lips together smugly, holding up his handiwork for Nate to see. He'd sharpened the branch segment at one end into a rough stake. *Not going to win him any ribbons at the Fair, that's for sure.* "Let me do you a favor. You want to be a martyr so bad? Here's a sacrifice they'll remember for at least a week."

Nate tried to scramble back, but his fingers slipped in the mud. He could only watch as Peter carefully planted a foot on his chest to stop him from moving, forcing a low gurgle from Nate's torn throat.

"Throat cut, staked through the heart. You are staying dead." He positioned the stake carefully above Nate's heart, raised it over his head, and stabbed down.

Nate distantly heard bones crack. The pain was all-encompassing, jerking through his body with a force that threw Peter back. The loss of his weight was no respite. The pain was too intense, too intrusive.

Too strong.

Chapter Twelve

The soil beneath him felt warm. Nate could feel it where his blood had seeped into it, feel the warmth as it called to the branch still in his chest.

This was good because everything else was numb. Colder than numb. *Shock? Maybe exposure?*

He should probably do something about the stake in his chest. Nate felt for it, but found he couldn't move his fingers. *Not a good sign.* Nate took a deep breath, found that he couldn't do that either. *What is going on?*

Calm down. It will be okay. I shouldn't be removing the stake anyway. Puncture wounds, you need a doctor to do that. A paramedic. We covered that in first aid, right? And throat wounds... I probably didn't want to be breathing with that wound.

Never mind that he shouldn't be breathing at all.

Nate resolutely quashed that thought. *There's an explanation. I just have to find it.*

The clearing was absolutely still. The rain had stopped entirely and even the wind had died down. Those sleeping in wait beneath the surface of the earth shifted restlessly, but made only the slightest vibrations in their discontent.

Peter was gone.

Nate felt for his presence, but the strands of magic had been cut when Peter cut his throat. *Fled? Sounds right— He's not the kind to fight his own battles.* Instead, he'd trust the trap he'd set for Ben—

There was an abrupt rustle in the trees, urgent footsteps. Nate's fear mingled with relief. *Right on cue—*

"Jesus Christ, Nate."

Not Ben. Gunn.

Nate felt disappointed—and immediately guilty. *Fine way to thank him.* Gunn had worked hard to keep Nate out of this situation. The officer was already moving, even as he scanned the clearing, making his way to Nate's body with unprofessional haste.

There was a strange resignation in Gunn's eyes, the muscles of his mouth tightening as he crouched beside Nate. "Once. Just once, it would be nice if somebody listened to me." He reached over, cold fingers oddly gentle as they closed Nate's eyes.

Nate was unimpressed. Gunn should at least have taken his pulse first—

Then as Gunn lifted Nate's hand to inspect the crisscross of lines there, Nate realized that he could still see the officer.

That's not—

Possible? But it was happening, so it had to be—

Hello? Some attention here? Nate tried to move the fingers of the hand Gunn held, but his limbs were so heavy and useless, they didn't even feel like his. *C'mon, Gunn. I'm sorry I got myself into this, but ignoring me's not going to help any—*

There was no sound that Nate heard, but Gunn dropped his hand, pulling a gun from his pocket seemingly instantaneously.

"Show yourself."

Ben melted out of the shadows, seriousness giving his habitual quietness a hard, unforgiving edge. "Gunn."

"Bennet."

There was a long moment of silence. It was obvious that Gunn didn't like any of Saltaire's brood, but Nate had not realized how mutual the feeling was. Then Gunn stepped back, lowering his gun. "We're both too late. Your friends worked him over good. Blood magic, and they took precautions against walking."

"I'd like to see him for myself."

Gunn shrugged. "I'm not going to stop you."

Ben didn't move. "Nate warned us. Peter left a trap for me in the park."

Gunn's head snapped up at the name. "Did he now?"

"It must be tied to my presence. You should leave."

"And let you have all the fun? You're out of luck, Hawick. I am not in the mood for any self-sacrificing vampire theatrics tonight."

"And I'm not in the mood to talk reckless officers out of their habit of self-endangerment," Ben said, tugging his own pistol out of his inside jacket. "I need one of them alive."

The soil rippled the instant Ben crossed the invisible circle around the oak. Clawed hands rose out of the soil, followed by dirt-covered torsos. Peter had buried his revenants only deep enough to protect them from sun and the attention of others, the damp soil offering no resistance as the snarling vampires pulled their way to the surface.

Gunn took out two with clear headshots even before the first had pulled himself to his feet. Ben shot another, winging a second and finishing him with a direct shot through the heart. Gunn added a third to his total, before the remaining revenants closed in on them. In seeming concert, vampire and officer both switched to melee weapons. They didn't talk, but there was a distinct pattern to their movements. Ben's expression closed off and hard and Gunn's businesslike, they made short work of Peter's preparations.

Either the necromancer had gravely miscalculated, or Nate had not given Ben's determination enough credit. Ben sliced through one wild, attacking vampire before spinning to block the attack of the next one, nothing left of the shell-shocked expression Nate had last seen on him. He fought with a chilling mixture of brutality and practicality.

Nate reached down further into the comforting warmth and familiarity of the soil. Was Peter right? Had Ben's refusal to engage with the world and his emotions protected him while trusting his emotions and trying to help had only got Nate—

Dead?

Nate shied away from the thought. *I can't be dead. Ethan, Ma—what am I going to tell Ma?*

The soil was warm, giving way for him. He could feel it, smell it. Nate took a moment to savor that fact. It was real. *He* was real. *This has to be a mistake.* How many times did people tell him to think things through? He could work this out—

The sounds of fighting had ceased, the only noise in the clearing a soft, feminine whimper that ended in the snapping of bone. Nate instinctively pulled back from looking, but he could hear what followed.

"Drinking from her? That wise?" There was a pause, and the sound of cloth moving, Gunn cleaning his combat knife on the clothes of some hapless victim. "You know where she's been."

"Necromancer's bonds work two ways," Ben said. "Nate also showed us that." Nate felt his arms lifted, placed on his chest, Ben's cool hand coming to rest over his own.

There was the sound of a match striking, a moment of concentration, and then Gunn breathed out. The weight of it said much. "For what it's worth, I'm sorry. I kind of liked the kid."

"I don't want your pity."

"I don't do pity." Another long pause. "Hawick, when this started, I was sure you were behind this. I was wrong. That's all."

Ben's hand gripped Nate's with a tightness that might have hurt. "Can I have a moment?"

"I'm gonna have to call the office. You got about twenty minutes before the cleanup crew arrives." Nate felt the vibrations of Gunn's footsteps as he walked away.

This is my chance. If anyone's going to hear me now, it's Ben—

Nate could feel the Ben's body tremble as he sat beside him, but it took the choked sound that escaped the vampire's throat for him to recognize it as grief. Nate felt something in himself give way. *It's true then.*

I'm dead.

* ~ * ~ *

"Gunn. How long until your unit arrives?"

"Ten minutes. Why?"

"Stay with him? There's something I need to do."

Leaving. Nate shouldn't feel so hurt by that. *I shouldn't feel hurt at all! I'm dead.*

It was harder to hold his thoughts together under the weight of the realization. Ben gave him some focus, but as he stood, even that receded.

Dead. Whatever energy had been keeping his consciousness together was fading and with it, Nate himself.

Gunn and Ben's conversation seemed only mildly important. "You're going after the necromancer? Now? By yourself?"

"I'm not asking you to come with me."

"Doesn't the old stiff have an opinion on this?"

"He has bigger problems. Nate broke the wards on our house."

Gunn whistled. "Every vampire in the city must know his wards are down, and he's let you out to go hunt a necromancer by yourself? What is he thinking?" A beat. "You're doing this without his permission."

"Just stay with him."

Gunn's weight came to rest on the ground beside Nate. "Hawick. He doesn't tolerate failure."

"He's taken precautions. In the event of my failure, his safety will not be at stake."

"Hunting without his protection." Gunn's snort was approving. "Aren't you the reckless one?"

"You won't change my mind." Ben's reply was raw. Defensive.

Nate remembered Hunter's protective presence. *He didn't just defy Saltaire. He defied Hunter, too.* But even that fact didn't reach below Nate's surface. *I really am dead.*

"I don't want to." The ground vibrated as Gunn shifted. "De Silver's got tricks up his sleeve. We combed this park twice, once in daylight, once in the dark, and found no sign of either of them. If the kid hadn't hit the emergency button on his GPS, we'd still be looking. That's either time mastery, or some heavy masking."

"Both of which take energy."

"Nothing worse than a cornered and desperate necromancer."

"Nothing worse for *Peter*."

Ben's steps faded away into nothing. Nate felt them disappear. It was harder to focus with each step, and as he ceased to feel Ben altogether, Nate gave up trying. *I'm dead. Dead people don't think. They just stop.*

The earth was comforting and solid. Nate let his awareness drift. The doctors had said that for Pa, it had been just like going to sleep. And sleep—sleep seemed pretty good right now.

Chapter Thirteen

The water was wrong.

The discordant tinkle was too shallow to be a soft summer shower and too uneven for the uniform hum of proper rain. It only sounded like one thing.

Nate ignored it. *I'm dead. Dead people don't pee.*

He focused instead on the sun. The light stretched through him, filling him with delicious warmth. He tried to float on it, to grasp the feeling of contentedness, but the spell had been broken. He could still feel the sun, but now he was aware of something pressed uncomfortably into his back. A weight lay over him, thick and scratchy.

Scratchy? Nate tried to line up his thoughts. He and Ethan had sat either side of Ma in the same pew every Sunday until he'd graduated high school. Not one of the succession of pastors who'd droned earnestly about salvation had said anything about eternal life itching.

This time the sound that interrupted was unmistakable.

"But that makes no sense." *Why would angels need to flush?*

"Fuck."

There was the metallic scrape of a hastily drawn zipper. Nate blinked his eyes open, taking in a stained and dingy shower curtain just before someone thrust it aside. Gunn smirked down at Nate. He'd switched out his habitual jacket for a dirty white T-shirt, and vines inexplicably surrounded him.

"Finally decided to rejoin the conscious? Just as well. Another day and I'd have had to harvest an organ or two as rent."

"Gunn?" Faded blue tiles filled the bottom half of the wall, the remainder a sickly off-white floral print that now looked closer to off-gray. Clearly a bathroom. A bathroom that was overdue a cleaning. A bathroom Nate had never seen in his life. "Am I in your bathtub?"

The officer snorted, leaning against the door. "I'm impressed you could find the tub under all of that."

"It's cold," Nate said. "And the tap's digging into my back."

"That'd do it."

There was a pause as they contemplated the "all of that."

Thick green ivy filled the tiny bathroom. A few tendrils extended over the side of the tub toward the door, but most swarmed toward two tiny glass windows, forming a literal green curtain. The ravenous vines pushed their way out the window to the wall beyond. Nate got the distinct impression of red brick, the rumble of the subway and sunlight, glorious and giving.

"Something you forgot to mention, Nate?"

If Nate made an effort, he could raise his arm, but the ivy pulled at his skin. Lifting the vines, he discovered that the vines started where Peter had gouged his skin with the knife. "That's not possible."

"You're lucky to be here at all," Gunn said. "No energy, magical or otherwise. If I hadn't noticed you were putting down roots when the boys gave the okay to move you, you'd be a jar in the vault, waiting until your next of kin picked you up."

Nate's fingers closed around the vines on his wrist. "Next of kin. You didn't—"

"Contact them? How?" Gunn set his foot on the edge of the bath and leaned in. Nate remembered just how uncomfortable the officer's focus could be. "You gave a false phone number and address on your job application, and no one with your surname lives in that county."

"Unlisted," Nate rasped. "Pa hated telemarketers." He put a hand to his throat. "Got some water?"

"To drink?"

What kind of a question is that? "Yeah, to drink."

"Don't think we're changing the subject." Gunn took a glass from the battered cupboard that clung to the wall above the sink on a single hinge.

The water was cloudy and the glass chipped, but Nate decided not to push his luck. He sipped slowly. The cold water soothed his throat. "No great mystery. I told Ma I work at a café. She thinks I'm a waiter. I don't want her to know about the club."

Gunn snorted. "Your night job's the least of your problems now. What are you—some kind of dryad?"

"Dryads are girls. And legends." The reality of the glass in his hand reassured. Nate glared at the officer. "I'm *normal.* I mean—human."

"Yeah. And I'm a nice guy."

Nate set the empty glass down in the mass of vines. Not that he had a choice. He couldn't see his chest, let alone the side of the bath. "I mean it. My brother inherited the farm and the weird. I got the truck and the normal. This isn't supposed to happen." Steeling himself, he wrapped his hands around the vines attached to his hand and tugged.

They gave easily, like pulling weeds from Ma's vegetable patch, tickling as they went. The vines left behind smooth skin, raised and thick where the cuts were deepest. Nate flexed his fingers. *I'm normal.*

Gunn watched him from the side of the bath. "Sure about that? I'm only a seasoned veteran of the supernatural, but it seems to me those vines are doing you a favor."

"If you're such a seasoned veteran, maybe you should know." Nate heaved a bunch of torn leaves and vines over the side of the bath. The ceramic was an uneven brown, a patina of neglect that had taken decades to form. Nate shifted, felt the surface he was sitting on move. "You put me in dirt?"

"Hey. It was a lot of work carting all that up the stairs." Gunn fished a cigarette out of the crumpled packet on the sink, setting it between his teeth as he dug in his jeans for his lighter. "Department sprung for actual manure. Who'd believe people actually charge for shit?"

"You *planted* me in your bathtub?"

"Which I want back, by the way. I've been showering at the YMCA so often people are starting to think it's a lifestyle choice." Gunn tapped his cigarette ash directly into the sink. "You're welcome."

"For leaving me in a tub for—"

"Three days."

"*Three* days? Shouldn't I have received actual medical attention?"

"Medical attention's for the living. That no longer included you. Sorry, Nate." Gunn leaned back against the sink. "Life's a bitch. Death's her older, meaner sister. But hey, we got you before the ambulance did. This was totally off the record. Except for our records. Congratulations. You're a person of interest."

Nate looked down.

After a long moment, he continued his vicious assault on the vines. Most of the vines he ripped away were rooted in his chest and arms. No one had removed his jeans—*Thank God for that*—but Nate looked down at his chest with horror.

The thin pink marks were unrecognizable as arcane symbols of any kind, mottled skin almost completely healed. The stub of wood protruding from his chest, however, was something else. Nate ran his fingers over it, found it warm to the touch. "The fuck...?"

"Medics couldn't remove it without destroying your heart. Don't worry about it. You're absorbing it. No one knows how. If murder investigations didn't trump research, you'd have woken up to find yourself in three different dissecting trays."

"Great." Leaves rubbed at Nate's chin. Irritably, he raised his hands to the knot of vines at his throat.

Gunn's hand closed over Nate's with a force that hurt.

Nate gasped, surprised into looking up into the officer's tawny brown-gold eyes. *I didn't even see him move—*

"Leave that one," the officer said slowly. He looked at Nate a long moment, as if trying to bore his message into Nate's skull directly, and then let go.

Nate stayed still, uncertainly. This was—

He yelped. In his haste to stop Nate from ripping away the last of the vines, Gunn had lost his cigarette. Nate had just found it.

"Sorry," Gunn said with complete lack of sincerity. "But face it. Those jeans are on the way out. I'll pick you up a change of clothes at the Goodwill. But first—catch."

Nate threw up his hands in reflex. He blinked, looking down at the smartphone. "What's this for?"

"A phone. You use it to call people. In your case, your folks."

Nate bit his lip as his fingers closed tightly around the phone. He could picture Ma, wiping her hands on the dishtowel before picking up the kitchen phone, her face lighting up in a warm, wrinkled smile that faded as she heard his story. She would be so worried.

Ethan—if anyone would understand, it would be Ethan. But would sympathy change anything? "Maybe they don't wanna know. I mean—"

"For fuck's sake." Gunn was in Nate's face for the second time that day, one hand painfully tight on Nate's shoulder as he stabbed Nate's chest with his finger. "Listen, sweetheart. Sudden death's a lot to come to terms with, I know. But I don't have time to hold your hand and lead you through the five stages of giving a fuck. I need to know what you are and if we need to make arrangements for you."

Nate tried very hard to ignore the pointed edges of Gunn's teeth. "Arrangements?"

"Department Seven handles supernatural cases. That includes the monitoring and, if necessary, containment of said cases."

"Now I'm a case?"

Gunn held Nate's eye. "I didn't receive my badge for my reputation as a bleeding heart."

"I don't know what the more shocking revelation is. That, or the fact you know what a heart is—" Nate caught himself halfway through dialing the house number. "For the record, I am calling because I want to, not because you're intimidating."

Gunn resumed his place holding up the wall, one hand automatically patting his pocket for his lighter. "As long as you make the call."

"Some privacy?"

"Privacy's a human right."

"Department Seven basically equates to having a license to be an asshole— Ma! I wasn't, I— Sorry, Ma."

"Nate." She didn't scold him for his language. She didn't scold him at all. Nate heard the hitch in her voice as she greeted him. "Nate. Darling. Where are you, are you well?"

Gunn was right about the call. "Yeah. I'm fine, Ma. It's been an interesting week." Nate ignored Gunn's snort. "You don't have to worry about me."

"Of course I worry." She was getting into her stride now, initial relief giving way to alarm. "What with the news and the deaths and everything, and you not answering your phone!"

"I'm sorry about my phone, Ma—"

"Come home, Nate."

"I can't. I mean, not yet. I want to, but there's something I got to take care of here first."

Ma let out an exasperated breath. "You boys inherited Mitchell's stubbornness. It's no use trying to dissuade you, but you'll be careful?"

Nate smiled, suddenly finding his throat thick with emotion. "I'll do my best."

Gunn cleared his throat.

Nate turned his back on Gunn as much as he could in the cramped confines of the tub. Winding a finger around a tendril of ivy, Nate swallowed. "Actually, Ma— There's something I got to ask you. When— You remember when I left home? You said that I was your son, no matter what?"

The silence before Ma responded was confirmation enough. "Nate, what's happened?"

"It's obvious in retrospect. I mean, at the time, I thought you'd figured out that occasionally I like to fuck guys and—"

"Nate, filter."

"Sorry, Ma. I was— You totally weren't talking about me—um. You were talking about something else."

Her voice was gentle and sad. He could practically feel the brush of her cool fingers on his forehead. "My dear."

"Ma—what am I?"

"You're my son. You and Ethan are my very precious sons. That's all I need to know."

It was tempting, but Nate couldn't forget the threat leaning against the wall behind him, curled around a cigarette as he listened intently. "You've never worried that maybe I'm a monster? That I might hurt someone?"

"Oh, no, dear. Your father and I raised you better than that."

Tears stung his eyes sharply. He had to smile not to cry. "I love you, Ma. Also, I'm bisexual."

Ma was tolerant but firm. "Come home soon, Nate."

Hanging up on Ma was hard. It had been easier than Nate thought possible to settle into the familiar eddy of Little River, the whirl of emotions and disjointed reactions of his awakening soothed into stillness by that steady flow—

"I have never been happier to be an orphan."

"Fuck you."

—but the currents below the surface pulled him places Nate didn't quite fully understand. Returning home was easy, but not right. Nate held out the phone to Gunn. "Something wrong with your heating? It's freezing in here."

Gunn pocketed the phone. "Says the half-naked guy. Should have thought of that before you rid yourself of your vinery."

Nate pushed the tendril he'd been toying with away. "They're not mine."

"Sure. Kick back while I grab a blanket. You look like a guy who was found mostly dead in a park three days ago." He was gone before Nate could muster a "fuck you."

Nate wormed his way back against the tub. Physically he felt...exactly like a guy who'd been found dead three days ago. He shivered. At least the vines had been warm. Without the soothing sunlight to bathe him, his aching muscles and the many scrapes and cuts intruded on his awareness along with a hollow sensation that seemed to come from within.

His head felt light. Empty. *No shock there. I've been jerked so many ways, it's a wonder I can tell up from down.* A strange sort of coldness had settled over his heart. Ma's voice could call to him, Gunn might irritate him, but left to himself, Nate couldn't muster the energy or the interest to decipher the whirl of feeling.

I should care about this. Me being human—that's a big deal!

Nate shut his eyes. He probed deep within himself for some reaction, but all he discovered was numbness. *I've never been more exhausted. Even feeling's too much.* A tendril of memory stirred. *Nothing will ever be the same again. Nothing—*

He was asleep before he finished the thought.

Nate woke to the loving embrace of thick ivy and sunlight. Swearing profusely, he stripped himself of the cloying vines again. This time, Nate made it over the edge of the bathtub. His bare feet came in contact with something woolen. Gunn had indeed brought him a blanket. Folding it neatly, Nate set it on the edge of the bathtub and looked for his host.

Man. Condemning this place would improve it! Gunn's living room contained a couple of crates and a sofa that might have been scavenged from a war zone. Newspaper was laid thickly around the apartment, as either reading material or carpet. Multiple ashtrays, littered with butts, were positioned strategically amongst the mess, and an army of empty bottles was piled haphazardly against the wall. One of the crates housed a TV that predated the shift to digital by years.

There were only three doors. The first was a cupboard in which sundry items, including a broken broom and a stack of mildewing magazines, had been jammed with more thought to containment than organization.

The second was the kitchen. Nate stepped inside and immediately backed out. Something in the kitchen had *died.* He was sure of it. Careful to breathe through his mouth, Nate tried the third door. "Gunn? You—whoa."

This room was in stark contrast to the rest of the apartment. The walls were painted black and the double bed stood on actual carpet. Five sleek metal cases stood around the room, all padlocked, while the collection of crucifixes Gunn had alluded to were affixed to the wall at regular intervals, along with mirrors, ankhs, and posters of topless women who felt very passionately about firearms.

Nate stepped over the threshold. The room smelled vaguely of aftershave with an undercurrent of dried herbs. Objectively, it was the most welcoming room in the place. And yet, Nate had absolutely no desire to go inside. *Maybe I was too quick to dismiss the kitchen?* He turned toward it. *I can crack open a window.*

The kitchen sink repulsed and fascinated. The layer of scum floating on its surface was as thick as the algae on Drummond's lake. Nate poked the submerged cans and dishes cautiously, half-expecting the sink to erupt swamp-monster-like in response. *Risk pulling out the plug?*

"You only live once— Fuck it."

The sink gurgled horribly as the slime oozed away, revealing rusting cans, a couple of submerged bottles, and—shockingly—an actual fry pan and spatula. Nate struggled to turn the tap, letting the water run as he assessed the counter. He needed somewhere for the sink's contents, but where? The coffee percolator, the only thing in the room that looked like it received maintenance, stood surrounded by a veritable elephant's graveyard of mugs. Some held almost a full cup of forgotten coffee, some only the dregs; all had viscous streaks of brown crusted onto their sides.

"This is where coffee goes to die."

The remains of microwavable meals, stale crusts, and fossilized objects that had possibly once been food littered the other side of the counter. The table held empty cardboard beer boxes and a stack of bills secured to the table with a stained knife. Not thinking about what he was touching, Nate dumped a pile of crap from the counter onto the table. A crisp box of baking soda was under the sink, along with a sponge that had clearly never been used. Nate scrubbed at the cleared counter space. The baking soda instantly turned a cloudy gray. The veneer of dried brown stains and grease gave way to reveal a tired metal finish. Encouraged, Nate applied even more muscle to the scrubbing.

"The hell were you doing in my room?"

Nate caught his elbow against the edge of the counter as he started. "Christ, Gunn." Dropping the sponge in favor of nursing his stinging arm, Nate turned. "Some warning—"

The complaint died unvoiced.

Gunn was angry. No, furious. His wiry body tensed beneath his habitual bomber jacket, and his mouth was a sour line. He was ready to fight, even with the two shopping bags dangling from one hand.

"Answer the question."

"The question?"

Gunn slammed his hand down on the counter with enough force to rattle the coffee cup cemetery. "You went into my room."

"I didn't go in! I didn't even know it was your room– I just wanted to see behind the door," Nate protested. "Your opinion of your decorating's way overrated if you think anyone would want to enter that black hole. Seriously, it's like the void."

Gunn gave him a sharp glare. He dropped the shopping bags with a glassy clink and made for the room.

Using the counter edge to steady himself, Nate reached over to turn the tap off. "Careful. That sounded breakable."

"You want to talk 'careful,' how about not messing with a carefully warded haven? I got curses in here that could fuck you up for centuries." Gunn's voice sounded vigorously from within the room, accompanied by the crisp rattle of padlocks being checked.

Nate leaned against the doorway. *Gunn's messing with me. Has to be.* The reminder that he barely grasped the world he now inhabited was not welcome. "What was growing in your sink could fuck up someone's intestinal systems for just as long. Are you actively trying to attract roaches?"

"Wards are good enough to keep 'em out. Works on rats too— even New Camden rats, and that's saying something." Evidently satisfied that Nate had not looted his bedroom, Gunn reappeared in the bedroom doorway. He nodded to the bags at Nate's feet. "Beer's mine. Rest is yours. Hope you're not vegetarian."

The first bag was evidently from the Goodwill, a pair of cargo pants, a sweatshirt, and other clothing items. The second was immediately more interesting. Gunn's six-pack of beer and a brown paper bag containing a chicken and avocado sub on generously sliced bread. Nate's stomach instantly decided it was ravenous. "Yeah? This looks great."

"Deli by the station. They do coffee, too."

"Mmm."

Gunn smirked at him. "I was gonna bring you back some, but your snooping forestalled that. Seriously, don't mess with my stuff."

"Warhahunh." Nate swallowed his mouthful of sandwich and tried again. "Wasn't snooping. What's with your lack of a front door?"

"Lack?"

"Yeah. How'd you even get in here?"

Gunn dumped the six-pack down on the table and twisted a bottle free. "I don't need to ward myself out of my apartment."

"But there's no door—" Nate looked toward the empty wall with suspicion.

Gunn smirked at him. "No one sees the door unless I want them to."

Nate's stomach lurched uncomfortably. "What if I want to leave?"

"Sucks for you."

"You're keeping me prisoner? Isn't that the opposite of what the police should do?"

"When we do it, it's 'protection.'" Gunn reached for a bottle opener concealed amongst the mess on the table and ripped the lid off his beer. "Also, I'm not a very good policeman."

"You? I'm—" Nate came to an abrupt pause.

Gunn raised an eyebrow at him. "You're what?"

Nate set the sandwich down and bolted for the bathroom.

Beer in hand, Gunn watched from the doorway. "I don't mind you taking over my tub, but I warn you, I'm gonna want the can back."

Nate couldn't even muster a proper glare. "I know you're not even slightly sympathetic, but do you have to watch me puke?"

"Getting my money's worth. That sandwich was two bucks. If you're not going to finish it—"

"I am."

"You took two bites and threw up."

Nate's stomach reeled just thinking about the sandwich. "I'm eating it."

"Sure you are. Get back in the tub, and I'll turn the hose on you. You'll feel better."

"I'm not a plant, Gunn. I haven't eaten in days. I need to...work up to it."

"I'll get you some compost when I head out later."

Nate looked away from the toilet. "Later?"

Gunn wandered back into the lounge. "Gimme a break. We're all pulling double-duty."

His stomach still heaved, but Nate thought he was out of immediate danger. He leaned back against the bathroom wall, raising his voice to be heard. "What do you mean double-duty?"

"We can't all laze around like queens." Gunn's reply was muffled, and when he next stuck his head in the doorway, he was munching on Nate's sub. "Not with the largest undead emergency in history going down."

"That's my sand— The largest what?"

"Yeah," Gunn took another deliberate bite of the thick crust, wiping a smear of dressing from his mouth. "Turns out some hapless moron destroyed Saltaire's wards. Normally I would be all for this. If anyone deserves a hearty helping of aggravation in his afterlife, it's him. Sadly, every vampire in the city decided to add to my schadenfreude. For all his numerous faults, Saltaire is good at what he does. What he does is terrify the rest of them into behaving. He's old, powerful, and until three days ago, no one knew where he slept. Now we got alliances forming, turf wars being waged, and a new missing person every time we blink. I took out twenty plus creepers and a vampire queen single-handed last night, and we're no nearer a solution."

Nate felt sick all over again. "Violence *isn't* the answer?"

"Don't get smart. Saltaire's repaired his wards, but now that they know they can be broken, our vampires will be asking themselves how. If I'd been involved, I'd be hoping to hell no one realized I wasn't dead."

Nate's hand tightened over the remaining vine around his neck. "That's a very specific hypothetical."

"Isn't it?" Gunn's grin displayed wolfish teeth. "Far as I know, no one knows you survived the rite but you, me, and Research. I want to keep it that way."

Nate looked down at the scars on his chest. In the short time he'd been awake, they'd continued to fade. Most were barely visible, only the edge of the stake protruding above his skin. But he didn't need scars to remember watching Peter carve his skin.

Peter didn't know that Nate survived.

"What if he tries the rite with Ben—"

"That's Hawick's lookout. Kid didn't go into this business blindly. For Saltaire to turn him at all, he's got to have something. The survival instinct you lack, perhaps."

"Low blow." Nate had only died *once*.

"Yeah." Gunn stuffed the remains of the sandwich in his mouth. "I'm gonna catch up on some shut-eye. I don't care what you do, but keep it quiet."

It was very quiet. Even the sound of the cars on the street outside seemed muffled. Nate rinsed his mouth with the cloudy water from the bathroom sink. His stomach no longer heaved, but he felt weak, his skin clammy. A flicker of white pulled his attention to the mirror. Nate started. *I'm going to give myself a complex.* This was the second time he'd jumped at his own reflection.

Nate ran his fingers over his face. Even his advanced state of stubble didn't offset his extreme pallor. Beyond that, the face in the mirror still looked like him. Not "inhuman" or "dead" or "monster."

Then again, Hunter had looked normal too.

Nate tilted his chin up, trying to get a better look at the vine at his neck. In contrast to the light growth he'd pulled off his chest, the roots stretching over his skin were thick. Nate discovered that it hurt if he poked at it.

Was Gunn on to something? Having remembered how he got the injury, Nate no longer wanted to pull the ivy away. Instead, he retrieved the bag of goodwill clothing. *First step to feeling like me? Looking like me.*

Washing himself from the sink reminded Nate of the winter the pipes froze solid, and the entire family had to take baths in the copper tub Pa kept in the barn. "It was my grandfather's wedding gift to my parents," he'd explained. "A family heirloom."

Nate had nudged Ethan. "If it's in the barn, it's an heirloom; if it's in our rooms, it's junk."

Pa heard and relegated Nate to bathing last, when the water was already cloudy and lukewarm. He'd learned to wash quickly.

Trusting that the officer provided for himself where it counted, Nate investigated the bathroom cabinet and was rewarded with shaving gel and an electric razor. The goodwill clothes smelled like mothballs, but Nate was glad just to be out of his jeans. Cargo pants might be dated, but Gunn had estimated his sizes accurately. With the belt and a clean T-shirt hiding the stake, Nate felt more himself than he had in days. He could even muster a smile at his reflection.

The smile faded as he prowled the apartment. The park was harder to shake off on the inside. Remembering that he'd had designs on the sink, Nate returned to find that murky water had pooled at the base, the sink clogged with bits and pieces better left unidentified. Nate rolled up the T-shirt sleeves. *Challenge, distraction, it was all the same.*

* ~ * ~ *

"Hey, Nate. You want some fertilizer to go with your com—" Gunn emerged from his room, finger combing his shaggy hair into some semblance of order, only to come to a halt. "What the triple-fuck have you done to my apartment?"

Nate sat up on his heels. "You hardly recognize the place, right?"

The living room looked pretty good, if he did say so himself. The floor could use a more thorough scrubbing, but he'd swept up the ash and dirt, put all the bottles in orderly rows next to the newspaper, and shifted some of the dirt from the bath into a crate to make a home for some of the vines. The ivy definitely approved. Nate had positioned it so it caught the last of the midafternoon sun, streaming through the apartment's no longer as grimy windows.

Gunn looked wordlessly from the ivy to the ordered bottles. "You have no idea how hard finding a place this bad was, and you're ruining it."

"Ruining it? You could explode a bomb in here and the place would look better."

"My point exactly. Damnit— If you needed a coping mechanism that badly, I'd have given you the beer. This?" Gunn waved his hands at the stack of crisply folded newspaper. "This crosses the line."

Nate used the back of the sofa to lever himself to his feet. "Who's coping?"

"Dying's hard, but you're hardly the first to do it." Gunn returned to his room. His voice came back through the door, accompanied by the metallic click of a case unlocking. "Take a tip from an old hand. Make peace with yourself as quickly as possible and get on with stuff. Softening the blow never works out well. Sooner or later, you got to come to grips with the stone-cold truth—you were a stone-cold corpse. Sucks, but you don't want to take it out on me."

Nate glanced around the apartment. *He can't be serious.* "You're telling me you like living like this?" he asked, standing on the threshold of Gunn's room.

The officer knelt before one of the larger cases. It held a collection of firearms, knives, and—was that a *mace?* In stark contrast to the rest of the apartment, the weapons gleamed. "I'm not here to enjoy myself. I got work to do." Gunn secreted the weapons on his person with the ease of long practice. "Work that can't be done by someone who is comfortable. Ponder that and leave the kitchen alone."

Nate watched Gunn weigh the mace and replace it in the case. "You live in an apartment one phone call away from getting condemned because you're worried about going soft?"

"One of the reasons."

"Suddenly I feel like I'm not the person with the most issues in this apartment."

"Save the flattery. You're not my type." Having armed himself, Gunn relocked the case and stood. He didn't look that different from when he'd first emerged from the room, but somehow he radiated purpose. Was that simply Nate's knowledge of what the loose-fitting bomber concealed, or the sunset slowly fading in the window behind him? "That sweatshirt I bought you? Put it on."

Nate retrieved the garment from the bathroom. "It's a little tight. Granted, better than catching a cold but—" Sweatshirt sleeves pulled up to his forearms, Nate stepped back into the lounge. "What the hell is wrong with me? I can't believe I fell for that."

The hall was empty. Gunn was gone and with him, the door.

Nate had already started tidying the kitchen, but now he cleaned it out of spite. He might have done it regardless. Seeing the effect his efforts had on the small space gave him a feeling of control over his circumstances. That it would annoy Gunn was only the icing on the cake. *Or maybe*—Nate wrestled with a particularly nasty burnt-on glob on the frying pan—*maybe Gunn's right. This is a coping mechanism.* The thought was not comfortable. Now he had to avoid thinking about the officer in addition to his own death, and Nate redoubled his efforts.

A few hours later, Nate discovered he had bigger problems.

It started with the niggling suspicion that there was someone in the apartment. Nate snorted as he first noticed it. "You can come in. The cleanliness won't hurt you."

There was no surly comment in reply. Nate wiped his hands on his cargo pants and went into the living room. "Gunn?"

No one there and no sound of movement from the other rooms. Nate hesitated. *Clearly imagination...* But some instinct kept him where he was.

There was a scratching sound. It sounded like claws raking over stone, searching for weakness. Nate's eyes locked on the wall. Gunn's words replayed in his head. *Works on rats too—even New Camden rats.* He'd dismissed Aki's accounts as pure exaggeration, but suddenly Nate was no longer sure...

An outline flickered onto the wall suddenly. A nondescript door, complete with security chain, yellowed paper detailing the building's emergency exits. As Nate watched, it flickered in and out of being there, gaining permanence the longer the thing scratched—

Chipping away at the wards? Nate watched, unable to move. Only when the door creaked with the pressure of something pressing against it from the outside could Nate back away.

God. What is that thing? It sounded like a wild animal—werewolf? Vampires were supposed to deter them, but if the city's population of vampires were fighting each other…or worse, what if it *was* a New Camden rat?

His gaze fell on the door to Gunn's room and hastily Nate flung the door open. *Please work.* If Gunn thought the disruption of the wards was just Nate messing with him—

There was a crunching sound behind him as the lock gave. Hand still on the door handle to Gunn's room, Nate turned.

The door that swung open looked only slightly more battered than the surrounding hallway. Nate didn't have the chance to appreciate his first view of Gunn's apartment door, however. The figure glowering at him from the doorway demanded his attention.

"I had hoped I would not have to speak with you again," Saltaire said. The vampire seemed to fill the entire doorway, the night's shadows lending him extra height and breadth.

Nate swallowed. He'd have taken the werewolf any day. "I'd have liked that, too."

"There's no time to waste on inanities. Come." Saltaire's tone was imperious. Not cruel, but so arrogant it made no difference. And layered through it, that irresistible note that made anything but obedience an impossibility.

Nate went.

Chapter Fourteen

The car waiting at the end of the block was sleek, black, and anonymous, but Nate recognized it as the car that had taken away the guests at the anniversary dinner. His heart sank. *Saltaire planned this?* Being alone with a vampire was bad enough, but a vampire with a plan...

Nate glanced down the deserted street. *Run? It's stupid enough it might work.*

As if sensing Nate's thoughts, Saltaire looked over his shoulder with a sharp glare. "Get in."

Only when the seat belt clicked shut around him in the back seat of the car could Nate think again. By then, the motor purred expensively. Saltaire nodded to the driver, and the car pulled out onto the street.

Nate's fingers closed around the seat belt. Saltaire's silent presence gave the voluminous backseat a claustrophobic feeling. He watched the vampire out of the corner of his eye.

Saltaire sat still and silent, one hand resting on his knee. *I guess a vampire wouldn't need a seat belt.* Nate grimaced. Of all the things to think of, his mind focused on that?

"The time for any levity has long passed." Saltaire looked past Nate to the car's tinted windows. "Look on the consequences of your reckless impulse."

Like I have a choice. Any relief from not having to look at Saltaire's grim form quickly dissipated with what Nate saw beyond the window.

New Camden was many things—loud, frustrating, bewitching, contentious, contradictory—but it was never quiet. Never empty. Never like this.

"What's happened? Where is everyone?" Without the flicker of the gaudy neon signage, downtown was unnaturally dark. Even with the car between himself and the night, Nate still fought a shiver.

"The citywide curfew was instigated two nights ago, when the quarrels of our kind claimed their first human casualties."

Broken glass glittered like teeth in a broken storefront. Nate shivered. "Deaths? How many?"

"Too many. De Silver got his wish for chaos, though for what purpose remains unclear." Nate felt Saltaire's gaze and turned to meet his stare. "What is his plan?"

"I don't know."

"And yet you helped him."

The seat belt cut into Nate's skin as his hands closed around it in fists. "I had as much choice in that as I did getting into this car!"

Saltaire's lip curled. "You are weak-willed enough that your resistance would be negligible."

Weak-willed—is he seriously blaming me for not being able to resist his power?

Sirens sounded nearby, the call immediately taken up across the city. *Someone else in trouble.* Nate turned to look out the window again. *That my fault too?*

The car halted before an ornate metal gate, twice as tall as Nate and with far more wrought iron flourishes. Nate wrapped his arms around himself and watched as Saltaire leaned into the open driver's window.

"You will return home, mindful of your safety. When you have seen to your protection, you will sleep. You will forget driving me tonight. You will forget our passenger."

Nate let out a breath, casually pressing the SOS button on his wristband. A quick glance down did not reassure. *Out of battery?* Just his luck. Dying twice was serious overkill. "You know—"

"Follow me."

And no one ever saw me again.

The gates were so heavy they left thick hollows in the ground where they rested. Saltaire lifted them without effort, revealing rows of gravestones. They were old, the slabs that covered the graves cracked and the names on the stones weatherworn and faded. Moss grew on them, and Nate could hear the gentle swish of leaves in the wind somewhere close. That made him feel slightly better, even when Saltaire walked into a path of pitch shadow.

Nate stumbled. *Stairs?* "A little warning," he muttered. The urge to follow the vampire was insistent, even in the shadow, and Nate felt for the next step with his foot.

"Your delay affords you no advantage. Hurry."

"Bite me." Unsteadily Nate took a blind step forward. Then a second. The stairs were uneven, the stones sunk with age or worn through years of use. “We can’t all see in the dark.”

Saltaire was silent until Nate reached the top of the stairs. “He reacts as though he might be hurt by falling, and his eyes are blinkered by the dark.”

Hunter’s reply came from beyond Saltaire. “Curious. Could it be that he is not dead?”

“He is of no use to a necromancer alive.”

“He is dead.” The third voice was savage in its insistence, thick with grief. “I saw him. I know.”

Ben. Nate felt a stabbing pain shoot through him. *So I can still feel. Good to know.* Pulled onward by Saltaire’s command, he joined the vampires. They stood beneath a streetlight that, judging from its ornate metal frills, had been installed as part of the cemetery’s original trappings. Through its steady glow, Nate could see a wide paved courtyard, edged by vaults and tombs.

And Ben.

Instinct had warned Nate thinking about Ben would be too painful. Just the memory of Ben kneeling beside him in the park hurt worse than his own death. But now, without any words spoken, Nate felt a compulsion stronger than Saltaire’s control. He couldn’t look away.

It was everything he’d been afraid of. Ben had shut down entirely. Paler than either of his companions, his eyes were shot through with red and his jaw unnaturally set. His expression wasn’t emotionless. It was that of someone who’d had every shred of feeling forcibly wrung from him.

Nate took an involuntary step toward him. "Jesus, Ben—"

"Stay away from me."

Nate stumbled. A physical blow could not have hurt any more than those four words.

"Was it necessary to bring this...travesty here?" Ben didn't look at Nate but at Saltaire.

"De Silver's discarded tool is our best chance of finding him." Saltaire stood at the end of the circle of light as though he commanded far more than the three before him. "And we must find him."

"He killed the others before he used them," Hunter agreed. "They told us nothing. That Peter tried to prevent Nate rising—"

"Means that he feared what would happen if he did." Ben's expression contorted between grief and repulsion. He struggled, shutting his eyes and swallowing. When he met Nate's gaze, his expression was clear. "Do what you must."

Nate felt cold throughout. *Ben's making himself like Saltaire—he's giving up!*

"Look at me, Nate." The order registered resentfully, even as Nate obediently raised his head. Had the horror he felt for Ben robbed Hunter of his usual persuasiveness? "Answer my questions truthfully, holding nothing back. What is Peter's object?"

"Ben should have been at the park to see me die. Peter was looking forward to it." Hearing his voice answer with sentences he hadn't thought of was chilling. Nate fought to interpose his own words. "Apart from that, he didn't share specifics. I heard a lot about how Saltaire never appreciated him, not a lot about his future plans."

"Revenge then." Hunter eyed Saltaire. "Perhaps you should have given de Silver the raise he wanted?"

Saltaire's facial muscles tightened. "He didn't ask for a raise. He asked to be turned."

Ben and Hunter glanced at him sharply.

The elder vampire carefully folded his coat over a nearby gravestone and began to roll up his sleeves. "I consider my refusal perfectly justified. Given how de Silver has misused the power of a necromancer, he is the last person to be trusted with compulsion. No, my policy is firm."

This is not a board meeting! Nate watched Ben, anxious for any sign that he found Saltaire's statement alarming. Instead, he saw something even more chilling. Ben's hand was on his hip, as if it rested on a hilt that wasn't there. It was a gesture that Nate remembered well. *That's how Saltaire stood at the house.* There was only one reason Ben might have adopted a habit that ended hundreds of years before he was born. *How deeply is Saltaire controlling him? Is there anything of Ben left in there—*

He sneezed.

All three vampires regarded him sharply.

"...excuse me." Nate wiped his nose on the back of his sweatshirt. The vampires still stared at him. Nate glared back. *What? It's not as if Saltaire gave me time to pack!*

"In cases of recent death, the body remembers," Saltaire said at last. "It's an echo."

"It was three days ago," Ben said. "That's not recent." He stood still, his body tensed, and he stared at Nate with an intensity that kept

Nate locked in place. “He’s shivering. He couldn’t tell his body to do that.”

“You said yourself.” Hunter’s tone was sympathetic. “You found him dead.” He turned back to Nate with a businesslike tone. “Nathan, that sweatshirt does nothing for you. Take it off.”

The cold registered before Hunter’s words did. *So much for Hunter losing his edge!* Nate dropped the sweatshirt to the paved courtyard. *It’s not enough being alone in a cemetery with three vampires, I have to be shirtless, too*

Hunter whistled. “His heart!” He looked over at Ben. “No wonder you said he wouldn’t walk.”

Nate closed his fingers over the last knob of the still-protruding stake. “It doesn’t hurt,” he said. “It’s just there.”

Ben gulped hastily and turned his back.

Nate took his hand away. He’d thought waking up dead was bad, but discovering he now made people actively nauseous? *I have got to stop thinking that things can’t get worse because they keep getting worse.*

“Strange.” At least Hunter didn’t seem in danger of losing his lunch, or whatever the vampire equivalent was. Nate took a step back as Hunter’s cold fingers brushed his chest. “He’s healed. You can see where the cuts were but not enough to identify them.”

“De Silver did not want to leave any traces of his work,” Saltaire decided.

“But to heal dead flesh…” Ben shook his head. “It doesn’t make sense.”

“He graduated with honors,” Saltaire told him. “Got a perfect score on his employee aptitude test."

Hunter's mouth twitched. "That should have been the first warning sign. Still, you're right. We're not dealing with a garden-variety necromancer here."

Nate choked. "Sorry," he said. "I just. I'm living in a world where there is such a thing as a garden-variety necromancer."

The three vampires regarded him in silence. Hunter's generous mouth smirked, Saltaire scowled, and Ben—

Ben looked like his internal narrator was struggling. "You're not. Living."

"You'd think I'd remember that. I mean, the dying. Left an impression." Nate's hand went automatically to his neck. He felt the rough knot of scar tissue as he swallowed, but the vine seemed to have deserted him. *Just as well. This is weird enough.* "I'm wasting time. Let's get on with this."

None of the vampires moved.

"You're offering to help?" Hunter tilted his head.

"You want to stop Peter, right?" Nate put his hands in the pocket of his jeans and tried to project a calm he didn't feel. "So do I."

"Looks like something can be said for my policy." Hunter glanced at Saltaire. "Since we all seem to be in agreement...?"

Saltaire inclined his head.

Hunter wiped the knife he held on a handkerchief. "Hold your hand out, Nathan. Palm up."

"What are you doing to him?" Ben's question was sharp. Nate stared at him, hand already outstretched.

"Finding out exactly what Peter was attempting—" Hunter was

interrupted.

"He is dead, Bennet. It doesn't matter what Hunter does to him." Saltaire paused, bringing the full weight of his stare to rest on Ben. "Your emotional attachment clouds your perception. What you see here is nothing, a mere shadow." He nodded. "Hunter, proceed."

"Ow!" Nate jerked his hand back too late. Hunter had pressed the knife into his palm, leaving a red mark.

"Second thoughts?" Hunter wiped the knife clean again.

"Warn me next time." Nate watched, fascinated despite himself, as the blood oozed upward toward his wrist.

Hunter's smile was faint. "Be as you were."

"Just what exactly—tickles!" And that wasn't all. Either vampires had the edge on necromancers in the magic department, or seduction wasn't the only thing Hunter excelled at. Red lines now crept over his skin, settling into a pattern Nate had last seen carved into his skin as he died. Nate bit his lip and dug his hands into his pockets in an effort not to claw at his chest. *Not good. So not good.*

Hunter waved a languid hand toward Nate. "Ben, you were the only one to see him. Does this look accurate?"

Ben drew a deep breath before joining Hunter at the circle. Like Nate, he had buried his hands deep within his pockets. He gave Nate's chest a careful examination then nodded. "As far as I can tell," he said. "I was distracted at the time."

Distracted? "Sorry my death was so inconvenient."

Ben's mouth tightened. "You know that's not what I meant."

"Don't engage with the shadow, Bennet." Saltaire watched the proceedings from the edge of the circle. He paused often to look beyond them, into the dark. "What can you read, Hunter?"

"It's complex." Hunter's cold fingers probed the phantom wounds. It didn't hurt, but Nate's brain told him that it should. He was very glad when Hunter finally left off his examination, the wounds fading back to healing tissue. "I'd need a reference book to identify the spell for sure, but it looks like an equilibrium principle, wound with a substitution rite."

Nate wrapped his arms around himself. "Substitution?"

Ben frowned. "Why would Peter want to use Nate in a substitution spell aimed at us?"

"He's tried the direct route and failed." Hunter shrugged. "Substitutions aren't only permanent swaps like changelings. He may have intended Nate to take your place as the intended target in a spell, or increase the force of a command to bring you to the park."

Nate shifted. "Are you saying Peter wanted to use me as a living voodoo doll? Because needle play is extra."

Hunter smiled. "I will miss your unique way of looking at things, Nathan."

"Stop flirting with the shadow, Hunter." Saltaire folded his arms meaningfully. "You waste valuable time. From what you've derived, de Silver was in the final stages of a complicated ritual when he was forced to cut—"

"My neck."

"—things short." Saltaire glared at Nate before turning back to Hunter and Ben. "That is an open link. As Nathan demonstrated at the townhouse, that link goes both ways."

Nate paused. *Is this punishment for breaking the wards?*

Ben was very still. "You think that we can use Nate—"

"Nate's shade. He's dead, Ben." Hunter placed his hand on Ben's shoulder. "I know it's hard, but this way, Nate's death can be his revenge."

Death. I am starting to get very sick of that word. "Some narrative exposition for the audience, please?"

Ben's choked laugh was unexpected. "The link goes two ways. Meaning that we have an unparalleled opportunity to strike Peter—but it means destroying you."

"What's left of him," Hunter added quickly.

"Without the bond between you and Peter, you'll probably dissipate," Ben said. "Disappear. This bond is the source of the energy holding you together."

"Once wasn't enough. I have to die again?" That really did not seem fair.

Ben bit his lip, pale eyes tracing Nate's face. "There's something about this that isn't right. The way he's acting. You've noticed it, haven't you? He's lucid, reacting to the things we say."

Hunter patted his shoulder. "A skilled necromancer can trap the soul within the body indefinitely. In the case of a master, the victim might not even be aware he's dead."

"Even if I'd missed the actual dying part, I'm pretty sure I'd know." Nate shivered. "You only mention it every other second."

"You see?" Ben said. "He has successfully processed the events of the park. The physical reactions, the healing—"

"Peter was the youngest ever candidate to pass the Arcane Teachings exam," Hunter cautioned. "If anyone could pull off healing dead tissue—"

"When would he have had the chance?" Ben looked to Saltaire. "Peter was long gone when I left the park, and I left Gunn with Nate."

Saltaire shifted impatiently. "The place I found him had Gunn's traces all over it."

"That's what I mean! Gunn's not going to miss a necromancer paying him a house call!" Ben waved his hand toward Nate. "What if you're wrong and Nate isn't being sustained by magic leeched from Peter?"

Nate stared. Ben was pale still, and there was a sharpness to his voice that stopped it from being calm, but there was emotion in his eyes that hadn't been there earlier. *That's—for me?*

Saltaire glanced at Nate and then dismissed him with a shake of his head. "You're clutching at straws, Bennet. If he possessed any talent capable of withstanding de Silver, we would have sensed it."

"Godfrey said he had latent talent," Ben persisted. "Magic can take many forms. Some types are triggered by trauma. What if Nate's death unlocked his own power? It would explain why he's walking after Peter's precautions—"

Saltaire shook his head. "The chances of that are one in a million. No, de Silver chose Nathan because of your bond, and through Nathan we have a chance to strike at him. Hunter—"

"You can't do the rite now!" Ben planted himself before Saltaire. Nate couldn't see his face, but he held himself up despite the older vampire's gravity. "You could be killing an innocent person!"

Nate felt his heart speed up. Hearing the urgency in Ben's voice alerted him to his own peril.

"And every moment we delay affords de Silver time to gain more victims." Saltaire picked up a long, thin object placed on the ground with Hunter's supplies. It was curved, and it was only the way that Saltaire held it, ready to use, that enabled Nate to recognize it as the blade he'd wielded at the mansion. "There is a quick way to end this. Emeric."

The hand on Nate's neck was a surprise. He hadn't noticed Hunter stand behind him. "I am sorry it had to end this way, Nathan." Hunter's fingers stroked Nate's neck, gently, even as he caught the sword Saltaire threw him.

"Hunter, stop." Ben took a deep breath, turning back to Saltaire. "Listen to me. This is wrong, and you know it. If Nate survived Peter's attack—"

Saltaire's hand came down on Ben's shoulder like a vice. "Do not presume to order me. You will listen, Bennet. And you will watch." Saltaire motioned toward Nate and Hunter, and Ben clumsily wheeled around, like a marionette with tangled strings. "Look deeply. This is what comes of allowing oneself to form foolish bonds."

"No—" Ben had to force the word out, but he wasn't allowed more than that.

"You will not interfere," Saltaire ordered.

This is it. Dying the first time, when he hadn't known what was happening until it was too late, was easier. This time, Nate felt himself numb with fear.

Fear of what? There is a lot worse out there than Gunn's bathroom! And if Peter can't hurt anyone else, it's worth it right?

It did not feel worth it.

"You're sure this will stop Peter?"

"You're not simply stopping Peter," Hunter assured him. "You're saving lives, Nathan."

Saving lives? Nate got off on helping people. This should be his ultimate dream, right? Riding through the empty city in Saltaire's car, Nate would have done anything to put things back to normal. Now that he had the chance, why did he hesitate?

As if on cue, a siren whined in the distance.

Nate winced. *Okay, universe. You've made your point.* He bit his lip, looking back to Ben. Nate was more interested in people than statistics, but Ben was a bigger picture person, he was sure of it. "Can't argue with saving lives, right?"

Ben flinched.

The effects of three days of grief were vivid in his extreme gauntness and sickly pallor. Nate took a step toward him, needing to reassure him.

Hunter stopped him with a warning hand on his arm. "You'd just make this harder than it has to be."

As if there's any way this won't hit him hard. Anger hit Nate suddenly. How was it fair that Ben who felt things so deeply was going to feel more pain than any one person should? *It will crush him.*

"Why do you delay?" Saltaire sounded impatient. *Typical.* Ben could hope for no understanding there. Saltaire would keep him close, unwilling to risk him forming another unwelcome attachment and Ben...

Would Ben even try to fight it? If following Saltaire into mindless obedience could end his grief—

Nate felt a cool trickle of fear across his shoulder blades. *Don't think that! He has Hunter!*

"I think we can allow Nate a minute to make his peace with death." Hunter sounded extremely unbothered. *That's not going to win him any points with Ben!*

Killing me is not going to win him points with Ben. Nate caught his breath. In three days, Hunter had not made the slightest impact on Ben's grief. *Could that mean—?*

Nate's head snapped up to stare at him.

Ben pressed a hand across his mouth. He sagged against an invisible barrier, the long hair of his fringe hiding his eyes. *Fighting emotion.* Emotion that hadn't been there before he'd seen Nate. *If I die that part of Ben goes too.*

After that, it was easy. They'd covered this in training. Knee to groin, twist hand. When Hunter dropped the sword, Nate kicked it as hard as he could. It slid through the barrier, sliding across the smooth stones to vanish in the shadows.

Not covered in training: Hunter's hand locking in the hair at the base of Nate's skull and forcing his head down so his neck was exposed and Nate couldn't pull himself free. "Points for trying. But a vampire's not so easily disarmed." His voice had a thickness Nate recognized as fangs.

"He doesn't want to die!" Ben gasped his words, forced them out against the pressure of Saltaire's icy displeasure. "If you kill him now, it's murder!"

Hunter didn't reply, but Nate felt the fingers in his hair relax slightly. Affection for Ben?

"It is your duty, Hunter." Saltaire's command was firm.

It was nice while it lasted—

Nate felt Hunter's shrug, then the tightening of his fingers. He tensed, trying not to remember the woman in the park, but it was too late. He could already see what it would look like as Hunter tore his throat out—

The gunshot was entirely unexpected.

Nate was on the stones, knees stinging in protest of the shock landing, head ringing with the sound before he realized what he'd heard.

Saltaire was poised to fight, and Ben whirled about to face this new threat. Hunter's mouth twisted, and Nate, looking up at the vampire, got a very thorough view of his fangs as he cradled the hand that had held Nate against his chest. "Why waste words when you can waste bullets, Isaiah?"

The reply came from above one of the neighboring crypts. "I skinned you. Not a wasted bullet in my books."

Gunn! Nate cautiously tipped himself forward onto his knees, getting ready to move. *Gunn won't let Saltaire kill me—if only because I'm more annoying alive.* That should not have been reassuring.

"What are you doing here?" Saltaire demanded.

"You thought I wouldn't notice you crashing through my wards with the subtlety of a goddamn bulldozer? Thanks for fucking up my apartment, by the way. Really appreciated." Gunn dropped out of the shadows to land heavily on the stone of the courtyard. He rested his handgun on his shoulder, and his teeth glittered in the night as he grinned. “A proper family gathering. Doesn’t it just take you back?”

“Your timing, as ever, leaves much to be desired.” Saltaire had drawn himself up with the dignity of age.

“Really? ’Cause I think I arrived just in time to be witness to your killing of an innocent.” Nate watched with dismay as Gunn lowered his gun to pull a cigarette from his pocket. The officer obviously felt at ease in the cemetery, but Nate was only too conscious that he was still within Hunter’s reach. “Auckland Protocol’s only good so long as you don’t kill the living.”

Saltaire snorted. “He hardly qualifies as innocent.”

Dracula has a point. “You knew I was alive this entire time?” Gunn was more interested in lighting the cigarette than denying Nate’s accusation, and Nate balled his hands into fists. “And you let me think I was dead?”

Gunn exhaled smoke. “I never said you were dead. Just that you had to get over being dead.”

“But—”

“I’m a jerk, Nate. If you haven’t figured that out by now—” Gunn shrugged.

“Gunn confirms it!” Ben turned quickly to Saltaire. *Compulsion not in effect when Hunter’s not trying to kill me?* “Nate did not survive via Peter’s magic—”

Saltaire shouldered past Ben, marching toward Gunn. “All that confirms is that he is not human, and thus not protected by the Protocol.”

“Doesn’t make him fair game for your hunt.” Nate could think of nothing worse than having Saltaire up close and personal, but Gunn seemed to relish it. He stood taller, a smirk playing on his lips as he made his argument. "Kid's been under my observation since he woke. Only danger he poses is to dust bunnies and my patience. Class Two, at his very worst. That means he falls under the mutual coexistence clause."

"That's your game?" There was something odd in Hunter's tone. "City Hall's not going to care about the fine print with a necromancer on the loose."

"They will if it gives them the leeway to punish those responsible for the necromancer." Gunn's glance to Hunter was unhurried.

That's it—the thing that's off about this whole situation. Nate got to his feet. *No one here is surprised by any of this.* Gunn's calculated insolence, Saltaire's contained fury, Hunter's studied detachment, even Ben, listening intently. *This argument's been had before.*

"You won't sway us with idle threats." Saltaire loomed. "I know the Council personally. They are grateful for our work keeping the city safe."

Gunn snorted, shaking the ash from his cigarette. "Yeah, they're grateful while you're *there.* Don't have much choice, do they? But afterward they wonder... And you have an awful lot of deaths to explain. I'm sure the Council is going to enjoy hearing why the best defense the city has gave its biggest threat a steady paycheck—"

Saltaire reached across and snatched the cigarette from Gunn. He stamped it out on the paving stones deliberately. "You do not threaten me, Isaiah. I need explain to no one. The loss of one life is negligible, when compared to saving dozens more."

Without his cigarette, Gunn's fingers twitched in the night air, momentarily at a loss. Shoulders tensed, Gunn settled on toying with the pistol he still held. "Wanna put that to the test? Let's find out how the Council feels about sacrificing civilians for the greater good."

"Just whose side are you on here?" Suddenly, Nate was not feeling very safe.

"The only side he's interested in. His." Ben's low murmur caught Nate's attention. Ben stood, arms folded, beside the circle. Nate hadn't heard him move, but seeing that the vampire had positioned himself to block Gunn's line of fire at Nate made him feel warm—then immediately worried.

Is it going to come to that?

"You know, Isaiah—"

"Stop fucking calling me that, *Emeric*."

"*Isaiah*. There is a third option." Gunn scowled, but Hunter did not let that deter him from slinking closer, or from laying a hand on Gunn's arm. He stood on the other side of the officer from Saltaire and looked across the courtyard to a monument that fell just within the circle of light. "It has been long since we hunted together."

"For good reason." Gunn shook him off. "I don't share your nostalgia for the past."

"But you do want to find the necromancer."

Saltaire had turned to look where Hunter had. Something in his posture relented. "You suggest we combine forces?"

"Our personal vendettas aside, we have a vested interest in ending the necromancer," Hunter said, voice low and persuasive. "I think—"

Nate didn't hear what he thought. His eyes had fallen on the monument that had caught Hunter's attention.

It was pure sentimentality, an angel with her head bent in earnest prayer, one hand resting on the head of the lamb that stood at her feet. Rainwater had left trails stretching from her empty eyes to her chin so that it really looked like she'd been crying, but the rest of her stone form was mottled with the inevitable New Camden grime. The grave had not been totally neglected. It was kept clean of the ivy that wound around nearby tombs, and the weeds had been pulled out, leaving the dedication readable, even in the dark.

Nate felt dizzy.

Isaiah Gunn

1910-1936

Sorely Missed.

Chapter Fifteen

The sirens wailed nearer. They'd been growing steadily more insistent. Now they were unbearable. Nate gritted his teeth. It wasn't bad enough he didn't know what he was, whose side anyone was on or even what was going on. *No, there had to be fucking sirens, too.*

"Sounds important," Hunter observed, as though the high-pitched noise didn't stab into his skull with every passing second. "Perhaps you should go do your job, Isaiah."

Gunn didn't move. "And risk Saltaire declaring martial law the moment my back is turned? No, my job is here."

Saltaire's opinion of the barb did not show on his face. "If you have a better means of finding de Silver than using Nathan, I would like to hear it. Otherwise, I think the fact there was interaction between de Silver and this" —Saltaire cast for a suitable word— "*man* before his death disqualifies him as an innocent party."

Nate raised an eyebrow. *Man? I've been promoted.*

"We introduced them," Ben said with sudden fierceness. "At the house party."

The glance Saltaire gave him was a rebuke. "Circumstantial. No one would consider that—"

"I sent de Silver to Nate on business." Hunter leaned back against Gunn's memorial. "Naturally, the fact I had no idea he was the necromancer at the time won't stop Isaiah from making all the capital he can of that." His hand came to rest atop the lamb's head.

Nate winced.

Gunn, patting his pockets for a cigarette that wasn't there, noticed. He glanced down. "Hate that fucking lamb," he said conversationally. "I'd destroy it if I didn't think they'd replace it with something worse."

"Cherubs," Hunter said immediately. "With round cheeks and little wings. Very touching."

"Next fucking leave I get, I'm going to Romania and pissing on yours—"

Hunter grinned. "You'll never find it."

"What are you?" Nate knew drawing attention to himself was a mistake, but he couldn't hold back the question. "I thought—" He stopped. Ben had warned him that Gunn wasn't his friend. Was this what he meant? "Are you a vampire, too?"

Gunn stared at him with open disgust. "I take back the beer I drank in your honor. Come on, Nate. Do you not remember me visiting you on the roof in *broad daylight?* What about when I handed you a crucifix? Am I a *fucking* vampire—"

"Gentlemen." The single word, delivered by Saltaire, was a crushing rebuke. "Our delay only affords de Silver further victims."

"So we should get to the bottom of the connection quickly." That was not the conclusion Saltaire intended, but Ben hurried onward before he could protest. "Nate, what happened when Peter visited you? Were there other meetings?"

"I only remember that and the park." Nate thought back. Had it really only been a week ago? “He seemed normal. We talked about insurance. Gave me his card and everything.”

“A card?” Ben and Hunter shared a look. “Nate, do you have it on you?”

So glad I remembered my wallet. The wristband had eliminated the need to carry cash, but his wallet had been a birthday present from Pa. Nate had tucked it into the cargo pants when he’d changed out of his jeans.

The card had gotten damp in the river, but was still in one piece. In the light of the moon, runic patterns the same shade of red as the blood magic threads were visible.

“Put it down,” Hunter warned. “Handle it as carefully as you can.”

As Nate obeyed, the park lurched around him. He had a sudden view of lights, a smooth bedspread and a coffee table spread with maps and notebooks. He looked down in confusion at the bathrobe draped around him and then looked up to an ornate mirror hanging on the wall. Peter’s shocked face stared back at him. “Jesus Christ.” He dropped the card. Instantly, Peter’s frown was replaced by Hunter and Ben, looking down at him as he sprawled across the cemetery’s paving stones.

“Are you okay?” Ben knelt beside him.

Nate inhaled deeply, shutting his eyes. When he opened them, the cemetery was still there. “Not hurt. Shaken.”

Ben helped him sit. “You saw something when you touched the card.”

Nate nodded, letting out his breath. “Peter. In a room. I don’t know where, but it was nice. Big."

"The card was Peter's way to control you," Ben's hand settled on Nate's arm. "As long as it was in your possession, he could influence you." He raised his voice. "Which clearly rules out collaboration."

"Too bad, so sad." Gunn's grin was triumphant. "Looks like you're out one sacrificial victim, Saltaire."

Saltaire looked grim. "The Council will be very impressed to hear you had the key to finding the necromancer in your possession for three days and didn't notice."

Nate gingerly returned to his feet. "The key to finding Peter?"

"The card has his magic all over it," Ben explained. "Very careless of him to forget it."

"Maybe he counted on Gunn finding the body?" Hunter smirked.

Gunn growled. "I am going to take that lamb and stuff it up your—"

"Enough!" Saltaire silenced everyone with his heavy glare. He looked again to the card, lying on the stone where Nate had dropped it. "Godfrey is exhausted. He needs time to recover from restoring our runes. Time we don't have."

"Department Seven employs several magic-users," Gunn said. "Why I bother pointing this out knowing you'll discount anyone I suggest is beyond me, but—"

"I can do it."

Nate turned to stare at Ben. He was conscious that he wasn't alone. The simple statement seemed to have caught the others off guard. "You studied magic?"

Ben nodded. "At first I just wanted to follow my father into the domestic side of ARX, but as I learned more, I discovered I liked it. There's something really special about seeing a spell come together." His smile was wry. "Sort of like real-life D and D."

Total geekpire. "Should have known."

Hunter frowned. "You haven't talked about your studies—your magic—in all this time, Ben."

"No point." Ben's expression was rueful, the most like him Nate had seen him that entire night. "The magic I studied with Godfrey requires living energy."

"And how are you going to power this spell?" Saltaire was unimpressed. "You're not alive."

"Nate is."

"Me?"

Gunn patted his jacket pocket, pulling out a crumbled cigarette carton. "Kid can't do magic. You heard him earlier. Thought I was a damned leech!"

"He can if I help him." Ben raised his voice. "We've done this before."

"Just like at the park." Nate tried to will himself confident, no mean feat given that Saltaire was looming aggressively between them. "I can handle that."

The smile Ben gave him made it all worth it. "Good. I'll need—"

"Not so fast." Saltaire folded his arms. "Before I agree to this, I want to be sure your priorities are in the right place, Bennet."

"My what? I want to stop Peter—"

"That I believe." Saltaire's stare was unflinching. Nate felt its reflected glare, wondered at Ben's ability to stay where he stood. "But the past week has taken a heavy toll on your judgment and, I fear, your loyalty."

Nate watched Ben's shoulders tense as he drew himself up. *This is not going to end well.*

Instead of the explosion Nate feared, however, Ben answered in a tight, collected tone. "You want me to prove myself. Fine. What would you have me do?"

Saltaire did not speak. He simply raised his eyes to look at Nate.

Nate took a step back. *Nope, not ending well at* all.

"Nate?" Ben had turned at Saltaire's pointed stare. "I can't hurt him. We need him in one piece to work the—" He paused, alarm flashing across his face. "You can't ask me to compel him! He trusts me!"

"And how am I to trust you otherwise?" Saltaire waited.

I'm missing something. In his peripheral vision, Nate could see that Hunter had straightened up from the statue, openly staring. Gunn's cigarette trailed smoke, entirely forgotten as Gunn watched the exchange with narrowed eyes. Nate felt an urge to laugh. *They must know that won't work. That Ben* can't *compel me.*

And as the silence stretched out, Nate realized, *Ben didn't tell them. All this time, he's been protecting me—from his family.*

Ben looked down, shoulders hunched as he battled to control his emotion. It took him another long moment to turn. His eyes met Nate's with an intensity that startled. "Nate. I'm so sorry." His eyes were not sorry. They were steady, trying to communicate. "Earlier, you made Hunter drop a sword. Find it. Give it to me."

Nate felt like a hand had squeezed around his heart. Hunter

standing behind him with a drawn sword was nothing to the danger he now felt. *They're vampires. They must know I'm faking*. And then they'd know—what? That Ben had only pretended to obey Saltaire? That Ben had chosen Nate over obedience to his Sire?

Nate's foot caught on an uneven stone edge, and he lurched awkwardly forward. That seemed to satisfy their audience. Nate heard Hunter exhale and then his footsteps as he crossed the courtyard.

"It hurts now, but you'll look back on this one day and know you did the right thing."

"You don't understand. I *promised* him I'd never compel him!"

Hearing that note of unhappiness in Ben's voice made it hard for Nate not to turn, but he forced himself to continue onward. *The sword slid somewhere over here.* But Ben didn't want the sword. *Is he buying me time to get away?* It would not take Saltaire long to become suspicious. Nate could feel the weight of the senior vampire's gaze on him, even as he stepped out of the lit circle and into the dark. *Vampire night vision. Gotta be.* Nate reached the edge of the courtyard and knelt to explore the garden beds with his hands. *So much for escape.*

"I knew Saltaire was cold, but Benny, I am impressed. Aren't you just a regular chip off the old icicle."

"Unless you'd like me to make Nate stab you with the sword once he finds it, I suggest you don't make me *cross*, Gunn." Ben took a deep breath. "I'm going to need some of Godfrey's supplies."

Hunter's voice sounded distantly. Nate looked up to see that he'd opened the door to a vault. "Anything in particular?"

"Some *twigs* if you can find them." Ben's voice was pitched oddly. Nate could hear him clearly, even on the other side of the clearing. "They don't have to be big. It's not about size after all, but *belief.*"

Ben was obviously trying to tell him something, but what? Nate obediently felt in the bushes for dirt. *I hope he doesn't think I'm going to have time to whittle a stake out of a bush over here. Saltaire's watching me like a vulture!* Nate risked a quick look over his shoulder.

Vulture was right. Saltaire stood with his arms folded. With his dark clothing and the shadow exaggerating his sharp angles, he waited with predatory intent. *Is he always this kill-happy or am I just lucky?* The large marble cross of the grave behind him only added to Saltaire's somber authority. *Judge, jury, executioner and undertaker. Truly a package deal—*

Cross! That's it! Nate scrabbled in the bushes. He snapped off a short twig, using his nail to punch a hole through it. A second twig made the base of the cross, and Nate carefully removed the leaves. *Is this really going to help me?*

"He delays long."

"You said yourself earlier," Hunter told Saltaire as he placed what looked like a fishing tackle box beside Ben, "Nate can't see in the dark."

Nate's fingertips encountered the cold metal of the sword handle. *Just in time.* He stood, walking slowly back across the courtyard.

Something of Saltaire's heavy presence had diminished. Nate

was still aware that Saltaire watched him closely, but the heaviness to his movements was gone. Risking a sideways look at the man, Nate was shocked to realize that Saltaire was shorter than him. *Makes sense. People were shorter in the past. Not that it matters. He can still kill me any number of different ways.* "Here's the sword," he said with what he hoped was the right amount of resentment.

Ben took it brusquely. "There's a broom in the vault. Find it and bring it here. A flask, too."

"Don't bother thanking me or anything." Behind Hunter, the door to a crypt stood open. Obviously the vault. Steeling himself, Nate stepped inside.

A candle burned in a lantern hung on a hook from the ceiling, clearly illuminating the tomb. Built into each of the surrounding walls were three stone caskets, and a fourth casket, much grander than the others, took center space. The air was thick with the old-leaves smell of the manor.

A vampire's home away from home? Three of the caskets would hold coffins for the vampires to sleep in during the day. The fourth? The stone lid of one casket had been pushed aside. Within it, Nate could see suitcases, a collection of musty looking books, the flask Ben wanted and even a first-aid kit. *Prepared for any contingency?* Nate picked up the flask, glancing over his shoulder.

Ben was explaining to Hunter the dimensions of his intended spell, while Gunn scratched his neck and Saltaire paced the edges of the courtyard. "Yes, it takes time, but for the results to be accurate, prior cleansing is *key.*" He looked calm and confident.

Nate had to suppress his grin. *He's got a plan.* Taking the broom from behind the door, Nate paused. A heavy iron key rested in the inside lock of the vault. *What on earth is the plan?*

Under Ben's directions, Nate swept an area of the courtyard with the broom. "When people talk about magic in the same sentence as brooms, you don't expect to end up sweeping."

Ben's smile was thin. "Clearing away negative energies is vital to accurate spell-casting. And on that note—" he handed Nate a bag of salt "—scatter this in a counterclockwise circle around you, then three times over your shoulder."

Nate did exactly as instructed. "It's always counterclockwise. What do you have against clocks?"

"To go counterclockwise is to go against the natural flow of energies, in the process diverting them to your own purposes." Ben lit the candles he'd placed around the edges of Nate's salt circle and stood. "The chalk work requires a practiced hand. I'll do that. Nate, scatter this at the perimeter of the circle, a few drops at a time only." He casually passed Nate the holy water.

Nate fought to keep his face straight. Ben had just handed him the vampire equivalent of kryptonite, and no one had said a thing! *Unbelievably, the plan was working.*

Hunter leaned over Ben's shoulder to watch him work. "I'd forgotten how neat your sigils were," he observed. "But you're a little rusty. Look. You've reversed your seals."

"That's the difference between living magic and blood magic." Ben continued to draw on the stone. "I'm not going to forget how to order seals in a year, Emeric. They are exactly where I want them to be."

Hunter raised an eyebrow. He looked again at the interconnecting circles and paused. Nate saw him glance at Ben with sudden suspicion. *That's it. We're done for.*

Instead, Hunter's hand rested lightly on Ben's arm for a moment before he turned to approach Saltaire. "This is going to take a while to set up," he said, throwing Saltaire an ironic salute. "Permission to patrol the perimeters of the graveyard?"

Saltaire frowned at him. "No need. De Silver's a coward. He would not dare approach us alone. He'll come with revenants of such number we could not fail to miss them, or he'll wait till daylight."

"I don't know." Gunn stubbed out his cigarette on a nearby angel. "Plotting his revenge while sitting right under your nose in board meeting after board meeting took nerve if you ask me."

Saltaire's look was withering. "We did not ask you."

"Maybe we should." Hunter held up a hand as if to ward off the glare turned on him. "Gunn's methods are ramshackle at best, but he does have access to means we do not. It is unlikely—*extremely* unlikely—but just possible that Gunn may have heard something useful to us."

Gunn snorted. "And what, you think I'll cough it up if you ask nicely? I would sooner volunteer to be a chew toy for a pack of werewolves—"

"We will not be indebted to one who allows his grievances to impede his judgement." Saltaire was coolly repressive. "Not only is he too reckless, but he cannot be trusted—"

A tug at his leg brought Nate's attention back to Ben. He sat on his heels, pointing down at the chalk circle.

Nate's eyes widened. Taking advantage of the others' distraction, Ben had written him a message on the stone. *He wants me to what?* Nate looked up to meet Ben's eyes. "You really think this will work?"

Ben nodded, quickly leaning forward to scrub away the words. "Trust me."

Nate discovered with a burst of warmth that he did. "Absolutely." He finished sprinkling the holy water, setting the flask down.

To Nate's untrained eye, Ben's spell looked like the time he'd tried to do his math homework on the school bus. It was a pentagram with circles instead of points, and overlapping rings wound round with rows of runes.

Ben didn't seem to see anything amiss with his work, however, directing Nate to stand in the circle in one arm of the pentagram. "If the three of you can stop rehashing old arguments for a moment, I'd like to get on with finding our missing necromancer." Ben stood in the circle opposite Nate, pointing to one of the two circles that made up the pentagrams base. "Hunter, if you stand here, then I'll want Gunn there—"

"Hold the fuck up. Why am I included in this spell?"

"You're the control." Ben frowned at his sigils, absently wiping his chalky hands on his hoodie. "Me, Hunter, Saltaire, and Nate have all interacted with Peter. It's possible that might interfere with the spell."

Saltaire took up the last circle without prompting. "I don't remember Godfrey's seeking circles being so complex."

"I've modified it to include a second spell." Ben placed Saltaire's sword in the very center of the pentagram. Very carefully, using the fabric of his hoodie to shield his hand from touching the paper, he placed Peter's card on top of it. "Peter was my donor and before that, my tutor. I know his methods. The more I think about it, the less likely it seems that he would forget anything that puts him at a disadvantage. This is a guard to prevent any backlash from activating the link."

Are we performing magic or running tech support? Nate wiped his sweaty palms on his pants. Ben had told him what to do, but not why or even what to expect. All he knew was that he needed to be ready to act.

Ben caught his eye again. "When I chant, I want you to watch me closely. You need to place your hands on the ground as soon as you see me do it. Your energy and my knowledge will activate the spell."

"You will do nothing to interfere with the proper workings of the spell." Forget compulsion. The glare Saltaire fixed Nate with was impulse all of its own. "You will give Ben your full focus, and you will not seek to harm any of us."

That would have been the end of everything—if not for the makeshift cross in Nate's pocket.

Ben knows Saltaire. Nate forced himself to stay calm, and face Ben across the pentagram. *He knows what he is doing.* As Ben started the chant, he found the even, measured words had a soothing effect on his nerves. When Ben knelt, placing his hands on the chalk-covered stones, Nate did the same. He felt energy pulse beneath his fingertips, the cold stone suddenly warm, and snatched back his hand in alarm.

No one noticed. They all watched as the sword shifted on the stone. It didn't hesitate, gaining speed as it slid quickly toward—

"Ben!"

Gunn caught Nate's hand before he could step out of the circle. "Ha! Now there's a twist you didn't expect!"

Hunter slammed his foot down on the hilt of the sword. "Interference. There's no need to read too much into it. We'll get a map and try again—"

"No," Ben said slowly. "Gunn's right. Peter's substitution rite was aimed at *me*."

Gunn's laughter broke the silence that followed Ben's statement. "This is the best!"

"What is going on?" Nate looked helplessly at Ben. "I thought Godfrey was supposed to make it so you couldn't be Peter's target again."

"The rite in the park." There was a note of fury undercutting Ben's calm. "He used your death to reopen a link with me."

Gunn slapped Nate on the back. "Don't feel too bad. After all, Bennet thought nothing of compelling you to regain brownie points with Daddy Dearest over there." His grin deepened. "Daddy Dearest who has made his feelings on necessary sacrifice in order to bring de Silver down very clear."

"You know that we would not sacrifice Bennet!" Hunter retaliated immediately. "He is family."

Gunn's grin was thoroughly unpleasant. "You wouldn't. Saltaire's yet to say anything on the subject—and he doesn't have a great track record where *family* is concerned."

Saltaire hadn't moved. His stony face reflected nothing of his thoughts, his gaze fixed on the sword. "Is this de Silver's objective? To force me to kill part of myself to destroy him..."

Hunter's laugh was forced. He looked from face to face, as if hoping to convince himself. "Even less reason then. Don't give de Silver what he wants!"

"Are you crazy? Ben is—Ben!" Nate sought frantically for an argument that could withstand the ancient sorrow carved on Saltaire's face. "After everything he's done for you, everything he's been through—you can't kill him!"

"Can and will." Gunn's grin was vicious. "De Silver's made a bad mistake if he thinks Ben's status will protect him. You've never hesitated in the past, Saltaire. Why now?"

"Isaiah, what happened to you has no bearing on this." Hunter interposed himself between the officer and Saltaire, as if he could physically block the other's words. "You cannot let yourself be swayed by guilt or duty, Saltaire. Bennet's worth is far greater than either—just think of all his knowledge, his training!" His words were hurried, robbed of their usual persuasive power. "He may have made a few mistakes, but who among us has not? He is young, he will learn—"

"He is dead." The words might have been carved in stone and dropped, echoing like thunder through the courtyard. "He has been dead this last year. No one is more aware of that than Bennet." Saltaire looked up at last, finality written all over his features. "His distaste for his half-life, his inability to reconcile himself to his new existence... No, it is better that it should be this way." He nodded, as if he conferred a blessing rather than a death sentence. "Bennet's second death will be his revenge."

Bile burnt the back of Nate's throat as he swallowed. His stomach roiled, everything in him revolting against those words. The lack of emotion in Saltaire's voice—the voice of a man who had already accepted his loss—was more terrifying than the revenants' blind hunger.

The argument continued around them, but Nate, struggling to keep the contents of his stomach down, kept his eyes locked on Ben. Hunter launched an impassioned appeal, taking a step toward Saltaire; Gunn smirked as he turned to watch. Saltaire, glowering, lifted his gaze off Ben to reprimand them—and Ben acted.

"Now!"

Nate pressed his hands to the circle. This time, the energy surged out of him in a rush, leaping into the ground. The chalk marks around Saltaire unfolded into thick masses of green vine, twining rapidly around him.

The vampire clawed at them. He jerked one vine out by its roots, but two more filled its space immediately. "Bennet, you dare—" A fresh growth wrapping around his mouth choked out the end of the sentence.

He will kill us both. But there was no time to think. Nate braced himself for what was quite possibly the last thing he would ever do—charging Gunn.

"What the—" Nate had never seen Gunn surprised. He did not have time to appreciate it. He tackled the officer, barreling him toward the open vault door.

The officer caught the edge of the doorway, just preventing

himself from hitting the ground. “Nate,” he growled. “You are not going to live to regret that—”

Hunter was unprepared for Ben’s assault. Thrown, he collided with Gunn before he pulled himself back to his feet. Ben followed his attack on his brother with a shove that sent Hunter and Gunn sprawling to the vault floor. Ben slammed the door shut, and Nate scrabbled in his pocket for the key. *Dead. We are so very, very dead.*

The lock clicked shut.

“We did it?” Nate sagged against the vault door. “There’s no way—”

“We have to get out of here.” Ben pushed Saltaire’s sword into Nate’s hand and shoved him toward the path. “That won’t hold Saltaire long—”

“Indeed.” Saltaire’s voice was cold contempt. “I wonder that you thought it would hold me at all, Bennet.”

Vines so thick he couldn’t move his legs still wound around Saltaire, but he’d freed one arm and used it to pull the plants away from his face. His mouth was a sour, downturned line, grimmer than any of the surrounding graves, and the anger in his eyes was enough to cause first-degree burns. Nate’s hand instinctively reached for the twig cross in his pocket.

“I was hoping to delay you.” The very fact that Ben could say those words in an even tone, despite the furious vampire before them and the muffled shouts from the vault was impressive. “That’s all.”

“You cannot delay a death that already happened, Bennet. I thought you understood that.”

“You’ve never lost an opportunity to impress how meaningless our existence is." Ben's voice was firm, but his shoulders shook with the effort of meeting Saltaire's stare. Nate stepped closer to place his hand on Ben's shoulder in wordless support. "That the only way we could redeem ourselves was by joining your fight. I believed you, did my best to please you. If it never felt right, that was a problem with me. But Nate changed that." Ben found Nate's hand, squeezed it. "Nate trusts me—"

"You dare speak to me of trust after your actions? Your abandonment of your responsibilities for base *lust*?" Saltaire spat the word, shredding a vine with his fists. "If Austin could see you now—"

"My father would understand." Ben possessed an iciness equal to Saltaire's own. "He believed in me. You never have." It was a year's worth of stored anger, freed all at once, the words coming faster than Ben could voice them. "Only allowed what freedom you chose, watched constantly, held up to standards that you decided— I thought you were protecting us, preventing us from becoming monsters! Or are you afraid that with the power to choose, we might question your methods, your decisions, force you to admit you can be wrong—"

"Silence." Saltaire ripped the last of the vine away. "You turn your back on me after all I have done for you?" His voice was clipped, shorn of any trace of emotion. "You would reject your family, Godfrey, Hunter, the sire who brought you back from the brink of death?"

Ben's fingers clenched tightly around Nate's wrist. "If it's the only way I can be free—"

"Very well." Saltaire waved a hand as if he commanded an

audience of hundreds. “I cancel any remaining obligation between us.”

Does he mean that? Ben’s free? Nate glanced at Ben but found him stock still, braced for something still to come. Nate felt dread settle in the base of his throat, making it hard to breathe.

“And I withdraw my protection.” Saltaire’s hand settled on his hip where his sword once rested.

“Nate.” Ben shoved him hard, sending him stumbling toward the edge of the courtyard. “Run.”

“What? I’m not leaving you here with him! Who knows what he’ll do?”

Ben gave him another push. “Which is exactly why you should run!”

Saltaire bowed his head. “Without my protection standing between him and the monster within, Bennet will be as wild and savage as a freshly turned revenant—and as hungry.” He regarded Nate without pity. “You would do well to run. In this graveyard, the only thing that can sustain the beast is you.”

He wouldn’t. Nate looked from Saltaire’s implacable expression, to Ben’s face, white with fear, and discovered that he would. “You are one seriously sick fu—”

“Nate, *please*.” Ben’s voice cracked with the strain of the words. He had hunched over, his fingers dug tightly into the skin of his arms in an effort to delay the change overtaking him. His body shook with effort, and Nate knew that, weakened by days of grief, Ben could not hold out long. “Run.”

The word had the thickness of fangs.

Nate ran.

Between the small pools of light offered by the intermittent lamps, the cemetery was dark with uneven stone. Nate lurched from uneven paving to nearly invisible steps, catching himself on the corner of unseen tombs.

This is never going to work. He'll catch me immediately!

Already it felt like Ben was right behind him. Every rustle of a branch sounded an alarm, the beating of Nate's own heart sounded like footsteps. *Not Ben—the vampire.* Nate swallowed. Saltaire might lie, but Ben's fear was far too convincing. Unwanted, the memory of Ben's teeth pressed against his neck returned.

No. I can't let it end like this. Ben's guilt would destroy him. *Exactly what Saltaire wants.* Nate's lip curled, even as he half ran, half skidded across a patch of stone worn smooth with wear. *He's counting on us being too afraid to think—*

Nate glanced around. It was hard to tell, but it seemed like he was in the more frequented part of the cemetery, with orderly rows of graves. *I need to be back in the old part.* Nate turned. *If I can find another vault to shelter in—*

Ben was already there.

He stood still, but his slight smile deepened as Nate stumbled back in shock, displaying the edge of his fangs.

"Jesus, you move fast." Nate stepped back. "Ben. Let's not do anything you'll regret."

Ben's smile, even full of fangs, was inviting. Nate had to force himself to step back.

"I mean it. Yeah, I'm sure I look great right now, all tasty and full of blood, and I'm really not helping. Uh." *You can't reason with a revenant. Even Gunn said so.* Nate glanced around, desperately searching for something that might help. A gap between two headstones suggested a path. Nate glanced back—and discovered Ben only inches away.

"Oh fuck."

Ben didn't try to close the distance between them. He was content to prowl around Nate, keeping him in constant motion as he tried to keep up with Ben. *Playing with me? Or tiring me out?* Neither option was good. *Think! There's got to be something I can— The cross!*

Scarcely daring to breathe, Nate moved his hand to his pocket, ready to draw out the cross.

And in that moment, Ben darted forward.

Nate raised the sword he held reflexively. With his other hand tangled in his pocket, his swing was clumsy.

Ben had no problems avoiding it entirely, ducking under the sword and knocking Nate's legs out from under him. The force of the impact cost Nate his grip on the sword. He heard a distant metallic clatter as Ben kicked it somewhere into the dark.

Ignoring the ache in his shoulder, Nate rolled onto his side. *Gotta think*. Forcing his unresponsive body to his knees, Nate needed both hands to stop from pitching forward. The graveyard dipped crazily. Pain pulsed through his skull, but it was an afterthought unconnected to him or the fear that coiled in his stomach. *Think*.

Ben was waiting for him to stand. Any hope that he retained a shred of self-awareness and restraint vanished as Nate took in Ben's slow grin, and his eyes fixed on Nate's mouth.

Raising a hand to his mouth, Nate's fingers came away bloody. *Just what we need.* Still if it was the blood Ben was fixed on, maybe—

He flicked the spilt blood to the ground and then threw himself to the right.

He didn't get two steps before Ben seized him. Nate's taller build was no protection against a vampire's strength; Ben slammed him against the nearest tombstone.

Nate fell to his knees. Gasping and acting only on instinct, he hauled himself back to his feet, only to be grabbed and thrown again.

And again.

Until Nate couldn't force himself to rise.

This is it. Nate shut his eyes as he felt Ben's fingers skim his forehead, shuddering as they brushed his hair from his forehead with a gentleness that hurt more because of the reminder that this wasn't Ben.

Satisfied that Nate would not escape, the vampire knelt, cradling Nate in his arms as he prepared to drink.

A siren's wail split the air.

Just my luck. Last thing I'm gonna hear is sirens. But Nate couldn't even find it in him to care.

The vampire hesitated. After a moment's thought, it took hold of Nate by one arm, dragging him into the shadows at one end of the clearing. The smooth stone gave way to the tug of bushes, the vampire evidently fearing discovery.

Not that it matters. No one'd get here fast enough. Nate choked weakly as the vampire seized him by the throat, hauling him upright only to immediately press him against a tree trunk. One hand automatically locked on the vampire's wrist in a futile attempt to free himself. *Only person who could help me right now is Gunn—and I helped trap him in the vault myself!*

His free hand scrabbled frantically for anything that might help. Nate encountered the rough ridges of bark and ivy.

Ivy?

The vampire growled a warning. Leaning in, he sucked at Nate's split lip, the sharp point of his fang just pressing into Nate's skin.

Nate fought desperately to keep his fear in check. *Ben won't hurt me.*

But this wasn't Ben. His inner vampire had taken control.

No. He didn't hurt me at the club. He won't hurt me now. Nate took a deep breath. *He's still in there somewhere. I just have to bring him out.* As Ben's tongue probed his wound, Nate's hand reflexively tightened, and he found himself clutching the ivy like a lifeline. Gunn's bathtub, wreathed in vines, jumped into Nate's head suddenly, and he imagined a layer of vines restraining Ben. *If only—*

Leaves rustled suddenly, lifted by the breeze.

Ben snarled, jerking back abruptly. He wrenched his wrist out of Nate's grasp, flinging him to the ground as he slashed out at something in the dark.

Nate let himself sink to his knees in the soil. He could hear the vampire snarl, the tearing of vine, but there was no sound from his opponent. Nothing but the gentle whisper of the leaves.

Leaves that rustled without wind to move them.

Nate found the raised edge of the stake. He could feel its warmth even now.

There was a thud as Ben fell. Grounded now, the vampire struggled even more violently, hissing like a cornered cat. It was no use. One by one, vines weighed down his limbs, until he lay still, a tight, angry, trapped bundle.

"That actually happened." Nate sucked in a deep breath and swallowed. Forcing his aching body to move, he crawled over to Ben. His hand shook as he placed it on Ben's chest, but his voice was steady. "Are you awake in there?"

The vampire hissed like an angry cat. The bundle twisted violently but could not free itself.

"Good. Well, not good. Last thing I want to do is hurt you in any way, but the last thing you want to do is hurt me so good on that front." Nate discovered it was easier to breathe now. "It's all right. I got this. I'm not going to harm you, and I'm going to make sure you don't harm anyone else." Nate patted what he thought was Ben's arm. "Not unless it's someone like Saltaire who is asking for it."

The memory of Saltaire was not welcome. Nate glanced around, but there was no ill will emanating at him from the shadows. *He wiped his hands of us when he unleashed Ben on me? Or is that too much to hope for?*

"Nate?" It was little more than a hoarse, strained whisper.

"Ben!" Nate turned back to the bundle beside him. "Are you okay? Are you—"

Every word seemed to be spoken with effort. "Be very careful.

The vampire—"

Ben. Nate breathed out, letting a hand rest on Ben's shoulder in relief. "I noticed the vampire. But between the two of us, I think we got him under control." He let the vines relax.

Ben leaned on Nate as he sat up. "This is the second time now."

"It's like I keep telling you." Nate squeezed his hand. "You can lean on me, when you need to." The vines gave easily as Nate lifted them off Ben.

"You did that?" Ben's voice held an indefinable note.

Nate's cracked lip hurt as he grimaced. "Not on purpose. I wanted to stop you, but I…I would never try to hurt you—"

Ben placed a hand on Nate's shoulder. "When this is over, we need to have a good long talk about what constitutes a *normal* human, Nate. Until then, I suggest we concentrate on getting as far away from here as possible."

Nate's breath caught in something between a laugh and a sob. His arms protested as he pulled Ben close, but Nate was too happy to care. "I'm so glad you're back to *you*."

Ben's hand rested on Nate's arm, and he leaned into his touch. "Me, too. But not so glad I want to tempt fate a third time. You've got a lot of faith in my self-control, Nate, but an open wound to a vampire—"

He stopped.

Nate relaxed his hold, scanning Ben's face for any clue to the problem. "Ben?"

Ben's fingers settled on Nate's cheek, tenderly inclining their foreheads together. "I lost control of the vampire, and you stopped me. Nate, if you had any idea just what you've done tonight—"

And before Nate could ask, Ben kissed him with an intensity that made further questions unnecessary.

Chapter Sixteen

"So," Nate said. "Approximately how much trouble are we going to be in once Hunter and Gunn get out of that vault?"

Ben did not slow his pace. He pulled Nate after him as he navigated the night streets. "Why do you think I keep telling you to hurry?"

"They're not going to kill each other, are they?" Even though they'd left the cemetery behind them ages ago, Nate glanced over his shoulder. "We should probably go back if they're going to kill each other."

Shorn of people and the lights of buildings, the streets were all alike in the dark. A car tipped on its side in a puddle of safety glass left a sour smell of burnt rubber and gas, and the crackle of a dying light bulb in the streetlight above them was the only other sound on the street.

"They won't kill each other." Ben didn't slow his pace at all. "They'd have no one to argue with."

Nate snorted. "With the way Gunn picks fights? That's not the problem you—" He collided with Ben's shoulder.

"Stay here." Ben let go of Nate's hand. "Don't move."

Nate glanced around them, but he was too late. Whatever the vampire had detected, he had no hope of picking it out of the surrounding night. "Again?" He turned back to Ben. "Just how many revenants—"

He was alone on the street.

Am I too trusting? Nate pulled Ben's ill-fitting hoodie more tightly around himself then shoved his hands into his pockets, stamping his feet in an attempt to keep warm. *Maybe it's my inherent good nature. I mean, there's got to be a limit...*

There was a sudden clatter ahead of him, and Nate turned to see a thin girl with pale hair that gleamed in the streetlight pick herself up from the asphalt. She took a moment to adjust her beret before sauntering up to him. "Aren't you lonely, out here all by yourself?" Her smile displayed teeth with too-sharp edges.

Nate stared. A seemingly endless walk through New Camden's streets had done nothing to diminish the memory of being face to fangs very much like those. Nate felt himself fascinated against his will. *Like a fucking deer in the headlights.* "Just passing through. I'm not what you're looking for."

Her smile was all secret amusement. "Don't be so sure of that." Her gaze flickered to his cracked lip predictably.

Nate was about to step back before he caught himself. *Don't move, Ben said.* "This is a really bad idea. I mean that in the nicest possible way."

"Counting on your friend?"

Fuck! I hadn't even heard him! Nate whirled around to find himself faced with another smirking vampire. This one had an eyebrow piercing. "Where did you come from?"

"He's cut and run. Left you high and dry while he saves his skin."

Eyebrow Piercing leered at Nate, displaying teeth that compensated for the lack of shock value by being extremely cruel, curved, and stained. "Hardly very friend-like behavior. But don't worry."

"I'm not worried."

"He's not going to get very far alone. *Our* friend will see to that."

There was a sudden thud from an alley behind them, ending in a voice raised in alarm. The sound came to a brutal stop.

Nate shuddered. "Christ—"

"Can't help you now," the girl said, drawing Nate's attention back to her. She'd gotten very close, and as he watched, she bared her fangs with a low hiss—

That suddenly became an anguished shriek.

Eyebrow Piercing was expecting Nate to run. He had to duck around Nate to see what had happened. "What the—"

The girl was roughly propelled toward him. Eyebrow Piercing caught her automatically. She was deadweight, and with a snarl, he dropped her, looking at the sword protruding from her back. "I knew something didn't smell right."

Ben smiled thinly. He didn't bother to waste time in taunts. His silence was daunting all on its own. Nate found himself unable to speak, watching as the two vampires sized each other up.

Eyebrow Piercing took in the dirt stains on Ben's left side and decided to chance it. He feinted towards Ben's injured side and then darted toward Nate.

Before Nate even registered the danger, Ben intercepted the other vampire. With a speed that left Nate with no idea how Ben had accomplished it, he held Eyebrow Piercing with one hand twisted back and Ben's teeth in his neck.

Nate swallowed. *If there was anything guaranteed to put you off a guy, this should be it.* This hadn't been their first encounter with other vampires on their walk across town. Ben had displayed a single-minded sense of purpose, dealing with them quickly and efficiently. He no longer tried to hide what he was from Nate—or even apologize for it.

No longer cares what I think of him? Nate's fingers dug into the fabric of his jeans in reflexive hurt. "Do you have to drink from them?"

Ben let the man slowly sag to the pavement. "Have to keep up my strength. You're attracting vampires like nothing else."

Nate winced. *Again, this is my fault?*

Ben turned his attention to the girl. He needed to place a foot on her back to pull out the deeply embedded sword. "Walk. I'll catch you up."

True to his word, he fell into step beside Nate barely a block later. "Are you all right?"

"Mentally, I know they're dead, I know they were looking to eat me, but when they die..." Nate shook his head. "Those two weren't revenants."

"With the city in chaos, younger vampires are grouping together to hunt." Ben looked straight ahead down the empty road. "Strength in numbers."

Nate snorted. *That worked well for them.* "Weird thing. She hissed at me when she got her fangs out. The last one did, too. That a vampire thing?"

Ben gave him a sideways glance, but Nate wasn't sure whether he was questioning Nate's state of mind or his vocabulary choices. "Instinct," he said. "Calls attention to your mouth, so your victim doesn't notice you're preparing to strike."

Forget feeling sorry for those things. "Are vampires turning into dust just in the movies?"

"Depends on the age of the vampire. If they're old enough that their corpse would dissipate on exposure to the air, then yes."

"So those kids back there—"

"A couple of months at most. More likely weeks." Ben turned his gaze back to the road. "You're taking this very calmly. We turn here."

Foster Ave? Nate looked from the old metal street sign to the long rows of apartment buildings. *That's all the way across town! Just how long have we been walking?* "You didn't see the freak-out when I first woke up."

"Even so." Ben's mouth twitched. Eventually he worked out what he wanted to say. "For all the credit you give me for self-control, I'm thinking you might have sold yourself short. You've got more strength than I think you realize."

Just when I thought this night couldn't get any more surreal. "A lot of that's you." Nate closed the gap between them, reaching for Ben's cool hand. "You're so all-or-nothing, it's impossible not to want to give your all in return."

Ben's fingers squeezed his. "That's a nice way to say I'm hard work."

Nate let his hand drop to Ben's ass. "Hard work's my specialty."

"That was terrible," Ben complained, but Nate noticed he didn't protest when Nate resettled his hand on Ben's waist.

"I kind of had to." Nate hesitated. "You're being very open suddenly. That's just an observation! I mean, I like it—"

"But you're wondering why am I so open about this knowing I can't erase your memory?" Ben's smirk was just as self-deprecatory as ever.

Nate had missed it. "I was pretty sure we'd settled that."

"We have." Ben squeezed his hand. "No. You've seen the vampire at its potential worst, and somehow you're still here. I suppose I don't have to hide it anymore."

Nate's heart beat emphatically. "I figured maybe you were trying to scare me off." *Or don't care enough to try.*

Ben leaned against Nate's side as he considered the problem. "You said you intended to be here and you are. Against every law of probability. Practically speaking, it seems I am stuck with you, so I'd better break you in as quickly as possible."

That was Ben for "I plan to keep you around." Nate was sure of it. "You say the sweetest things."

A siren flared up suddenly a few blocks away. The noise was startling in the quiet night. Nate tensed and felt Ben's hand tighten around his.

"It's moving away from us."

"Sorry." Nate fumbled for words. "The sirens. I—"

"Have never liked the sound," Ben repeated. "I know." His eyes were more gray than blue, luminous under the streetlights. "Because of your father?"

Nate blinked, startled. "Ethan and I were planting the apple trees, and all of a sudden, sirens. That's how we found out." He glanced up, but Ben's expression wasn't scornful. "Heart attack while Ma was getting the laundry in. It was already too late. How did you know?"

"I guessed. I've been thinking about that night—about you—a lot." Ben turned to scan the street. "It took me a long time to hear them without thinking of the night my father died."

"You died, too."

Ben's mouth twitched. "I'm not likely to forget."

"Too personal?" Nate bit his tongue. Ben had lost his entire second family just hours earlier.

But Ben shook his head. "You can ask. After everything we've been through, talking about these things with you... It feels right."

Right. Nate let the word roll over him, savoring it. *We feel right.* "How come you were turned but your father wasn't? Less injured?"

Ben shook his head. "Saltaire could have turned us both if he'd wanted. There was time. My father was a loyal ARX employee, skilled at what he did."

Nate glanced down at Ben. "Then why not both of you?"

"Saltaire's reluctant to turn anyone. Something that happened in his past. Hunter knows, but won't talk about it," Ben said. "My father had enough life left to ask Saltaire to save me. He'd— If he'd stayed hidden, he might have survived but—he died trying to save my life. That tipped the balance in my favor."

Nate squeezed his hand. "I'm sorry."

"You have nothing to be sorry about," Ben elbowed him in warning. "You're the exact sort of person Dad would have wanted me to meet. He was always pushing me to go out and try new things, have interests that didn't revolve around monster hunting and magic."

"Instead you're hanging out with a guy with an affinity for vines that has Department Seven baffled. I don't know if that's any better." Nate hesitated. "When you asked me at Century what I was, I really didn't know. I thought—"

"It's all right, Nate." Tired as he was, Nate couldn't complain when Ben leaned against him like he did now. "How could I ask you to trust me when I didn't trust you? Or even trust myself? If anything, I owe you the apology."

"Ben." Nate bumped him with his shoulder. "I know that you're crazy smart, scarily fast, and possess vampire powers I've never even heard of, but Saltaire is entirely out of your control." Nate hesitated. "You're sure he's not—"

"Positive." Ben nudged Nate in response. "If my grief after killing you wasn't enough to cause me to end myself, he counted on the city to take care of me. Stray vampires aren't exactly welcome right now. Department Seven is patrolling the sewers, citizens groups are checking graveyards for signs of disturbed graves, and no one with any sense is going to open their door to a stranger."

Nate frowned. Saltaire letting them go had not been the break he imagined. "So what are we going to do? It's going to be dawn soon."

"I don't understand you, Nate. Here we are, in a deserted street at night in New Camden, hungry revenant capital of the world. You're hurt, exhausted, and bleeding, and it is *my* safety you're worried about? I got you killed!"

"Peter killed me. Not you."

"But aiming at me. The spell proved that. All this time—"

The spell. Nate stopped to look at Ben. "Back in the cemetery, when you did that finding Peter thing. Did you know it was going to point to you?"

Ben shook his head. "I expected Peter had rigged something to cover his tracks and let you catch the blame. It would suit his sense of humor to have us do his dirty work. You're not changing the subject. My actions have consistently led you into danger—death!"

"Dead despite you." Nate made his voice gentle. "You went to an awful lot of trouble to protect me."

"For all the good that did." Ben wasn't having any of it. "You should be angry, scared, traumatized. At the very least, you should be conflicted!"

Nate hesitated. "It's hard to explain, but I was aware in the park. Afterward, I mean. I heard you and—" It was still hard to think of the naked pain in Ben's voice without hurting. "Grief like yours is… I couldn't doubt how you felt after that."

Ben had gone from leaning on Nate to dead weight. "You *heard*? But—"

Nate placed his hands on Ben's shoulders to steady him. "I don't know how. It's a lot weird, but that's how I knew I was dead. When I couldn't make you hear me. I—"

Ben cut him off by hauling Nate into the relative shelter of a traffic bridge. Before Nate could question the relocation, Ben tugged him down to mouth level. His fingers gripped Nate's arms so tightly, not even a crowbar could have come between them. His mouth sought Nate's with urgency, and with single-minded purpose, Ben set about making up for the park.

"I have to warn you," Nate said at last, stroking Ben's hair. "That if you want me to consider you a threat, then that is not going to do it."

Ben had relented his attack, allowing Nate to pull him into a hug. "All I want is right here."

Nate felt a warmth that soothed even the tired ache in his bones, but this happiness was still so new that he didn't trust it. "And Hunter? I mean—sorry, I shouldn't—"

"Hunter," Ben said slowly. "It's strange. He was kind after your death. Thoughtful, attentive, even charming. Everything I like in him. I understand now what you mean about him feeling more than I thought."

Nate couldn't speak. He couldn't even breathe.

"The thing I most wanted—and it didn't even touch me inside." Ben sat up, looking at Nate with a puzzled expression. "And you make me feel without even trying. It doesn't make sense, but there it is." He elbowed Nate in the ribs. "And if you want this to continue, stop distracting me. It's later than I realized. We're not going to reach my Dad's apartment before dawn."

Nate followed Ben to his feet. "A new plan?"

"Let me think." Ben stepped out from the bridge, scanning the surrounding areas. "Do you see any ivy? If you did what you did earlier with those vines—"

Nate looked around. As he took in the bridge they'd sheltered beneath for the first time, he felt a shock of recognition. "I know this place." With growing confidence, he looked around. "That's the path we walked from the station, this is the under bridge that Mandy's scared of." Nate scanned the sky. *Still time?* "Her building's not that far from here."

Ben bit his lip. "I won't be a danger to anyone."

"You won't be." Nate took his hand firmly. "I've got you."

"Nate?" Mandy answered the door armed with a frilly low-cut teddy, dressing gown, and a rolling pin. "What are you doing here? You shouldn't scare people so early in the morning. It's not even light yet!"

"That's kind of the point," Nate started. "Listen—"

"Are you all right? Where have you been? Your manager getting murdered is all over the news! Aki said—"

"Denise?" Nate's breath caught. The memory of Denise's body sliding to the floor now made horrible sense. "She can't be— She's Denise!"

"You didn't know? Nate, what's been happening to you?"

That was a very good question. "I guess I was slated to be the necromancer's next victim. Only it didn't work that way. I've been in hiding. But you, Aki, Bea, you're all okay?"

Mandy wiped her eyes on the sleeve of her exceedingly fuzzy dressing gown. "If being worried sick was an actual medical condition then we'd be in trouble," she said. "But we're fine."

Ben shifted restlessly. "Time," he said quietly.

Mandy noticed him for the first time. "Who's this?"

"Ben." Nate took a deep breath. "This is going to sound bad

but–"

"I'm a vampire." Ben's matter-of-fact announcement made Nate's heart sink.

"But not the usual kind of vampire. He saved my life several times over tonight just getting me here!"

Mandy had drawn back at Ben's words, looking from him to Nate with increasing panic. "There's no such thing as a good vampire, Nate! He's bewitched you or—" She swallowed. "Are you—"

It took Nate a moment to catch her fear. "He didn't turn me! Look—you can feel my pulse for yourself." Nate held out his hand, but Mandy didn't take it. *Just as well Ben insisted we stash the sword before making our house call. No way would that have gone over well!*

"Regardless of what happens to me, Nate will be safe," Ben assured her. "And I am powerless to enter your apartment without invitation."

"But once you're in you can come back anytime?" Mandy clutched the rolling pin tightly. "I'm not falling for that—"

"The invitation can be rescinded," Ben said. "A simple online search should provide a dozen methods, or I can show you one before we leave."

Nate put a hand on Ben's shoulder. "He's my friend," he told Mandy. "And he doesn't have very long. I'll take full responsibility for him while he's here. Seriously, we can just stash him in a bathtub until dark, and then he's out of your hair, I promise."

"Your friend?" Mandy was so surprised that she lowered her rolling pin. "Vampires are not friends!"

"Ben is," Nate said firmly. "Seriously. He's put himself in danger to protect me, even got kicked out of his family when he stuck up for me! Mandy, I know how much family means to you, so when I tell you that Ben has nothing—"

Ben squeezed his hand. "I have you," he reminded Nate. "That is far from nothing."

Nate could only stare at him. The simple sentence delivered in Ben's matter-of-fact tone had thrown him absolutely.

Mandy was likewise startled. It was a long moment before she reacted, swinging the door shut. Before Nate could protest, the sound of the safety chain sliding back provided an explanation.

"I must be out of my mind!" Mandy stepped back. "Come in. Both of you. My mother will—"

Nate caught her up in a tight hug. "Thank you, Mandy. You don't— You're the best."

"Right. Well." Mandy, almost as pink as her dressing gown, waved them toward a closed door. "The spare room. Quickly, before I think twice about this."

The spare room was extremely spare. The double bed had sheets, a single quilt, but not much else in the way of furnishings. Nate drew the curtains shut and looked back to see Ben winding himself up in the sheets.

"Will this be enough?"

"If you help me finish this it just might be." Ben lay down flat on the bed. "Make sure my head is covered, and then wrap me once more with the quilt."

"Right." Nate knelt next to him on the bed. "You're not going to suffocate?"

"I can't." Ben hesitated. "Promise me you won't look. I know you know I'm dead but... Seeing it is—"

"You don't want me to see you dead?" Nate leaned in pressing a quick kiss to Ben's forehead. "You don't have to explain." The knowledge that Ben cared how Nate saw him, even in these grim circumstances, was somehow immensely reassuring. He drew the sheets over Ben's head, draping the quilt over his still form. "How's that?"

No response.

The room was unnaturally still.

There was a slight knock. Mandy pushed the door open. "It's dawn. Is he—"

"I don't know." Nate looked down at the outline of Ben's form beneath the blankets. "I guess we won't know till tonight."

Mandy wrapped her arms around herself, suppressing a shudder. "I didn't know what else to do, so I made coffee. I mean, vampire in my apartment, the last thing I should be doing—"

Nate forced himself to stand and smile. "Coffee sounds great."

In addition to the coffee, Mandy made toast and eggs, filling Nate in on the news he'd missed as they ate. "Century's closed. All the clubs and most of the bars are. Aki's sleeping on Bea's sofa while he waits for the situation to stabilize."

"Man. Aki and Bea? If I didn't know the situation was serious already, that'd do it." Nate scanned the headlines of the newspaper in his lap. "This just gets worse and worse..." *Mounting victims, Council in Chaos: No Confidence Vote, Missing People Hotline deluged with calls...*

"It's hard to believe that you're all right." Mandy's eyes were red-rimmed, and she blinked rapidly as she held her coffee mug. "I mean, after that Department Seven officer said you'd called them about the necromancer...well, it was hard not to think the worst."

Their breakfast cluttered the kitchen table, some pussy willow twigs in a vase and a pink-and-white striped tablecloth Mandy had probably run up herself on the old Singer sewing machine sitting beside the bread bin. It was a world away from the sleek surfaces of the club, but Nate's training stood him in good stead all the same. He reached over to pat Mandy's arm automatically. "It was a close thing. I've spent the last three days under police protection, trying to hide the fact I'm still alive from the necromancer." Nate gave Mandy a heavily edited version of events, trying to keep as much of the supernatural events—especially Ben's strange link to Peter—out of it as possible.

He was glad that he did. Mandy gnawed at her lip as he talked, hands clutched together. "Weren't you terrified? I would have died!"

"Not with Ben there," Nate said. He looked down. The coffee reflected back his smile, and Nate picked up the mug, still astonished that he had it in him to be giddy despite the night they'd had. "I knew he wouldn't let anything happen to me."

Mandy blinked at him and then smiled, a little too rapidly to mean it. "You look like someone's who's been up all night. I can loan you a towel if you want a shower."

A shower? "Hell yeah." Nate gulped down the coffee and helped himself to the eggs. "You don't know how good that sounds."

Mandy laughed. “I think I have a good idea. You know, if you give me your clothes to wash, I could even have them dry for you before sunset.”

A hot shower, the prospect of clean clothes, and no one trying to kill him or Ben. “That would be amazing. But what about your job? I don’t want to get you in trouble.”

Mandy shook her head as she stood. “You really are out of it. It’s Saturday, Nate.”

Nate insisted on washing the breakfast dishes, while Mandy flitted around, putting plates away and worrying about him overtiring himself. Daylight had reached the windowsill and crept over the counter, lighting up the vintage cola bottles that Mandy collected one by one.

“I like washing up,” Nate said. “Something about the combination of hot water and detergent...I feel more relaxed than I have in days.”

Mandy beamed at him. “It’s really nice having you here. With everything that’s happening...I do love Bea and Aki, but they’re so morbid right now I can’t hang out with them! If it wasn’t for work, I wouldn’t see anyone. I wish you could stay—” She caught herself. “But you have plans, don’t you?”

“Ben won’t stay anywhere that he might endanger anyone,” Nate agreed as he handed Mandy the final saucepan. “He says he’s got a place he can go to rest while we figure out a way to stop the necromancer.”

"Wouldn't it be safer to leave that to the authorities? Nate—You're just an ordinary person!" Mandy paused mid-saucepan to stare at him. "Anything could happen!"

Nate let his soapy hands rest on the counter. "Not totally ordinary. My family doesn't like to talk about it but—we're different. Not like a vampire or a werewolf is different, but...somehow I think I'll be all right." Nate shrugged. "Even if I wasn't— I'd still have to help, you know?"

He was half braced for Mandy's repulsion or anger. Not the dishtowel. "I was so upset when you disappeared! And now— I can't believe you want to go out there again! Don't you care what might happen?"

Was this how Ben felt, on the other side of Nate's hurt? "Mandy, believe me. I care. That's why I have to do this. Somehow, I got caught up in the necromancer's plans, and I think I can do something to stop him. I can't promise you I'll be safe—but I can promise you I'll be careful."

"Boys!" Mandy flung herself after the dishtowel. Nate suddenly found himself with his arms full, breathing in Mandy's floral perfume as she cried on his shoulder. "I'm sorry," she said at last. "I really didn't want to cry on you."

"Don't feel bad," Nate said. "I think you needed that."

"I really did." Mandy rubbed at her eyes. "I've been so tired lately. I can't sleep. What with the news and not knowing..."

"Go back to bed," Nate told her. "I can figure out the shower and the washing machine myself and knowing you've got someone else here might help you sleep."

Mandy wiped her eyes and nodded. "You'll still be here when I wake up? I— Stupid question."

If the dishwater had felt good, the shower was happiness overload. Nate stood beneath the showerhead, letting the heat and water pressure soak in. Alive. Safe.

Tired.

Reluctantly, Nate turned the water off. The towels smelled of Mandy, or at least of her favorite brand of detergent, and Nate dried himself, fully aware that he must smell like a florist's. With the towel looped securely around his waist, he picked his way across the living room to the spare room. No sound. Presumably Mandy had managed to fall asleep.

Ben's cocoon looked even more pathetic in the dim light. Somehow, although there was room on the bed, Nate preferred to sit on the floor beside the bed. For the first time, it really sunk in.

Ben was dead.

Am I selfish to want to keep him like this? Nate leaned against the side of the bed, looking up at the ceiling. *If he hates being a vampire so much...*

Something inside him rode up in immediate denial of that thought. Nate snorted. Other people could argue about whether it was right or wrong. He just knew that he had to do it.

As he settled himself against the bed, Nate breathed in the rich loam. The smell was quickly becoming not only familiar but welcome. *I like it, but will Mandy appreciate it?*

Eyeing the floral motif of the curtains, Nate shook his head. He doubted Mandy's love of flowers extended to having an apartment that smelled of soil. *Better open the window,* Nate decided as he shut his eyes for only a moment. *Let in some air—*

* ~ * ~ *

An unexpected noise. Midday sun filtering through the curtains. *Gunn doesn't have curtains—*

Nate blinked blearily around him, becoming aware of his surroundings. No clothes. The thick smell of ripe dirt. "Ben!"

The bundle on the bed was just as Nate had seen him last. Nate tentatively stood up, feeling the burn in muscles that had not entirely recovered from the previous night. *I'm too young to feel this old.*

A small pile of clothes beside the door caught his attention. Nate picked them up. *Still warm from the dryer— Mandy must have just put them here.*

Somehow, the act of putting fresh clothes on did more to make Nate feel awake than the nap he'd just taken. Slinging the towel over his shoulder, Nate pulled open the door carefully. He glanced back over his shoulder to check that Ben hadn't moved before it registered.

He's not asleep. He's dead.

This really had to stop.

"—want to speak to the officer in charge," Mandy said. "It's important."

Nate froze. Last thing he wanted was to interrupt—

"I saw the news reports. The vampire you're looking for? I know where he is so won't you just— No, I'm not interested in the reward! I have to speak to Gunn! Please, it's very important— It's a friend of mine!" Mandy sounded strained. "Yes, I'll hold."

Nate took a step back from the door.

He nearly couldn't breathe. Everything crowded in on him at once. Gunn looking for Ben, what he'd do with the knowledge of the connection between Ben and Peter—

It can't end like this. It won't end like this!

There was only one way out.

Nate drew the curtains, pushed the window open. Making sure the duvet was still wrapped tightly around Ben, Nate heaved him over his shoulder.

The fire escape was a rusted ladder that clung to the wall like some kind of alien vine, rust stains spreading over the wall like moss. Nate didn't allow himself time to wonder if it would hold both of their weight. It had to. That was that.

Ben was not heavy even with the addition of the duvet, but he was awkward to carry. Nate had to hook an arm around him tightly to manage the escape ladder and drop the remaining way to the ground. Once there, he could balance Ben over one shoulder, but increased ease of movement did not compensate for other problems.

We stand out like a fucking red flag. Nate ploughed determinedly down the path, pretending not to notice the stares or the people stepping into the road to get out of his way. With the city on vampire watch, Nate was not going to get far carrying a person-sized bundle.

Nate crossed one road and turned down a side road. *If I can find a park—*

What then? I don't know how I did what I did in the cemetery—I don't know anything about how the vines work!

"Fucking hell!" The whine of sirens coming closer was the last thing Nate needed. He quickened his pace to a jog, searching urgently for something, anything that could help.

This is not how I wanted to see my first werewolf!

Crouched behind a Dumpster, Nate watched two uniformed police officers confer beside the car they'd just exited. Beside them was an animal, far too big to be a normal police dog—possibly too big for even a normal wolf.

"Officer Kenzie will accompany me," the first man said. "You stay here and—"

"I know how a search works, Ramírez." The second officer waved his handheld. "I'll hold the perimeter, you find Gunn."

The wolf barked in response and set off down the pavement, the man with her jogging to catch up.

We are in serious trouble. Nate possibly had a chance of dodging the patrol cars if he stuck to the alleys and side streets, but the distinctive smell of vampire would lead the werewolf right to them. *Think! There's got to be something...*

Calm down! You're not going to help Ben by freaking out like this. Nate took a deep breath. Usually he found the smell of leaves comforting, but the knowledge that it brought them closer to discovery entirely undid its soothing influence. There was something different about the smell, too. A stale sickly sweetness, like potpourri gone wrong.

Frowning, Nate cast a look down the street to check for cars, before pulling himself up to look over the side of the Dumpster. It was filled with garden castoffs. He dug past the faded azalea blossoms at the top—*Someone just tore out a perfectly good bush? What a waste! Seriously, some people shouldn't even have gardens*—to the tightly packed leaves and grass cuttings at the base. Nate looked over his shoulder to Ben, propped against a neighboring fire escape. *It's a long shot...but it's our only shot.* "I'm really, really sorry about this, Ben. Really."

Nate was still apologizing five blocks away. "I swear it's nothing personal. I just— Well, I couldn't think of what else to do. In the same situation, you'd...well, okay, you would have a safe place and a spell already worked out."

There was a shout behind him and a whistle blown.

Nate ran down the pavement. No time now for weaving in and out of side streets.

Pedestrians glancing up at him in annoyance looked down the street behind him, and their expressions changed to panic.

Department Seven. Nate adjusted his hold on his bundle as he ran, fully expecting to feel the teeth of the werewolf on his legs.

Instead, there was a growl behind him and then a soft body tangled beneath his legs. Nate hit the pavement face-first with enough force that he skidded, losing his hold on his precious bundle.

Ignoring the pain, Nate pushed himself up off the sidewalk to see the parcel several meters ahead of him. Grunting, he tried to haul himself up onto his elbows, only to be met by a low growl as the werewolf positioned herself between him and the bundle. She gave the bundle a brief sniff and then turned to Nate, snarling in warning not to move.

Nate stared. "And I thought vampires had teeth."

She growled.

The werewolf's jaw put Nate's terrifying nightwalk into perspective. And this was in broad daylight! "Was that disrespectful? Sorry. I just—haven't had the opportunity to see teeth like yours up close before." Nate wiped grit from his chin. There was blood on his hand. Nate was grateful that the werewolf appeared better trained than the vampires he'd encountered the previous night. "I got to say, you must have one hell of a dentist. Your teeth are amazing."

The wolf barked at him. It was a short bark, and she sat, looking down at him, her ears cocked.

Nate didn't have time to wonder what this meant. There was the clatter of footsteps on the pavement behind him and a very familiar voice. "Good girl, Kenzie."

The wolf snarled as she relinquished her guard position over the bundle, but Gunn ignored her. Nate instantly forgot any relief he felt at seeing that the officer had escaped from the vault with no apparent damage as Gunn reached under his jacket and pulled out a stake.

"No! You can't!"

Halfway to his feet, the werewolf caught Nate's arm in its jaw and firmly pulled him back from the officer.

"I can't destroy the necromancer currently terrorizing an entire urban population? I got to question your priorities, Nate—and your knowledge of my character." Nate's heart lurched as Gunn gripped the edge of the duvet and pulled, upending its contents onto the footpath.

The bundle of branches and leaves looked even more pathetic spilled over the pavement.

The wolf barked again, a high-pitched yelp that sounded almost like a laugh.

"Not a word of this, Kenzie, unless you want to spend the night in the pound." Gunn rounded on Nate. "And you. Unless you want to get very personally acquainted with this stake, I suggest you tell me where Bennet is and make it fast."

If it hadn't been for the wolf behind him, Nate would have stepped back. "You already know that won't work on me."

"Don't think that because I don't know what you are, I can't hurt you." Gunn's anger at Nate's intrusion into his safe room was nothing to him now. "I got ways, Nate. Tell me where Bennet is."

"So you can kill him?"

"So I can save people's lives! We got a necromancer loose in the city. Someone who takes power from death and a large urban population ripe for the taking. De Silver's hidden himself so well an entire department of magic users can't locate him. His link to Bennet's the only thing we got on him. You have to see how this adds up."

"I'm not letting you kill Ben."

"You think I'm the only one looking for him? De Silver's out there, too. And let me tell you, compared to being found by the necromancer, I'm the better option! Do us all a favor, Ben included, and tell me where he is!" Gunn's argument would have been more effective if his hand wasn't around Nate's throat.

"Promise you won't hurt him?"

"For fuck's sake. Kenzie, please tell me you got a lead on this idiot's scent."

The wolf had been watching the exchange. She barked, getting to her feet.

Gunn shoved Nate away from him. "We've wasted enough time. Let's go."

They set off at a jog back down the way Nate had come. Nate ran after them. "Please! You've got to listen!"

"You're into vampires this much, there are clubs you can go to," Gunn yelled back. "Obstructing justice on the other hand—"

Nate gritted his teeth and forced his aching body after the officers. They easily out-distanced him, but Nate knew that there was only one place Kenzie's nose would take them. *Ben. I'm so, so sorry—I never wanted this!*

His heart sank as he rounded the corner of the alley to see Gunn holding the sheet he'd left Ben wrapped in, the wolf and the other officers Nate had seen earlier with them.

It's over—

"Of all the boneheaded stunts!" Gunn glared as he saw Nate approaching. "Our one shot at finishing the necromancer and you left him in a fucking Dumpster?"

"And they say that romance is dead," Ramírez observed with a snort.

"Don't know what you're laughing about! We have a necromancer out there still—one who now has exactly what he was after!"

Nate's heart thudded painfully. "You didn't—"

"Find your boyfriend? De Silver beat us to it. Nice work, Nate. I'm sure Bennet will be really thrilled about that for the rest of his brief existence." Gunn dug a cigarette out of his jacket, jerking his head toward Nate. "Cuff him."

Ramírez stepped toward him. Nate was too surprised to protest. "You're arresting me?"

"You got rights. You want to hear them?"

"But—"

"Acting like a lovestruck fool isn't against the law—yet," Gunn said in a tone that made Nate feel he might be safer behind bars. "But impeding an officer in the course of duty is. Let's see how much *you* enjoy being locked up."

Chapter Seventeen

"Don't take this the wrong way, Nate, but orange? So not your color."

Nate started, hitting his head on the bunk above him as he stood up. "Aki! What are you doing here?"

Aki grinned unrepentantly through the bars of the holding cell. "A situation like this, of course I'm going to gloat! What kind of a friend do you think I am?"

Beatrice snorted beside him. "Mandy called in tears to tell us she had inadvertently launched a police hunt. We tried station after station looking for you." As if Beatrice and Aki weren't incongruous enough in the stark police station corridor, Beatrice held a houseplant. "And here we are."

"This isn't a housewarming! I'm not staying here!" Aki and Beatrice looked exactly the same, but the bars between them were solid proof that things had changed. *How much do they know?* "Did Mandy—" Nate paused as the plant Beatrice held registered. "Is that my spider fern?"

"Rescued it when Century got evacuated." Aki patted the backpack slung over his shoulder. "And I got some of your clothes in here. I knew you'd need them."

Nate rested his hands against the cell bars. "This is— I can't believe you guys would do this for me."

Beatrice looked at her nails. "We are, for reasons unknown even to ourselves, somewhat fond of you."

"You're not going to get in trouble for this? I've not exactly been arrested before, but I don't think criminals get care packages," Nate protested. "I haven't even had my phone call."

"The entire station's in an uproar." Aki glanced back the way they'd come. "No one stopped us coming in here. They didn't even ask our names."

"Shocking, really. I'd complain if I didn't think they'd confiscate your vine."

"Fern," Nate corrected. "A spider fern. Each offshoot—" He stopped himself. "I'm really glad you saved it, but why bring it here?"

Aki and Beatrice eyed each other. "I'll leave Cassandra here to explain." Beatrice passed the spider fern to Aki. "Take care of yourself, Nate. Try not to get in too much more trouble. Mandy has cried so much she left mascara stains all over my shirt."

Nate watched Beatrice make her way down the hall. "Mandy's upset."

"Yeah," Aki said, glancing at Nate hesitantly. "She realized pretty quickly that she'd fucked up, but you can't exactly tell a police search you changed your mind. And she's been under a lot of pressure. I couldn't tell her why I knew you were all right, so this entire time, she's been imagining disasters happening to you and working herself up. Bea and I were cracking jokes, trying to cheer her up, and she snapped at us for being insensitive. Insensitive, me? If there was a prize for being sensitive, I would take first—"

"You knew I was all right?" Nate's fingers tightened around the bars. "Did Gunn tell you?"

"No. I just—knew." Aki took a deep breath. He looked directly at Nate. "I've—been meaning to tell you this for a while now, but never knew how. After you told me about your brother, it should have been easy, but...it had been so long, I thought you'd resent me for keeping it a secret."

"Aki," Nate said, reaching through the bars to place a hand on Aki's shoulder. "You're my best friend, and I'm really glad you're here, but I have no idea what you're trying to say."

"Let me say it then!" Aki swallowed. "I see things, sometimes. Before they happen. Or I get feelings—premonitions."

"You do?" The relief was almost dizzying. Aki wasn't normal. Aki would understand. "Listen. I—"

Aki held up a hand. "We can talk later. I knew you were fine because I knew you would need the spider fern. So I brought it."

Nate blinked. The yellow-green striped leaves were a welcome sight in the gloomy jail, but Nate would have preferred a way out. "I can think of a lot of things I need right now. A spider fern is not exactly top of the list."

"Trust me on this," Aki said. "You and your stupid plant are on the top floor of some building. It's tall and you're—"

A large hand clamped down on Aki's shoulder. "Sharing visions without a license, Mr. Fujino? That's an instant five hundred dollar fine." Gunn's grin was decidedly unpleasant. "Maybe you'd like to describe what you saw to Officer Simeon."

The thin man who stood noiselessly on Aki's other side indicated this was a rhetorical question.

Aki slid the backpack off his shoulder. “Catch you later, Nate.”

“I’ll take those.” Gunn shouldered the bag and gave the fern a dubious glance. “A goddamn houseplant?”

“Careful with it! That fern has great sentimental value.”

“It would have to.” Satisfied the plant was all that it seemed, Gunn nodded to the cell door. “Get him out of there,” he ordered another uniformed arrival. “Don’t try anything, Nate. Kenzie bites.”

The woman was five feet tall, a full head shorter than Nate, but he didn’t doubt Gunn’s warning for an instant. Instead, he walked the short distance to the interrogation room.

“Sit.” The room was bare except for a table, four chairs, and a water cooler. *Just like every TV interrogation room ever.* A case of life imitating art or vice versa?

“Scram. I’m taking this.” Gunn planted himself in the chair on the opposite side of the table.

Kenzie folded her arms. “Procedure clearly states—”

“Since when do I give two shits about procedure? Your nose is needed in the field, Kenzie.” Gunn folded his arms on the table, tawny eyes fixed on Nate. “We’re not to be disturbed for anything less than a code three, please.”

Kenzie’s mouth twisted as she saluted. “Your funeral. Sir.”

Nate jumped at the slammed door, but Gunn shrugged it off as he did his subordinate’s obvious dislike. “You’re in luck, Nate. Contrary to expectations, the city has yet to fall to legions of the undead, there is no detectable spike in dark magic levels, and the majority of our citizens still possess their own mind and soul. The necromancer must wait until night to complete his rite."

"There's still time to stop it?"

Gunn lolled back against his chair. "So you do want to stop him. I was starting to wonder, after your actions in the graveyard."

With a reflexive stab of guilt, Nate remembered the graveyard. "Is Hunter— I mean, you didn't—"

"Kill him?" Gunn's lip curled in disgust. "The guy compelled you, you know he compelled you and you still...?" He kicked a foot up on the table. "It was difficult. I was tempted, very tempted, but my duty to the city restrained me. And speaking of duty, let's discuss yours to your fellow citizens."

Nate flinched. "I couldn't let Ben die! He said you'd kill him."

"And? You got to admit it would solve all our problems."

Nate slammed his hands down on the table. "There's no way I'm letting that happen! Ben's a person, not a monster—and a good person at that!"

"Spare me the love confessions. I got enough on my plate without adding nausea." Gunn's other foot joined the first on the table. "Though, you solved one problem for me. Couldn't decide whether to book you for criminal mischief or contempt. We can write you up as gross stupidity."

"It's not stupid to want to protect someone," Nate shot back. "As a police officer, you're meant to save lives!"

"Not at the cost of other lives. But hey. We've got time." Gunn folded his arms behind his head. "Tell me how handing over Bennet to a necromancer, someone who takes power from death, is going to save his undead life."

Nate slumped forward against the table. “I just thought if we could last till night, Ben’d know what to do. I had to try.”

“You saw the ritual. Got any idea what de Silver wanted to accomplish?”

Nate frowned. “In the park he said I was going to help him take back what was his.”

“Ruthless and vague. The worst combination.”

Nate persisted. “They’re both ARX employees, right? Maybe there’s something there.”

“We can’t wait till nightfall to grill the old leech.” Gunn drummed his fingers on the edge of the table. “And we’d be more likely to get tears from a rock than we would any kind of help from that fossilized fuckwad.”

“I don’t mean professional jealousy.” Nate leaned forward. “It could be vampire related. De Silver asked Saltaire to turn him—”

Gunn’s laugh sounded like a shot in the small room. “And they said the necro was smart!”

“Peter doesn’t feel about death the same way most people do. From his admittedly twisted perspective—”

Gunn jerked his feet off the table. “Saltaire didn’t found ARX because he likes working with the undead. He loathes them. Hates them the way only someone who has been alive centuries can hate. That includes other vampires.”

Nate watched Gunn pull out his lighter. “But Hunter and Ben—”

“You can’t be alive as long as Saltaire and cling to sanity alone. Not that he is the bastion of mental clarity, but having them around gives him the illusion of humanity.”

"Maybe Peter thought—"

"That he could be the next vampire son? Yeah, not happening. Even if he fit Saltaire's ridiculous criteria, asking to be turned's an instant no." Gunn spoke with absolute certainty.

"Is that what happened to you?"

Nate knew the question was a mistake at once. Gunn's fingers tightened around his cigarette, the only movement he made. Then he smiled, showing teeth that definitely didn't belong in a human mouth.

"Maybe it's time. That old can of worms has been festering long enough."

"I didn't mean—"

"Shut up, Nate. You're going to learn something about the stupidity of trusting a vampire." Gunn stood, leaning a leg on the chair he'd just vacated. "I first met Saltaire when I was nine. My mother worked nights, so there was nothing to stop me from sneaking out and looking for trouble. I found it. Broke into a warehouse a vampire colony used to store their coffins; Saltaire saved my life. I thanked him by trying to kill him. Guess he liked my proactive attitude." Gunn flicked the ash from his cigarette. "He did everything short of formally adopting me. Put me in school, taught me how to fight the undead, even summoned Hunter back from Europe to complete my training. I lived with the bloodsucker." Gunn's expression twisted. "Called him 'father'—idiot that I was, I liked the man. Had every expectation that when my number was called, I would be joining Hunter as part of Saltaire's vampire family—and he let me think that, too. Said he was proud to call me son. God. It makes me sick."

Nate shifted. The atmosphere in the interrogation room was approaching claustrophobic levels. "I didn't mean to bring up bad memories."

"Maybe that was the problem. I was too sure of myself, and that made me reckless. I got myself into trouble a few times, and Saltaire took me to task for it. I didn't take his warning seriously—why should I? Hadn't seen my mother in years, and the only people I met were part of the night world. I was eager to be a fully fledged member of the company. And then it happened. Wanting to prove myself ready, I got in over my head. I'll spare you the gory details." Gunn tapped his cigarette against the end of the table. "Upshot was Saltaire found me fatally wounded and left me to die."

"Jesus—"

Gunn watched the glow of embers at the end of the cigarette with a thin smile. "Said if I was this reckless in life, there was no way I could hold myself back in death. That turning me would make me a monster, but at least I could die like a man. And then he walked away."

Nate swallowed.

"Lacked focus!" Gunn snorted. "I was focused as I died. Focused on my anger, my hate for the man who had betrayed me. And bleeding out on the floor of the same warehouse where I met Saltaire, my hate called something out of the dark." Gunn glanced at Nate carelessly. "You probably covered demons on the job. This one was old. Whispered promises of vengeance. All I had to give it was everything I was."

Nate couldn't move, not even to blink. All he could do was stare at Gunn, the pressure building in his lungs squeezing his chest.

"Maybe it was weak. Maybe I was hungrier. All I know is that the only thing left of Isaiah Gunn, sorely missed, and the *lemure*, missed by fucking no one, is me, a thing that wears Isaiah's shape and occasionally has his revenge." Gunn leaned over the table, stabbing his finger into Nate's chest. "Stay away from the undead, kid. We'll take everything you have, and then some."

"Don't think he's joking. Gunn's responsible for more gray hairs in this department than the ghouls we chase, and that's saying something." Kenzie had returned with a quietness at odd with her stocky build. "You'd think he'd get enough suffering from the job, but no. Feeds off victims, perps, his own colleagues..."

"Misery is misery." Gunn leaned back to eye the woman.

Including his own? Nate frowned. "Does that explain your apartment—"

"I told you to scram, Kenzie." Gunn raised his voice to drown out Nate.

She held out a paper. "New developments."

Gunn glanced at it and folded it into his jacket pocket. "I don't know who is causing who misery here. Nate, this won't take long. Rack your brains for anything you might have forgotten to mention. I'll be back to hear it in a minute."

The room did not feel any more welcoming without Gunn. Nate walked the length of it, pausing at the mirror. In movies, there would be a second room behind it, with people watching. *Is that why I feel so on edge?*

He returned to his seat, picking up the spider fern. Nate stroked a frond thoughtfully. It was in good shape considering everything. Dirt a little dry, but it had been looked after. *I owe Aki thanks. Or maybe Bea is a gardener?*

The interrogation door swung open. Nate looked up, but no one entered. *Not locked?* Fern under one arm, he stuck his head out the door. The officers passing up and down the corridor were too busy to even glance his way.

The men's room was just there.

The fern needs watering...and it's not like I'm going far. Gunn would be angry, but angry was Gunn's default setting. "I'm not running," he told the mirror. "Just going to the men's."

Nate wiped his hands on the towel glancing around. *This is all wrong. I should have been arrested a second time by now.* Maybe they were counting on the orange jumpsuit Nate wore to stop him from getting out unnoticed? *Most prisoners don't get a change of clothes brought to them by their friends—*

Nate stopped. He leaned his hands on the edge of the counter to steady himself.

Aki said he saw the future. What if—he saw me walking out of here?

Ma would kill him. Gunn would kill him!

Ben—

Nate took a deep breath and stepped into a cubicle. *Don't think. Do it.*

A few minutes later and with the spider fern clutched tightly against his rumpled sweater—Aki's foresight not extending to ironing—Nate walked out of the station as casually as he dared.

* ~ * ~ *

Ethan took the news that Nate was on the run from the law and desperately in need of his help with mild surprise. "Spider fern's fine?"

"Yes, your stupid plant's in great condition." Nate drew a deep breath. Hearing his brother's voice, the same as it always was, moved him unexpectedly. He tried to remember everything he needed to ask. "But if I am going to get out of this, I need your help. Ben needs your help. His life depends on you!"

"Camden's too far."

"I know. Ethan, I need your advice."

There was silence on the other end of the phone, but he could picture his twin's confusion. People were Nate's department. They both agreed on that.

Nate glanced around. The payphone he was using to call home was open to the rest of the street, a simple fiberglass hood over the clunky old phone. A garbage truck moved down the street, its attendant crew in their fluorescent jackets the only people in sight. "I woke up to find I was growing ivy. Not in a garden. Out of my fucking chest. I put down roots. I think and plants do things!"

Ethan's measured reply came after a moment of thought. "And?"

Nate shut his eyes. "And I need to know how I can use this to find Ben."

"Never asked before."

It was true. Nate bit his lip. He was aware of Ethan's difference, but never wanted to know specifics. “This was your thing,” he said. “Like the farm’s yours. I guess—sometimes I felt like the plants were more important to you than I was. I didn’t like being in a competition I couldn’t win. So I—ignored it.”

“Didn’t say anything.”

Nate’s smile was rueful. He’d never realized that his brother could sound so—human, hurt and surprised. “I’m stupid, I guess. I mean—you’re my brother. Nothing can change that.”

“Nothing.” Ethan’s tone was firm.

I really need to go home. “I miss you. You know that, right? I don’t often say it, but—”

“You say it. Without saying it.”

Nate blinked rapidly. *I cannot cry now. I have to hold it together.* A flash of red drew his attention further down the street. An overly big dog sprawled on its side beside a rubbish bin. Not unusual—New Camden had a large population of strays. But this dog was large and...apparently unbothered by the fact that there was a large and noisy garbage truck moving down the street.

I’ve seen that dog before. The wolf accompanying the two police officers. The teeth of the woman who interrupted Gunn’s interrogation.

I didn’t escape—they let me go.

Counting on Nate to lead them to Ben?

First things first, I need to find him! “Ethan.” Nate lowered his voice. “How do you do things? Plant things, I mean.”

“You know how. You’ve done it.”

“On purpose, I mean.”

Ethan's snort was fond and unhurried. "Think like a plant."

"Like a plant." *Getting angry won't help*. "How do I know how plants think?"

"Listen to them." Ethan's shrug was audible, his tone signaling that he had reached the limits of what was for him, a long conversation. "They're always talking. You hear them, right?"

Hear them? Nate swallowed. Memories of fifth grade, Ms. Sparks sarcastically observing that Ethan was off in his own world again, while the rest of the class tittered, and Nate went red, angry at both his classmates and his brother for letting himself be so easily made a target. Ethan had shrugged off Nate's hurt, going back to staring dreamily out the window. "All this time—you've been listening to plants?"

"Said so, didn't I?" Ethan was definitely losing interest with the call.

"Wait! I need your help! Please, Ethan—I have no idea what I'm doing!"

Ethan paused. Finally, with a sigh, he delivered his advice. "Ivy's an invasive species. Careful where you grow. It chokes natives."

"That's not exactly—"

"Watch your soil too. Need a gravel base. Good drainage. Too wet, your roots rot."

"I need—"

Too late. Nate was answered by the dial tone.

He stared helplessly at the receiver he held in his hand. *I'm on my own.*

Almost.

The breeze lifted the leaves of the spider fern to scratch against each other slightly and Nate smiled despite himself as he lifted it off the top of the payphone. As he turned to leave, he noticed that the wolf had crept closer. *Following me.*

"I'm warning you now, I have no idea what I'm doing," he told her. "And that's me being honest. This entire situation is beyond me."

The wolf watched him with eyes that did not register either surprise or hostility. Nate walked a block, before glancing back over his shoulder to see if the wolf followed. She had.

It should not have made him feel better, but it did. Gunn was taking a massive risk on Nate. He had to be confident that Nate could lead them to Peter.

And if he could do that...

"No one else is getting hurt because of my decision. Not Ben, not anyone." *Listen to the plants, huh.* Nate tucked the spider fern against his chest as he picked up his pace. *I know just the tree to talk to.*

The oak felt cold beneath his fingers, having absorbed the chill of the afternoon. Despite the cool edge of the bark, Nate found that he could breathe out. This was familiar.

This was where I died.

He set the spider fern down between the roots so that he could place both hands against the tree. The rough surface was exactly as he expected it. Nate leaned his forehead against the oak, shutting his eyes.

"Fuck."

What exactly was he expecting? Nate hadn't heard the oak the night they'd sheltered beneath it. He hadn't heard it when he'd spent hours trapped against its trunk in Peter's world between life and death. And he hadn't heard it when he'd died, too concerned with the fact that Ben hadn't heard him.

Ben.

Not being heard in the park was nothing compared to waking up to find yourself Peter's prisoner. *He'll think I betrayed him.* Nate scrubbed a hand over his face so hard it hurt. *That I might have planned this.*

Even if that wasn't true, Nate's deliberate choice had endangered Ben. *I have to find him before night. If I don't—*

A rustle called his attention to a yellow shred caught in the branches above him. Crime scene tape. Department Seven had picked the ground over several times by now, any trace of Peter's magic already taken back to their labs for analysis. Assuming Department Seven did analysis.

"Is magical analysis a thing?"

The wolf sat at the edge of the clearing. She had her eyes shut, apparently peacefully soaking up the late afternoon sun, feigning complete disinterest in Nate's actions. Only her ears, at rigid attention, indicated that she was keeping close tabs on everything Nate did.

Like there's anything to keep tabs on! Nate slumped against the oak, shutting his eyes. The sun's inexorable progress across the sky brought them ever closer to night. Time was running dangerously low.

I don't know where Ben is, or how to find him...and I'm wasting time with every minute I'm here. His hand, pressed against the oak, encountered a break in the oak's rough bark. Opening his eyes, Nate saw a raised bump. Impossible now to know whether it had been the result of pruning or a storm, the outer ridge of the scar felt polished under his fingertips, weathered into something smooth by age. Inside, the texture was closer to fine sandpaper. It reminded Nate of the stake in his chest, and he pressed his other hand to the hard edge he could still feel beneath his skin. *Does a tree hurt...?*

There was a twinge of something. Pain. Holding his breath, Nate kept the hand on his chest where it was and pressed his other palm flat against the tree.

The feeling was stronger. A physical ache Nate could feel in his own bones, the raw edge of an open wound.

Nate pulled his hands back. "Jesus. That's the rowan, isn't it?" He stepped back, craning his neck to look up.

Not being able to see the place where the rowan had been torn from didn't shake the impression Nate had received. The oak felt the rowan's absence like a physical wound.

"That doesn't make sense." The rowan grew like a parasite on the oak and not even a beneficial one. There was no reason for the oak to miss it...and yet it did. Nate knew that.

"Fucking hell." Nate wiped suddenly clammy palms on his jeans. *Listening is what I wanted! Why am I freaking out?* The oak had been easy to understand, underneath its pain the steady endurance of decades. It didn't have thoughts as Nate understood them, but it had something.

And that something resonated deeply within him.

Nate took a deep breath. "It's a tree. I am not afraid of a tree." Especially not the oak. Its solid strength had sustained him through two terrifying ordeals. He squared his shoulders and planted both hands firmly against the oak's trunk.

It greeted him with the warmth of the sun on its leaves. The sweet smell of photosynthesis invited him to drift on the afternoon. The light would soothe hurts. He could forget everything and merely be.

Is this why I've never been good at mornings? Nate preferred to sleep with the curtains open, so that he could bask in the early morning sun. He felt its tug inside him, wanting to relax.

I can't. I have to find Ben. Nate bit his lip. How did you communicate immediate danger to a plant?

Down. The thought came from outside his mind, directing his attention to the cool soil beneath. While the leaves basked, lightly rustled by the late afternoon breeze, the roots worked. Each tendril brought back different information. Moisture, flavor of the soil, needed nutrients, temperature, and lingering traces of something rotten.

Rotten? Nate kicked off his shoes and tucked his socks into his pocket. His feet felt cold in the soil, but right. He flexed his toes in the dirt, found it easier to imagine roots creeping beneath.

The earth was torn here, many root tendrils still protesting their ill use. Something had roughly churned the soil and left decay in its wake. *Revenants!* Nate flinched, but when danger was not immediately forthcoming, he made himself relax. No revenant would have escaped Department Seven, not when they employed a werewolf.

He sifted through the sour traces of the revenants. Nothing concrete remained, but they had permeated the soil with their presence, many of the root ends rotting. But as Nate explored the minute strands, he found that life was returning. Insects, attracted to the decay, had brought life with them.

The oak extended its many years, the knowledge of seasons passing in a similar cycle. The decay would soon become compost, fruitful food for the surrounding plants. Death, life, death, life, and death in life. It was strong in the knowledge of this truth, and Nate felt that same strength within himself. He had the weight of decades behind him, of branches that had withstood storms that drove people to hide indoors and roots that ran deep. The warmth of the sun calmed and refreshed him, and despite the few hours' sleep he'd had, Nate felt better than he had all week.

There was a dull ache at his side. Nate felt in his pocket, discovered the twig he'd taken from the flying rowan. He'd never got around to burying it as he'd intended. Clearly, Aki hadn't checked the pockets of the clothes he'd grabbed, or washed them. Nate smoothed his thumb over the rough surface of the twig. *Never thought I'd be grateful for Aki's sloppiness.* Although the twig was dried, its already battered leaves cracking as he pulled it from his pocket, some memory of life still clung to it. Holding it cupped in his hands, Nate shut his eyes and drew the sunlight into himself. He felt it play over his face, saw it behind his closed eyelids. The sunlight pooled in his hands around the twig, knowing before Nate did what he wanted.

Grow.

The thought was clumsy, falling short of what was happening within his palms. The toughened twig relaxed, the dead parts of it repurposed as the warmth flowed through it, becoming the energy needed to push out delicate green buds.

Cradling the twig against his chest, Nate sought a handhold in the oak's bark. The trunk was too wide, the branches too high for him to climb, and the bark wouldn't hold his weight. Nate knew that, but he still felt a ridge at the right height beneath his hands and feet, and he pulled himself up into the cradle of the oak's branches.

"No wonder this hurt."

The removal of the rowan had left light gashes in the oak's bark. Peter had dug it out with a knife, careless of damaging the oak. Most of the loam that had collected in the hollow between the branches was lost, but there was enough left for Nate to pat into a raised mound to plant the restored rowan. Pressing his hands on either side of the plant, he imagined setting down roots, pushing the image onto the plant. When he took his hands away, the rowan twig was a plant.

Nate touched the white blossom carefully. *First right thing I've done all day.* By restoring the rowan, it felt like he'd repaid the protection it granted. Some of the pressure on him eased. For the first time, it occurred to him to wonder how Peter had got up there. *No way the oak helped him.*

A ladder would be seen. But Peter had somehow buried the revenants entirely unnoticed. "Someone had to have seen something!" But they hadn't. How was that even possible?

Nate swallowed. The way the crew at Century had looked past

him, coupled with his collision with the guy in the park—

"Kenzie. I think I got what Gunn is after."

The wolf stood, ears pricked in expectation.

"When Peter brought me here the second time, he said he was between life and death, and that's why I was the only one who could see him. That's how no one's been able to find him— He's not living or dead. He's somehow in between."

The wolf barked. She turned, darting toward the park gate.

"Wait!" Nate swung himself over the edge of the hollow. "I'm coming with you!"

The fall was harder than he expected, and Nate stumbled. By the time he got to his feet, Kenzie was gone.

Gunn's got what he wants. He'll leave Ben alone, right? Yeah, not happening.

If only Saltaire had been right, and Peter had used me as a substitute for whatever he's doing, Ben would be safe right now! And he'd know what he was doing. Me, on the other hand... Nate exhaled.

And paused.

It's not Peter I want to find, but Ben. And Nate had found Ben once before, even without understanding how bonds work. *If I can do it once, I can do it again.* Nate stretched out his fingers in search of the thread.

It was harder when he knew what he wanted to do. Nate had to stop several times to wipe his palms on his jeans, as he tried not to think about what the absence of a thread might mean.

He's alive. Well, the vampire equivalent of alive. He has to be.

Peter's waiting for night. That's got to count for something, right? Nate shut his eyes, leaning back against the trunk of the oak. *How did I do this?*

He'd felt the tug of the thread before he'd seen it. *But Peter had been doing his necromancy shit.* Nate's fingers sought the scar tissue at his neck. *I can't replicate that!*

His breath caught. Something had stirred beneath his fingers. An ache, not yet healed. Nate recognized traces of the same wrongness that had lingered beneath the oak.

If Nate kept his fingers pressed to the scar, he could feel the faint stirrings of the threads Peter had used to orchestrate his plan. Shutting his eyes, Nate stretched out the fingers of one hand. He found a thread midair.

It wasn't there when he opened his eyes, but Nate could still feel it. It dragged on the ground, loosely discarded.

This is it. Nate swallowed. The sun was starting to set, the shadows in the park growing with every second, but he remembered very well how his tugging at the string had called Peter's attention to it. *I can't rush this.*

Moving carefully, Nate followed the invisible thread through the city. Patrol cars passed him, but no one gave him a second glance. Nate hoped that Gunn was busy chasing up his new lead. The idea that Nate might have slipped a second time into Peter's half existence was terrifying.

Don't think.

It was now entirely dark. The sun gone, Peter was free to do whatever he wanted. Was his ritual about to be completed and Ben discarded?

Don't think. I'll find him—I have to!

Nate stopped. The thread had been leading him down one street for the last half hour. Before him rose a sight known to everyone in New Camden. "The Grande Hotel." It couldn't be, right? The Grande was too well known, too famous...

"Or is that why?"

No one would consider it. It was just too audacious!

But if there was one thing Peter had in buckets, it was audacity. *If you were going to take over a city, why not do it in luxury?*

"Jesus." Nate shouldered the fern and began to run. "Christ."

Aki had seen Nate at the top of a tall building.

Chapter Eighteen

A "closed" sign hung on a velvet rope behind the automatic doors, but the lobby lights were on, and the delivery entrance was unlocked. Nate slipped through the door. Immediately, the stench of revenants greeted him.

At least I know I'm in the right place.

Holding his breath, Nate made his way across the marble expanse of the reception room. The light let him see where he was going, but it also left him exposed, unhappily aware of every shadow in the room. A sudden movement to his side had Nate whirling around to face the reception desk—and his shadow.

I'm not going to find Ben if I jump at myself! Nate tried to will his racing heart into a calmer state. His eyes traveled down the length of the reception desk until it settled on a long shape, too solid to be a shadow. Unwillingly, Nate stepped toward it.

A pantyhose-clad leg was just visible on the marble floor behind the reception, half out of the modest business heel beside it. Nate didn't need to lean over the marble to know that woman was dead, but he had to know how.

Her face was turned aside, for which he was grateful, but the gaping rent in her neck was enough to shake Nate's newfound certainty. He was going up against monsters.

All the more reason to do this right. Nate took a deep breath. He couldn't let the man responsible for this and so many other deaths control Ben's fate—or his own.

Leaving the woman felt wrong. *It's not for long. Big place like this, there'll be deliveries, people coming and going...even in a state of emergency.* Nate turned toward the elevators. Did the fact no one had found the woman mean Peter had only just put his plan into action? Or did he no longer care about discovery?

The gentle glow of the fire escape sign barely touched the edges of the marble paneling that bordered the three elevators, making the light of the swiftly alighting elevator shine with all the abruptness of a searchlight.

He knows I'm here.

There had to be stairs. Backtracking to the lobby, Nate rushed through the restaurant and pushed through the swinging doors into the kitchen. He gagged. The pungent smell was even worse here. Spider fern clutched clumsily against his chest, Nate pressed his free hand over his mouth and forced himself to continue. A door with an electronic lock drew his attention, and he tried it without success.

Footsteps echoed in the deserted restaurant. Coming toward him?

Think like a tree, Ethan said. *How is that advice? What good will photosynthesizing or putting down roots do?* Nate thought of the oak, impassive in the face of Peter's unnatural machinations, and twisted the handle again. He couldn't deny that he would rather like to borrow its unmoving strength—

Was that it? Nate breathed in, firmly planting himself in his imagination inside the oak itself. When he pressed his hand around the door handle, it was with the weight of years of patient growth. Against that wooden pressure, the handle snapped.

I owe Ethan an apology—

Later. The snap of the handle had called attention to the kitchen. Nate pulled the door shut behind him and started up the staff stairs.

All too soon, he could hear footsteps below him. Nate grabbed the rail and swung himself up the stairs, desperate for more upward momentum. Ugly brown stains jumped out at him from the walls as he passed, indicators of what would happen if he were caught. *Can't think of that.* Nate stumbled, using the railing to haul himself upright. *Keep moving—*

He was face to fang.

"Fuck!" Nate flinched back.

The revenant was so still he hadn't seen her. Now she moved, the strength of her grip on his arm explained by her blue security uniform.

Nate thought oak but was barely able to manage more than a spindly branch. He shook her off, but the guard kept coming. Nate took a step back, found himself balancing precariously on the edge of the stairs. The revenant saw her opportunity in the moment Nate needed to steady himself. She leapt, and they both fell.

Nate reached out a hand to grab the railings. It stopped his roll but cost him the spider fern, the pot jerked from his grip. He heard pottery crack as he clung to the railing.

The revenant growled low as she got to her feet, sizing Nate up for another pounce. Her mouth dripped red, and Nate felt an answering pain flare across his shoulder. *Shit—she bit me?*

The revenant watched Nate feel his shoulder with intense concentration, tracking the red-smeared hand avidly. One arm now hung awkwardly, but it didn't seem like she felt it.

Nate swallowed. *Dead. Doesn't feel pain—doesn't get tired either.* The footsteps of the revenants who'd chased him into the stairway slowed as they approached. They knew their prey was cornered. Nate could barely think beyond the ache where he'd collided with the railings. Run? He would struggle to stand.

The female revenant hissed a warning. Her prey was not going to be stolen. She charged.

Nate's eye fell to the spider fern, scattered at her feet. Did he think it, or did the plant react? Either way, as Nate clutched his shoulder, blood winding a sticky, trickling trail down his arm, vines suddenly filled the stairwell. The female revenant screamed in fury as a vine snagged her arm before it could connect with Nate. A second, then a third vine wrapped around her body, dragging her back down the stairs.

Nate levered himself to his feet. *The other two—*

They'd only paused long enough to dismiss the threat the plant posed. The meanest of them shouldered past his companion with enough force to knock him down. He didn't give the security guard a glance as she fell, stepping over a stray tendril of fern.

Nate snorted tiredly. "The dead don't learn." Just like Ben had said. He bit his lip as the man was swathed in choking vines that whipped up out of seemingly nowhere. Locked around his throat, the vines, slowly, inexorably, pulled him down. Too slowly.

"We don't have time to waste." A vine met the third revenant, spearing straight through his stomach. *Drop him!* Nate thought viciously, stepping over the woman, no longer even visible inside her cocoon of plant. As the sound of cracking bone reverberated through the stairs, he limped over to the fire door. *Strength of ages. I'm a fucking oak.*

Amazingly, it worked. The door cracked, and Nate glared at the empty hallway. *Where's Ben?*

The doors of the rooms he passed were mostly open, bedclothes in disarray and belongings scattered. Seeing people's possessions abandoned so abruptly reminded him too closely of the woman in the lobby. *Don't tell me they were here when Peter moved in...* Nate trudged down the hall, keeping his gaze straight ahead, but the thought had taken root. *Where are they now?*

An entire hotel could produce an awful lot of revenants...

At last. Nate seized on an employee only entrance with relief. The creepy atmosphere of the deserted halls was getting to him. *Housekeeping, please don't let me down—*

Behind the door was a second set of stairs and the staff elevator, complete with cleaning trolley and laundry chute. Nate squeezed past the trolley to hit the buttons. *Where am I going?* In the lobby, he'd seen the lights of the elevator start near the top. *Penthouse?* The brief flash of Peter's surroundings had definitely been grand enough. Nate hit the button. *Aki said "top."*

He was still reviewing all of the ways in which this was a huge mistake when the elevator arrived at the top floor. There was no bell to announce its arrival, presumably to ensure the housekeepers did not disturb the guests. *The little touches. No wonder it's the best hotel in the city.*

Nate found himself looking down a distinctly businesslike corridor. The door on his right was solid fir. *Costs a fortune to install something like this—and they put it here, where no one will see it?* The gilt letters, "manager's office" went someway to explaining the luxury, but Nate shook his head as he continued down the corridor. It was another world.

Even here, the traces of violence showed.

Three ugly holes marred the elegant wallpaper. Gunshots, Nate saw as he drew closer. From the angle, they must have come from there—

Security.

A man sprawled across the floor. He wore the same blue uniform as the woman, a gun lying on the floor next to his mangled arm. He didn't react to Nate's gasp of shock.

"Nice zombie. No attack."

He didn't react at all. The air smelled of blood and gunpowder, but it was sour, not putrid. The man was dead, but he wasn't rotten like the revenants. Nate paused a moment out of respect.

A sudden movement made him flinch. It took him a moment to realize there was no accompanying sound, or flesh-mangling teeth. Instead, in the center of the room, not far from where the man had fallen, was a series of television screens. Closed-circuit TV. Nate swallowed. If he could find Ben—

"I'm warning you now, don't even think of mauling me." Very carefully he edged around the man, stepping over an upturned chair.

Guy must have been sitting at the feeds when he was attacked. Jesus Christ—what a way to go.

The screens were grainy, flickering between seemingly endless empty hallways, entrances, and exits. Nothing remotely useful.

Do vampires even show up on these things? Nate dug his fingernails into the skin of his arm. *Focus! You have to do this.* Now that adrenaline was fading, the ache in his shoulder was starting to become more persistent, and he could feel the start of a headache. Grimly, he focused on the screens. *There has to be something here...*

"Fuck. He didn't!" The image on the grainy camera was clear. A huge room, possibly a ballroom. A huddled, frightened mass of people, trapped within a large circle. Nate leaned in, but all he got was the impression of runic traces before the camera flickered onto the next room. *Hundreds of people—the hotel guests.* "Trapped."

Food for Peter's revenants? Or fuel for his magic? Nate reached for the phone attached to the control desk. No dial tone. The computer screens flashed a 404 error at him—all but one.

Nate tilted the laptop screen back so that the document was visible.

It's the SOB from the Insurance. Routine adjustments— Must have been planning it since the new system was installed last year. 03:15, fire alarm. The team supervises the evacuation, I try to raise the fire department. Communications cut, net out, cell phones blocked. Didn't mess around. Tried to radio my team, but it was too late. I saw them picked off one by one over the cameras, couldn't do a damn thing! All the while, the guests are running down the stairs, only to be herded into the ballroom like lambs to the slaughter. Fire doors lock automatically. Once they were in the stairs there was only one way to go. Nothing my team could have done. Good people, all of them. Didn't deserve that.

Captain goes down with the ship. Gonna try

Nate breathed out slowly, looking back at the still form. The Grande's Security Chief never had the chance to try plan B.

If a team of trained professionals couldn't stop Peter... Nate looked back to the wall of monitors. This time, what he saw made his heart jolt. "Ben!"

The vampire slumped forward in an ornately carved chair at one end of a long dining table. Before him was a thick candle burned almost to its base. Its flickering light exposed the thick rope tying Ben to the chair. There was no one visible in the room with him, but as Ben's head lolled back at an entirely unnatural angle, Nate could picture all too clearly the revenant holding his head back.

"Show me where he is, damnit!" Why weren't these labeled? *There has to be a map somewhere, some kind of key!* "Come on!" Nate scanned the screens. Ben was entirely defenseless. Nate could picture the revenant's teeth too clearly. "Please! Something I can use—"

"I'm not sure who you think you're talking to." The voice was callously unhurried. "But I can assure you no help is coming. Hello, Nathan— I'm sorry." Peter's smile was as insincere as his apology. "Nate."

Two revenants flanked him, wearing the same blue uniform as Nate's companion. Peter raised his hand, and they stepped through the door, their eyes traveling immediately to Nate's bloodied arm.

Don't look at the gun. Nate took a step back, slowly. Rather than his habitual paisley, Peter was wearing the clothes Nate had last seen on Ben. That made Nate even angrier. "You told me you wanted what was yours. You didn't say anything about killing an entire hotel!"

Peter raised an eyebrow, watching the revenants spread out to circle Nate. "I'm a necromancer. If that doesn't imply death, I don't know what does."

Nate's foot bumped into the edge of the gun. He snatched it up before either revenant could stop him. "The people in the ballroom. Let them go."

Peter's eyes flickered over the gun. "You noticed my little ace then."

"This isn't a game. But if you want to play, I think gun trumps ace."

"Are you sure?" Peter nodded to the security guard. "That didn't help Hensen, and he knew how to use it."

"Hensen didn't know that to kill a revenant, you aim at the heart or you decapitate them. 'Course, I'm not aiming at them." Nate steadied the gun at Peter's chest. *Thank everything that he hadn't injured his dominant arm.* "You have a heart, I'll hit it."

"You really don't want to do that." Peter leaned a shoulder against the door. His hands were in his pocket. The revenants went still. "For many reasons. Not the least of which is—"

"Hands where I can see them."

Peter blinked. For the first time, there was a flicker in his composure, but it was gone as he smiled, wiggling his fingers as he held them up. "Nothing up my sleeve."

"You're a murdering bastard, fine. Don't have to be an ass about it." Nate couldn't hear any movement from the revenants. Good. "Let those people go."

"Or what? You'll shoot me?" Peter smirked. "My hand on their leash is the only thing keeping the revenants in check. Shoot me, you unleash a feeding frenzy."

It sounded plausible. *Too plausible.* "You're just saying that. You die, the energy keeping the revenants goes too. All our problems solved." Nate preferred a shotgun, but he was confident that at this close range, he would not miss.

That uneasy flicker traveled across Peter's face. He wasn't smiling now. "Nothing's more dangerous than ignorance. I never understood that until now. Your reasoning's off on so many levels. You know nothing about how necromancy works!"

"I don't know magic." Nate's stiffly held arm protested, and the ache was back in his shoulder, but Nate ignored them, keeping the pistol trained. "But I know how to shoot. Untie Ben or you find out how well."

Peter frowned. "Ben's entirely safe with me. My revenants are guarding him. With our link, I'm not about to let anything happen to him. That should be obvious even to you."

"Maybe you should have made it more obvious to your revenants," Nate said. He jerked his head toward the monitor. "Look! That's not part of your plan, is it?"

Peter frowned. "The revenants are entirely under my control. They do nothing without my say-so."

"Then what's that?"

Peter glanced at the monitors. It didn't take him long to spot the danger. His face contorted with fury. "You don't—" He drew his arm across his chest in an abrupt jerk. On screen, a chair toppled. Heedless of the gun, Peter ran out the door. "Can't rely on anyone!"

Nate glanced at the revenants. They stayed where they were, only their eyes following Nate toward the door.

No time. Nate ran after him. "We're not done!"

"If we're not fast, we will be." Peter flung open one door, stepping into a wide lobby area. He sprinted across the lush carpet to throw open the door of an exquisitely outfitted meeting room. Nate got a brief impression of a bright mirror and the long meeting table reflected in it, reminiscent of the dining room at Hunter's townhouse. The air was thick with the aftertaste of smoke and incense, while a complex pattern of lines traced over the polished wooden floor, reflecting at crazy angles by the mirrors stacked carelessly against the walls of the room. Then Nate caught a glimpse of a slumped form stained with red.

"Is he—"

"Dead." Peter tipped the body over with his foot. Any relief Nate felt at seeing the unfamiliar face of a revenant was lost at the sight of the damage done to it.

I don't think I'll ever unsee this. God. His throat had been torn out, an ugly wound that made Nate glad the revenant's eyes were unseeing. Nothing deserved to feel that, not even a monster.

The second revenant cowered at the far end of the room. It shrunk as Peter approached, hissing weakly as it pressed itself back into the corner.

"Hungry?" Peter's voice was like a whip held tight. Ravenous appetite or not, the revenant was in danger now. Which left the single form slumped in the chair.

"Ben!" Balancing the gun under his arm, Nate placed his hand on Ben's neck. The skin was clear, unbroken. *Please, please let him be okay—*

But how did you tell if a vampire was hurt?

Nate set Ben back against the back of the chair so he could see him. The clothes he wore were loose on his form, resulting in wrinkles that could have disguised any number of fatal wounds. *Peter's. Obviously.* Nate pushed the thought aside. He couldn't get sidetracked when he had to find out if Ben was hurt.

He is always pale, but this is ridiculous. Ben's skin seemed to have taken on a translucent quality. His hair was thistle-soft, and Nate absently smoothed it down. Ben was warm to touch. *A bad sign? He hadn't felt like this in the cemetery.* He looked even thinner as Nate patted the clothes. No obvious sign of injury, but he was still, his chest barely moving as he breathed in and out. *Please be all right.*

"That's right. You eat or starve at my command." Peter had reduced the revenant to a whimpering mass on the floor. "And only mine." He drew his fingers together, gathering strings that Nate could not see. He didn't watch the revenant get unsteadily to its feet. He didn't need to. "Wounded?"

"I can't tell," Nate said. "What did you do to him? He's not moving at all!"

"The ritual I enacted was particularly draining. More so than anticipated. Fortunately, I need him unharmed, not conscious."

Peter shrugged, drawing himself up to sit on the edge of the table. "Now that we've dealt to this little alarm, you may as well *give me the gun.*"

Nate's gaze had fallen automatically to Ben's still form, but Peter's voice called his attention immediately. *That tone. I've heard it before.* But not from Peter. It sounded like—

That's not possible. There's no way!

Peter smiled, the movement drawing Nate's attention to his mouth—and the mirror behind him. He could see his own confused face, and Ben's unmoving form in the chair. But Peter...

Peter had no reflection.

"Impressive. Maybe you're not the complete novice I took you for." Peter kept his eyes locked on Nate. "But still useless. You can't resist a vampire with Saltaire's power behind him, whether Gunn's helping you or not." Peter swung his legs and slipped lightly from the table. He smirked at Nate's shock. "Of course, I know. The only way you could have survived your death in the park was via proxy, and I'm sorry, but you think of that? I'm not buying it."

His teeth were the same bone-white of Nate's nightmare.

Nate swallowed deliberately, trying to clear his head. A strangely fuzzy feeling replaced the dull ache. Where Saltaire's words had resonated immediately with his body and Hunter had simply bypassed his brain, Nate felt no inclination to listen to Peter at all. "You said—"

"Give me the gun. You have to, Nate. No one can resist me now. Not you, not that leech Gunn, soon not even Saltaire himself."

"Saltaire," Nate said, his voice thick. "He's your target?" He had to struggle to think, his voice thick with the effort of getting every word out. The putrid smell of the dead revenant was becoming unbearable.

Peter's smile was almost beatific. "He said I was incapable of wielding a vampire's power. He's going to regret that."

"This is all an ego trip?"

"Is it egotistical to want a father?" Peter flung his arms out angrily. "Saltaire promised family and then changed his mind the first time I did something he didn't like!" Even knowing he would not see the reflection, Nate's eyes went to the mirror. He could see Ben, even the revenant pressed against the wall, its eyes locked on Peter, but the necromancer wasn't there. "Look at me when I talk!"

With guilty surprise, Nate looked back, catching Peter's triumphant smirk.

"That's better. No, Nate. I *earned* this. All those years of playing the good foster son, of perfect scores on tests, and meekly taking orders like the model employee. I only ever asked for one thing from him. One thing! I didn't even make vacation requests! And he said no! I wasn't worthy of joining his little family. He owes me for all those wasted years, all that sacrifice—and I intend to make sure he pays his debts. The gun, Nate." Peter held out his hand.

Nate licked dry lips. *What do I do?* Any second now, it would become apparent to Peter that his compulsion didn't work on Nate, and when that happened? Nate shivered. The park came back to him in an immediate rush of cold, and Nate reached to take the gun out from under his arm with a clammy hand.

"Delaying does no good. Gunn's not coming to your rescue this time," Peter said, hand still outstretched. "Accept the inevitable."

It's always a stake in books, Nate swallowed. *But I bet a bullet works just as well—*

There was a light pressure against his injured arm, the fingers squeezed lightly.

The rush of relief was so strong that Nate swayed on his feet. His mind raced with a million thoughts, most of them "Ben!"

"You've made your point," Peter said. "I'm getting impatient now, Nate. I've been waiting for this a very long time. Give. Me. The. Gun."

Nate felt the light touch against his hand a second time. He thought it felt firmer, a clear command. Head suddenly light, he held out the pistol.

"Finally!" Peter dropped it into his pocket without a second thought. "Clearly I still have fine-tuning to do. First time I've used compulsion on an actual live person," he added for Nate's benefit. "Once again, you turn up exactly when I need you. It's like we were made for each other."

"I'd sooner fuck one of your stinking revenants," Nate told him. "And before you get ideas, necro is not one of my kinks."

Peter needed a dull second to stare at Nate before he laughed. "It shouldn't be a surprise that your mind would go there," he said. "Considering your job. But I don't need to know about your...kinks."

"You asked." Nate deliberately kept his gaze off Ben, finding him instead in the mirror. He hadn't moved. *Did I imagine that touch? Or—*

"I referred to your habit of anticipating my needs. Worming your way into Bennet's affections, leaving him where I could easily collect him—"

"It was that or let him be taken by Gunn!" Nate said hotly, conscious that Ben could hear. "Nothing to do with you at all!"

The touch of the revenant on his shoulder reminded him that he didn't want to anger Peter just yet.

"I'm not so sure about that," Peter said. "Once is chance, twice a coincidence. Three times..." He frowned at Nate. "I didn't anticipate needing to repeat the rite, and Hawick's grave is so well guarded I'll never steal more bone. I only had one other option, and you arrived even before I'd worked out how to set a trap for you."

There was another slight pressure on his hand. Nate moved his hand slightly, so he could squeeze back. He felt better even if he didn't know what Ben wanted him to do. "Trap?"

"No loose ends in dark magic," Peter said. "The timing of your arrival alone..." He stretched out a hand toward Nate and then thought better of it, returning it to his hip as he sized up Nate. "There's more to this. Though what... Maybe I won't kill you just yet."

The word was no surprise, but it still gave Nate a cold shock, hand immediately going to the scarred tissue of his neck. "That's your answer to everything."

"I'm hurt. After my work in the park, I'd think you could appreciate my art." Peter turned for the door, his back momentarily unguarded.

Now! Nate tensed, ready to move.

A firm grip on his hand kept Nate where he was.

Nate glanced down at Ben, caught a glimpse of the revenant

standing behind him in his peripheral vision. He swallowed. *Maybe I don't want to make any sudden moves.*

"I won't keep you long." Peter reached the door. "Your unanticipated cooperation means I'm not quite ready for the rite, but putting everything together won't take long. The Grande keeps a good stock of candles in for weddings and there's salt in industrial quantities in the kitchen. The only difficulty is chalk, and I," he patted a pouch at his waist, "make it a practice to always keep a generous supply on my person." Looking up to deliberately catch Nate's eyes, Peter stared at him. "You will *stay here* until I return."

Nate lowered his head in what he desperately hoped was a convincing show of grudging obedience. "I will stay here."

"Isn't it easier when you don't fight me? I won't keep you long."

"Wait!" As Peter turned back, annoyance clear on his face, Nate jerked a head toward the remaining revenant. "Aren't you forgetting something?"

"You don't have to worry about him," Peter said dismissively. "He'll not attack you unless I want him to."

Not even remotely reassuring. "How sure are you about that? He keeps touching me." The revenant had moved back, playing the part of a docile puppet, but his eyes continuously darted back to the red smear down Nate's arm and its source, the dark blotch on his shoulder.

Peter stepped back into the room. He narrowed his eyes at the revenant, sizing up the creature's apparent obedience against the hunger of its mouth. With a single finger, he signaled it to move. "Don't get any ideas. I'm leaving it outside the door—and I'll send more to join it."

No sound had ever been more welcome than the click of the door shutting behind him. Nate waited until Peter's brisk footsteps faded, before bending to his companion. "Be—"

A kiss answered that question. And the next. Nate put his arms around Ben, breathing him in with a heady rush. He hadn't dared hope for this, the impossibility of it filling him with even more fear, but Ben was there, real, and kissing him with a warmth he had never before possessed.

Nate broke the kiss to pull Ben even tighter with his good arm, burying his nose in the vampire's neck. The scent of old leaves lingered, but it was faint, overlaid with something new. Whatever it was, it lacked the putrid notes of Peter's creations, and the last of Nate's fear melted away. "You're really—"

"Not so tight." Ben squeezed him warningly. "I don't have a vampire's strength to protect me from your hugs anymore."

"So it's true. Peter stole your vampire...ness." Nate relaxed his hold on Ben, but kept his arms around him.

"Hunter was right about it being a substitution rite, but wrong about its purpose." Ben frowned at Nate. "Let go of me. I want to look at your shoulder."

"It looks worse than it is," Nate assured him, but still let Ben seat him in the recently vacated chair. "A revenant got me in passing. It barely even hurts."

"You're a terrible liar," Ben said. "And even if you weren't, the way you've been holding it so stiffly says volumes. Still, it could be a lot worse." He let go of Nate's shoulder. "As soon as we get the chance, Neosporin. You can't take chances with dark magic."

"And you?" Nate squeezed his hand. He needed the physical reassurance that Ben was there after the sheer hell of the last day. "When I first saw you, I thought—" He stopped. Seeing Ben, tired but apparently fine, was such a struggle for his mind to accept that he didn't want to jinx it by voicing his fears out loud.

Ben seemed to understand, smoothing Nate's hair out of his eyes with a surprisingly gentle touch. "I didn't spend a year as a vampire without learning how to play dead. I'm tired. The rite—well. Becoming a vampire was bad enough, but to reverse the process... If I was offered a hot bath, a bed, and a mountain of Tylenol right now, you would be escaping Peter on your own."

"See if I ever hike across the city to rescue you again." But Nate felt better than he had all night. He didn't think he'd ever heard Ben joke before. "What's the plan?"

"The plan?"

Nate crossed to the door, kneeling to look beneath it. "He wasn't kidding about leaving revenants outside. I see three of them."

Ben joined him at the door. "Now that Peter wields a vampire's compulsion, he has almost complete command over the dead. I won't be able to wear down the revenant's orders a second time. We need a more direct approach." He looked at the table. "Figures the only piece of furniture able to be used as a barricade would be too heavy to lift. Even the two of us couldn't budge that."

"That's no problem." As Nate passed him, he couldn't resist patting Ben's arm again. *Really here.* "I learned something new. Watch this."

The strength came readily now, antique candelabra and starched linen tablecloth falling to the floor as Nate heaved it upright.

Ben carefully maneuvered himself out of the way of Nate's heavy burden. "All right," he said as he watched Nate carefully line up the table to block as much of the doorway as possible. "I'll admit that is an impressive trick."

"It's almost too bad we can't see out. Peter's face when he comes back to this..."

"Serves him right for underestimating you so badly." Ben's hand found Nate's. "Though he won't make that mistake a third time. We have to get you out of here."

"What about the people in the ballroom? We can't leave them."

Ben frowned. "People?"

Nate explained what he'd seen over the monitors. "Peter said that if he went, the barrier preventing the revenants from attacking those people would go too."

"Unfortunately accurate," Ben said. "To create the numbers of servants you describe, Peter must have drawn on the revenants own life power before he killed them. Less of a drain on him, but they won't die when he does."

Nate's heart sank. "And there's nothing we can do to stop him?"

Ben folded his arms around himself. "You keep looking at me like you think I'm going to fix this. I'm not— I'm human now, Nate. I don't have the power to challenge Peter or his revenants or—anything."

Nate snorted, shrugging out of his jacket. "You will never be 'just human,' any more than you were ever 'just a vampire.' Seriously, Ben. You know more about Peter and how he works and how we can stop him than anyone in this building."

Ben stood still as Nate draped the jacket over his shoulders. "The dramatic irony here is blinding, but you're right. I'm thinking like a vampire. That's not going to help us now." He looked up at Nate again, his old command back in his eyes. "Tell me how you found the hotel and everything that happened since you set foot inside."

Chapter Nineteen

The Grande's doors were too well oiled to squeak. The only indicator that the door had been opened was the sudden shift in air and the silence that followed. Finally, Peter spoke, his teeth gritted.

"Very funny," he said. "But this isn't going to keep me long. You. Get to work."

Nate, standing with his palms against the table, felt the efforts of the revenants to budge it. "I don't think so. Not solid birch." He glanced over his shoulder to Ben. "He's giving them verbal orders now. Think he's rattled?"

"Ignore him. I need you over here." Ben had appropriated the clear space left by the table to set up a magical circle of his own. With the mangled revenant at its center, he'd used its blood to draw a double circle crossed by a triangle, three candles he'd stolen from the candelabra at each corner. "Bring that mirror with you. Put it there, with the rest."

The mirrors were propped up against the remaining chairs to form a circle around Ben's runes. "You want to see what it looks like from all angles?"

"Maximize the impact. The reflections add power, as if we're doing this rite multiple times. We don't have very long, so we've got to make sure this counts." Ben beckoned Nate to stand with him in the circle.

Nate hesitated. The dead revenant was right there. "I miss when we felt sorry for the revenants."

"There's no time to be squeamish. The revenant was created by Peter; we need it to act as our conduit into his power."

"Can we at least cover him? I mean—he can be a conduit with dignity, right?"

Ben looked at him a long moment. "The tablecloth."

The thick linen made at least a reasonable shroud. Nate wrapped him carefully. He knew it was ridiculous to care, but somehow he felt it made amends in some small way for what they were about to do. "Done."

"So am I." Along with the candles, Peter had forgotten a half-full box of matches in the room. Ben lit the last one and stood. "Give me your hands."

Nate choked on the rancid air. His eyes were watering so badly it took him two tries to find Ben's hands. "If I never smell another necromancer again, it'll be too soon."

"Easy," Ben soothed him. "I need you to remain calm. Focused."

A wooden crash shook the entire room.

Nate's head jerked toward the door. "Fuck. He improvised some sort of battering ram—"

"*Focused,*" Ben repeated. "I'm going to concentrate on our defenses. You're going to undo what he's done."

If Ben hadn't held his hands so tightly, Nate would have stepped back. "You're kidding! Me, undo what a master necromancer did? I don't know the first thing about this crap—"

"And that's your strength," Ben assured him, raising his voice as the sound of another charge striking the table filled the room. He pressed on in the gap between blows. "You don't know what the rules are, which means you'll see opportunities I don't. More importantly, you'll see things Peter hasn't foreseen."

Nate stared at him helplessly. "I don't know—" The memory of being out of his body was back. He felt the weight of unresponsive limbs and the chill of a night that cut beneath the skin. "Anything I've done has been mostly panic. This is— I don't think I can do this."

"You found me in the dark entirely on instinct," Ben reminded him. "You resisted Peter's efforts to kill you without any help and found him when Gunn, a seasoned veteran, couldn't. You did all that on your own. Think what you'll do with help."

Fuck me. Nate's heart squeezed tightly. *This is everything I wanted.* Ben trusting him at last. *No way can I stop now.* "Undo what he's done?"

Ben squeezed his hand before shutting his eyes. "Start with the revenant. Find something you can engage with and go from there." He looked calm, as if he were settling into a daily meditation session, not reacting at all as the crashes outside became more frequent. "You said it smelled bad?"

"Worse than bad." Nate took a deep breath and shut his eyes, mirroring Ben. "Disgusting. Rancid. Foul. Decayed. Unless you want me puking all over your circle, we might need to find another in." But the rotten core kept calling Nate's attention back. It was what kept the natural decay in its unnatural state of putrefaction. He shuddered, imagining what it might feel like to be trapped in that half-life state, unable to escape a shell rotting away from the inside out, and felt something echo within him. "No. Hell no. A world of no—"

"Calm, Nate. Tell me what's going on."

Nate opened his eyes, surprised to find that he'd shaken one hand free of Ben's, and it now clutched the cut on his shoulder. "The revenant. When she bit me, I think she got some of him in it." *There's not enough Neosporin in the entire universe—*

"There's your in," Ben said with triumph. "Take it back, Nate. Make it yours." Outside, the revenants charged against the overturned table with enough force to make the lights of the room swing, and Ben shut his eyes again, face assuming a mask of calm.

"Make it yours?" Nate drew a deep breath as he followed suit. *That'd be great on a motivational poster, but in terms of actual help...*

The rot left by the revenant's bite stretched out in thin tendrils that looked almost like roots. Making this a weed? *That's easy at least. To deal with a weed, you pull it out.* There was a sharp twinge from his shoulder as he yanked at the dark roots, but almost immediately, the dull ache rescinded. Instead, he felt faint vibrations from the threads he held.

Threads...or roots? If he didn't think of them as Peter's puppet strings but as roots stretching out, it was easier to follow them down.

"You've found something?"

"Yeah," Nate said slowly. "I think I have." He kicked off his shoes, and when that wasn't enough, pressed his hands to the wooden floor.

Beneath its layers of varnish, the wood remembered the sun and sky and wind moving through waving needles. It welcomed Nate, inviting him to share its memories. Nate breathed in the scent of thick pine, reminded automatically of Christmas on the farm. Adding the security and warmth of family to the pine's forest, he surrounded himself with the hardy armor of the evergreen before turning his attention down.

Roots stretched deep, spreading in all directions. Nate could feel the sharp preemptory tug as Peter ordered the revenants outside the door. Instinctively, he shied away, digging deeper.

"He really got into this place good."

There was no end to the tendrils. Some were faint, dissolving at the slightest touch of Nate's roots. Others were well traveled, offering resistance as Nate traced their path. He felt something flinch back. A revenant, with enough awareness to resist his pull.

"No, you don't—" Now that Nate could see that the revenant was riddled through with rot, its hunger and hate didn't scare him. He stretched out with the warmth of the sun in his roots, taking firm hold of the struggling revenant. *Tinder fungus,* he thought, felt the burst of life as the plant took rapid hold of the revenant's already decaying center, felt it give way to withered bark and spent autumn leaves.

"I've got this!" It was impossibly easy now, the roots spreading of their own volition. They instinctively sought the rot, knowing it left fertile soil for their own tendrils to sprout, forming waves of delicate orange shells that spread of their own accord.

Nate breathed in the smell of mossy soil and growth. Leaving the fungi to follow at its own pace, he dove down to the heart of the knotty roots. Peter's threads were thickest here, strengthened by use and meticulous repetition. No mold here, but a thriving network of vine.

The ivy came easily, spreading more rapidly than Nate could keep up with. He waited, trusting the searching devouring vine to tell him—

"There."

The ballroom air was stifling, dry with stale fear and unmoving air. A particular plant was needed, hardy enough to thrive in the difficult conditions, but giving enough to offer necessary shade to those trapped. *Poplar? Willow?* Nate pushed, but there was not room for the plants to find purchase. *Something more extreme?* But Nate struggled to find the right thought for cactus. *There's got to be something!*

Trapped revenants strained against cords growing increasingly tight around them, and Nate absently sent tendrils of vine their way. As their energy dissipated into delicate oyster mushrooms and dried leaves, Nate felt the plants energy feed his own and thought of the rowan. He was a parasitic plant, leeching power from the existing network of roots, but what he really needed was something with power of its own that would resist Peter's rot even more.

What's a rowan without an oak? Confident now, Nate threw out his branches. The floor cracked beneath him as roots spread wide, drawing strength from the very foundation of the building. Methodically, he tore through the runes imprinted into the floor of the ballroom, determined not to leave even a single patch of the circle remaining.

"Nate!"

The plants were beautiful and right, filling the air with the exhilarating smell of ozone. Nate reached up, instinctively searching for the sun. The barriers he encountered were nothing, easily giving way to his push.

"Stop him! If you don't, we're all dead!"

"That's enough, Nate."

Sound fell upon him, like the gentle patter of rain in spring, but less consequential. No need to rush now. The rot was almost entirely replaced by living, thriving plants with their own push to grow. Nate looked over them fondly, feeling their life as his own. The excitement of new growth, or leaves unfurling to feel the air for the first time—

Sudden pain seared through him. Nate gasped, cradling his hand protectively. A large section of roots had been slashed haphazardly. Even as he drew back, another hack left a fresh section of root raw and bleeding.

"Do that again and you're dead, Peter."

"I warned you. If you won't stop him, I will."

"You'll do nothing." The angry rustle of branches tossed by a storm before the lilting rain returned. "Nate? Listen to me. Concentrate on my voice."

It was the rot. To resist the plants pull, it had sliced itself free of his vines before they could take root.

You're not getting away. Nate gritted his teeth, the throbbing pain cutting through the peace of his forest. He could feel the rot's influence even if he couldn't take hold of it. He would not let it spread that poison again. Grimly, he searched his network of vines for something that could take hold of it.

"It's time to come back."

How had he missed it? A dark patch of mold remained, right at his center. Nate stretched out with his root tendrils and encountered a warmth that came not from the sun, but from inside. No wonder the fungi had not been able to take root here. That heat alone would repel them.

"Nate." That same warmth brushed across his forehead. For a moment, all he saw was sunlight filtered through the leaves, a feeling of satisfaction that stretched all the way down his branches to settle lazily in his stomach. Nate frowned. He needed to remove the rot before it could gain another stronghold, but he was strangely reluctant to attack this growth. As he gathered up its roots, he felt an answering ache within.

Pruning makes a plant stronger, he promised the close-twining vines. *It hurts now, but without this parasite holding you down, you'll grow tall.* Thinking of sunlight and straight branches that resisted the breeze, he began to tug at the parasitic plant's tendrils.

"Oh god. Nate, that hurts—"

"Give it up! He can't hear—won't hear you! Face it, the only answer is to destroy the monster—"

"You're the only monster present." That grim note registered, bringing the conversation suddenly nearer to Nate. Sifting through root and rot and the still throbbing pain of torn vine, he tried to follow the voice. "Nate— You wouldn't let me hurt you. I know you don't mean to hurt me. But you have to stop now."

"Ben." The word was hard to say, forced out of a throat dry as peeling bark in summer.

"That's right." Again, there was that warmth at his forehead.

Nate felt it whisper lightly through his leaves. "I've got you."

Nate allowed himself to unfold into the warmth before he realized. This was the parasite! Its tendrils curled more deeply, as it latched on to his strength. *Like I'm falling for that.* Now that he was aware, he could see the rot that laced through its vines. Ruthlessly, he gathered a branch and struck, right at its center.

The pain was surprising. It echoed in and outside of him, a scream that traveled down to shake his roots. For the first time, he realized what precarious soil he was perched on. The excitement of new growth could not withstand this new assault, and his power was dwindling, plants withering and fading in its wake.

Fuck that rot. Gripping his injured branch, Nate rallied his strength for a renewed attack and came up—empty. As the new growth retreated, decay blossomed in its wake, souring the air with its passing. There was no way to check it, Nate's roots dissolving faster than he could pull them. Already he could feel a hollowness spreading through his center. *Where was the sun now?*

"Easy." The warmth was back, the parasite soothing even through the pain that pulsed through their tangled roots. "I can help."

"You're healing him? Bennet, are you mad? Our only hope is that he'll expend himself before dawn—"

"Shut up."

A surge of energy washed over him. The warmth eased the numbness in his roots, and Nate glanced down. "What the fuck?" Instead of the trunk he was expecting, he saw pale growths that contrasted oddly with the thick vine that hung over them, or the clumps of roots that clung to them like spiderwebs. "I don't understand."

"Breathe out." The voice was immediately beside him. There was a forced note to its calm that called Nate to look even through his alarm. "You'll be all right, Nate."

Nate. The name called him one way, even as instinct called him another. "You want me to relax so you can get your roots in. A parasite—" With his strength fading fast, he couldn't sustain a parasite. He had to destroy it—

"Look at me." A firm hand guided his gaze back to eyes the gray of the sky before rain. Ben regarded him seriously, looking in his eyes for recognition before continuing. "Not all parasites are bad. Remember the rowan?"

Nate shook his head to clear his vision. Ben's form merged crazily with that of a tree. A branch had speared him through, a red stain seeping down his arm where the wood had pierced skin. "Ben. Your arm." It was there even when he looked again. Nate tried to stand, felt an answering tug. The branch was his.

"Don't." Ben's voice was firm.

"But that's— I hurt you!" How had this happened? It was all wrong.

"You've done worse than that! Look at this place!" Peter's angry voice sounded from across the room. "Look at me!" Most of the lower half of his body was dead wood, and he struggled to free himself from vines that withered even as Nate watched. Mold and dry rot riddled even the part of his body that was still Peter, the bruised flesh on his shoulder an explosion of toadstools.

Nate swallowed. "I never meant— I didn't want—" The vine fell away, revealing Peter's rotten core. Suddenly, he recognized the rot. "I tried to kill you."

"Ignore him, Nate. He's as good as dead now." Ben's touch was light on his skin.

Skin. Not bark. "You don't understand." He was a person. "I would have killed him—killed you!"

"But you didn't," Ben said. He was tired but calm, Nate could feel it even through the branch that held him pinned. "You realized what you were doing and you stopped."

It was hard to argue with him, not when Nate could feel the coldness spreading out from his hollow center. He rested his head against Ben's hand in mute apology. "I didn't hear you at first. Only saw the rot."

"I can take care of myself," Ben assured him, squeezing Nate's fingers lightly. "Let me take care of you."

It was hard to move, with his roots hugging the wooden floor tightly and the weight of the vines on him. Nate didn't even try. He simply shut his eyes, trying to relax.

"Thank you." He felt Ben almost immediately, the warmth of his energy traveling swiftly right to Nate's most vulnerable core.

Instinctively, he wanted to flinch back, to fight it. *Parasite!* his mind screamed. *Don't let it get deep!*

Too late. Ben put down roots as naturally as if he'd always been there. Nate felt the warmth spread out, realizing with an incredulous feeling, that it filled the hollowness inside him.

"See? Just like the park." Ben relaxed, leaning against him.

Nate opened his arms to receive him, realized that he could move unimpeded. The branch that had transfixed Ben was an arm again. "Twice now we got a flying rowan to thank."

"Thank is not the word I'd use." Nate felt the tear as Peter ripped himself free from the surrounding vegetation, but it didn't hurt. Looking down, he saw only bare feet, the warped floorboards of the meeting room covered with dead leaves and gnarled roots indicating where Peter's circle had been. The linen that had clothed the revenant sprouted a few button mushrooms, the lingering smell of compost the only other trace of it remaining. "In fact, I have a few more I'd like to share with you. Rot in hell, freak."

After everything that had happened, Nate couldn't bring himself to care about the gun that Peter held. It looked inconsequential compared to the lifetime of growth he'd experienced. *An entire forest's worth of time...* Not even the blaring sirens that had been background noise for some time could break this calm.

Ben draped himself across Nate, a welcome weight. "Not without killing me," he said. "And that means killing yourself. You're homicidal, Peter. Not suicidal."

"Exactly. Which is why I won't be aiming for your heart." The click of the safety coming off intruded uncomfortable reality into Nate's attention. "I hadn't planned on quitting this body so soon, but in its current state, it's inevitable. The fact that I can get back at the two responsible for robbing me of my justified revenge at the same time is only further incentive. I *hate* loose ends."

The tension in Ben's arms made Nate feel cold. "The risk alone doesn't justify it—"

"Risk?" Peter's smirk was pure triumph. "You forget. With my rite completed, I'm the vampire. There are only two ways to kill me—and bullets aren't one of them. I'll survive this. You won't."

Nate let Ben tug him to his feet. "Run?" The word was quiet enough Nate had trouble hearing it himself.

"Won't get far," Ben warned. He cradled his arm against his body, the pallor of his skin indicating that he was at the limit of his endurance. "You?"

Nate remembered with a shock that Ben was injured. He stretched out but couldn't summon enough energy to rustle a leaf. "Nothing. Your arm—"

Ben shook his head. "Unimportant. We need—"

"I suppose it was too much to hope that you might accept this like reasonable adults," Peter said. "Fortunately, you don't have to—"

Three things happened at once.

The door at the far end of the room was kicked open. "Police. Freeze!"

Reflexively Peter's finger closed around the trigger. Ben's leg shot out before the gun had even fired, and Nate slammed into the ground to the sound of the bullet hitting the wall above their heads.

"Might as well yell, 'Police! Ignore us!'" Gunn shouldered his way past the officer crouched in the doorway, gun in hand, closely flanked by the woman Nate remembered from the station.

Gingerly Nate sat up, only to find the first officer's gun trained on him.

"Stay still!"

"New recruit," Gunn said in explanation. "Still breaking him in." Although his attitude was casual and he toyed lazily with his pistol, his eyes were alert, flicking from Ben's injury to Peter. "Not complaining that you led us to both necromancer and vampire, but would it have killed you to call earlier?"

It took Nate a long minute to catch his meaning, the shift in mental gears almost too much. "Bracelet's out of battery. And he cut the phone lines."

"So you improvised by putting a tree through a fucking wall. I'll give you that it's original." Gunn shrugged, casually sauntering into the center of the room. "But for future reference, something that gets more immediate attention would be great."

"There is not going to be a next time," Peter said tightly. He pointed his pistol at Ben. "Unless you want to be responsible for a human casualty, you will lower your guns."

Not even the rookie cop reacted.

"You smell any humans, Kenzie?"

"Only the one in uniform," she replied. She'd settled on Peter as her target, watching him intently. Instead of a gun, she held a Taser, though even that looked like an afterthought in her powerful arms. "Stinks of dark magic and vampire in here." Her nose twitched. "And pine?"

"I distinctly smell Christmas tree," the new recruit added.

Nate opened his mouth to explain, felt a warning squeeze on his shoulder.

"Why would a first-class hotel smell of shitty air freshener?" Gunn nudged something with his foot. It looked very like pine needles, but before Nate could defend the plant, Gunn's prowl had brought him into Peter's range.

"Stay back. I order you— *Stay back!*"

Nate slowly got to his feet, reaching for Ben's hand automatically. Peter must know that compulsion wouldn't work on someone like Gunn. A sign of how desperate he was?

"It might have worked with the power of a necromancer behind it," Ben said quietly, anticipating Nate's question once again. "But you burned through that."

"Don't come any closer! I'll shoot—"

"Try it. Could do with a laugh. After all, you've caused us a fuckload of trouble, de Silver." Gunn's sheer lack of urgency was what did it. While Peter struggled to resolve Gunn's threat with his attitude of disinterest, Gunn stepped straight up to him. The gun went off in the resulting struggle, but the bullet lodged harmlessly in the ceiling. Peter went down with a wooden clatter, Gunn forcing his arms behind his back to cuff him. "But all good things come to an end." He stuck his knee in Peter's back to lever himself upright, dusting off his hands on his tactical vest. "Get to work. You two are carrying him out of here."

The rookie cop covered Kenzie as she approached Ben. "Hands out, Vampire."

"What are you doing?" Nate protested, but Ben had simply held out his hands to be cuffed. "He's not—"

"You too, Blossom." Kenzie removed the third pair of cuffs from her colleague's belt, and they were around Nate's wrists before he'd finished processing the "blossom."

"Mr. de Silver," the rookie started. "You've got the right to remain silent."

"But that's about it," Gunn interrupted. "Turns out the city really doesn't like it when you murder her people."

Peter fought his unresponsive limbs and was able to heave himself onto his side. "This is highly irregular! I demand to know what I'm being charged with—"

"Everything," Gunn said. "But it matters that much to you, we can hash out the details on the ride back to the station. Let's go before you start wilting."

Kenzie and the rookie went first, carrying Peter. From the chest upward, he twisted, trying to free himself, but with his bottom-half gnarled wood and his hands in cuffs there was little he could do. Dead leaves and vines fell away as they walked, and sickly orange spots appeared across his skin, a sure sign of diseased wood. Nate and Ben walked behind them, and Gunn followed, covering all of them. "Don't even think about holding hands."

Ben's fingers immediately closed around Nate's, and they shared a faint smile.

I should feel more worried about this. Even with the cuffs on and Gunn's unpredictable presence at their back, Nate couldn't make himself worry. Not with Ben beside him, cool fingers twined through Nate's as if he had every intention of staying there.

"What the hell happened out here?" The luxurious reception space that Nate had briefly glimpsed was now a luxurious war zone. Toadstools peppered the walls and carpet, while shriveled vines bursting from walls and ceiling indicated where magical channels had flowed. Nate looked from the cracks that riddled the massive floor-to-ceiling window like an immense spiderweb, to the furniture overturned in the wake of the makeshift battering ram. "Ben. You weren't—"

Ben looked beyond Nate, not even hearing him. "The dawn."

The simple observation drew everyone's attention to the sky beyond the windows. It was gray, growing lighter by the second, the edges of the clouds on the horizon catching the light.

"Don't just stand there!" Peter flailed wildly, trying to prod Kenzie and the rookie into action with his arms. "Get me out of the light at once!"

"Put him down," Gunn ordered. His subordinates quickly obeyed, Peter's body hitting the lush carpet with a distinctly wooden thump.

"You can't leave me here! You have to help—"

No one moved.

Peter levered himself onto his side, dragging himself forward with handfuls of carpet. "You're all small-minded fools, jealous of what I dared to accomplish! Jealous that I defied him, that I did what none of you had the balls to! But I refuse to give in to an incompetent police officer and his sycophantic leeches!"

Gunn patted his tactical vest for the inevitable packet of cigarettes. "Called you sycophants. Remember that for the report, Clay. How we'll laugh."

"Fitting. Mockery is the refuge of the ignorant." Peter continued his desperate crawl toward the elevator doors. "But I'll show him. I'll show everyone."

Nate couldn't stand any more of it. He turned to Ben, wondering what comfort he could possibly offer, but Ben's attention was on the approaching dawn.

"Look." He stepped toward the window, hand resting against the glass. "The clouds…they're beautiful. They almost look pink."

Nate placed a hand on Ben's shoulder. "Red sky at night, shepherd's delight. Red sky in the morning…" He swallowed. "Shepherd's warning."

Ben leaned back against him. "Is this what that meant? I always wondered. But then I've never seen a sunrise."

The light hit then, catching the cracks in the glass and reverberating through the room. The gentle light that had bathed the clouds gave no hint of the viciousness of its attack. The sun overwhelmed.

Nate winced at its bright glare, but even with his eyes shut tight, he still felt it sweep over him and then settle in him. He gasped at the sudden pain of light concentrated directly within him. "Burning." *There has to be a way to fight it—* But the hand that clutched his burning shoulder didn't find blistered, raw flesh or any traces of the revenant's attack. *It healed?*

"There's a reason the sun is the greatest enemy of dark magic," Ben said. He hadn't taken his eyes off the rising sun, even though his cheeks were wet with the effort of looking at it. "Second only to fire as a purifying agent—" He gasped.

The next moment, Nate felt it too, tiny hot needles stabbing deep within his skin. The pain was intense, but it burned away almost immediately, taking with it the last traces of the rot. *Not rot—blood magic.* It was hard to move between the two worlds, and as Nate reached blindly for Ben, he searched with roots as well as hands.

He was rewarded by the cool touch of the rowan as it settled against him, its ever-present shade a welcome antidote to the fire of the sun. “I’m fine. Feel for yourself.” Ben’s fingers directed Nate’s to close around his wrist. “See?”

The sun washed over them, gentler now. In its wake, Nate could feel the lull of contentment as plants raised their leaves to the light and drank, the energy channeled back to the rest of the plant through countless veins in a rhythm similar to the steady beat that Nate could feel beneath his fingers.

“Your heart.”

“My heartbeat.” Ben’s smile unfurled slowly, like a fern frond in time-lapse photography. “I’m human—”

“This is your fault!” Peter swayed crazily in the center of the carpet, taking a tottering step and then another, gathering speed as he half fell toward them. “First you take my place as Saltaire’s protégé. Then, after I arrange your death, he goes and makes you family!”

Ben’s fingers fastened on Nate’s arm. “You were behind the attack.” His voice was steady as if this wasn’t entirely a surprise, but his grip on Nate indicated it still hurt.

“Your death should have reminded Saltaire of the fragility of humans, their impermanence. Still, your survival forced me to come up with my master plan. Feeding a necromancer’s power with that of a vampire— It should have worked perfectly!” More of Peter gave way with every step, skin flaking off, dissolving into pale, white ash, or withered leaves that whispered as they fell. “But you— I don’t know how you did this, but I promise you—” Peter’s voice was hoarse, the scrape of fingernails on tree bark as his chest and throat collapsed. “Both of you! This is not the end—”

The sunlight hit him directly, illuminating the edges of his remaining limbs just as it had the clouds. Then the tired wood and dried out twigs that remained fell in on themselves with barely even a sigh, muffled by the soft hush of falling ash.

The crackle of brittle leaves abruptly broke the silence.

“Find yourself a rake, Clay. I want a bonfire.” Gunn brought his boot down deliberately on the biggest branch until he heard the crack.

Nate watched, the sick feeling of earlier creeping back. “He’s really—”

“As dead as it gets. Trust an old hand at this.” Gunn began to wipe the dust that was Peter off his boot into the carpet.

“It’s not your fault,” Ben added quietly, touching Nate’s shoulder. “Peter brought it on himself. Blood magic is powerful, but that power is held in check by its vulnerabilities. The more power he amassed, the more Peter left himself open to exactly this.”

Nate bit his lip. He couldn’t deny how readily the plant had sought to destroy the rot. Almost as if it sensed a natural enemy. “I didn’t like the guy. But that was a hell of a way to die.” *Full of hate, right to the end.* “Do you think he’s ...”

“Coming back?” Ben’s expression was thoughtful. “Hard to say. With a strong purification rite, we can—”

“Less talking, more dissolving.” Gunn breathed out the smoke of his cigarette sourly. It mixed strangely with the odor of decay that lingered faintly. “C’mon. You’re a vampire. Make like a fifties housewife and dust."

Ben's face started to assume its habitual mask but paused somewhere between affronted and expressionless as Gunn's words registered. "Bad news."

"Guess the necro was telling the truth," Kenzie observed, retrieving the cuffs from the ground and looping them onto her belt. "Dunno about the other, but that one's human."

"Currently," Gunn said. "That could change."

Ben snorted as Gunn motioned them toward the stairs. "You can't charge me with 'not being a vampire,' Gunn."

"I'll think of something. It's a long ride back to the station."

Chapter Twenty

It was a long walk down the hotel's emergency stairs. Even out of the direct sunlight, Nate could feel its energy beneath his skin, soothing aching muscles, but it did little for physical exhaustion. "Is taking the elevator a crime now?"

"Building's been structurally compromised," Gunn said. "Don't know if you knew this, but throwing trees around the place tends to have a detrimental effect on things like walls."

Nate stopped so suddenly, the new recruit stumbled into his back. "The people in the ballroom. Are they—"

"Evacuated before we entered the building." Gunn shrugged. "For some reason, the chief doesn't like me mixing with the general public."

"I can't imagine why." Ben's arm brushed against Nate.

Nate smiled, grateful for the reassurance. As they continued their downward progress and the cracks in the walls became more frequent, Nate found the warmth of the sunlight cracking too. *I can't afford to fix an entire hotel! If we have to mortgage the farm again, I'll be indentured for life! That's if I even still have a job now.*

There was one bright spot during their walk.

"I don't believe it!" Nate let go of Ben's hand, taking the steps two at a time to reach the spider fern. It sat calmly on the landing, its pot cracked, but otherwise undamaged. In contrast to the last time Nate had seen it, choking the revenants and threading the entire stairwell with its offshoots, the fern had somehow tucked itself back down to normal size. Someone was going to have to take a rake to the dried leaves littering the stairwell, but the fern itself was fine. "It's not damaged at all!"

"So that's where the damn weed went." Gunn prodded Ben in the back, indicating that he should keep moving. "Wondered why it wasn't upstairs with you."

"Spider fern." Carefully, Nate cradled the fern against his chest. Its fronds felt dry. *Definitely time for another watering. Maybe back at the station?* Thinking of the station reminded him of how the spider fern had reached Nate in the first place. "You're not really going to fine Aki for trying to help, are you?"

"Turns out he's licensed." Gunn didn't try to disguise his annoyance. "Doesn't practice, so he's not known to the department. Said you should call him when you get back to New Camden."

"I'm *in* New Camden—"

"Trying to make sense of a psychic is never worth the headache," Kenzie observed. With the necromancer who had terrorized the city turned to dust, the officer was in a cheerful mood. Or did she just seem upbeat compared to Gunn's scowl? "Fujino might even qualify for the reward we had out for information that would lead to the arrest of the necromancer."

"Yeah?" Nate was all for anything that would decrease the amount of student debt Aki had to whine about. He waited for Ben to draw level with him on the landing. "Nice to see some good come out of this mess."

With his still cuffed hands full of the spider fern, Nate couldn't reach out his hand, but Ben seemed to know what Nate wanted, patting his arm in passing. "Not the only good thing, I hope." His smile was slight, but the most honest Nate had seen it.

"Definitely not."

"That's it." Gunn shouldered through them. "You're going back to the station in separate cars."

The station was equally chaotic the second time round. Nate and the fern found themselves back in the same interrogation room, though this time it was Kenzie asking questions, while an earnest recruit in a still-creased uniform sat in a chair in the corner taking shorthand.

"Are you sure it's all right to leave Ben and Gunn alone together? I mean—" Nate toyed with the nearest of the spider fern's leaves. "They really don't like each other."

"Gunn's an ass," Kenzie said, pushing a cup of coffee across the desk. "But even he's got limits. He won't kill a human."

For all that he despises Saltaire, he still keeps his rules? Nate nodded slowly. "Right." *The dead don't change—*

"Leech off them, prey on them, manipulate them, carelessly endanger them, or lie to them, sure. But not kill."

"How soon can I see Ben?"

"We just need both of your accounts. So long as there's no gaping irregularities and neither of you tries to lie or kill anyone in the precinct, you're good to go in a couple of hours." Kenzie settled into the chair opposite Nate with a paper cup of her own. "We got a couple hundred people who swear the only reason they got out of the Grande alive is the sudden manifestation of an oak. Hotel owner and his wife were among them. We can overlook a couple minor magical infractions. Now, tell me again how you made your way upstairs."

Reminding himself that this was routine procedure and the department needed to know, Nate gave the best account he could. Words did not do justice to how it felt to put out roots or vines, and he faltered, guiltily conscious of how unconvincing his story must sound.

Kenzie took it all in stride, blowing the steam from her cup but not drinking. "So, what we saw when we arrived, the necromancer in an advanced state of involuntary metamorphosis, that was you?"

Nate stared at her with dismay. "I don't know what those words mean."

"Right. Forgot you're self-taught." The officer considered Nate thoughtfully. "First time you'd done this?"

"I thought I was human until yesterday. This...I don't know how or what I did. I just know that I did it." Nate bit his lip. "Do you know— I mean, what—"

"What you are?" Kenzie shrugged. "There's no easy answers." She patted the manila file beside her, neatly labeled with Nate's name and numerical code. "There's almost as many types of supernatural creatures living as there are so-called 'natural' species—and let me tell you, a bunch of us would take issue even with that definition. Those kinds of labels exist mainly for the peace of mind of the day crowd."

"You can't tell me it doesn't matter."

"'Course it matters. You want to find out how much, go and tell a fifth-generation werewolf that he's legally no different from a ghoul turned five minutes ago. Just don't expect us to come sprinting to your rescue when you do." Kenzie tapped her pen against the desk. "I get that it seems like the end of the world, but in this business, everyone's got a secret or two. You learn to take things in stride. That includes accepting that there's questions you might never get an answer to."

"I think 'what am I' is a fairly important question."

"Didn't bother you last week, did it? And not knowing isn't impeding your continued existence now."

"That's not really helping." Nate paused. "Can I at least see my file?"

"It's not procedure, but you know what, Flower?" Kenzie handed the file over. "Since you asked so nicely."

Flower. Nate remembered the wolf's teeth and decided he'd been called worse. "Thanks."

There were only a few sheets of paper in the file, a computer printout of a person of interest report that included Nate's photo from the Century website, and sparse, handwritten notes in the boxes. In the additional comments box next to Nate's Class Two designation was "Amazing ability to not move for days. Check for roots before declaring dead." His order was listed as "plant-type," genus "fucked if I know." Nate stared at it helplessly. "Am I looking at a police report or a Pokémon card?"

"Actually," the new recruit said, still busily noting down every word. "The classification system was heavily based on the Monster Manual in—"

"Forget I said anything."

Kenzie leaned across the table to put her hand on Nate's. Her touch was warm and her eyes sympathetic without losing any alertness. "Look. After what went down at the hotel, you should be listed as Class Four or Five, but we're gonna make a case for the influence of dark magic momentarily making your latent ability not so latent. That puts you at a three with the potential for further awakening. All that means is that for the next six months, you're on probation. You check in with your assigned caseworker fortnightly. Otherwise you go on with your everyday life."

"It can't be that simple. I mean—you saw Peter! And the people in the hotel— They could have been seriously hurt!" Not even the spider fern made Nate feel better. He could still remember it as it choked the revenant in its fronds. "Something like that could happen again."

"And if it does, we'll know to pack a weed whacker." Gunn didn't knock, he just charged into rooms. "Got his statement down? Close enough. Sign it and get out of here, Nate."

"Now?" That surely couldn't be proper procedure.

But not even the recruit shared Nate's concern. "Take a look at it. My shorthand's terrible, but I can read it back—"

"Not in here! Take him into the stairwell or something."

The recruit opted for a cleaning supplies closet. Nate sat on a bucket, squinting at the paper while the recruit leaned in the doorway looking down the hall. "The mayor. That explains it. We'll have a press conference out front. Gunn's probably hoping to get you out before they set up their cameras."

Nate initialed the page as instructed and handed it back. "That seems unusually generous of him."

"Unusually generous, or he's banking on the frustration of the reporters as they realize they have nothing more exciting to take back to the papers than more photos of the mayor." The recruit shrugged. "Either way, you want to make the most of this opportunity to get out while you can."

"Is that really all right? I mean—my statement—"

"Kenzie can smell a liar," the recruit said readily. "And if we have further questions, we'll find you."

"I don't have a phone. I'm not sure I still have an address—"

"We'll find you," the officer said with confidence. "I'll show you the back door."

He meant it as reassurance, but somehow Nate did not feel any better. "Ben?"

The officer hesitated. "Vampire's going to take a while. There's—well, there's got to be testing. This has never happened before. When someone becomes a vampire, they stay a vampire."

"Where is he?"

"They took him to Research. That's in the basement." The officer jerked his thumb down the corridor. "Take the stairs on the right, and prepare for a long wait— Research hurries for no one."

In contrast to the station above, Research had all the clinical atmosphere of a hospital and none of the people. Once the receptionist had ascertained that Nate had no appointment and no credentials, she ignored him, and he sat on an uncomfortable plastic seat, spider fern on his lap, breathing in the mingled smell of bleach and formaldehyde.

Smells like high school science. Nate bit his lip, thinking of the collection of things in jars that Ms. Grizwold kept in the equipment room. *Ben's not going to end up in a preserving jar, is he?*

Finally, a door opened.

"Ben!" Nate got to his feet immediately. "Are you all right?" It was hard to tell if Ben was tired, or if the dullness was the effect of the fluorescent light that made everything in the underground room look the same dirty shade of gray.

"I wasn't sure you'd wait." Ben's smile followed on a time-delay.

Definitely tired. Nate's first impulse had been to hug him, but instead he took Ben's hand, leading him toward the door. "No way I was leaving until I knew you were okay," he said. "C'mon. You look like you need some fresh air."

Ben didn't look much better above ground, though the novelty of seeing things in sunlight brought back some of his energy. "It feels different after dark," he said as Nate gently guided him out of the center of the pavement before he could get trampled by other pedestrians. "I can't get over how many people there are, or how relaxed everyone is."

"They're not usually this cheerful," Nate assured him. "It's just because the necromancer's gone and the curfew is lifted. Seriously, this time tomorrow and you'd never know there had even been a state of emergency."

Ben gave no sign he'd even heard. "I could stand here people-watching for hours."

"Somehow I doubt that." Nate deposited Ben at an outdoor table set up by an optimistic cafe owner in anticipation of spring temperatures. "I'll be right back."

What kind of sandwich did Ben like? Did he even eat sandwiches? Nate scanned the selection in the display cabinet with a growing sense of dismay. *What do I know about Ben really, despite the vampire thing?* And now he wasn't a vampire. *I know he's strong,* Nate reminded himself firmly. *I know he is a geek with an internal narrator and used to read comics.* He glanced back to see Ben wrapping Nate's jacket more tightly around himself as he watched the passing pedestrians. *I know he needs me.*

"One tuna salad on rye, please." Everyone liked tuna, right? "And, uh." Nate had spent so long on Ben's order that he'd forgotten to choose something for himself. "Chicken and cheese on—actually, make that the vegetable wrap."

Nate carefully balanced a tray with the sandwiches, two coffees, and an excess amount of sugar and creamer back to the table. "I didn't know what you liked, so I had to guess—"

"Food?" Ben sat up immediately.

"The tuna's for you, but if you don't like it, I can—"

"Tuna's my favorite." Ben tore into the sandwich with a speed that proved the truth of that statement.

Nate sat down opposite, picking up his own sandwich.

"Hungry?" He was starving himself, but remembering what had happened the last time he'd tried to eat anything, he approached his wrap in small, careful bites.

"You have no idea." Ben paused to swallow before continuing his sentence. "I think the only reason I got out of the lab was that my stomach growled. Suddenly everyone remembered there's a reason you don't want a hungry vampire on your hands."

"But you're not—"

"It's complicated," Ben said. "The only thing the practitioners who looked at me agreed on was that there was no way this should be possible. They ran tests, of course, but the results were inconclusive—The lingering traces of Peter's work."

"Didn't the sun get rid of that?"

"I was exposed to more of him that you were." Ben paused to take a bite of his sandwich. Then another. "And you don't spend a year being dead without some carryover." It seemed he'd taken the edge off his hunger. Now he ate in small, evenly sized bites, working his way from the inside of the sandwich to the edge. He left the crusts on his plate, picking up the second half of the sandwich as he talked. "The problem is they couldn't tell whether they were seeing the aftereffects of Peter's magic or something else."

Research needs to see him now. Nate watched Ben pause his methodical consumption of his sandwich to pick out the lettuce. *He doesn't eat like a vampire, he eats like a freaking five-year-old.*

"It was while they were discussing possible detoxification rituals that my stomach growled, and they decided to give me time to flush the death out of my system naturally," Ben finished, with what seemed a sudden realization of how closely Nate was watching him. "Nate?"

What does it say that even exhausted and with a mouthful of tuna salad, I think the guy is cute? Nate reached over to brush a crumb off Ben's cheek. "And that's that? You're really—"

"Free to go." Ben looked at Nate quizzically.

Nate sat back in his chair. "You had something on your face." He waved to Ben's reflection in the cafe window.

Ben glanced sideways and froze.

"Ben?" Nate was on his feet at once. "What is it? You saw someone? Him?" *Was whatever Peter did starting to wear off?* Nate glanced around, desperately. If he was fast, he could bundle Ben into a tablecloth—

"Is that—me?" Ben's hand hesitantly went to his face. Nate watched as the reflection traced a hand down his cheek with a serious expression. "I—didn't recognize myself." He put the sandwich down and leaned toward the window, obscuring his reflection from Nate.

"Are you all right?" It was hard to judge from Ben's shoulders, but Nate thought the answer was "no."

"I look like a stranger." Ben put out a hand to the glass.

Nate stood behind Ben, looking into the window. He put his hands either side of his shoulder. "You look pretty good to me."

Ben's mouth twisted unhappily. "Next to you, I look dead."

"It's just like you said. You don't spend a year as a vampire and not have some hangover," Nate told him, hoping he was right. "A proper meal, a decent sleep, you'll be yourself in no time."

Ben turned back to his sandwich, but he kept stealing sideways glances at the glass as he ate. “And who is that? I feel like I don’t even know anymore.”

“That’s my line,” Nate told him, patting his shoulder as he went back to his seat. “You’re still the same person you were as a vampire—and before being a vampire even. You don’t forget that sort of thing. It’s like falling off a bike.”

Ben looked away from his reflection to raise an eyebrow at Nate. “Don’t you mean ‘it’s like riding a bike’— You don’t forget?”

“You don’t forget falling off a bike.” Nate pushed Ben’s plate toward him before he could look back at the window. “And stop that. I think we’re freaking out the waitress.”

“Here.” The key turned reluctantly, and Ben had to lean on the door with his shoulder to get it open. Stale air wafted out to greet them. “This is it.”

The apartment had been left in a state of hasty abandonment. Big pieces of furniture, such as a blunt table constructed out of hefty Norwegian fir remained, but the shelves of the matching bookcase were bare. Boxes, in various stages of packed and unpacked, were stacked around the combination dining room and living area.

“Jesus Christ.” Nate felt like he was intruding. The room was big. Big enough to fit not only the farmhouse’s kitchen, living, and dining room, but the bedrooms as well. “What does this take, the entire floor?” When Ben had said he owned a building, Nate had pictured something small. Manageable. This was an apartment building with a penthouse at the top.

"Not all of it," Ben said. "Some of it is roof." He picked up a saucer left on the table and put it down again. "Some friends of my father moved in after we went. We left them the furniture and all the basic things—sheets, towels, cutlery. When they moved out, this was all supposed to go into storage, but Dad decided to wait and see if the next tenant would want it. There wasn't one." He licked his lips, glancing toward Nate. "That's why it feels so..." He waved his hand in a motion that encompassed the starkness of the bare furnishings, the clutter of the boxes, and the cold feeling of neglect that had settled over the apartment with the dust.

Nate realized a moment too late that Ben was worried about his reaction. "I like it. Seriously. Those windows— You must have an amazing view."

"Yes." Ben immediately navigated through the boxes to open the curtains. "Obviously, the windows need cleaning but—"

Nate put his arm around Ben's shoulders. "Windows are easily cleaned. A week or so to get settled in and this place will be amazing."

Ben didn't lean into the touch, but he didn't attempt to shake off Nate's arm either. *Too much? Or just input overload?* Nate watched him closely. *It's got to be a lot to process.* He squeezed Ben's shoulder lightly before letting go. "First things first. Let's get some fresh air in here." He started opening the windows.

Ben watched him for a moment before turning back to the boxes. "There's so much to do," he said. "We'll need new wards. Water, electricity, and gas will have to be turned on. Groceries—" He disappeared into another room.

Nate finished opening the last window before following. A desk of the same dark wood and large proportions as the dining room table took up most of the room, but Ben struggling to lift a box out of a cupboard caught Nate's attention. "Give me that." He was not surprised to discover the box contained candles and herbs. "Spell-casting supplies? Where do you want this?"

"The dining table." Ben rested his hand briefly on Nate's arm. "It's central to everything."

"Doing the whole apartment?" Nate glanced down at Ben. Was he going to exhaust himself?

"I want us to be safe." The instant Nate placed the box on the table Ben started digging through it.

"Can I help? One person— That's a big job."

He half expected Ben to refuse, but instead he frowned, unpacking the contents of the box onto the table. "Actually, yes. I want paper. There should be a notepad somewhere on the desk. A pen, too."

"Got it."

Everywhere else in the apartment was bare wood or carpet, but the rug in the study had been left. It was easy to see why. It was thick, and Nate was willing to bet it would feel fantastic underfoot. "Focus!" Pad and pen were easy to find. Nate returned to the living room where Ben had made a pile of candles and salt and was sorting through the herbs. "Got what you need?"

"For the moment." Ben took the notepad, immediately opening it to a fresh page.

Nate leaned over Ben's shoulder. "A list maker? Somehow I'm not surprised."

"You make it sound like a bad thing." Ben didn't look up from the notes he was jotting. He ripped out the page and gave it to Nate. "Here. These are some basic household tasks you can start on. You'll need my father's papers to handle the electricity and the rest of it, but I'll look for those tomorrow."

Ben's assumption that Nate would help with cleaning should have annoyed. Instead, Nate felt warm inside as he pocketed the list. *This is the most like himself I've seen him since Research.* "And you?"

Ben was busy on a new page. "Basic wards against dark influences. I need to go shopping before I can do a proper cleansing."

"Is getting some rest on your list?"

"Once we're secure. The salt goes—"

"Counterclockwise." Nate squeezed Ben's arm. "I know."

Ben did not say how much salt, so Nate erred on the side of generosity. By the time he'd circled back into the living room, Ben had started his own circuit, candle in hand, chanting something that sounded like Latin.

Nate didn't want to interrupt. He looked down at his list. "Why am I not surprised?" Making an inventory of needed cleaning supplies was ahead of making up a bed or food. *Trust Ben to put himself last.* "Yeah, no." Nate tucked the paper back in his pocket. He had a different list in mind.

* ~ * ~ *

"Nate, have you seen the—" Ben stepped through the bathroom door to be greeted by steam. "What are you doing?"

"Running a bath." Nate shook out the bathroom rug before

placing it by the tub. The boxes had been packed with ease of unpacking in mind. Nate had discovered the plastic bag of toiletries tossed carelessly within the mirror cabinet. The towel was among the bed sheets. The rug had been hardest to find, in the bottommost box in the master bedroom closet, and Nate smoothed it out as he stood. "A bath for you, so you know."

"I don't follow." Ben looked down to the notebook he held.

"I'm not thinking sexy bath times," Nate assured him. "You're tired, and I don't know anything better for that than a hot bath. I figured you could relax while I finish the bedrooms."

Ben stared at him for a long moment before collecting himself. "There shouldn't be any sort of bath times. How did you turn the water on?"

"It went something like this." Nate leaned over and turned on the sink.

"But that's not— I haven't called water. I haven't even called electricity yet." Ben trailed off, looking to the ceiling with an immediately confirmed suspicion. "This apartment should not have power."

"That is the last thing you want to complain about, seriously." Nate tested the water temperature. "Needing power and not having any? That's a problem. Next you'll be complaining about the gas being on—"

"The gas!" Ben disappeared out the door again.

Nate stood, drying his fingers on a towel and waiting. The bathroom was a definite step up from crashing with Gunn. Polished quartz surfaces everywhere and mirrors with surfaces that didn't mist. After a moment's thought, Nate opened the cabinet, letting the door obscure the mirrors. Ben didn't need his reflection to confront him again.

"The gas is off exactly like it is supposed to be," Ben announced. "And maintenance isn't answering the phone. I find that suspicious."

"It'd be more suspicious if they did answer the phone. This time of night, normal people are off the clock."

Ben looked out the window at the night sky. His surprise was easy to read. "That's why Dad's lawyers aren't picking up. I thought—"

"That we'd uncovered a secret plot to steal your utilities?"

Ben frowned at him. "Laugh all you like, but we've had cases hinge on less. I don't like this. If someone's been staying here—"

"You notice anything weird while doing your wards?"

"No. But—"

"Can anything get in here that we don't want in here?"

"No." Ben pursed his lips. "Are you saying I'm being irrational?"

"I'm saying you're tired." He'd been pale earlier. Now, Ben was only a few shades shy of funerary marble. "I agree this is weird, but we can look into it tomorrow. Now, you need to relax. That's not going to happen unless you let it."

Ben's mouth pursed, about to argue. Then abruptly the fight went out of him. "Maybe you're right. I feel—like I have to keep going, because if I stop, I might not be able to start again."

"Hey." Nate shifted his hand to brush Ben's hair out of his face. "I'm not going to let that happen, okay? We'll get you feeling yourself again. A bath, a beer, a good f—night's sleep." Nate awkwardly buried his hand in his pockets. "Then we'll handle the big stuff."

Ben looked at the bath. "I suppose it couldn't hurt."

"Then I'll leave you to it," Nate said. "Yell out if you need anything. Or just to let me know you're still alive."

Ben, about to pull his T-shirt off, paused. "I survived attacks by werewolves, demons, and other vampires. I'm not going to be killed by a bathtub!"

"With how tired you look, I don't want to take any chances."

Ben raised an eyebrow. "And I'm supposed to believe that you have no interest in seeing me naked?"

"Added perk." Nate picked up Ben's notebook and waved it at him as he stepped out the door. "Remember. The goal is to relax. Not think of more things to worry about."

Maybe working the cleaning shift at Century hadn't been a complete waste of time. Nate smoothed down the duvet of the master bed with professional attention. The bed looked comfortable, sure. But it also looked...strange.

Nate sat on the end of the bed, running a hand over the covers. *The only strange thing here is the fact we only recently survived a necromancer and I am choosing to stress about a bed.* "It's a nice bed." A great bed. The sort of bed that you could only expect in a top-class hotel—

"Is that it?" Nate glanced around the room.

Ben's father had possessed a good eye for contrast. The stark wooden bedframe and the industrial design of the bedside lights worked perfectly together. Likewise, the alternating white and black of the walls, carpet, and bedding gave the room more punch than you'd expect from a generic hotel room. But there was no evidence of the room being lived in. None of the minutiae of life that accumulated where people were.

After a moment's thought, Nate put one of the pillows at a crooked angle. "There." Now it looked like a bed you could sleep in.

I am overthinking this too goddamned much.

Nate levered himself to his feet. There was nothing more he wanted than to fall into bed himself. *And what a great surprise for Ben that would be. I invite myself into his house, fall asleep in his bed...all I need is to wreck his chair and eat his porridge and we got a regular fairy tale.* He was definitely overtired.

Going for food was the next logical step, but Nate didn't want to leave Ben alone in the bath. He wasn't entirely convinced that the other man was capable of staying awake long enough to enjoy the relaxing effects of the bath. He rapped on the bathroom door in passing. "Still alive in there?"

"As far as I can tell." Ben's reply sounded faintly tolerant.

A good sign, right? All he needed was some time to recover his equilibrium. Until then... Nate made up the spare bed quickly, trying to push back the suggestion at the back of his mind. *I'm doing this for Ben, not for me.* Ben needed to know he could say no at any stage, take back his space. *I won't mess this up by moving too fast.*

The opening of the door behind him made him start. "Geez. You walk like a ghost!"

"Technically, ghosts don't walk." Ben, towel draped over one shoulder, considered the bed. "I wasn't expecting to find you in here." His hair was towel dried, mostly weighed down with moisture, but enough dry strands escaped that Nate wanted very much to smooth them down with his fingers.

"Yeah. I figured maybe you'd want some space." Nate sat back on the bed, drawing one leg up to tuck under him. "I mean, you're pretty tired, and I don't want to rush things."

Ben settled his arms around himself and leaned against the doorframe. "Back in the bathroom. You were about to say I could do with a good fuck."

Should have known he'd catch that. "Yeah, I was."

Ben tilted his head back, weighing Nate. "Not interested in me now that I'm no longer a vampire?"

"What? No!" Nate was on his feet immediately. "I just thought—I didn't want to assume! I mean—"

Ben waved him to sit back down. He perched on the end of the bed as Nate sat awkwardly. "I had to ask. You've been acting strangely since we got back to the apartment, and I'm trying to work out why."

"Just because you've never seen me on good behavior doesn't mean I can't be a gentleman if I want." Nate felt himself turning pink at the look Ben gave him. "Anyway, right now I'm more interested in taking care of you."

"Your need to be needed?"

Nate winced. "No! I—really do want to be here for you, whatever way you need. Including giving you space if you need it." He gripped the edge of the bed tightly. "Yeah, I made this bed up hoping you'd ask me to stay even if you didn't want to—do anything tonight."

Ben blinked. "I didn't think to ask. I just—assumed you'd stay. We should talk about this—"

"But neither of us is in any condition for a heart-to-heart right now." Nate gave in to the temptation to reach out and run his fingers through Ben's hair. "Look. I figured we could take it slowly. Get to know each other a little. Maybe even—"

"Fuck," Ben supplied, helpfully bland.

Nate gripped his shoulder in warning, but it was too late. Ben saying the word gave his entire body an illicit thrill. "I don't want to fuck you, Ben. I want to push you to your limits and beyond."

"Nate." Ben drew a sharp breath. "I—"

"You remember the first night? I told you then you needed to let go." Nate crawled over the bed. He placed his hands squarely on Ben's shoulders, beginning a massage. "It was true then, and it's even truer now. But it's got to be what you want, too."

His imagination or did Ben relax? No—the other man definitely leaned back as Nate's hands continued their work. "I don't know what I am, who I am, or even why my apartment has power. What I want is—"

Nate snorted despite himself. "I know. Look, I don't expect you to have it all figured out. Which is why I just want you to know that I'm here if you want me to be." He gave Ben's back a last hard rub and then let go. "Why don't I take a shower and leave you to think about it?" he said. "And don't go overthinking this. One night at a time."

"You'll be here tomorrow, no matter what I decide." It could have been a question, but there wasn't a note of uncertainty in it.

Nate nodded. "Until you tell me to leave," he said. "I mean it."

Chapter Twenty-One

Finding Ben's towel had been easy, but finding a second took effort. As Nate stripped, he couldn't get his mind off the implications. *It really is just like someone arranged stuff so they could come and go here.* He bit his lip. *Maybe—*

Ben said his wards were good. I can't protect him from overthinking if I immediately start it myself. And it was a crime to be thinking about anything but this bathroom. The deep counter before the mirrors looked to be carved from the solid block of quartz that produced the walls and floor. A deep bathtub, encased seamlessly in that same quartz, stretched the entire length of one wall. The bathroom fittings emphasized the beauty of the polished stone with their bluntness. The metal taps and showerhead were set directly into the wall above the bath, while the toilet was equally minimalist. The bathroom was showcase standard, but the rug turned it into porn for home-designers. Thick and soft, it amply protecting Nate's bare feet from the chill of the stone.

Nate turned both taps on and stepped under the showerhead without testing the water. The necessity of immediate readjustment kept his thoughts occupied awhile, but eventually Nate settled back under the water with a sigh.

"God."

What was he even doing? Coming on to Ben that strongly… No matter how cool he acted, Ben had been a virgin before they met. Add in some completely justified emotional turmoil, a total change in lifestyle, and good old-fashioned exhaustion and you had a bad case of manipulation waiting to happen.

"But what else can I do? I can't just say 'Hey, here's my number. Call me when you're no longer a mess!'"

His words sounded—scared. *Is Ben right? I need to be needed? Or am I afraid that now he's human and can have anyone he wants, he'll figure out I'm not that great?*

Nate scrubbed viciously at his skin but the thoughts went too deep. *I really am a horrible person. Knowing I should go, and I still find excuses to stay.* It wasn't Ben. It was him. Nate didn't want to leave.

The rustle of the shower curtain being drawn back made him start. "Jesus, Ben! Some warning."

"I knocked. You didn't answer." Ben peeled his T-shirt over his head.

Nate's eyes immediately locked on the pale skin left in its wake, enjoying the smooth expanse of chest. *He's taking his clothes off,* Nate's brain helpfully supplied. "I didn't hear."

"I know," Ben said. "It confirmed what I already suspected." His hands rested at his fly, drawing Nate's attention to the tight bulge nested there.

Nate steadied his hand against the bathroom wall. "Really."

"Really." Ben's tone was not the tone of someone who didn't know what they wanted. It dragged Nate's attention up to catch the smirk as Ben continued. “You were distracted. Overthinking. Worried. Doing, in fact, all the things you were so keen for me to avoid.” He raised his chin, challenging Nate. “Am I wrong?”

Nate felt his cheeks ignite. “No, you pretty much got me pegged.”

“Not yet.” Ben undid the zipper and pushed his trousers down. Nate made a movement toward him, but Ben held up a hand. “Stay there.” He perched on the bathroom counter to pull the trousers off, revealing one lean leg at a time.

What the fuck is he trying to do to me? Nate reached automatically for his hardening cock. He caught himself just in time. “Ben. You don’t have to do this.”

“I know.” Nate’s movement had caught Ben’s attention. He paused to swallow, color creeping into his cheeks despite his outward composure. “Halfway through trying to work out what I want, I realized that I missed you. Logically, I knew you were right there in the bathroom. Then it hit me.” His fingers toyed with the elastic of his briefs. “I don’t have to be logical tonight. Or strong. Or even sensible.”

“Fuck.” Never in his life had Nate had more trouble staying put. “Ben—”

“Touch yourself,” Ben told him. “I can see how much you want to. I want it, too.”

Nate’s hand needed no more encouragement, sliding over his shaft with soapy ease. “Knew you got off on control.”

Ben leaned back against the mirrors with a smile that did dangerous things for Nate’s ability to keep standing. “You were right about that. Which means there’s a chance you’re right about other things. Slower, Nate. Tease yourself."

Nate groaned. Ben, giving orders without the fear of compulsion behind him, was hot beyond imagination—and he was telling Nate to go slow? *Fuck me. I've created a monster.* He grasped his cock tightly as he slowed his rhythm. "What…other things?"

Ben shrugged, but Nate noticed that he shifted on the counter to accommodate the tightness of his briefs. "That I needed to unwind but didn't know how. Was going to keep going until I hit a wall. And I would hit it. That was inevitable. But if I hit it with you—" Ben slid off the counter. "Maybe the impact won't hurt as much."

Nate watched Ben stalk toward him, reminding himself to breathe. "You criticize my technique, and then you say you want me to be your air bag. I don't know how to take this."

"I was thinking safety belt."

"That's really not much better."

Ben pinched his arm. "Stop talking and kiss me."

Nate happily obeyed, brushing Ben's hair out of his eyes before leaning over the edge of the bathtub to take Ben's lips. But there was nothing sweet or gently exploratory about Ben's response, the other man crushing their mouths together as he sought Nate's tongue.

Damn! Nate couldn't fight his body's impulse to draw Ben close. The hot pressure of the shower on his back contrasted with Ben's touch in the best possible way. The gentle caress of Ben's cotton briefs against his skin quickly became a rough hasp as the fabric pressed against Nate's damp body. "Fuck, Ben." Nate broke the kiss, needing air badly. "Just what do you want to do?"

Ben leaned against Nate to steady himself. He was breathing

quickly too, skin flushed pink. “You said you want to make me lose control. Hope you didn’t think I’d make it easy for you.” He dug his fingertips into Nate’s shoulder, just enough to sting.

Nate squeezed Ben’s hips and picked him up. He placed him in the bathtub, Ben’s surprise at his relocation allowing Nate to press him up against the wall without protest. “I like a challenge.”

“What challenge?” Ben looped his arm around Nate’s neck. “You’ve been doing a lot of thinking of your own, pushing yourself to be here for me. I don’t know whether it’s because you care or you’re just as scared as I am about what’s on the other side of this collapse, but—” Ben let one hand follow the rivulets of water down Nate’s chest. “—either way, that’s left you open.” Ben’s hand reached the trail of hair at Nate’s navel, and they both felt it as Nate’s cock twitched just from the anticipation of Ben’s fingers around it. “Needy.”

It’s on now. “Want to see needy?” Nate placed his hand over the bulge in Ben’s briefs, roughly sliding up and down his length. When he reached the base, he paused to tug Ben’s balls. “You like that?”

“Fuck.” Ben gripped Nate’s shoulders, bracing a leg firmly against the back of the bath, eyes shut to avoid the water. Off-balance and blind, it would have been a crime not to take advantage.

While his hand continued to jerk Ben through the cotton, Nate attacked his mouth, catching his lips with the light edge of his teeth. As Ben gasped and turned up his face to meet him, Nate kissed him deeply.

Ben’s slick mouth was a pleasant contrast to the warmth of the shower, but the scrape of his teeth as he caught Nate’s tongue only added to the heat spreading through Nate's mind. Nate pushed the elastic band of Ben's briefs now, eager to remove the one remaining barrier between them.

Ben caught his wrists. "Leave it."

Nate couldn't have heard right. The wet cotton was practically transparent, revealing Ben's erection as it strained against the fabric. It did nothing it terms of modesty.

Ben drew a deep breath. There were imprints in his lip, where he'd bitten down.

Fuck me. Fighting his reactions? The realization went straight to Nate's cock. Ben was confident in his control. To need the briefs as an additional check meant he must be in serious need.

Nate could relate. His arousal was demanding urgent attention, but he couldn't give in to the temptation to touch himself. He had to hold on. Reaching behind Ben, he fumbled for the shampoo bottle on the bath ledge. He gave Ben's erection a last caress before dumping a handful of the cool shampoo into his hand.

"Jesus." Ben swayed as Nate pressed the cool liquid over his heated skin. His body arched up as Nate's hand traveled down. The shampoo clung to Ben's skin with the smoothness of fresh sheets, the chill quickly lost to the heat of his body.

Nate watched his fingers travel Ben's taut stomach. "I love your body. I mean, look at this." As Nate's hand roughly massaged Ben's skin, his body instinctively arched to greet him. "I could never get sick of touching you." He pulled back a hand to add another handful of shampoo to Ben's stomach.

Ben ran a hand down his own chest, and then it was Nate's turn to feel the sensation of soap sliding across his skin like a whisper. With a grunt, he pressed his body against Ben's, enjoying the silken glide of skin against skin.

It would have been easy to come like that, just from the sheer rightness of it, but tonight wasn't about easiness. Nate pulled back. "What do you want?"

Ben took a moment to steady his voice. "There's lube in my clothes. Throw it here."

Nate snorted. "You *planned* surprising me in the shower?" He stepped onto the bath mat, bending to sort through Ben's discarded clothes.

A soapy hand gripped Nate's ass cheek, giving it the same rough treatment Ben's balls had received earlier. "It didn't take long to realize what I wanted. After that, things followed logically."

Logically. The thought of the cold bite of lube inside him, followed by Ben's heat—Nate scattered Ben's clothes, searching. Finally, his fingers locked around a small bottle. It was a generic brand, the plastic seal still intact. Nate craned his neck to look back at Ben. "You went out to buy lube to surprise me in the shower?"

Ben held up his hands to catch the tube. "Is that a problem?"

"What you lack in spontaneity, you make up in other means." Nate let his gaze linger pointedly over Ben's briefs. Not until Ben blushed did he toss the bottle.

As Ben moved to catch it, his foot slid in the newly slippery bath. He kept his balance but lost his composure, having to brace his feet on either side of the tub. He used his teeth to tear the seal. "Hands to yourself," he told Nate, tipping the contents of the bottle into one hand.

"Fuck."

Rather than slick his cock like Nate had anticipated, Ben's hand slid along his own crack before disappearing beneath the briefs. He leaned forward, probing his entrance, knowing the position left him precariously balanced.

Nate's hand was on his cock without any conscious direction on his part. "Jesus, Ben."

Ben continued to work himself, impatiently shoving the back of his briefs down. He glanced back over his shoulder as he added more lube to his hand. "Gonna last long enough to take me, Nate?"

"Not a problem." Nate climbed back into the tub.

Ben braced himself against the bathroom wall as he continued to stretch himself. "I said—"

"No hands. I know." Nate knelt in front of Ben. He pressed a gentle kiss to Ben's thigh before turning his attention to sucking at his balls, trapped but visible beneath the entirely damp cotton.

"Nate! You— Oh fuck."

Nate grinned around his work. The briefs clung to Ben like a second skin, offering no protection at all from the heat of Nate's mouth. He shifted deliberately between Ben's balls. The fabric must have been unbearable, its rough grip only acerbating the effect of Nate's tongue on incredibly sensitized skin. "Like that?"

Ben made a strangled sound, hand hovering somewhere above Nate's head before he caught himself.

Who is needy now? Nate smirked against Ben's flesh, continuing to tease his tongue around the edge of his briefs. If Ben thought the tightly constricting cotton would help him hold on, he was going to be mistaken—

Ben grunted as his hips jerked, an involuntary sound so much at odds with his usual composure that it spoke straight to Nate's cock. He sat back on his heels to watch.

Ben had given up on leisurely teasing. With another generous handful of lube, he worked himself further apart. Just like it had their first night together, the intensity of Ben's need had overcome his reserve. Emotion played freely across his face. His cheeks were red, half-lidded eyes dropping back to rest on Nate's cock with flattering consistency.

Imagining me inside. Nate lazily ran his fingers along his erection, feigning a casualness he did not feel. Knowing that every movement of Ben's fingers brought them closer to the hard fuck Nate craved...

"How do you want me?"

It should not have been possible for Ben to look embarrassed with his cock visibly hard and pressed tight against the briefs, but somehow he still managed it. "On your back. Like—"

The first time. Nate hit the water and stepped out of the tub. He quickly swept their discarded clothes aside, clearing a space on the rug.

Ben peeled his briefs off. His cock sprung up immediately, but Ben hesitated. Nate stretched out his hand to draw him out of the tub, trusting that the physical contact would speak across the sudden divide between them.

It worked. Ben folded into Nate with abandon, kissing him

hungrily. Hands roamed freely, contest forgotten in the thrill of reunion. Or so he thought—

"So hot." Ben's teeth grazed Nate's neck. There was no mistaking his tongue for the vampire's fangs, but Nate didn't miss the undercurrent of danger. Ben going after what he wanted was a turn on in itself.

"Aim to please." Nate squeezed Ben's ass, nudging him forward.

Ben caught his hands. "Patience. You're testing my control, remember?" That smirk was worth the sudden loss of contact as Ben carefully positioned himself above Nate.

Nate ran his hands along Ben's thighs. He wanted to control, that was obvious. But that didn't have to mean distance. "Oh, fuck. Ben." It took a Herculean effort to stay still as Ben mounted him, levering himself down with painstaking care—or devilish intent to torture. Nate's heels slid over the stone floor, unable to find purchase. "Shit. You feel so—" His hips jerked up involuntarily.

Ben stayed still, though Nate could feel intimately the shift and tension of his body around him. He threaded his fingers through Nate's, locking both of their hands together. His hair brushed against Nate's forehead as he leaned forward. "No letting go."

Nate tipped his mouth up. "No letting go," he said into the kiss. He wasn't sure if Ben heard him, but the result was the same either way. They began to move.

How is it we have a rhythm already? Nate rubbed a circle with his thumbs on Ben's palms, hips moving in the same lazy pattern. They hadn't coordinated it; there were no false starts. They just knew how to move in time, at a slow pace, letting the need catch up and overtake them. Even their breathing seemed to be in perfect time. It was hard to be sure whose moan belonged to who. Nate felt the wonder build, along with a warmth that was all Ben. The physical need, always there, flared up between them, taking with it all the tiredness, the cold, the uncertainty of the last few days. Nate didn't even notice when the fear went, given entirely to a building want. His body moved without his input, knowing what he needed.

He felt a shock as Ben let go, hands immediately seeking to replace the contact by gripping Nate's chest. "God, Nate. I need more—"

Nate held his hips, crushing them together, but it seemed that only increased the fire. "Stand."

Ben braced himself against the bathroom counter and made space for Nate between his legs. Nate ran his hands down the curve of Ben's spine, feeling the willingness in his body. Another night, he'd have played with that, but now, just seeing Ben's eyes track down his body in the mirror, totally exposed but too far gone with need to care, was enough. Raising Ben's hips, Nate thrust into him.

There were moments after that. Ben's fingers closing over his, the string of incoherent words that let Nate know he'd found Ben's spot, the blurry lights dancing across his vision. Mostly though, it was his body and Ben's, working together in a way that did not require fear, doubt, or even thought.

Only when the aftershocks had started to fade did it occur to Nate that he'd lost control. He planted a kiss to Ben's shoulder in apology, letting his hand travel down Ben's chest, intending to take care of him. The hot stickiness his fingers encountered indicated that he already had.

"You weren't kidding." Ben's voice sounded hoarse, but the fact that he could form words at all was a challenge. "I don't think I've ever felt anything that intense...that good. And we're going to need another shower."

"See what happens when you lose control?" Nate turned off the taps, ignoring the scattered clothes and damp towels all over the floor. They could deal with that tomorrow.

"A mess and a water bill, apparently. I— Some warning would be nice!" But despite his words, Ben rested against Nate's chest as Nate picked him up, the willingness with which he let himself be carried speaking volumes for his content.

"Here's your warning." Nate fumbled for the bathroom door even as he planted a kiss against Ben's neck. "Hope you're ready for round two."

~~*

"We find the coffeemaker and beans without trying, but can we find a single frying pan?" Nate carefully lifted the pots out of the box he'd just removed them from. "I question the priorities of your mystery guest."

"Maybe maintenance will have some insight." Ben sat at the breakfast table, hair still damp from the shower he'd taken. He held a mug of coffee in one hand, a pen in the other. His notebook was in front of him. "If you'd let me call when I woke up, we might already have this figured out."

Nate knelt to place the pots inside the kitchen cupboard. "You really complaining about spending a few more hours in bed? You needed the rest."

Ben's bare foot nudged Nate's rear. "Watching you on your knees, it occurs to me there's more productive things we could be doing than looking for a frying pan."

Nate leaned back on his heels. "Yeah?"

Ben blew the steam from his coffee as if he wasn't blushing. "Would you like me to make you a list?"

Nate grinned. "Actually, I would."

"After I've called maintenance." Ben took a swig of coffee and stood. "My coffee had better still be there when I return."

Nate smirked. "No promises."

As soon as Ben was out of the kitchen, he took a sip of coffee. Too bitter for his taste, but he thought he could get used to it. Setting the mug back on the table, Nate opened a cupboard, looking for a place for the rest of the cookware. "Fuck me."

It was the frying pan.

It sat in the center of the cupboard, a single plate resting beneath it. The spatula was balanced on it, and a knife and fork stood upright in the glass beside it.

Nate reached out to pick it up and then stopped. On its own, it was nothing, but with the towel...

"Ben!" He'd been too focused on getting Ben the rest he'd needed the previous night to dwell on the implications, but now Nate could see that there was one person in New Camden with knowledge of the apartment and a very good reason to be using it illegally. "You're right, this is weird—"

"Stay in the doorway." Ben stood in the middle of the room, looking at the desk. "Something's wrong."

Nate stayed put, watching Ben crouch. "But your wards— We'd know if they were broken, right?"

"This was inside when we got here. Only last night, I was tired—too tired—to sense it. Nate, this might be dangerous, but can you remove this chair?"

"On it." The chair was heavy, but Nate set it aside without a problem. "I don't feel anything."

"It's under this." Ben jerked back the rug in a neat movement.

Nate looked down at the rusty stains with a dizziness that had nothing to do with his lack of breakfast. "Christ." And he'd blithely encouraged Ben to relax, all the while this...thing...was there! "That's a trap?"

"A latent spell. Activated when the intended target stands on it." Ben's mouth was thin. "I'll be right back."

Nate stayed put. It wasn't like the circle was going anywhere, but all the same, he didn't want to turn his back on it. "You could have been killed. Or worse. And all because I wanted to take it easy—"

"You forget. It's entirely due to you making me get rest that I discovered this now when I have the energy to deal with it." Ben held a bucket. "Not last night when I would have been too tired to resist its magic." He carefully poured its contents onto the circle.

Instantly, the surface of the floor bubbled and hissed. The smoke that rose formed a human shape, diving frantically for Ben. Nate snatched Ben back against him, and they watched the thing evaporate into nothingness.

“Was that” —Nate swallowed— ”Peter’s ghost?”

“A fragment of his consciousness. Planted here to possess me when I stepped onto the circle.” Ben pulled on plastic gloves. “Open the curtains. We want as much light in here as possible.”

Nate did as told, glancing back to find Ben already scrubbing vigorously. “Is that bleach?”

“Not as effective as holy water, but a good second choice.”

“And that’s really going to be enough?”

“Possession of that sort requires a weakened target.” Ben’s scrubbing came to a halt. “Peter knew me well enough to know that my instinct would be to work so that I didn’t have to think. That I would come here exhausted and distracted. He didn’t anticipate you.”

“You’d have noticed this sooner without me distracting you.”

Ben shook his head. “I think—”

The front door echoed with the sound of a tree falling. They both jumped.

“I got this.” Heart still racing with their near-escape, Nate made for the door. It rattled again as he approached. *Fuck. They trying to break the door down?* Nate dismissed the thought. Whoever was on the other side of it, they were not harming Ben. “You’d better not—”

Instead of the apparition Nate was expecting, he faced a tall, broad-shouldered figure, accompanied by an earthy smell that left no doubt of its reality.

The man blinked back at him. Also tensed for danger, he had a shovel resting on his shoulder in a way that radiated implicit threat. “Nate.”

"Ethan?"

His mouth, the mirror of Nate's, twitched in a slow smile, his hazel eyes showing uncharacteristic amusement. "Who else?"

"I don't believe this!" Nate threw his arms around his brother. "What are you doing here? Scratch that. How did you even get here?"

Ethan endured the hug with the same stoic indifference with which he greeted most of Nate's ideas, but Nate felt the slight pressure of Ethan's hand on his shoulder, and knew he'd been missed. "Drove."

"Drove? But that would have taken—" Nate stepped back to scan his brother's face. Ethan didn't show any of the signs of someone who had driven all night to reach the city. *But then again, he wouldn't, would he?* Nate bumped Ethan's shoulder. "You jerk. Ask before taking my truck out of state!"

From Ethan's slight smile, he knew Nate was not annoyed. "'M asking now."

"That doesn't count. Just because you're older…" Seeing Ethan framed by the apartment building interior and not by the greenery of the farm or the homely wood of the farmhouse was a trip. The jacket he wore added unnecessary bulk to his already wide shoulders, and dirt from the farm caked his boots. He'd probably gone straight from mulching to the truck. "Why did you bring a shovel?"

Ethan shrugged. "Time you came home."

"Home?" When Ethan made up his mind, that was it. No argument would ever change his mind. Nate wasn't even sure he wanted to. The simple word had evoked a rush of longing. *Home.*

A sharp movement called Nate's attention to his side. Ben had joined them.

“Right.” Nate let go of Ethan. “This is Ben. Ben, this is—”

“Ethan.” Ben’s smile was brittle. “Your brother.”

“Yeah.” Was he thinking of Hunter? Did he miss him? Nate ran his hands through his hair. “I was looking forward to introducing you guys. I didn’t think it’d be so soon.”

Ben took a step toward him. “Would you like to come in?” he said to Ethan. “The place isn’t much right now but—”

“Truck’s downstairs,” Ethan said loudly. “I’ll wait.” He turned, Ben’s invitation stumbling to a halt behind him.

Nate put his hand on Ben’s shoulder. “My truck gets towed or ticketed and you’re never borrowing it again,” he called as Ethan ambled toward the stairs with a speed entirely disproportionate to that of the New Camden city meter officials. “I’m not kidding, Ethan!”

The stairwell door swung shut behind him. “Brothers,” Nate said turning toward Ben. “So—”

He was met by Ben’s polite mask. “I thought we’d have more time.”

“So did I.” Nate took back his hand.

“I won’t keep you,” Ben said. “Obviously, your family is worried, and you want to see them.”

“Yeah, I do.” Nate followed Ben toward the spare room. His backpack was exactly where he’d left it, on the floor beside the bedside table. “But they can wait a day or two. Until you’re settled in.”

“Your brother’s not going to wait two days.” Ben waited until Nate had shouldered his bag and then passed him the spider fern.

"Ten seconds later and I think he'd have broken down the door."

"He gets like that," Nate agreed. "He's not good at meeting people."

A horn sounded loudly from the street outside. Reluctantly, they turned toward the stairs.

* ~ * ~ *

Ethan had parked over a good chunk of sidewalk. He leaned against the driver's side window, ignoring the glaring pedestrians forced to squeeze past.

"This isn't Little River! You can't just park where you feel like it—Geez!" Nate turned to Ben. "I guess—"

"I can give you my number," Ben said. "This isn't good-bye."

Nate took a deep breath. "Truck's got more than one seat."

Ben blinked. His shoulders were hunched defensively. It took a moment for Nate's invitation to register, but when it did, uncertainty and hope flashed through the blank mask he wore. "You really mean that?"

Nate squeezed his hand. "It's a lot to ask at such short notice," he said. "But yeah. I've been thinking for a while now that I'd really like to take you home to meet the family. I mean, we're not perfect, and the house is small—"

"I want to come."

"And there's nothing to do, but the farm—" Nate slowed to a stop. "Right," he said, aware that he was grinning far too widely to be cool. "Just give me a minute."

Ethan looked pointedly as Nate swung open the passenger door.

“That little,” he said, “took that long?”

“Stop moaning. We’ll be out of the city soon.” Nate placed the spider fern in the passenger seat, carefully buckling the belt around it. “Ben’s coming, too,” he announced, shutting the passenger door. Nate slung his pack into the back seat and turned to Ben. “This is your chance to reconsider,” he said, holding out his hand.

“That might be your best line yet.” Ben used Nate’s hand to swing himself up into the back of the truck.

As soon as he heard the door shut behind Nate, Ethan pulled into the road. Nate was used to his brother’s impatient driving habits, catching Ben before he could lose his balance. “I should probably have warned you,” he said, settling an arm around Ben. “That it’s a really long drive.”

Ben discovered that with a bit of wriggling, he fit perfectly against Nate’s side. “Perfect.” He shut his eyes.

Nate felt as if he were sunlight inside and out. It took him a moment to realize why that was strange. For the first time since he’d felt it that night in the club, he was entirely free of the lingering influence of the premonition. Nate tangled his fingers in Ben’s hair. *I will never be the same again.* It was true. Something within him had irrevocably changed. It was more than the knowledge of what he was. The Nate who had preferred comfortable ignorance could not have weathered the storm Ben had brought. *Nothing’s going to be the same.* What lay ahead was uncharted territory. Once again, Nate was entirely in over his head, only this time, he didn’t mind. He leaned down to kiss Ben’s forehead.

“You owe me a new coffee,” Ben said without opening his eyes.

"Yeah, yeah." Nate leaned back in his seat so he could catch Ethan's expression in the rearview. "What do you say, Ethan? The diner off the thirty-eight? You liked their waffles right?"

"Hated them," Ethan said immediately. "Tasted like plastic."

Not everything had changed.

About the Author

Gillian St. Kevern is an author of paranormal romance and urban fantasy. Originally from New Zealand, she currently lives in Japan and has visited over twenty different countries. Her writing is a celebration of the diverse people she meets.

As a chronic traveller, Gillian is interested in journeys rather than endings, writing characters that grow and change to achieve their happy ending. Her stories cross genres, time-periods and continents, taking readers along for an unforgettable ride.

Email: gillian.stkevern@gmail.com

Website: www.gillianstkevern.com

Twitter: www.twitter.com/GillianStKevern

Facebook: www.facebook.com/gillian.stkevern

Mailing list: www.gillianstkevern.com/newsletter-sign-up.html

Pinterest: www.pinterest.com/gillianstkevern/

Goodreads: www.goodreads.com/author/show/8337607

NineStar Press, LLC

www.ninestarpress.com